MODERN SARAH

When God delays,
His promise is never denied.

A Novel

By

Holly Bogdan

Modern Sarah

This is a work of fiction. Any resemblance to actual persons, living or dead, is purely coincidental. The characters, events, and settings are products of the author's imagination, though inspired by biblical texts.

Scripture quotations marked (NKJV) are taken from the New King James Version®. Copyright © 1982 by Thomas Nelson. Used by permission. All rights reserved.

Scripture quotations marked (NIV) are taken from the Holy Bible, New International Version®, NIV®. Copyright © 1973, 1978, 1984, 2011 by Biblica, Inc.™ Used by permission. All rights reserved worldwide.

Cover design: Developed in collaboration with Tanjot Kaur Gill

ISBN 979-8-9997091-0-3 (pbk.)

DEDICATION

For every woman who has ever waited,
wondered, and wept.
May you always trust the God who never forgets
His promises.

CHAPTERS

Act I - The Promise

The Lord's Covenant with Abram

After this, the word of the Lord came to Abram in a vision:

"Do not be afraid, Abram. I am your shield, your very great reward."

But Abram said, "Sovereign Lord, what can you give me since I remain childless and the one who will inherit my estate is Eliezer of Damascus?" And Abram said, "You have given me no children—so a servant in my household will be my heir."

Then the word of the Lord came to him: "This man will not be your heir, but a son who is your own flesh and blood will be your heir." He took him outside and said, "Look up at the sky and count the stars— if indeed you can count them." Then he said to him, "So shall your offspring be."

Genesis 15: 1-5 (NIV)

CHAPTER 1

The College Years

Freshman Year—University Student Center

The smell of burnt coffee and microwaved popcorn filled the student lounge as Sarah balanced a heavy stack of books on her hip, scanning for an empty table. Her first semester was already overwhelming, and she hadn't met many people yet.

"Hey, you can sit here!" a cheerful voice called out. Sarah turned to see a petite brunette waving her over. Her energy was warm and bright, like sunshine cutting through an overcast sky.

"Thanks," Sarah said, dropping her books on the table with a relieved sigh.

"I'm Lottie," the girl said, extending her hand. "Lottie Franklin. Business major. Over-caffeinated. Chronic over-achiever." Sarah laughed, already feeling lighter. "I'm Sarah Cohen. Also business... also over-caffeinated."

As Sarah sat, another girl approached, carrying two iced teas.

"Lottie, your tea…" she stopped and smiled at Sarah.

"Oh, hi! I'm Mara."

"Mara's my roommate and spiritual counselor," Lottie joked, winking. "She keeps me from flunking accounting and from losing my soul."

Mara grinned. "Mostly the soul part."

They all laughed.

Within minutes, the conversation flowed as if they'd known each other for years. They talked about classes, hometowns, bad cafeteria food, and dreams for the future.

"I want to build something," Sarah said thoughtfully. "A business. A legacy. But I also want a family. Someday."

Lottie nodded. "Me too. In that order though. Career first. Husband much later. And maybe kids after." Sarah caught something softer behind Lottie's smile, though she couldn't name it then. She didn't know that Lottie's bold plans came from old hurts. Lottie rarely talked about her childhood, but sometimes when she fell quiet, Sarah wondered if all that drive and independence were really just a promise she had made to herself long ago: never rely on anyone else to hold you together.

Mara, who knew Lottie more, smiled knowingly.

"Sometimes God surprises us with His timing."

They laughed, unaware that this was the beginning of a friendship that would shape each of their futures in ways none of them could predict.

Sophomore Year—Southern Christian University, Dallas

The dorm room was dimly lit, bathed in the soft glow of a string of twinkle lights across the window and the open pizza box that sat like a trophy in the middle of the floor. Sarah, Mara, and Lottie were sprawled across mismatched pillows, their legs tangled in fleece blankets as laughter echoed off the cinderblock walls.

It was their sophomore year, and they'd spent the evening watching old rom-coms, mocking the unrealistic plots while secretly loving every minute.

"I swear," Mara said between bites of crust, "if one more movie ends with a man chasing a woman through an airport, I'm done."

"Hey," Sarah smirked, "I like a dramatic gesture. Not that I'd want one, but it's cute... in theory."

Lottie rolled her eyes. "You two are such hopeless romantics." Sarah narrowed her eyes playfully. "Oh come on, Lottie. You're telling me you don't want some man to make you the center of his world someday? Don't you wanna' get married someday?"

"Nope, not anymore" Lottie said, not missing a beat. She reached for her sparkling water. "Not planning on it. And kids? Also scratched off the list."

Mara sat up. "Wait, seriously? When did this happen?"

"I'm serious." Lottie's tone wasn't defensive, just matter-of-fact. "I love my life. I've decided this year I love being in control of my time, my energy, my goals. And I've seen too many people lose themselves trying to be everything for everyone. I'd rather be everything for myself....and for the Lord. I would love to be like Paul the Apostle, dedicating my life to being the best I can be in my career, my ministry and every aspect of my life, without marriage or kids in the picture."

Sarah was quiet for a moment. "So... you've really thought this through."

"More than you know," Lottie said. "I'm not saying love isn't beautiful—for other people. But I've got plans. Big ones. And I don't want anything tying me down."

Mara gave a half-smile. "Well, if you change your mind, you'll have two wedding veterans to help plan it all."

Lottie laughed. "If I change my mind, I'll send out a press release. Until then, you two can be the queens of love and lace."

They all laughed, the kind of laughter only college roommates know— deep, honest, and fleeting.

But Sarah tucked the moment away. Because even then, something in Lottie's voice sounded less like conviction and more like protection, a wall carefully built. And Sarah knew from her own life that walls often had cracks.

The Pact is Born

Between studying for mid-terms, Mara closed her journal and turned toward them, a playful glint in her eyes.

"Okay, serious question—where do you all see yourselves in ten years?"

Sarah grinned. "Married. Two kids. Maybe three."
Lottie chimed in quickly.
"Single. Traveling. And friends who make me laugh until I can't breathe."

Mara smiled thoughtfully. "Married, yes. And ministry. Maybe counseling couples. Something where I can help people rebuild what the enemy tries to destroy."
The room grew quiet for a moment, not heavy, just reflective.
Then Lottie clapped her hands together.

"Alright. Dating Pact time." Sarah groaned.

"Oh no, what now?" Lottie grinned.

"If none of us are married by 30, we move to the same city, live in some fabulous downtown loft together full of wine and takeout, and act like one giant, weird family." Mara laughed.

"That sounds terrifying and amazing."
Sarah shook her head, but she was smiling.

"I'm not waiting until 30."

"You don't have to," Lottie agreed, "but it's a backup plan. Just in case God's timetable doesn't match ours."
Sarah leaned back against the pillow, her voice softening.
"Sometimes I wonder if I want marriage so badly because I miss family more than I even realize."

The other two grew quiet, understanding instantly.
Sarah rarely talked about her parents' absence, but they all knew how much she carried it.
Lottie reached up and squeezed her foot gently.

"Your story isn't over, Sarah."
Mara added quietly, "And God sees you. Even in the waiting."

Sarah nodded, blinking back sudden tears.

"I just hope He hurries up."

They all laughed again, but beneath the laughter, their hearts carried the silent ache every twenty-year-old woman carries when dreams feel so close and so impossibly far at the same time.

After the laughter faded, Sarah lay awake while Lottie and Mara whispered about classes and boys. She stared at the ceiling and breathed out a quiet thought only God would hear. She wanted a husband and a family one day, but underneath it all, what she really wanted was to know that she was not forgotten. That the prayers she tucked away at night were safe in His hands.

As they prepared for their nightly prayer circle, Mara reached out her hands. Sarah took one. Mara took the other. Lottie stood a moment, arms folded. "I'll sit this one out tonight, if that's okay."

Sarah blinked. "Wait, you're not joining?"

Lottie smiled politely. "You know I love you both. But asking God for a husband or kids? That's just... not where I am. Not anymore."

Mara hesitated. "You don't even want to ask? Just in case you change your mind?"

Lottie shrugged. "I'm asking for other things. Peace. Purpose. Maybe to not be defined by someone else's timetable."

She stood back, watching as they bowed their heads. Sarah noticed that she stayed silent, no whispered "amen," no hands clasped. Just presence.

Mara prayed softly:

"Lord, You know the desires of our hearts. You placed them there. Prepare us for the men You are preparing for us. Protect our hearts. Teach us to trust Your timing. And remind us that You are faithful— even when we're impatient."

When Mara finished praying, Sarah and Mara whispered 'amen' and let the room settle into stillness. Sarah kept her eyes closed a moment longer and whispered again into the dark. Please don't forget me, God.

Outside, the wind rattled the window just enough to remind her the world was wide and waiting. Inside their small dorm, three girls drifted to sleep, each holding a different hope close to her heart.

Senior Year, Spring Semester

The sun had barely set as Sarah sat at the tiny corner table of the coffee shop just off campus, her iced latte untouched, condensation pooling beneath the cup.

Across from her sat Mark. Tall. Clean-cut. Polite. One of those "on paper" guys who checked every reasonable box her friends and family had gently suggested. He led Bible study. He served at church. He said the right things.

But tonight, his face was drawn tight with tension.

"Sarah," Mark began, his voice careful, "I've been praying a lot about... us."

Sarah's stomach clenched. She'd known this conversation was coming for weeks.

"And?" she asked quietly.

Mark exhaled. "I don't think I'm the one you're supposed to build a life with."

The words, though not surprising, still hit hard.

Sarah kept her voice calm, even as her chest tightened.

"Because?" Mark fidgeted.

"You want... things I don't think I do. A home. A house full of kids. That life."

Sarah's throat thickened, but she pressed on.

"You don't want a family?"

Mark hesitated, then spoke softly.

"I want ministry. Travel. Freedom to serve wherever God calls. Kids... that would anchor me. I don't feel peace about that kind of future."

Sarah nodded slowly, her worst fear quietly confirmed.

"We've talked about this before."

"I know." Mark looked pained. "I kept hoping maybe one of us would bend. But the truth is I think maybe God wired us differently."

She stared down at her untouched latte, swallowing hard.

"I appreciate your honesty."

Mark leaned forward slightly.

"You're going to make an incredible wife and mother someday. But it won't be with me."

Sarah forced a small smile, her heart cracking as she whispered:

"Then I pray God brings you someone who shares your vision."

He reached for her hand briefly before pulling back.

"And I pray the same for you."

The Quiet Grief

Later that night, Sarah lay curled in bed, staring at the ceiling fan as it spun in quiet rhythm.

Mara and Lottie texted supportive messages, both offering to come over, but Sarah had declined. She needed to sit in it.

She whispered into the dark:

> *"Lord, am I asking for too much?*
> *Am I wrong to want a family so deeply?*
> *Is this my fault somehow?"*

No answers came.

Only silence.

And yet, beneath the ache, she couldn't deny that small, stubborn seed that had always lived inside her, planted since childhood, the one that refused to let go of the dream of building a family.

> *One day.*
> *Please, one day.*

CHAPTER 2

How Sarah Meets Abe

The Introduction—Dallas & Manhattan

The FaceTime call connected as Sarah curled up on her couch, balancing her laptop on her knees and sipping some chamomile tea.

Lottie's face appeared, bright and energetic as always.

"Hey stranger!" Lottie beamed.

"Hey yourself," Sarah smiled. "I feel like we've both been living at our offices."

Lottie laughed. "That's adulthood, isn't it?"

Sarah nodded, glancing at the Manhattan skyline behind her. She had only been living in New York for a year but was finally starting to feel like she belonged.

"So," Sarah said, "what's the big reason you wanted to video chat instead of just text?"

Lottie's eyes sparkled mischievously. "Well... I miss seeing your beautiful face." "Oh, be serious, Lottie! Okay, I miss you too. But seriously, you hardly do video calls, so what's up?"

Realizing that she had been caught, she gave up, "I may have someone I want you to meet."

Sarah raised an eyebrow. "Lottie…"

"Hear me out!" Lottie said, holding up both hands. "You remember Abe Abrams, right? From my church in Dallas? The business guy?"

Sarah thought for a moment, vaguely recalling Lottie mentioning his name in passing years ago.

"Vaguely."

"Well," Lottie continued, "he recently relocated to Manhattan for work, some huge renewable energy startup. He's single, loves Jesus, funny, stable, wants a family someday—Sarah, seriously, he's solid."

Sarah raised a skeptical eyebrow. "You're trying to set me up with someone who's only lived in my city for two weeks."

Lottie grinned. "Exactly. He needs friends. You need a husband."

Sarah laughed, rolling her eyes.

"Oh my gosh."

"Look, no pressure," Lottie said, now softening her tone. "But seriously, I think you two might click. At the very least, it's coffee. You don't even have to wear heels."

Sarah exhaled, biting back a smile.

"All right. Coffee. No heels."

After their video call with Lottie, Sarah hesitated for a day before finally texting the number Lottie had sent her. Abe replied within the hour, polite and warm. Their messages were short—mostly logistics about times and places—but there was something steady in the way he wrote. No flirty jokes. No overly familiar emojis. Just a simple, "Looking forward to meeting you, Sarah." It felt old-fashioned in a way that made her heart settle, even if only for a moment.

The Coffee Meeting—One Week Later

That Saturday morning, as she put on mascara and tied her hair back, Sarah caught her reflection and paused. What if he was disappointed? What if she talked too fast or her laugh came out too loud? What if he was perfectly polite and never texted again? For a split second, she considered cancelling. But then she remembered his final text from last night: "Excited for tomorrow. Rest well." And something deeper whispered, go.

The cozy corner café was warm against the cold drizzle outside as Sarah arrived, nerves fluttering in her chest.

Abe was already there, standing to greet her as she approached, tall, clean-cut, with kind eyes and a confident but calm presence. He extended his hand.

"Sarah?"

"Yes. Hi."

"It's great to finally meet you. Lottie talks like you walk on water, so I figured I should see for myself."

Sarah laughed immediately, the tension easing slightly.

"She exaggerates."

"That's what she says about me too, so we're even."

They sat, ordered coffee, and within minutes, the conversation slipped into a surprisingly easy rhythm—books, careers, faith, travel, the strange loneliness of being new to a city.

Abe asked genuine questions, listened carefully, and laughed at all the right moments without feeling performative.

"You moved here for work?" Sarah asked.

"Yes," Abe nodded. "I was recruited by an energy investment group here. Long hours, big challenges, but... I love it. It's such a neat story...I'll have to tell you about it some time."

"I'm looking forward to that! So, you've made the big move to Manhattan," she said. "Do you see yourself settling here long term?" Sarah asked.

Abe grew thoughtful.

"Honestly? I'm not sure yet. Career-wise, yes. But honestly? Where I live isn't as important as the family I build. A home where faith is lived, not just spoken. Where children grow up knowing they're wanted and seen."

He paused, searching for the words.

"God told Abraham, 'I will make you the father of many nations.' And while I don't claim to be that man, I do believe God puts dreams in our hearts that reflect pieces of His design."

Sarah's breath caught for a moment. She wasn't prepared for how deeply his words resonated.

"You really think that's still possible in today's world?" she whispered.

Abe smiled gently. "I don't think anything is impossible with God."

"What about you? Family? Marriage?"

Sarah exhaled.

"That's always been my dream. Career has been great, I've been really blessed. But marriage, kids—that's always been the end goal."

Abe nodded.

"Then maybe we have something in common already."

They both laughed softly, but beneath the lightness, something rooted itself quietly—a spark neither of them wanted to rush, but neither could deny. As they said goodbye, Sarah felt a small flutter of hope in her chest. But as she walked back into the drizzle, she tucked her hands into her coat pockets and sighed. He seemed almost too good to be true. She had learned the hard way that first impressions were only the beginning. Only time would tell if kindness was who he really was, or just who he was trying to be.

Later That Night—Lottie's Text Thread
Lottie: *Well???*

Sarah: *Coffee lasted 2.5 hours*
Lottie: *That's a good sign!!!*
Sarah: *We're grabbing dinner next week!*
Lottie: *I'm already picking out bridesmaid dresses*

Sarah laughed as she read Lottie's reply, her heart warm for the first time in a long while.
Maybe... just maybe.

CHAPTER 3

The First Date

Little Candle—Lower Manhattan

The restaurant was small, warm, and full of quiet charm—exposed brick walls, soft candlelight, and the faint hum of jazz playing somewhere in the background. The kind of place where the city faded away and the world shrunk down to just two people at a table for two.

Abe and Sarah sat near the window, tucked into a cozy corner. Their glasses of wine reflected the flickering candle between them.

"I love this place," Sarah said, her eyes scanning the room. "It feels like a secret."

Abe had picked it. Simple but thoughtful. Not showy. Comfortable.

"It's even better in person," Abe smiled as they sat.

"I always believe the first impression a man makes with a restaurant says a lot."

Sarah laughed softly. "And what impression are you hoping to make?"

Abe grinned. "That I'm a man of good taste and better company."

The banter came easy between them. Lottie had been right, there was a natural rhythm already.

As they worked through their appetizers, their conversation shifted into deeper waters.

"Do your parents live here in the city?" Abe asked gently.

Sarah's smile faltered slightly. "No... actually, they were both killed a few years ago. A drunk driver."

"I'm so sorry." His voice softened.

She nodded. "Thank you. It still feels strange sometimes, like I suddenly got cut loose from my anchor. That's part of the reason I moved to New York...to escape the bed memories back in Dallas."

Abe paused, then offered quietly, "I understand that more than you might think."

Sarah looked up, surprised by the gentleness in his voice.

"My parents passed too. My dad first—heart attack while I was preparing to go to college. My mom a year later."

"So young," Sarah whispered.

Abe nodded. "Yeah. It changes you. The world feels thinner. Like you're walking without a net."

Sarah exhaled deeply. "Yes. Exactly that."

Abe sipped his wine slowly, then looked up at Sarah with a half-smile. "You know, I almost left Dallas for college."

"Oh yeah? Where to?"

"NYU," he said, a wistful tone in his voice. "I got accepted senior year. Even had a scholarship lined up. But my dad had just passed, and I couldn't leave my mom alone. So, I stayed."

Sarah's eyes softened. "That must've been hard."

"It was," he nodded. "But even back then, I had this pull toward New York. Couldn't explain it. Still can't. Just always felt like something important for me was waiting there."

She smiled. "Maybe it wasn't a place. Maybe it was a person."

They sat in quiet understanding for a moment, two people who knew something most people their age hadn't yet tasted: the ache of living without the safety net of parents.

Abe smiled softly. "I guess that's one more thing we have in common."

Sarah returned his smile. "Maybe we both know what it's like to build something new without the safety net we expected to have."

Abe nodded. "And maybe we both believe God still writes good stories, even with missing chapters."

The ease between them deepened in that small admission. Something unspoken passed between them—not romance alone, but a recognition of shared strength.

As they finished their entrées, Abe's gaze shifted out the window for a moment, watching the blurred glow of city lights. Then he turned back toward her, his tone softening.

"Do you ever think about the future, Sarah? Like... really think about where all this leads?"

Sarah set her wine glass down gently. "Sometimes. But lately, I'm more curious about where your future is headed."

Abe chuckled, but there was a weight in his eyes. "Honestly? I've always had this sense—like God's given me a vision that's bigger than just my career. Not just success, but legacy."

"Legacy?" she echoed, intrigued.

"Yeah." He paused, choosing his words carefully. "I want to build something that outlives me. Something that multiplies. Companies, sure. But more than that—people, families, communities. A kind of ripple effect that keeps expanding long after I'm gone."

Sarah studied him for a moment, surprised by his conviction. "That's... beautiful, Abe."

He smiled, but there was a vulnerability beneath it. "I don't talk about it much. I guess I've always felt called to something that feels... almost impossible sometimes. Like I'm supposed to create a future that blesses far more people than I'll ever meet."

Sarah's heart stirred at his words. She had dated men before—successful men, ambitious men, but none had spoken about their future like this. Not from ego, but from purpose. But as she listened, a small part of her wondered if anyone could truly live with that kind of purpose forever. Dreams felt beautiful at dinner tables with candlelight. Living them out every day was a different story. She admired his faith, but she also wondered if he ever woke up afraid, the way she sometimes did.

Abe looked at her more intently now. "I do want a family someday. Children. Not just one or two. I always imagined a house full."

Her breath caught slightly. "How full are we talking?" she teased gently, her voice light but her pulse quickening.

He laughed softly. "Enough that the house always feels alive. Enough to pass something on."

Sarah smiled, her eyes glistening. "I've always wanted to be a mom too. That's been part of my dream as long as I can remember."

Abe reached across the table and took her hand, his touch warm and steady. "We'd make a good team."

Sarah smiled at his words, but deep down a quiet fear pressed against her chest. What if she couldn't give him that? What if their dreams only matched on the surface but cracked underneath when life didn't cooperate? She tucked the fear away behind her smile. She smiled again, quieter this time. "I think we would."

The Unfolding Connection

They continued talking long after their plates had been cleared. Careers. Childhoods. Travel. Church. The kind of honest, effortless conversation that feels both familiar and new.

By the time they stepped back out into the cool evening air, Sarah found herself smiling more easily than she had in a long time. As they stood to leave, Abe moved to pull her chair back but knocked his knee against the table leg. He winced and laughed softly, rubbing it. "Graceful, I know," he joked. Sarah laughed too, grateful for the tiny moment that reminded her he wasn't perfect either.

Abe glanced at her as they walked toward her building.

"Would you be open to doing this again?" he asked, not pushing—simply hopeful.

Sarah laughed softly. "I was hoping you'd ask."

They paused at her front door, standing just close enough for the electricity between them to hum quietly.

"I'm glad Lottie suggested this," Abe said softly.

"Me too."

Neither moved to end the moment quickly. Finally, Abe simply whispered, "Goodnight, Sarah."

"Goodnight, Abe."

As she stepped inside and closed the door behind her, Sarah leaned back against it, her pulse still steadying.

She pressed her back against the door, closing her eyes for a moment. Her heart was light, but beneath the glow lay a small ache she couldn't quite name. He was kind. Intentional. Almost too perfect. She whispered into the quiet room, "Please let this be real, God."

The Same Night—Lottie's Phone Call

Sarah practically floated into her apartment that night, kicking off her heels with a little spin before collapsing onto the couch, heart still racing. Without even taking off her coat, she grabbed her phone and hit Lottie's contact. Lottie answered on the second ring.

"Well??" Lottie squealed before Sarah even said hello. Sarah burst out laughing.

"Okay... I think you may have actually nailed it."

"I knew it!" Lottie practically shrieked. "Tell me everything. Start from the beginning."

Sarah curled up on the couch, grinning ear to ear.

"We sat for almost three hours. The conversation never even dipped once. It was... easy. He's so kind, Lottie. Like, *genuinely* kind. Thoughtful. Confident without being arrogant."

Lottie let out a long, satisfied sigh.

"I love it. Okay, I'm not saying I'm planning your wedding yet... but I'm definitely picking out your engagement photoshoot outfits in my head."

"Stop!" Sarah laughed. "Don't jinx it!"

"Okay fine—but come on, you felt it, didn't you? That spark?"

Sarah paused, her voice softening, "I did."

"And you're attracted to him, right?" Lottie pressed.

"Be honest."

Sarah giggled, "Lottie, he's adorable. Like dangerously handsome and doesn't even seem to know it."

Lottie let out a dramatic gasp, "I'm so happy I want to cry."

Sarah laughed again but grew thoughtful.

"There's something different about him, Lottie. He really wants a family one day. He even talked about legacy and purpose. It wasn't cheesy...it was sincere. It was like...God-centered."

Lottie momentarily grew quiet, then whispered, "Sarah...I think God may be writing your story."

Sarah exhaled deeply, feeling a little overwhelmed but incredibly hopeful.

"We'll see," she whispered. "But for the first time in a long time...I feel like this might be the beginning of something."

The Next Morning—Saturday

Sarah was pouring herself a cup of coffee when her phone buzzed. She glanced at the screen, her stomach flipping slightly when she saw Abe's name.

She grinned and answered, trying to sound casually composed.

"Good morning."

"Good morning," Abe replied, his voice warm. "Did I wake you?"

"Nope. Just surviving my usual weekend caffeine addiction."

He chuckled.

"Glad to hear it. I was debating whether to call or text, but this seemed worth a real call."

Sarah leaned against the kitchen counter, heart fluttering.

"Oh? And what's so important it warranted full voice contact?"

Abe smiled on the other end, his tone playful but sincere.

"I had a really great time last night, Sarah."

Sarah's heart swelled a little more.

"So did I."

"I'd like to see you again," Abe continued. "But this time I was thinking...if you're open to it, I'd love for you to come to church with me tomorrow. Then maybe grab lunch afterward?"

Sarah blinked, pleasantly surprised.

"You want to take me to church on our second date?"

"Well," Abe chuckled, "if you're going to know me, you should know my church. Fair warning: the pastor tends to get...enthusiastic."

Sarah laughed.

"Sounds like my kind of place."

"Perfect," Abe said. "Service starts at 10. I'll text you the address."

"I'll be there."

As they hung up, Sarah stood for a moment, holding her phone to her chest, her coffee entirely forgotten.

Church and lunch. This felt different. Good different.

Sarah's Prophetic Dream

The apartment was still and quiet when Sarah finally drifted into sleep. But somewhere in the dark, a dream found her. She was standing under a night sky more expansive than anything she had ever seen. Stars glittered like sequins on velvet, thousands upon thousands of them, pulsing with light.

Then she heard it, a whisper, barely audible but unmistakable:

"So shall your children be."

She looked down. Her hands were empty. Her belly flat. Alone, in the middle of a vast field, with stars singing overhead and no one to hold. Then she jolted awake, breath shallow, heart racing. It was just a dream. But something in her spirit trembled.

She got up, padded to her desk, and opened her journal.

Lord, what are You trying to tell me? If this is a promise, why does it feel so far away? Am I just making this up? Help me believe again. She closed the journal and whispered aloud, *"Please, God. I don't want to be disappointed. Not again."*

CHAPTER 4

The Church Date

Sunday Morning—Cornerstone Church, Manhattan

Sarah arrived a few minutes early, stomach flipping as she stepped onto the sidewalk. She felt underdressed, overdressed, and unprepared all at once. Dating apps had never felt this intimidating. Church with a near-stranger felt like letting him see something raw in her before she was ready. Abe was already waiting outside, dressed sharp but simple in a navy sport coat and open-collar shirt. He smiled as soon as he saw her.

"You look beautiful," he said warmly.

Sarah blushed, catching her breath. "You clean up pretty well yourself."

He shifted awkwardly, brushing his coat sleeve as if realizing it was lint-speckled. "Sorry, I came straight from prepping slides for Monday's board meeting. Didn't even check myself in the mirror," he said with a crooked smile, rubbing his neck. "And I might've spilled coffee on myself earlier."

He offered his arm, and together they walked inside. The sanctuary was larger than she expected—modern but warm, with soft lighting and a small worship team already playing softly as people found their seats. As they settled in, Sarah whispered, "You're sure this isn't some sort of evaluation and assessment by your church?"

Abe smiled.

"No evaluations. Just grace."

The music swelled as worship began, and for the next twenty minutes, Sarah felt her heart soften as the congregation sang—the familiar lyrics washing over her like comfort. But part of her wondered...was she being moved by God...or just caught up in the moment?

The Sermon

When Pastor Wells took the stage, Sarah smiled at his youthful energy, Bible in hand.

"Today," he began, "we're going to revisit one of my favorite stories in all of Scripture—the story of Abraham and Sarah."

Sarah's head snapped slightly toward Abe, eyebrows raised. Abe grinned and whispered, "Total coincidence."

The pastor continued, voice full of passion.

"God made a promise to Abraham—that he would become the father of many nations. But Abraham and his wife Sarah had to wait. And wait. And wait. For years, they saw no evidence of the promise. They wondered if God had forgotten them. But God never forgets His promises."

Sarah listened, captivated—both by the sermon and the strange, gentle tug in her own chest.

"Sometimes God's timing makes no sense to us. But He operates outside of time. His delays are not His denials. And when God finally delivered His promise to Abraham and Sarah, it produced laughter— the kind of joy that only comes from impossible things becoming possible."

Sarah swallowed hard, her throat tightening unexpectedly. She hadn't expected to be so moved. She almost thought this was a setup.

As the congregation filtered out, Sarah and Abe walked together in comfortable silence, each lost in quiet thought.

Finally, Sarah broke the silence.

"Well. That was...oddly specific."

Abe chuckled. "I swear I didn't plan that."

Sarah smiled but looked up at him, her voice quieter.

"Do you ever wonder what kind of story God's writing for you?"

Abe paused before answering.

"I do. Often."

He glanced at her, sincerity radiating in his voice.

"And I have to admit...I've been wondering lately if maybe... you're part of that story."

Sarah's heart skipped, but she quickly redirected with a soft smile.

"You always sound so sure. I usually take the long way around hope. Well, let's at least get through lunch before you start making any divine appointments."

The Lunch Date

The restaurant was quiet for a Sunday afternoon, with soft jazz playing in the background and the occasional clink of silverware. Sarah sat across from Abe, still glowing from the morning's church service. The sermon had been surprisingly personal—about legacy and God's promises echoing across generations. It had stirred something in both of them.

They were halfway through their meal when Abe grew quiet, gazing at the small window beside them.

"What are you thinking about?" Sarah asked gently.

He hesitated, then smiled, his tone a little quieter now. "You know...I don't talk about my dad much. But today's message really brought him to mind. And I've been meaning to tell you how I landed in New York."

Sarah leaned in. "I'd love to hear about your dad."

Abe nodded. "My dad was a quiet man. Steady. Faithful. He worked in energy infrastructure, helping build pipelines and clean-energy facilities in rural areas. He believed deeply that access to power could change people's lives. But he never got to see the big dream come to life—the idea of a community-owned energy grid powered by renewables. I shared with you last time that he died of a heart attack when I was still in college."

"I remember...I'm so sorry, Abe," Sarah said softly, her eyes full of compassion.

"Thanks," he said. "What's wild is...as I was getting ready to graduate, I got recruited by a small but ambitious investment group out of New York. Their pitch? They wanted to fund the future of energy—real innovation, not just profit. It was like someone picked up my dad's blueprints and said, 'Let's go.'"

Sarah blinked. "Wait...this is the firm you're still with? And just moved to New York for?"

"Yeah. And get this—the senior partner? He worked with my dad once. He recognized my last name and told me my dad's vision was ahead of his time. Said it was why he took a chance on me and reached out." Abe's voice caught for a second. "I moved to New York not just to take the job—but to finish what my dad started."

Sarah reached for his hand across the table. "That's incredible, Abe."

"I want to build something that lasts, Sarah," he said.   "Not just investments. A life. A legacy. Something our kids will be proud of one day."

She smiled, not just moved by his words, but feeling her heart knit even more tightly to his.

"Now I see why you want a big family."

Abe smiled warmly.

"Yes. Marriage, kids, the whole messy, beautiful thing. Legacy matters to me. Though... I've also wondered...what if it doesn't happen for me?"

He gave her a sideways glance. "Would I still be enough?"

Sarah's voice grew quieter.

"Let's trust God and his process, and...I want that too."

He studied her for a moment, then said gently, "We're not too different from Abraham and Sarah, you know. Dreaming about promises we can't fully see yet."

Sarah smiled, her chest fluttering again.

"Let's just hope our waiting season is a little shorter than theirs."

Abe chuckled softly.

"Amen to that."

Later That Evening

As Sarah settled into her apartment that night, she texted Lottie one simple line:

I think this could be something real.

Her heart whispered a silent prayer as she set her phone down:

Lord, if this is You...let my faith outlast my fear. Even if You say 'not yet.'

CHAPTER 5

The Moment of Knowing

Two Months Later—Early Spring

The park was just beginning to bloom again as Abe and Sarah walked side by side, coffees in hand, enjoying the first real hints of spring warmth after a long Manhattan winter.

Sarah looked radiant even in her casual Saturday clothes—hair pulled back, sunglasses perched on top of her head, her laughter soft and easy as they meandered along the paved path.

"So," Sarah said playfully, nudging him, "are you going to let me win this time or are we still pretending we're both equally good at Scrabble?"

Abe chuckled.

"Hey, I can't help it if you keep drawing terrible letters."

"Excuses," she teased.

He laughed but said nothing for a moment, his heart growing unusually full as he watched her light up.

I'd prayed for someone like this, kind, resilient, easy to talk to. But even in my best prayers, I hadn't imagined someone quite like her.

Abe had dated before. He'd even thought he might have been in love once or twice. But nothing had ever felt like this—not just comfort, but peace. Not just attraction, but calling.

Sarah stopped briefly to admire a cluster of blooming cherry blossoms, closing her eyes as a light breeze carried the petals gently across their feet.

Abe studied her carefully, quietly.

This is the one I want to build a family with. The one I want to walk with into every season—good or hard.

Without thinking, he whispered, almost to himself,

"I want to marry you," Abe said, almost before he realized the words had formed.

Sarah turned, the surprise in her eyes softened by something deeper.

"What did you say?"

Abe hesitated, then chuckled, suddenly self-conscious. "Did I say that out loud?"

She nodded slowly. "You did."

A long pause.

"But I'm not scared. Maybe I'm just getting ahead of myself."

Sarah's eyes twinkled but her voice grew soft.

"Not getting ahead of me."

They stood for a beat, both quietly aware that the conversation had just tipped into deeper waters.

Abe reached for her hand, squeezing gently.

"Let's enjoy this season a little longer first. But yes—I'm already plotting."

Sarah exhaled, her heart skimming the edge of panic and peace. This was the moment she'd dreamed about, but now that it was here, she wasn't sure if her heart was ready to believe it could last.

Still, something inside her settled. Not with certainty. But with trust. The she laughed.

"I figured."

They continued walking, hand in hand, the air filled with unspoken promise—both of them fully aware now that their love story was unfolding under a much bigger Author's pen.

Later That Night—Abe's Apartment

Abe sat at his desk long after Sarah had gone home, opening a simple leather-bound notebook where he scribbled personal prayers and reflections.

He wrote one quiet sentence at the bottom of a new page:

Lord, thank You for Sarah. If this is Your will—prepare my heart, prepare hers, and prepare our future. I trust Your timing.

He closed the book, smiled, and whispered aloud, "I think she's the one."

One Weeks Later—Guy's Night Out

Sarah stepped into the dimly lit restaurant where Abe had invited her to meet "the guys." The place had a warm, masculine feel—dark wood, leather booths, and the quiet buzz of after-work laughter.

Abe spotted her instantly and stood to greet her.

"You made it," he said with a grin, kissing her cheek.

Sarah smiled but whispered playfully, "Are you sure I'm ready for this initiation?"

Abe chuckled.

"They're harmless, I promise. Mostly."

He led her to a long booth where three men already sat—all early-thirties, well-dressed but relaxed, each sizing her up with friendly curiosity.

Abe made the introductions.

"Sarah, this is Eli, Jordan, and Marcus—my new partners-in-crime I met through a small group at church."

Each man shook her hand in turn, exchanging polite smiles.

"We've heard a lot about you," Eli said, his grin teasing.

"All good things, of course."

Jordan leaned in conspiratorially.

"And we've been waiting to meet the woman who's tamed Abe Abrams."

Sarah laughed, already sensing the good-natured tone.

"Tamed might be a strong word."

Marcus added, "We're really just here to make sure you're not secretly a Knicks fan. Dealbreaker."

Sarah grinned. "Thankfully, I have no strong opinions on basketball. You're safe."

As the evening unfolded, Sarah held her own—answering questions about her job, her upbringing, her faith. She was honest, warm, and poised, but also quick with her wit when the teasing escalated.

"So what's your biggest flaw, Sarah?" Eli asked with mock seriousness.

Sarah sipped her drink thoughtfully.

"Probably… my inability to say no to dessert."

Eli laughed heartily, "Oh, what a weakness! That way, you'd always have a full meal whenever you eat."

"Yes, I like to eat and be well fed", Sarah replied, enjoying the light banter.

Jordan raised his glass.

"A woman of priorities. I respect that."

Abe watched the exchange with pride. He loved seeing Sarah handle the playful gauntlet with grace.

The Unspoken Evaluation

Later, as Sarah excused herself to the restroom, Marcus leaned toward

Abe.

"You did good, man," Marcus said, his voice low and sincere.

"She's solid."

Jordan nodded.

"She's the real deal."

Eli added, "And you're glowing like you already bought the ring."

Abe chuckled, not denying it.

"Maybe I have."

The guys raised their glasses in a quiet, unofficial blessing over the table.

"To Sarah," Marcus said softly.

"To the next chapter," Abe added.

As They Left

Walking home hand-in-hand later that night, Sarah looked up at Abe with a sly grin.

"So... did I pass?"

Abe laughed.

"You more than passed. You raised the bar."

Sarah squeezed his hand playfully.

"Good. Because I kind of like you."

Abe kissed her hand.

"I kind of like you too."

Two Weeks Later—Ring Shopping

The small private jeweler was tucked away in an unassuming building—the kind of place you only found if someone gave you the address directly. Abe wanted something personal, meaningful, and not off the rack.

As he opened the door, Marcus stood up from the waiting couch and grinned.

"You ready for this, man?"

Abe smiled nervously.

"Thanks for coming. I figured you'd keep me from doing something reckless."

Marcus chuckled as they shook hands.

"You know we drew straws, right? Jordan and Eli were terrified they'd end up having to make sentimental judgments."

Abe laughed.

"Well, you're the most emotionally stable of us."

Marcus raised an eyebrow.

"Or the one most likely to cry while you propose."

"Fair."

The jeweler emerged, greeting them with quiet professionalism. Abe explained what he was looking for—classic, elegant, but unique.

"I want it to feel timeless," Abe said. "Not flashy. Just...right."

As tray after tray of rings appeared on the counter, Marcus watched his friend carefully.

"You nervous?" he asked under his breath.

Abe exhaled.

"Not about marrying her. That part's crystal clear."

Marcus smiled, nodding.

"She's the real thing."

Abe stared down at the display of glimmering diamonds.

"She's the answered prayer I almost didn't know I was allowed to ask for."

Marcus's expression softened.

"You've both walked through loss. But maybe that's part of why you found each other."

Abe nodded, his voice quiet.

"God didn't waste our waiting."

Marcus smiled.

"Sarah's gonna love whatever you pick. But more than that— she'll love the man who's choosing her."

Abe smiled, his nerves giving way to quiet certainty. Finally, after several rounds, Abe pointed to one.

Simple.

Oval cut.

Delicate band.

A quiet elegance that felt exactly like Sarah.

"This one," he said.

The jeweler smiled. "An excellent choice."

Marcus looked at the ring, then at his friend.

"Okay," he said softly. "Now I might be the one who cries."

Abe laughed, sliding the box closed.

"Save it for the wedding."

As they stepped back onto the Manhattan sidewalk, Marcus patted Abe on the back.

"You're about to change both your lives, man."

"I know," Abe said, grinning. "And I can't wait."

CHAPTER 6

The Proposal

Brooklyn Bridge Park—Late Afternoon

The golden glow of the setting sun reflected off the East River, turning the Manhattan skyline into a living painting. Sarah walked beside Abe, their hands naturally intertwined, as they made their way along the quiet path. Tourists and locals milled about, but in this moment, Sarah felt like they were the only two people in the world.

Abe had been unusually quiet all afternoon—thoughtful, almost nervous—but she hadn't pressed him. She liked that about him. He never filled silence just to avoid it.

They stopped near a bench overlooking the water. The breeze lifted her hair as Sarah looked out across the city they were both falling in love with. Abe stayed behind her for a moment, taking in the sight of her standing there—strong, independent, beautiful. His partner.

"Sarah," he said softly.

She turned, smiling at the tenderness in his voice. "Yeah?"

He stepped closer and reached for both her hands. "I've thought about this moment for a long time."

Her heart skipped. She blinked, breath catching slightly.

"I know life won't always be easy. I know we'll face things neither of us can predict." His voice was steady now, full of quiet conviction. "But I also know that I want to face all of it—with you."

Sarah's eyes glistened as her smile trembled. "Abe…"

"I want to build a life with you. Not just a career, not just a beautiful home, but a family, a legacy. The one we talked about that night at Little Candle. I believe God has written something for us that's bigger than we can imagine. But I don't want to write it alone."

Slowly, Abe reached into his jacket pocket and pulled out a simple, elegant ring—a single diamond, set on a delicate gold band.

He lowered to one knee.

"Sarah Cohen," he whispered, emotion thick in his voice. "Will you marry me? Will you let me love you, lead you, wait with you—and build the kind of forever only God could've dreamed up?"

Tears spilled freely now as Sarah nodded, unable to speak at first. She finally whispered, "Yes. Yes, Abe, I will."

He slipped the ring onto her finger as they both laughed through their tears. Standing, Abe pulled her into his arms, and they held each other in the fading light, as if anchoring themselves to this moment.

In her heart, Sarah felt something she hadn't fully known before: *This is the man I'll wait with. And this is the man I'd waited for.*

She'd always imagined she'd cry the day she got engaged—just never like this. Not with such peace. Not with such surety. This wasn't the end of longing—it was the beginning of something truly beautiful and God-ordained. This was peace.

The sun dipped beneath the skyline, casting a last golden breath. And somewhere in Sarah's spirit, she heard it—not words, but a knowing: *The promise has only just begun.*

A Dallas "I Do"

Engagements were in the air, but Mara had managed to beat Sarah to it and sent out her wedding invites for just a few short months away. Sarah and Abe were newly engaged, so never a more perfect time to travel to Dallas to participate in her best friend's nuptials.

It had been years since Sarah walked through the grand stone archway of the Bella Donna chapel, but the moment she stepped inside, it felt like stepping into another world.

Lavender-scented candles flickered in the sconces, sunlight spilled through stained-glass windows, and every pew was filled with people who had watched Mara and Jared's love story unfold. Sarah smoothed the soft emerald fabric of her bridesmaid's dress, exhaling slowly. The hush before the wedding march began always made her emotional.

And then it started—the music, the rise of the guests, the hush of anticipation.

Mara appeared at the top of the aisle, radiant in a flowing lace gown and veil that shimmered in the sunlight shining in from the windows. Jared, her groom, looked stunned. Sarah glanced over at Abe, who had flown down with her just for the weekend. He was seated in the second row, pressed into a tailored navy-blue suit, his tie just slightly askew. He caught her eye and gave a small, boyish smile.

She smiled back.

After the ceremony, guests gathered outside for a candlelit reception under a canopy of twinkle lights and paper lanterns. Long wooden tables were filled with platters of brisket, cornbread, and peach cobbler—Texas charm at its best. Laughter echoed under the stars, and a bluegrass band strummed upbeat melodies while Mara clung to Jared during their first dance.

Lottie stood beside Sarah, holding a champagne flute and dabbing at the corner of her eye with a tissue.

"That dress," Sarah whispered. "She looks breathtaking, like a genius work of art."

"She looks like she won the lottery," Lottie replied, her voice soft with sincerity. "Jared's a good one."

Sarah turned to her. "So...who do you think will be next?"

Lottie snorted. "Please. I'm only here for the cake."

Sarah gave her a playful nudge.

Lottie lifted her glass. "One down, one to go. But don't get your hopes up. I'm still not the white-dress type."

Sarah raised her brow. "You were the one who helped pick this venue."

"Yes, and I have excellent taste. Doesn't mean I want to be the one walking the aisle."

As the words left her mouth, her eyes lingered on Mara and Jared—their foreheads touching, their steps slow and unhurried in the warm night air.

The Dance

Sarah finally found a moment alone with Abe near the bar.

"You clean up well," she teased, eyeing him over her glass of iced tea.

He tilted his head. "You didn't tell me your best friend throws such beautiful parties. Or that you'd look like this in satin."

Sarah blushed. "It's the lighting."

"No," he said, a little more serious now. "It's you."

Their gazes held for a moment longer than either expected. The music shifted to a slow song. Abe offered his hand. "Come dance with me?"

She hesitated—not because she didn't want to. "You sure you're ready for my two-step skills?"

"I'm brave."

They stepped into the soft candlelight, moving slowly in rhythm with the music. His hand rested gently on her waist. Her head leaned against his shoulder. The night felt impossibly romantic—the kind of night you want to bottle forever.

Midway through the song, he murmured, "You think Mara and Jared knew this was it when they first met?"

Sarah glanced toward the head table where Mara and Jared were laughing with friends. "Hmm, she said the moment she prayed for a husband, Jared showed up a week later. Like an answered prayer walking through the church doors."

Abe nodded thoughtfully. "When I pray, I don't always get answers that fast."

"Me neither," Sarah said. Then she looked up at him. "But sometimes the answer is standing right in front of you."

He smiled. "Now you're just flirting."

"I might be," she said, teasing again.

He leaned in, lips close to her ear. "I'm really glad you invited me, Sarah."

"Of course! I'm really glad you came."

As the song ended and the dance floor buzzed again, neither one pulled away too quickly.

Window Seat Dreams

The hum of the airplane engines blended with the quiet rustle of passengers settling in for the flight. Sarah leaned against the window, still clutching the wedding program from Mara and Jared's ceremony. She hadn't wanted to toss it—something about the simplicity of their vows and the sparkle in Mara's eyes made her want to keep it as a memento.

Abe slid into the seat beside her, placing a water bottle in her cupholder. "Hydration," he said, grinning. "Doctor's orders."

"Thank you," she said, smiling. "That was some weekend, huh?"

Abe leaned back and sighed. "It was. That whole reception felt like something out of a rom-com. Mara and Jared are the real deal."

Sarah nodded, then glanced at him sideways. "Do you ever think about what kind of wedding you'd want?"

Abe looked amused. "We just left one and you're already planning the next?"

She laughed. "Just wondering. You have proposed after all!"

He considered. "Something simple, probably outdoors. Maybe in a garden or vineyard. Not too fussy. But lots of music. Great food. And friends and family everywhere."

Sarah tucked her legs underneath her, facing him. "You ever picture the person standing across from you?"

Abe's eyes met hers. "Not anymore because I know it's you."

A slow smile spread across her face, heat rising to her cheeks.

"What about you?" he asked. "Big wedding? Ballroom? Central Park horses and carriages?"

She mock-gasped. "How did you know?!"

He chuckled.

"I used to dream of that kind of thing," she admitted.

"But now…it's more about the person than the production. I just want to look across the aisle and *know*. You know?"

"I do."

The plane bumped slightly with turbulence, and their shoulders brushed. Neither moved.

Sarah looked down at the wedding program in her lap and traced the calligraphy. "I loved their vows," she said softly. "So honest. So intentional."

Abe nodded. "You and I would write our own."

Sarah looked up, surprised. "Really?"

"Absolutely. Vows shouldn't be recycled. If I'm standing there, I want every word to count."

She gave him a long look. "I believe you."

They flew on in companionable silence, but everything felt a little more defined. A little more real.

As they began their descent into LaGuardia, Abe glanced out the window, then back at Sarah.

"Just think," he said. "The future Mr. and Mrs. Someone could be flying home from a wedding just like this... and not even realize they're writing their own story."

Sarah smiled. "Yeah. I think I've heard that one before."

CHAPTER 7

The Wedding Dress

Two Week After Mara's Honeymoon

Sarah kicked off her heels the second she walked through the door and flopped onto the couch with a sigh of relief. Before she could even close her eyes, her phone buzzed in her bag. She fished it out and smiled when Lottie's name popped up, quickly followed by a FaceTime invite.

She hit "accept," already bracing herself for her friends' questions.

"Finally!" Lottie's voice burst through. "I've been pacing around my apartment like it's the finale of *The Bachelor*. We need the full download—now."

Sarah laughed, tucking her hair behind her ear. Before she could respond, Mara's face appeared on the call, her skin sun-kissed and glowing with that unmistakable post-honeymoon bliss.

"Hi, bridesmaids," Sarah greeted, holding up her left hand and wiggling her ring finger for the camera. "Still engaged. Still real."

Lottie gasped dramatically. "We know that, Miss Cohen, we need details. But first, can we take a moment for Mara's wedding? Stunning. Like something out of a Southern fairytale."

"I'm still processing it," Sarah added. "You were absolutely glowing, Mara. I cried during your vows…and the first dance…and the cake cutting."

Mara laughed. "It was such a blur, but I loved every second. Jared keeps calling me Mrs. Thomas and it still feels surreal."

"Well," Lottie said with a grin, "Now it's your turn, Sarah. You're next! Any news on the date?"

Sarah tucked her legs under herself like she used to during college dorm nights, when the future was still foggy and full of possibility. "We're thinking early spring. Something local. Intimate. Maybe Central Park— Conservatory Garden, to be exact."

Mara squealed. "Stop. That's perfect."

"And," Sarah added with a smirk, "Abe and I want to keep things moving. So…I'm going dress shopping this Saturday. And you two better be there. No excuses."

Lottie gasped. "Girl. I've had a Pinterest board since 2017 titled *Sarah's Dress Vibes*. I'm ready."

"I already took Friday off so I can fly in," Mara chimed in.

"Text me the address—I'm bringing tissues."

Sarah felt a surge of warmth as she looked at her two best friends. "You know, it's kind of wild. From coffee-fueled all-nighters in college to weddings and dress fittings…"

Lottie grinned. "And soon…baby showers."

Sarah laughed. "One thing at a time, please!"

"Deal," Mara said, lifting her mug toward the screen.

"To the next chapter."

They clinked their virtual cups in unison—a toast to love, friendship, and everything still to come.

The Dress Appointment—Manhattan Bridal Boutique

The floor-to-ceiling mirrors stood like quiet sentinels, reflecting Sarah as she stepped out of the fitting room. She paused, smoothing her hands down the bodice of the lace gown, feeling the delicate threads beneath her fingertips. It was as though the dress breathed with her, whispering secrets of every bride it had ever held.

Lottie's eyes brimmed with tears the instant she looked up.

"Oh, Sarah…" Her voice trembled with a joy too big for words. Beside her, Mara clasped her hands against her chest, shaking her head in wonder. "We can stop right here," she declared, her voice bright with conviction. "That's it. That's your dress."

Sarah turned slowly, the gown swirling like cream stirred into coffee. For a moment, she barely recognized herself—the woman in the glass looked softer somehow, luminous and rooted all at once. A small, tearful laugh slipped past her lips. She felt her chest tighten with an emotion deeper than happiness. Something closer to grace.

Lottie moved around her in a quiet circle, her fingers brushing the scalloped hem, the intricate lacework at the sleeves. "The neckline… the sleeves…the way it falls," she breathed. "It's as though it was sewn for your story alone."

Mara nodded slowly, taking in every fold and shadow. "Classic, but it still feels like now. And the back?" She exhaled. "Utterly stunning."

Sarah smiled, her eyes damp with gratitude. "You two are dangerously good for my ego today."

Lottie shook her head, a grin breaking through her tears. "We're just good at seeing what's true."

In the background, the boutique attendant stood quietly, arms folded over her measuring tape, a small smile playing at her lips. "You really do look radiant," she said softly, as though speaking a blessing into the room.

As Sarah turned in front of the mirror, the lace catching light like morning dew, her breath caught. Tears rose unbidden, burning softly behind her lashes.

I never imagined I'd find this so quickly...or that God would write this story so beautifully. Each thread felt like a promise kept, each fold a whisper of mercy long prayed for.

Lottie noticed the way her friend's shoulders trembled and stepped forward, resting a gentle hand there. "Hey," she said, her voice low and kind, "it's okay to feel overwhelmed."

Sarah tried to answer, but her words came out hushed and broken. "I just...I never thought I'd reach this moment."

Not because love felt impossible, but because hope sometimes felt like a luxury she wasn't sure she could afford. Some days, belief was a battle waged quietly, under blankets and tears and silent prayers. Mara stepped closer, her voice steady with fierce affection. "You deserve every bit of this, Sarah. I'm sorry your mom is not here for this. She would be crying big tears of joy I'm sure."

A tear slipped down Sarah's cheek as she whispered into the quiet hum of the boutique, almost to herself, "I do miss her, but God is so good to give me friends like you."

Lottie squeezed her hand, her thumb tracing slow circles against her skin. "He is," she said softly. "And Abe is a good man. The two of you...you're building something rare and holy."

The boutique attendant approached with quiet reverence, clipping the final veil into place. The delicate tulle framed Sarah's glowing face like dawn rising over still waters. For a long moment, all three women stood in silence, letting the beauty settle over them like a blessing.

Finally, Lottie spoke, her words brushing the air like a prayer. *"I just want you to remember this moment forever,"* she whispered. "Before babies and boardrooms and life gets loud... remember this mirror. This beginning."

Sarah nodded, her gaze steady through her tears. "I will."

She drew a long, trembling breath, then let the words fall from her lips with a smile, quiet and sure.

"Okay. This is the one."

Premarital Counseling, Church Office—One Month Before the Wedding

The small office smelled faintly of old books and freshly brewed coffee, a comforting scent that seemed to settle over the room like a quiet blessing. Behind the broad wooden desk hung a large wooden cross, catching slants of morning light that fell across Pastor Wells' calm, lined face. His presence felt like an anchor in the gentle hush of the early hour.

Sarah and Abe sat side by side on the worn leather couch, their knees brushing every so often, their hands naturally intertwined. Outside the window, traffic moved steadily down Lexington Avenue, but here, time felt slower, softer. Sarah watched Pastor Wells flip open his notebook, his wedding band glinting as he turned the page with deliberate care.

"This part isn't about finding problems," he said, his voice low and rich with kindness. "It's about giving your marriage a strong foundation before you walk into the covenant."

Sarah smiled, tilting her head in quiet gratitude. "We appreciate you doing this with us."

"It's my honor," he replied, his eyes warm. He studied them for a moment, as though memorizing their joined hands and youthful hope before he asked, "Tell me, what are you both most looking forward to?"

Abe turned towards Sarah, and though he said nothing for a moment, his eyes spoke with quiet certainty. "Building a life together," he finally said, his voice husky with sincerity. "Building a home."

Sarah felt tears prickle at the corners of her eyes. She swallowed, her thumb stroking the side of his hand. "Being a family," she whispered.

Pastor Wells nodded thoughtfully and leaned forward, elbows resting on his knees. "And children…is that something you both desire?"

The question settled heavily in the small office. For Sarah, it was a beautiful weight. Her heart fluttered against her ribs as she answered, her voice soft but unwavering. "Very much."

Abe nodded beside her, squeezing her hand gently. "We've both wanted children for a long time," he said. "As many as God sees fit to give us."

Pastor Wells' eyes crinkled as he smiled, folding his hands together before him. "That's beautiful." He paused then, letting the silence stretch a moment before he continued, his voice gentler now, edged with quiet wisdom. "But I always ask this next part carefully— are you prepared for the reality that sometimes the road to parenthood doesn't unfold easily?"

The words were not harsh, but they were honest. Sarah and Abe exchanged a glance. In that single look passed so many unspoken things: hope, fear, a brave, tender faith. No one had ever put words to the fragile vulnerability beneath their dreams until now.

"We trust God's timing," Abe said, his tone low but steady. "Even if it looks different than what we expect."

Sarah turned their hands palm to palm, pressing her warmth into his. "And we'll walk that road together."

Pastor Wells nodded, a flicker of emotion crossing his face before he spoke again. "Good," he said softly. "You're already learning one of marriage's hardest truths…waiting together is one of the greatest acts of faith. And one of the greatest acts of love."

For a moment, no one spoke. The hush of the office grew deep, filled with something sacred and unspoken, the quiet presence of God settling around them like dawn mist on open fields.

Finally, Pastor Wells flipped to a fresh page in his notes and smiled. "Now, one quick question about the ceremony itself. Do you plan to use traditional vows, or would you like to write your own?"

Sarah and Abe shared a small, knowing smile.

"We actually talked about that already," Abe said, his voice lighter now.

Sarah nodded. "We'd really like to write our own."

Pastor Wells' smile widened. "Good. I always love hearing personal vows. They give your guests a glimpse into your hearts—and honestly, they serve as beautiful reminders for you when marriage gets real."

Abe chuckled, leaning back slightly. "More real than seating charts and centerpieces?"

Pastor Wells laughed softly, the sound rich with pastoral affection. "Far realer. But far better too." He closed his notebook and bowed his head. "Now let's pray over your union—and the family God will build, in His way, and in His time."

And in that quiet office, with hands joined and eyes closed, their hearts brimmed with something bigger than hope.

Expectation. Surrender. Love.

CHAPTER 8

The Wedding Day

The Following Spring—Central Park Conservatory Garden

The Conservatory Garden shimmered like a dream whispered into bloom. Petals fluttered in the breeze, soft as breath, their colors blushing beneath the afternoon sun. Somewhere between the canopy of trees and the trailing wisteria, violins hummed a tune that wrapped itself around the guests like silk.

People hushed as they took their seats, glancing up at the sky, as if even the heavens had paused to bear witness.

Behind a curtain of white satin, Sarah stood motionless.

She clutched her bouquet the way a sailor might grip a lifeline—not from fear, but from wonder. Her veil trembled slightly as she adjusted it again, her fingers clumsy with nerves. She did not feel like a bride. She felt like a child dressed in a grown woman's story.

Lottie leaned in, tucked a stubborn curl behind Sarah's ear, and whispered, "You okay?"

Sarah tried to nod. The motion came slow, as though she were waking from a long, impossible dream.

"I keep thinking this can't be real," she said, voice barely louder than the rustling leaves.

Lottie smiled, her eyes warm. "It is real. And you, my dear, look exactly the way a miracle ought to."

Sarah let out a breath she hadn't realized she'd been holding.

"Do you think I'll get it right?" she asked, almost too quickly. "You've seen me—all of me. My ambition. My need to control everything. The way I calculate, plan, perfect."

She laughed, but the sound trembled in her throat.

"What if I ruin it? What if I ruin *him*?"

Lottie didn't answer right away. She simply drew Sarah into a half-embrace, her forehead brushing lightly against Sarah's temple.

"Sarah," Lottie said softly, "you are not perfect. You never have been. But you love that man with your whole, complicated heart. And he loves you—not despite who you are, but *because* of it."

Sarah blinked fast, but the tears were already rising.

Lottie touched her cheek. "The rest," she said, "God's got."

That broke something in Sarah—gently, like a shell cracking open to release light.

She laughed, then wept, then laughed again.

"You're my best friend," she whispered, clinging to Lottie's hand as if letting go would unravel her.

"And you're mine." Lottie kissed her knuckles, then pressed both palms to Sarah's cheeks like a mother might do before sending her daughter into the world. "Now go. Go become the wife you prayed you'd never have to become alone."

Sarah was headed towards the door, then turned back to say,

"Remember our pact? If we were still single at thirty, we'd all move in together and become the sassiest, weirdest little chosen family in a downtown loft full of wine, takeout, and maybe one too many cats?"

Lottie laughs. "I don't remember the part about cats, but that probably fits."

"Well," Sarah continues, "I'm sorry to break the deal. I guess that leaves you to find the loft. Just promise to save us a guest room—you know, for emergencies or very bad Tuesdays."

As they laughed together, the music shifted. The notes grew taller, fuller, wide enough to walk inside. The moment had come.

Lottie bent low to adjust the train, her hands practiced, reverent. She leaned close and breathed words that were both instruction and benediction. "Walk slow. Breathe deep. And when you see him standing there—waiting—remember this isn't your ending. It's only chapter one."

Sarah nodded, lips trembling. And then she stepped forward.

The crowd rose as one, like a great sea drawn by the tide.

Sarah's heart pounded in her ears, but her steps were steady. The path stretched before her like a promise—framed by blooms, anchored by a thousand silent witnesses. She barely noticed them.

Because at the end of the aisle stood Abe.

His eyes caught hers, and she forgot to be afraid. He smiled—not broadly, not theatrically—but with the kind of smile that had steadied her through sleepless nights and early morning doubts. It was the smile that told her, *You're safe. You're home.*

The world narrowed to that single line between them.

Behind her, Lottie stayed just out of view, tears catching in the corners of her eyes. But she did not wipe them away. Instead, she whispered a prayer that rose like incense.

"Let their love stand every storm, Lord. Let laughter find them in ordinary rooms. Let forgiveness run faster than anger. And give them joy, not just in the easy seasons, but even in Your long waits."

The wind answered with a hush.

And for one sacred breath, the garden stood still.

"Let their love stand every storm, Lord. And give them joy in Your perfect timing."

The Empty Chairs

As Sarah walked down the aisle, she caught sight of Abe standing at the altar, his eyes locked on hers. Joy, nervousness, hope, all of it swirled between them.

But as she reached him and they stood hand-in-hand, her eyes briefly flicked toward two empty chairs near the front—reserved, but unfilled. Lottie, standing behind her as maid of honor, had quietly placed white roses on the chairs earlier that morning.

One for Sarah's parents. One for Abe's.

As Pastor Wells spoke, Sarah felt her throat tighten, tears pricking her eyes—not just from joy, but from the bittersweet ache of their absence. Abe squeezed her hand gently as if reading her thoughts.

"They're proud of you, Sarah," Lottie had whispered earlier when placing the flowers. "They're here. Just higher up."

In that sacred moment, Sarah silently released both her grief and her gratitude into the warm breeze swirling around them.

Abe's Vows

Abe took Sarah's hands in his, smiling gently as he began.

"Sarah, from the first moment we sat across from each other at that tiny coffee shop, I knew my world had shifted. You were strong, kind, and—let's be honest—intimidatingly organized."

The guests chuckled as Sarah shook her head playfully.

"But what drew me to you most wasn't your career or your confidence. It was your heart. The way you see people. The way you love fully, fiercely, and sacrificially.

I promise to cherish you in every season—in the laughter and the quiet, in the long workdays and lazy Saturday mornings. I promise to always find ways to make you laugh, even when you pretend my dad jokes aren't funny."

Another ripple of laughter.

"I vow to walk beside you as your partner, your protector, and your biggest encourager. And when life brings us waiting seasons—because we know they'll come—I promise to never let you wait alone.

Sarah, you are my answered prayer. And I promise to spend my life loving you with the same kind of grace God has shown both of us."

Sarah's Vows

Sarah took a slow, steady breath as she looked up at Abe, her eyes shining.

"Abe, before I met you, I prayed God would bring me someone strong—and instead, He gave me someone steady. You are my safe place—my calm in the storm, my biggest cheerleader, and my built-in IT support for life."

Laughter bubbled again, breaking some of the happy tears in the audience.

"I promise to love you on the good days and especially on the days when we both forget to order groceries and live off takeout. I promise to always support your dreams—even if they involve more camping than I'm emotionally prepared for."

Abe laughed, his shoulders shaking slightly.

"But most of all, I vow to choose you. Every single day. Through the waiting, through the answered prayers, through every new chapter God writes for us. You are my favorite blessing, Abe."

Pastor Wells Seals the Deal

"By the power entrusted to me—and by the clear presence of God in this union—I now pronounce you husband and wife."

A collective gasp of joy and applause began to rise, but Pastor Wells held up his hand gently, his voice growing softer and more reverent.

"And what God has joined together, let no one separate."

Abe and Sarah turned to each other, eyes already glistening.

"You may kiss your bride."

Abe leaned in slowly, his hand cradling Sarah's cheek. The world around them seemed to blur as their lips met—a kiss not just of love, but of covenant. Of all the waiting, the wondering, the prayers whispered into silent nights…this was the moment those prayers found flesh.

The guests erupted into cheers. Lottie sobbed. Mara clapped through her tears. Even Pastor Wells smiled with paternal warmth.

As they walked back down the aisle, hand in hand, the sun broke through the clouds above the Conservatory Garden, spilling light across the path ahead.

And Sarah thought, through the haze of joy and nerves and disbelief:

This is the beginning of the promise.

The waiting may not be over.

But hope is walking with me now—in a tuxedo, holding my hand.

The Reception—The Parkview Rooftop

The rooftop ballroom glowed under soft string lights, the Manhattan skyline painting a breathtaking backdrop behind the glass. The night air was perfect, a warm breeze, just enough chill to keep everyone lingering outside between dances.

As guests filed out for the cocktail hour, Lottie hung back, watching Abe twirl Sarah gently beneath the ivy-draped archway for a private post-ceremony moment.

She sighed, then turned to Mara, who stood beside her in a sapphire bridesmaid dress.

"She did it," Lottie said softly. "Our girl."

Mara smiled. "She really did."

Lottie tipped her head thoughtfully. "Guess that makes me the last single lady standing."

Mara laughed. "For now."

"Don't get ideas," Lottie warned with a smirk. "I'm still very committed to my freedom. Weddings just make people temporarily insane."

Mara gave her a side-eye. "You cried during the vows."

"They were well-written. That's not romance—that's just good copy."

They both laughed.

The Core Circle

Sarah looked around the room, nearly overwhelmed by the sea of faces gathered to celebrate them. Friends, colleagues, family, church members—all pieces of the puzzle that had brought them here.

Lottie and Mara were seated at the head table, both still dabbing at their eyes from the ceremony.

Lottie leaned over, whispering to Mara,

"I give it three months before she's asking me for pregnancy advice."

Mara smirked.

"I give it two."

Sarah caught their exchange and laughed from across the table.

"Don't start placing bets on me tonight."

At a nearby table, Marcus, Jordan, and Eli were already halfway through their second round of toasts.

Marcus raised his glass.

"To Abe finally finding a woman who can beat him at Scrabble and keep him humble."

Eli chimed in.

"And to Sarah—may she continue to pretend to laugh at Abe's dad jokes for many happy years."

The table roared with laughter, Abe mockingly raising his glass in surrender.

Jordan leaned toward Sarah with a wink.

"Welcome to the brotherhood. You're officially one of us now."

Pastor Wells' Blessing

Across the room, Sarah spotted Pastor Wells chatting warmly with several of Abe's family members.

Sarah smiled to herself—grateful for how Pastor Wells had become a steady voice for both of them during their premarital counseling. His blessing earlier that evening still echoed in her heart.

Later that evening, he stood with a microphone, his voice carrying warmth and humor.

"Marriage, as you've already heard today, requires patience, humor, and a very good sense of direction—both spiritually and with your GPS apps. But what matters most is what I've seen in both of you: a willingness to surrender your story to the One writing it. And I have no doubt that the best is yet to come."

The guests applauded warmly, several already misty-eyed again.

The First Dance

As the music shifted to their song—soft, acoustic, romantic—Abe gently pulled Sarah onto the dance floor.

"I still can't believe you said yes," he whispered into her ear.

Sarah smiled as they swayed.

"I still can't believe you called me for a second date after I ordered dessert and an appetizer."

He chuckled.

"That's when I knew you were the one."

They moved together effortlessly, lost in each other while the world faded around them for just a moment.

As the reception wound down and guests slowly departed, Sarah and Abe stood hand-in-hand by the terrace railing, gazing out over the glowing city.

Abe whispered,

"Can I tell you a secret?"

Sarah smiled.

"Of course."

"This, right here, right now, feels like the first page of our real story."

Sarah's voice grew soft.

"Then let's write something beautiful."

They leaned into each other with a long, passionate kiss as the Manhattan skyline sparkled behind them—two hearts fully surrendered to whatever chapters God would write next.

CHAPTER 9

The Honeymoon

The warm ocean breeze hit them the moment they stepped off the plane, instantly washing away the final remnants of wedding stress.

"Do you smell that?" Sarah said, inhaling deeply.

"It smells like freedom," Abe grinned.

They made their way through the small Caribbean airport, luggage in tow, hand in hand. Everything about the trip felt lighter—the vows had been said, the rings exchanged, and now they were officially stepping into forever.

The resort was tucked against a private stretch of white sand, framed by lush palms and crystal blue waves. Sarah let out a soft gasp as they pulled up.

"Abe, this is... stunning."

"Only the best for my wife," he whispered in her ear, making her blush even after months of engagement.

The First Sunset

That evening, barefoot on the beach, Sarah and Abe walked hand in hand as the sun melted into the horizon.

"You know what the best part of this is?" Sarah asked.

"The view?" Abe guessed.

"No more wedding checklists," she said, laughing.

Abe pretended to sigh dramatically.

"I don't know. I might miss seating chart negotiations."

They both laughed, the easy joy between them flowing effortlessly.

As they sat down on a blanket with a small bottle of champagne, Abe raised a toast.

"To day one of the rest of our life together."

Sarah clinked her glass gently against his.

"To day one."

They sipped, leaned against each other, and let the sound of the waves speak for them.

The Adventures

The next few days were filled with spontaneous adventures just like they both had hoped.

Snorkeling along coral reefs, Sarah squealed into her snorkel when a school of brightly colored fish darted past.

Later, they tried paddle boarding—Abe falling repeatedly into the water while Sarah giggled uncontrollably from her still-standing board.

"Don't get cocky, Mrs. Abrams!" Abe shouted between splashes.

"I'm just naturally gifted!" she teased.

Their laughter echoed across the calm bay.

The Candlelit Dinner: Dreams Shared

On their fourth night, they dressed up for the resort's private candlelit dinner on the beach. The flicker of candles in glass lanterns illuminated the intimate table as waves gently lapped nearby.

As they enjoyed grilled lobster and fresh fruit, Sarah reached across the table, becoming more serious.

"Can I ask you something a little...heavier?" she said softly.

"Of course."

"What do you really want in life, Abe? I mean beyond this... beyond our marriage. What's the dream?"

Abe smiled thoughtfully, taking a sip of wine.

"I want to build something that lasts...not just in business, but in people. Whether it's the company I'm trying to grow now, or something entirely new, I want to help create opportunity for others. Make room for people who haven't been given a seat at the table."

Sarah's eyes softened.

"I love that about you."

Abe flipped the question back.

"What about you?"

Sarah exhaled, glancing toward the horizon.

"I want to make a difference in the business world too. But honestly? More than titles or bonuses...I want a life that matters. I want to lead teams with integrity. To mentor younger women like I once needed."

Abe nodded, his voice warm.

"And we will."

The waiter quietly refilled their glasses and disappeared, giving them privacy.

Sarah hesitated, then asked, "When do you want to start talking about a family?"

Abe smiled gently, not surprised.

"I want kids with you more than anything," he said, reaching for her hand, "but I also don't feel rushed. I want us to build our foundation first. Travel a little. Grow our careers. Take one year to just enjoy being married."

Sarah's shoulders relaxed.

"Exactly what I was thinking."

Abe grinned.

"Wow, look at that. We're already excellent at marriage."

Sarah laughed, eyes sparkling.

"We're definitely going to be insufferable newlyweds for a while, aren't we?"

"Absolutely."

Closing the Honeymoon

On their final morning, as they stood on their balcony sipping coffee, Sarah leaned against Abe's chest.

"Do you think God smiles at how this all came together, Mr. Abrams?" she asked softly.

"I do, Mrs. Abrams" Abe whispered. "And I think He's just getting started."

As the sun rose over the endless blue water, they stood together—not knowing that behind the sweetness of these first months would come the testing of every promise.

But for now, there was only peace.

CHAPTER 10

The First Apartment

Six Months After the Wedding—Their First Home

The apartment was small, but to Sarah and Abe, it felt like the beginning of everything. Warm sunlight poured through tall windows framed by white linen curtains Sarah had picked out during a whirlwind post-honeymoon Target run. The exposed brick wall behind their worn leather sofa added just enough edge to remind them they were still living in the heart of Manhattan. Hardwood floors, slightly uneven in places, creaked with charm beneath their feet.

Wedding photos lined the entryway wall—candid shots of laughter and dancing, the slow kiss under the Conservatory Garden archway, Abe twirling Sarah beneath a sea of twinkle lights. A framed copy of their wedding vows sat on a shelf near the kitchen, beside a bouquet of dried lavender from Mara's bouquet and a silver candleholder gifted by Lottie.

In the corner of the living room, a small sideboard doubled as a makeshift bar, stacked with champagne flutes and whiskey glasses—wedding gifts still wearing their delicate "Mr. & Mrs." tags. A Keurig machine nestled beside a trio of mismatched mugs labeled *Wife Life, The Groom Life, and Probably Wine.*

Above the TV, two simple black-and-white photographs hung in matching frames—one of Sarah's parents on their wedding day, the other of Abe's father holding a toddler-aged Abe on his shoulders. They had debated whether to hang those in the bedroom or the living room, but in the end, they wanted their parents' love to greet them every day, right where new memories were being made.

The kitchen was modest but full of character—white subway tiles, open shelving, and a row of cookbooks that neither of them had really opened yet. A cast iron skillet gifted by Abe's grandmother held court on the stove like it had seniority.

Sarah stood barefoot near the window one morning, coffee in hand, the city slowly waking around her. Behind her, Abe was reading the business section on the couch, his tie still hanging loosely around his neck.

"I love it here," she whispered, more to herself than to him.

Abe looked up and smiled. "It's not much, but it's ours."

She turned and smiled back.

"No," she said. "It's not just ours. It's everything we hoped for." And though their future still held questions, in this little apartment nestled among the noise and glow of the city, there was peace. A beginning. A promise quietly unfolding in picture frames and sunlight. They stood for a moment in the quiet of their new home, breathing in the promise of fresh beginnings.

Abe rested his chin on her shoulder. "I can see it all already."

"See what?" she asked.

"Our life here. Hosting dinners. Movie nights. Long conversations on the couch." He hesitated, his voice softening.

"And eventually... kids running through these rooms."
Sarah smiled, closing her eyes. "Me too."

They had already chosen the room that would one day be a nursery, the small second bedroom with perfect morning light. The room had no furniture yet, just a soft ivory rug, a rocking chair gifted by Mara's mother at the bridal shower, and a framed print leaning against the wall that read, *"For this child we have prayed."*

They had quietly envisioned what would fill the space: a crib by the window, a rocking chair in the corner, little footprints everywhere.
Sarah turned and looked up at Abe, her voice soft but full of hope. "Do you think it'll happen quickly?"
Abe met her gaze and smiled. *"I don't know. But I believe it'll happen. In God's time."*
She nodded, comforted by his steadiness. "I just feel like I've waited for this part of life for so long. I'm ready."
Abe kissed her forehead gently. "Then we'll wait together, however long it takes."
They held each other in the quiet warmth of their apartment, overflowing with possibility.
Outside, the city hummed with its usual rhythm, unaware that inside this small corner of Manhattan, a new chapter was beginning—one built on love, faith, and the fragile, beautiful hope of what was yet to come.

Eleven Months Into Marriage—Their Manhattan Apartment
Sarah walked through the door practically glowing.
Before Abe could even ask, she blurted out, "I got it!"
Abe's face lit up immediately.
"You got it?"
"The promotion. The big one! After six months of endless interviews they made me the Chief Marketing Officer!"

Abe crossed the room and scooped her into his arms, spinning her around as she laughed.

"Sarah Abrams, you're unstoppable."

"I'm exhausted, but yes—also unstoppable."

He grinned, lowering her gently.

"Do we have champagne?"

"I already bought a bottle on the way home," she said with a wink. "I had faith."

Later That Evening—Celebration Mode

Abe set out takeout from their favorite Thai place while Sarah poured champagne into two flutes. The soft glow of the city twinkled through their floor-to-ceiling windows.

As they clinked glasses, Abe added,

"I have something to share too."

Sarah raised an eyebrow playfully.

"Please don't steal my thunder."

"Not at all...I think we can share the stage."

He smiled, eyes gleaming.

"My latest funding round closed this afternoon. The last investor finally came through."

Sarah's jaw dropped.

"Wait—seriously?"

"Seriously. We're fully capitalized for phase two."

Sarah laughed, shaking her head.

"Look at us—corporate power couple."

Then Sarah's eyes lit up again, snapping her fingers.

"Oh! And guess what? The best part is...drum roll please...I get to hire my own assistant now!"

Abe grinned.

"Ah yes, your very own corporate minion. Don't get too power-hungry, Mrs. Abrams."

Sarah smirked, playing along.

"Please. I plan to be a very benevolent dictator."

Abe leaned in with a mock whisper.

"Promise me you won't make them get your dry cleaning."

She grinned.

"Only on Fridays."

They both burst into laughter as Abe raised his glass again.

"To hiring the poor soul who has no idea what's coming."

Abe leaned in.

"Not to brag, but we are crushing year one."

The Reflective Moment

Later, as they curled up together on the couch, Sarah rested her head against Abe's shoulder.

"Sometimes I still can't believe how different life looks now," she said softly.

"Marriage suits you," Abe teased, kissing her hair.

She smiled.

"Do you ever think about where we were two years ago? Just starting that coffee shop conversation..."

Abe smiled thoughtfully.

"I do. I think about how God wove all of this together. The timing. The open doors. The delays that led us here."

Sarah sighed contentedly.

"And this feels like the foundation we always said we wanted before starting a family."

Abe nodded slowly.

"It does. And I'm grateful we took this year to just... be us."

They sat in silence for a moment, watching the lights of Manhattan blink like distant stars.

Finally, Sarah whispered,

"Do you think it's almost time?"

Abe glanced down at her, understanding instantly.

"For us to start trying?"

She nodded, her voice soft but certain.

"I think so."

Abe smiled gently, rubbing slow circles on her hand.

"Yeah, maybe it's time. We should at least start practicing!" he added with a boyish grin.

Sarah exhaled, her eyes glistening not with fear—but quiet anticipation. Before she could reply, Abe leaned in and kissed her slowly, surely, and full of something deeper than excitement. It was gratitude. Desire. Hope.

He didn't rush. Just let the moment unfurl between them like a shared breath.

Then, without breaking their kiss, he shifted, guiding her gently backward until she was lying down on the soft, worn leather couch. His hand cradled the side of her face, his thumb brushing just beneath her cheekbone.

Sarah's laughter caught softly in her throat, a low, contented hum as she let herself melt into him.

"Right here?" she whispered teasingly.

Abe grinned against her skin. "We've got a perfectly good couch. And a perfectly good reason."

She giggled, wrapping her arms around his neck, pulling him closer. The city buzzed just beyond the glass, but in that small apartment— the one filled with wedding photos and waiting—the only sound that mattered was the rhythm of two hearts leaning into the future.

Whatever came next, they would begin it together.

Act II - The Waiting

Hagar and Sarah

Now Sarai, Abram's wife, had borne him no children. But she had an Egyptian slave named Hagar—so she said to Abram, "The Lord has kept me from having children. Go, sleep with my slave—I can build a family through her."

Abram agreed to what Sarai said. So after Abram had been living in Canaan ten years, Sarai his wife took her Egyptian slave Hagar and gave her to her husband to be his wife. He slept with Hagar, and she conceived.

Genesis 16: 1-4 (NIV)

CHAPTER 11

The Next Season

One Year Into Marriage—Saturday Morning

The rain fell in a soft, steady rhythm outside the apartment windows as Sarah stirred pancake batter in the tiny kitchen. The apartment smelled like fresh coffee, vanilla, and home—her favorite combination.

Abe stood behind her, wrapping his arms around her waist and resting his chin lightly on her shoulder.

"You realize," he whispered playfully, "that you just made enough pancakes to feed a small army."

Sarah smiled. "You know I stress-cook."

"Are you stressed?"

She hesitated. "Not exactly. Maybe...thoughtful."

Abe gently turned her to face him, his warm eyes searching hers.

"Talk to me."

Sarah sighed, resting her hands on his chest.

"I've just been thinking a lot lately...about us. About what's next."

Abe waited quietly, allowing her the space to gather her words.

"We've built such a beautiful rhythm together," she continued. "Marriage is...better than I ever dreamed. But I keep feeling this tug— like there's something missing. Or maybe not missing, but waiting."

Abe nodded, his expression softening with understanding.

"You've been thinking about starting a family again."

Sarah nodded slowly.

"Have you?"

He smiled. "Every day. I think we're ready now."

That surprised her. She blinked, her voice catching slightly.

"Really?"

"Of course." He took her hands in his. "Sarah, from the moment we sat across from each other in the coffee shop, I knew you were someone I could build a life with—not just share a life with but build one. And that includes children."

Her eyes filled. "I didn't want to rush you. I know work's been intense, and...I guess I was waiting for some kind of sign."

Abe chuckled softly.

"Maybe this conversation is the sign."

"Oh, thank goodness! I was hoping you felt this way. I talked to Mara this week," she said softly.

"Oh yeah?" Abe looked down at her.

"She and Jared are trying," she said, her voice light but tinged with something deeper. "They've only been married a few months longer than us and already started planning for a family already."

Abe was quiet for a beat. "How do you feel about that?"

Sarah took a breath. "Happy for her. Really. But also...like maybe we're standing still. Like everyone's moving on, checking off boxes, and I'm still just trying to figure out if I'm ready."

Abe shifted to face her more directly. "You don't have to compare, Sar. It's not a race."

"I know." She smiled faintly, but her eyes glistened. "It's just that Mara and I have always shared everything. College, late-night study sessions, crushes, even that awful temp job in college. And now she's ahead of me in something I've wanted for so long but was scared to say out loud."

"You've never been behind," he said, brushing a strand of hair from her face. "And if this is something you want, let's talk about it. Let's pray about it. Together."

Sarah exhaled slowly, as though releasing something she'd been carrying.

"I think I am ready," she whispered. "Scared, but ready."

Abe smiled and kissed her forehead. "Then let's do it!"

She laughed through the shimmer in her eyes, and he pulled her closer.

The Honest Fears

Sarah bit her lip. "Do you ever wonder... what if it's not easy for us?"

Abe's smile softened.

"Of course I've wondered. But I also trust that God knows the timing. We'll walk through it together…whatever it looks like."

Sarah exhaled, letting the quiet fear loosen its grip as his steadiness wrapped around her like a blanket.

"Okay," she whispered. "Then I think…I'm ready."

As they sat down to their breakfast—which now truly looked like enough food for an army—Sarah couldn't stop smiling. Neither could Abe.

"So," he said playfully, raising an eyebrow as he poured syrup onto her plate, "should we call this an official start to 'Project Baby Abrams'?"

Sarah laughed, blushing slightly.

"Let's call it...a very enjoyable new season of practicing with intention."

Abe winked in response, reaching across the table to take her hand.

"To new beginnings," he said softly.

Sarah squeezed his fingers and whispered back:

"To the next chapter."

Neither of them knew then how long the next chapter would stretch. But in that moment—full of hope, laughter, and love—they believed in the beauty of the season to come.

CHAPTER 12

The Waiting Begins

Six Months Later—Their Apartment

The faint sound of worship music played in the background as Sarah stood quietly at the bathroom sink, staring at the small white stick resting on the counter.

One line. Again. She closed her eyes for a moment and exhaled slowly, willing the tears not to come—at least not yet.
But even as the music played softly, a quiet voice crept into her thoughts.
Maybe this isn't God's will for you.
Maybe you're not meant to be a mother.
Maybe all the praying in the world can't change what He's already decided.

She gripped the edge of the sink tighter.
She had heard those thoughts before. Always subtle. Always in moments like this, when her faith felt thin and her heart felt raw. She knew they didn't come from God.

Abe knocked gently on the bathroom door.

"Hey, babe? Everything okay?"

Sarah took a breath and plastered on her practiced smile before opening the door.

"Negative," she said softly.

Abe didn't hesitate. He pulled her into his arms, wrapping her tight against his chest.

"It's okay," he whispered into her hair. "We keep trying."

Sarah nodded against him, but the lump in her throat wouldn't fully dissolve.

She wanted to believe him.

But the enemy's lie lingered like smoke in her chest, curling around the question she couldn't voice:

What if God never meant for us to have children at all?

The Early Months

After the first negative test result, they decided to wipe away all fear and joyously keep trying. The first few months had been full of laughter, excitement, and whispered prayers under starry skies. Every new cycle brought a flutter of anticipation.

They charted ovulation. Read articles. Downloaded apps. Took vitamins. Followed every piece of advice well-meaning friends offered.

Every month felt like another roll of the dice.

And every month ended the same way. With every disappointment, anticipation and faith died further.

The Quiet Adjustments

By month eight, Sarah had stopped buying pregnancy tests in advance. She waited until she was truly late—not just by a day, but unmistakably late—refusing to let hope rise too soon.

Her mind became oddly clinical, her heart quietly barricaded.

She tracked data points instead of dreams: basal temperatures, cycle lengths, luteal phases. She adjusted her diet, switched to prenatal vitamins, even gave up her favorite chai latte "just in case."

She joined a few online forums, but mostly lurked. The acronyms became second nature—TTC. BBT. CD14. DPO. Words that felt like a secret language of women holding their breath.

Abe tried to stay lighthearted. "Any luck?" he'd ask gently, hope tucked behind his eyes. She'd shake her head with a small smile that didn't reach her eyes.

And beneath it all, a quiet ache started to form—not sharp or sudden, but slow and constant, like water wearing down stone.

She hadn't cried. Not yet.

But some mornings, brushing her teeth, she caught her reflection and didn't quite recognize the woman staring back.

The Private Confession

Evening draped itself over the apartment in quiet layers. The dishes were done, the lights low, and the soft flicker of the television danced across the walls, unheeded. Outside, the world pulsed on—car horns, footsteps, a dog barking down the block—but inside, time had slowed. They sat curled into each other on the couch, a blanket across their knees, their bodies close and warm, but their thoughts drifting further apart than either of them wanted to admit. The silence wasn't new, but it had thickened.

Abe shifted beside her and turned, one hand sliding over hers, thumb stroking the knuckle absently.

"Sarah," he said gently. "Can I ask you something?"

She looked at him, her eyes already answering before her mouth could.

"Yes."

He hesitated, but only for a breath. "Are you okay?"

Sarah opened her mouth, then closed it again. She took a moment, her eyes fixed on a spot just beyond the room, as if searching for the truth out there might make it easier to say aloud.

"I don't know," she said.

Her voice cracked on the last word.

She wrapped her arms around herself, then quickly unfolded them, as though trying to decide whether to protect her body or free it from blame. "Sometimes I feel like my body's failing me," she whispered.

"Like I'm doing everything right but still being punished. Like I'm broken in a way no test can find."

Abe reached for her, both hands now cradling her face, his thumbs brushing the corners of her mouth where the words trembled. "Hey," he said, voice steady. "You're not failing. We're not failing."

She blinked hard. "But every month it doesn't happen, it chips away at me. A little more each time. I keep thinking I'll grow numb to the disappointment, but it always hurts. Always."

"I thought it would be easy," she added, almost to herself.

"I did too," Abe murmured. "But this…this doesn't define you. Or us. It doesn't change how much I love you."

She wiped her cheek quickly with the edge of her sleeve. "I just…I don't want this to become all we are. I don't want this to be the only thing we talk about. Or the only thing we pray for."

"It won't," he said.

And the way he pulled her into him—not as a solution, but as a shelter—made her believe it, at least for that night.

"We'll hold onto each other first," he whispered into her hair.

"Always. No matter what doesn't come. No matter how long the waiting lasts."

The Beginning of Waiting

Later that night, as they lay in bed, Abe reached for Sarah's hand, their fingers intertwining naturally in the quiet.

"Let's keep praying," he whispered.

Sarah nodded, her voice trembling but full of quiet faith.

"Lord," she prayed softly into the dark, "Your timing, not mine. But please…don't let it be too long."

They lay in silence for a moment, both listening to the stillness around them, hearts heavier than either wanted to admit.

Finally, Abe spoke again, his voice low but steady.

"Hey…what do you think about meeting with Pastor Wells sometime? Just to talk. To get some perspective."

Sarah turned slightly toward him, surprised but comforted by the suggestion.

"You think that would help?"

Abe squeezed her hand gently.

"I don't know if it will change anything, but I know he'll listen. And I think...I think it might help keep us grounded while we walk through this."

Sarah exhaled slowly, feeling a bit of the weight ease off her chest.

"Yeah. I think that's a good idea."

"I'll call him tomorrow," Abe promised softly.

They fell asleep still holding hands—not defeated, not desperate—but entering the season of waiting that neither of them yet knew would test every part of their faith.

Eight Months into Trying—Pastor Wells' Office

The cozy office smelled faintly of coffee and old books. Stacks of well-worn theology texts lined the shelves behind Pastor Wells, whose warm smile had not changed since their premarital counseling sessions.

Sarah and Abe sat side by side on the couch, their hands naturally intertwined as they always seemed to do when facing something heavy together.

Pastor Wells leaned forward in his chair, his voice gentle.

"It's good to see you both. I know you didn't come today just to say hello."

Sarah offered a thin smile.

"We thought we'd be coming here for baby dedication counseling by now."

Abe squeezed her hand.

Pastor Wells nodded, his expression full of empathy.

"The waiting is heavier than people realize, isn't it?"

Sarah swallowed.

"It's starting to feel...endless. Month after month. Hope rising, then crashing."

Abe added softly,

"We wanted to check in—not just for advice, but because we know we need to guard our hearts. This waiting is starting to chip at us."

Pastor Wells nodded slowly.

"You are wise to come. Many couples underestimate how spiritually vulnerable long waiting seasons make them."
He leaned back slightly, speaking with the careful pace of someone who had counseled many before them.

"Abe, Sarah—you both know that God made waiting part of His design. Think about Abraham and Sarah of Scripture. Isaac came after years of barrenness—but God wasn't late. His timing was perfect."
Sarah smiled weakly.

"We've thought a lot about our namesakes lately."
Pastor Wells smiled back.

"Of course you have. And I'm sure you've wondered: why would a loving God withhold such a good thing for so long?"
Sarah's eyes filled as she whispered,

"Almost every day."
The pastor's voice softened.

"Not every delay is God's denial. Some are divine appointments preparing you for something you cannot yet see."
Abe spoke quietly, his voice edged with weariness.

"But how do we keep our hearts from becoming bitter while we wait? What if it's not meant to be at all?"
Pastor Wells didn't hesitate.

"By anchoring yourselves in truth. God's truth. In the very first chapter of Genesis, we find His heart for humanity: *'Be fruitful and multiply.'* That was the first blessing spoken over mankind, before sin, before struggle. It's not just biology. It's identity.
He opened his Bible, tapping the page gently as if to underline the moment. Genesis 1:28 says *'Then God blessed them, and God said to them, "Be fruitful and multiply—fill the earth and subdue it". That's not a cruel command, it's a blessing. One the enemy has been trying to steal ever since."*
Sarah's eyes glistened, but she stayed silent, listening.

"The lie," Pastor Wells continued, his voice softening, "says not everyone is meant to bear children. That your longing is somehow selfish. That if it hasn't happened by now, it probably never will. But that's not God's voice—that's fear wearing a spiritual disguise."

He leaned in, lowering his voice to a near whisper.

"Biblical waiting isn't passive. It's not twiddling your thumbs until God shows up. It's actively trusting in God's promises. It's praying with boldness based on the promises of His Word, loving with vulnerability, and refusing to surrender your hope to disappointment. That's where your character is being forged."

He turned to Abe.

"Keep praying as if God has already answered your prayer and you are simply speaking it into being. And don't let the enemy write the end of your story just because God's promise hasn't arrived in your timing."

Then gently, to both of them:

"James 4 says, *'Resist the devil, and he will flee from you.'* This includes the lies he whispers in your waiting season."

A long silence followed, heavy but holy.

Sarah whispered, "So it's not wrong to keep hoping?"

Pastor Wells smiled.

"It's never wrong to hope in something God designed you to long for. Your womb is not forgotten. Speak life into your womb, that the will of God for your body is to be fruitful and multiply."

After a moment of silence, Pastor Wells stood.

"May I pray over you?"

They nodded, both visibly emotional.

He laid his hands gently on their shoulders and began:

"Lord, You are the God of Abraham and Sarah—the God who makes barren wombs fruitful and who fulfills promises in Your perfect time. You see every tear these two have shed. You hold every desire they've whispered. Strengthen their hearts. Protect their marriage. Guard their joy. And when Your appointed time arrives, may the miracle You have written for them shine even brighter because of this waiting. Amen."

A quiet peace settled over the room.

As they rose to leave, Pastor Wells looked at them both, his voice tender but confident.

"You are not forgotten. Your story is not over."

Sarah wiped her eyes and smiled softly.

"Thank you, Pastor."

"Thank you for reminding us who the real Author is," Abe added

Midtown Manhattan—Annual Girls Weekend

The three women had already tackled half of Fifth Avenue by mid-afternoon. Shopping bags dangled from their arms like trophies as they collapsed into a corner booth at a cozy café.

Lottie laughed as she kicked off her heels under the table.

"I swear, shopping used to feel like cardio in my early twenties. Now it just feels like survival."

Mara groaned playfully.

"My feet gave up somewhere around Bloomingdale's."

Sarah smiled, sipping her iced tea, grateful for these familiar rhythms with her closest friends.

After the server left them with fresh pastries, Lottie turned her attention to Sarah with a mischievous grin.

"So...you're coming up on your second anniversary, Mrs. Abrams."

Sarah laughed.

"Don't remind me. It flew."

Mara leaned in, her voice teasing.

"Which means...are we talking nursery colors yet?"

Sarah's cheeks flushed, but she didn't shy away.

"Well," she said softly, "Abe and I have talked. We wanted this first year to be just us. But...yeah. We've been trying."

Lottie's eyes sparkled.

"Ooooh. Now the fun begins."

Sarah chuckled, but her tone grew slightly more serious.

"I mean...I know it's not always as easy as people make it sound. I'm hopeful, but also realistic."

Mara nodded thoughtfully.

"Yeah. You never really know how your story's going to

unfold."

Sarah gave a small smile.

"We're praying God opens that door when the time is right."

Lottie squeezed her hand.

"Well, whenever it happens...I fully expect weekly bump photos. And full nursery consultation privileges."

"Deal," Sarah laughed.

Mara smiled, but Sarah noticed a heaviness behind her friend's usual sparkle.

After small talk and laughter, Sarah turned more serious.

"Okay—your turn. What's going on? You've been quieter than usual."

Mara exhaled, fiddling with her coffee sleeve.

"I wasn't sure if I should bring it up with everything you're walking through...but, we've been trying. For over a year now."

Sarah's eyes widened softly.

"Oh, Mara..."

Lottie reached across the table and squeezed Mara's hand.

Sarah's voice was full of empathy.

"You should have told me."

Mara's eyes glistened.

"I didn't want to add to your burden. You and Abe have already been so strong walking through your own waiting. I figured I could handle mine quietly."

Sarah reached over, taking both of Mara's hands.

"We're in this together. You've carried me through so many hard conversations. Now let me return the favor."

Mara wiped her eyes.

"I guess I didn't expect it to hurt so much month after month."

Sarah squeezed her hand gently.

"I know that feeling better than I wish I did."

She paused for a moment, then added softly,

"Abe and I met with Pastor Wells recently. And something he said really stayed with me."

Both women leaned in, instinctively knowing what she was about to say was something important.

"He reminded us that the first blessing God ever spoke over humanity was 'Be fruitful and multiply.' That it wasn't just a command—it was part of our identity, part of His original design."
Lottie's brows lifted slightly, and Mara nodded, listening closely.
Sarah continued, her voice growing steadier.

"He said the enemy tries to twist that—make us believe maybe we weren't meant to be parents. But that's a lie. God's design hasn't changed, even when the timing feels delayed."
She took a breath.

"He also said waiting isn't passive. That biblical waiting is active, choosing to trust, choosing to keep loving boldly, praying boldly, and not letting disappointment define our story."
Mara closed her eyes for a beat as the truth of it settled in then whispered, "That's powerful."
Sarah nodded.

"It was like...God was reminding me: You're not forgotten. Your womb, your heart, your prayers...He sees it all."
Lottie exhaled softly.

"I needed that too, honestly."
Mara gave a faint, watery smile.

"Maybe we all did."
Sarah nodded.

"We'll wait together. And we'll believe together."
For a long moment, the three women simply sat quietly, holding one another's hands—an unspoken sisterhood of waiting.
Lottie finally broke the silence with a soft, humor-laced sigh.

"Well, I guess we'll all have very full baby showers one day—even if we're eighty."
They all laughed—not because it was funny, but because the laughter softened the weight just enough to breathe.

Later That Evening—Sarah's Apartment

After leaving the coffee shop, Sarah invited Lottie back to her apartment for one more cup of tea while she waited to head to the airport for her flight back to Dallas.

The city hummed softly outside as they sat on Sarah's couch, warm mugs in hand.

Lottie glanced over gently.

"Hey...can I just say something?"

Sarah smiled faintly.

"Of course."

Lottie's voice grew tender.

"You handled that so beautifully today. With Mara. I know how heavy all of this is for you too...but you didn't make it about you. You just... sat with her."

Sarah exhaled, eyes misting.

"I think...I've finally realized that pain has layers. Mine doesn't cancel out hers. And hers doesn't diminish mine. They just...coexist."

Lottie nodded, emotion catching in her throat.

"You're becoming stronger through this, you know."

Sarah blinked away a tear.

"I don't feel strong, Lot."

"That's usually when you actually are."

They sat quietly for a few moments, sipping.

Finally, Sarah added softly,

"Pastor Wells said something during our last session that keeps echoing in my head. He told Abe and me: *'Sometimes your waiting becomes someone else's comfort.'*"

Lottie looked at her curiously.

Sarah continued, voice thickening.

"I used to think I needed my miracle first to help anyone. But maybe God is already using me right now...while I'm still waiting."

Lottie smiled, eyes brimming.

"That's the most beautiful thing I've heard all week."

Sarah wiped at the corner of her eye, voice barely above a whisper.

"I hope He still writes miracles for both of us."

Lottie reached over and squeezed her hand. "He will."

CHAPTER 13

The Assistant

Sarah's Offic—Midtown Manhattan

Hagar Daniels was five minutes early to her first real job. Not an internship, not campus work-study, not a temp gig answering phones for someone else's dream. This was a salaried role with benefits, a title—"Executive Assistant to the Chief Marketing Officer"—and a boss who, by all accounts, ran the most polished team in the building.

The elevator doors opened with a gentle chime on the 21st floor of Harbor Creative Group's Midtown office. Hagar stepped out, heart pounding but chin high. She wore a borrowed blazer, a tailored navy sheath dress, and the only pair of heels she owned—polished but discreet. A folder tucked under her arm held printed copies of her résumé and references, but she knew the content by heart.

A receptionist led her through glass doors into a conference room flooded with natural light, clean lines and warm neutrals. A minimalist's dream—like someone had edited out all the noise.

Noise. That's what her life used to sound like.

"You must be Hagar," said a woman in black-framed glasses as she opened the door. "I'm Dana, the office manager. Come in—Sarah's running a few minutes late. She had a breakfast meeting uptown."

Hagar nodded, stepping into the space with cautious confidence. She could feel the hum of ambition in the air. It felt good—like potential.

By the time Sarah walked in, crisp and cool in cream wool and espresso heels, Hagar had already been offered a tour, a latte, and a temporary desk.

"Ms. Abrams," Hagar said, standing as she immediately recognized the woman from her research. Sarah Abrams. CMO. Young for her role. Impeccably dressed in a pale blouse, tailored slacks, and a quiet air of authority that made you sit straighter without being told.

"Sarah, please," she replied, waving off the formality. She looked Hagar over quickly but not unkindly. "You're early. I like that."

Hagar smiled. "Habit. Being early was... safer."

Sarah raised an eyebrow, just slightly. "You'll fit in fine here. We move fast. And you'll be helping me stay ahead of things, so you'll be moving faster. Ready?"

"Yes," Hagar said quickly, offering her hand. "It's an honor to meet you."

Sarah's handshake was firm. "Come in, have a seat."

As Sarah led her into the corner office, Hagar took in every detail—the subtle floral of Sarah's perfume, the precise alignment of frames on the wall, the barely-touched bowl of green apples on the table.

This was a world built on control, and she was determined to belong in it.

They sat across from each other. Sarah glanced at a printed copy of Hagar's résumé but didn't dwell there long.

Her eyes lifted. "Before we dive in, can I ask...your name. Hagar. It's quite unique. Do you know what it means?"

Hagar nodded, her voice calm. "It's from the Bible. She was the servant girl God saw in the wilderness. My mom gave me the name hoping I'd remember that—even if the world overlooks you, God doesn't."

Sarah studied her for a quiet second, something flickering behind her eyes. Then she smiled softly. "That's a good reminder."
She leaned back, shifting into business. "So, Hagar. You're graduating next week, congrats. Tell me why you applied to Harbor."
Hagar swallowed her nerves and leaned in just slightly. "I've followed your firm's campaigns since sophomore year. I even built a class presentation around your 'Rise Without Limits' rebrand last year. It was smart, elegant—and it elevated the brand without overpowering it."
Sarah raised her eyebrows. "You presented that in class?"

"Yes. And got a 98," Hagar added with a quiet smile.
Sarah smiled back. "Good taste."
They both laughed gently. The atmosphere softened.

"And why this role?" Sarah asked. "Being an executive assistant isn't everyone's dream job out of school."
Hagar paused, choosing her words carefully. "Because I want to learn from the best. I know this isn't a 'creative' role, but support work done well can open doors—if I'm learning from someone I respect."
Sarah leaned back slightly, folding her arms. "You did your homework."

"I did."

"I don't sugarcoat things," Sarah said. "This role requires juggling chaos, discretion, 4 a.m. calendar changes, and putting out fires before they reach my desk. That doesn't scare you?"
Hagar's gaze didn't flinch. "No. I've already been juggling school, two jobs, and student loans. I can handle pressure."
Sarah nodded slowly. "You remind me of...me."
The comment caught Hagar off guard, and Sarah seemed to notice, amused.

"I mean that as a compliment," Sarah added. "I hired my first assistant thinking I needed a helper. But what I really needed was a partner who could anticipate what I didn't have time to see."

"I can be that," Hagar said, her voice firm and low.

There was a beat of silence between them—something unsaid but forming.

Sarah gestured toward a folder on the desk. "We've got three major campaigns launching this quarter. I'll need someone who can juggle high-stakes timelines and keep confidentiality like a vault."

"I can do that."

Sarah glanced at her watch and stood. "Thank you for your time. We have more interviews, but I'll be in touch soon."

Hagar rose to shake her hand again. "Thank you for the opportunity."

As Sarah walked her to the door, she said casually, "Hagar—just one more thing. Can you start Monday, if we make an offer?"

"Yes," Hagar said without hesitation.

"Good."

The Offer

Hagar was folding laundry in her tiny off-campus apartment when her phone buzzed.

Unknown Number.

She nearly dropped the warm towel in her hands.

"Hello?" she answered, trying to keep her voice even.

"Hi, is this Hagar Daniels?" The voice was familiar—confident, crisp.

"Yes, this is she."

"This is Sarah Abrams from Harbor Creative Group. I hope I'm not catching you at a bad time."

Hagar blinked. Sarah Abrams was calling her directly.

"Not at all," she managed.

"I'd like to offer you the executive assistant position we discussed. If you're still interested."

Still interested? She nearly forgot to breathe.

"Yes. Absolutely. I accept."

Sarah chuckled. "That was fast."

"I've never been more sure about anything," Hagar said, letting a rare smile take over her face.

"Great. I'll have recruiting email you the offer letter and onboarding paperwork now. And then come in Monday morning, 8:30 sharp. Let's get started."

"Yes, ma'am. Thank you. I won't let you down."

"I believe that," Sarah replied. "See you soon."

When the call ended, Hagar sat down in the middle of the floor and stared at her phone, grinning like a girl who'd just been handed the keys to something sacred.

She had a seat at the table now.

First Day at Harbor

The office was already humming when Hagar stepped off the elevator Monday morning in a structured blazer and a sharp pair of flats. She'd arrived twenty minutes early but still found Sarah seated at her glass desk, already on her second cup of coffee.

Sarah glanced up. "You're early."

"I figured it's better than being late."

"Always." Sarah stood and handed her a sleek black binder. "This is your onboarding packet. HR will do the boring stuff, but the real learning starts right now."

They moved swiftly—Sarah wasn't one to waste time.

She gave Hagar a tour of the floor, introduced her to the senior team in clipped but friendly tones, and by 10:00 a.m. had looped her into two internal meetings and tossed her a list of urgent scheduling changes.

"You'll need to reschedule my 2:00 with Garvey," Sarah said, typing as she spoke. "And find a time before Thursday to meet with the fundraising team."

"Got it," Hagar said, already pulling up the calendar.

"And if my husband, Abe, calls, patch him through no matter what I'm doing."

Hagar smiled faintly. "Yes, ma'am."

Sarah paused, giving her a look. "You don't have to call me that."

"Force of habit," Hagar said. "Old Southern roots."

Sarah let out a breath of laughter. "Fine. Just don't call me 'boss lady' either."

"Noted."

By the end of the day, they had developed a rhythm. Sarah tossed tasks, and Hagar caught them with precision. A quiet trust began to form, unspoken but unmistakable. When Sarah paused outside her office at 6:45 p.m., coat over one arm, she found Hagar still typing furiously at her desk.

"You don't have to stay this late on your first day."

"I know. I just wanted to finish this list you gave me."

Sarah studied her for a moment. "You're going to do well here, Hagar."

"Thank you," Hagar said, lifting her eyes. "I plan to."

Sarah gave her a short nod, then disappeared into the elevator.

Hagar leaned back in her chair, the city twinkling through the floor-to-ceiling windows beside her.

She was tired. But not the kind of tired that made you want to quit.

The kind that made you feel alive.

CHAPTER 14

The Trying

Manhattan Fertility Center

Sarah sat in the waiting room, fingers intertwined tightly in her lap, eyes fixed on the modern abstract painting across from her. The sterile white walls, the soft background music, the neatly stacked parenting magazines—it all felt both hopeful and suffocating.

Abe sat beside her, calm on the outside but gently squeezing her hand every few minutes like clockwork.

They had put off this appointment for months—convincing themselves it would happen naturally. But two years had passed since they first started trying. Month after month of negative tests. Silent disappointments. Quiet tears behind closed doors.

Abe gently placed his hand over hers, his voice soft. "We're here. That's the first step."

Sarah forced a small smile. "I know."

The door opened and a cheerful nurse called out, "Sarah and Abe Abrams?"

They rose together and followed her into the consultation room. After some brief paperwork, they were escorted into a consultation room where Dr. Malik entered moments later, smiling warmly.

"Good morning, Mr. and Mrs. Abrams," she greeted, extending her hand. "I know these first visits can feel a little overwhelming, but I promise—we'll walk through everything together."

Sarah exhaled slowly. "Thank you."

Dr. Malik reviewed their files and asked a few basic questions about their history. As Sarah answered, Abe watched her closely, silently proud of her courage even in this vulnerable space.

"So, tell me where we're starting from," she began.

Sarah took a deep breath. "We've been trying for almost two years now. Actively. We've been tracking cycles, doing everything we're supposed to."

"No pregnancies at all?" Dr. Malik confirmed gently.

Sarah shook her head with a strain of disappointment across her face.

"Have either of you had any prior testing?" she asked.

"Not yet," Abe answered.

"We see many couples like you," Dr. Malik said gently.

"Healthy. No obvious red flags. Sometimes the issue is simply unexplained. Sometimes it's timing. Sometimes we uncover something small we can address."

Sarah exhaled slowly at those words—as if permission had been granted to let go of the silent shame she'd been carrying.

"We'll start with bloodwork, hormonal panels, ultrasounds, semen analysis—the basics," Dr. Malik continued.

"We gather information first. That's how we build a path forward."

Sarah glanced at Abe, her voice barely above a whisper. "We were hoping...maybe we wouldn't need all of this."

Abe squeezed her hand gently. "It's okay. Whatever it takes."

Dr. Malik smiled. "You're not alone in this. We'll take it one step at a time."

As they left the clinic an hour later, neither spoke right away. The city's familiar energy surrounded them again, but for Sarah, everything felt slightly out of focus.

She finally whispered, "I didn't think it would come to this."

Abe stopped and turned to face her, gently brushing a tear from her cheek. "It's not the end of the dream, Sarah. Just a different road to it."

"I know," Sarah said softly. "I just never thought we'd need help. It always seemed like something that happened to other people."

Abe stopped walking and turned her to face him.

"We serve a God who works in both miracles and medicine."

Sarah blinked back fresh tears, her throat tightening.

"I'm scared."

Abe pulled her into his arms.

"So am I. But I believe this story's not over. And I believe it ends with laughter."

She nodded, but deep down, she felt the first crack of fear settle quietly inside her—the fear that the road ahead might be longer and harder than either of them expected.

The days that followed became a blur of lab appointments, ultrasounds, consultations, and nervous waiting for phone calls.

Terms like "low ovarian reserve" and "unexplained infertility" entered their vocabulary, filling the spaces between prayers.

And still, Sarah whispered nightly into the quiet:

"Your will, Lord. But please—let Your will include us holding a child."

Sarah's Work Gala

Sarah had a gala at her office to celebrate a major contract they'd just landed, one she had personally led to the finish line after six months of intense strategy, long nights, and delicate negotiations. At the gala,

Sarah dazzled. She moved through the room with practiced poise, shaking hands, giving toasts, laughing in all the right places, and accepting compliments with the kind of polish only women in power could perfect.

"You were incredible in that pitch meeting," a junior associate gushed. "Honestly, the client wouldn't have signed without your vision."

Sarah smiled graciously. "Team effort."

A client crossed the room and when she reached Sarah, she leaned in and said warmly, "You've got that glow about you tonight, Sarah."

Another colleague chimed in. "Wait— are you pregnant? Is that why your *glowing*?"

The question was casual. Light-hearted. But it hit her like a slap.

Sarah laughed softly, brushing her hair behind her ear. "No…just happily married and well-lit in these ballroom lights."

They chuckled, but someone nearby added teasingly, "Well, if you ever were expecting, I bet you'd keep it under wraps until the quarter closed."

Sarah smiled, all charm. "A woman's best kept secret is always timing."

A ripple of laughter. But inside, something in her fractured.

Just then, Abe appeared beside her, sliding his arm gently around her waist. "What has this swarm of women laughing over here?"

Sarah's colleague directed her next comment to Abe, "We were just wondering when you and Sarah were going to start a family. We love when new babies visit the office," she added with a smile.

"We are still enjoying our time together," Abe responded while smiling with his eyes at his lovely wife. "Now, you'll please excuse me," he said to the group with a boyish grin. "I'm stealing my wife for a turn around the dance floor."

They stepped away from the crowd, Sarah clinging to the reprieve.

"You okay?" he asked as he pulled her into his arms to dance while reading her carefully.

She nodded, eyes bright but distant. "Just...glowing, apparently."

Abe gave a soft smile. "You always are."

But the moment the music stopped, Sarah and Abe parted and she slipped into the restroom for a break. Immediately she stepped into restroom, her smile dropped.

She stood alone at the sink, gripping the cold marble with both hands. Her reflection stared back, flawless makeup, perfect dress, victorious in every professional sense.

But the ache wouldn't leave.

She whispered to herself, "God, I'm tired of pretending this is fine."

And for a moment...just a moment...the weight of success without fulfillment nearly stole her breath.

Three Months Later—Virtual Call with Pastor Wells

The video call screen glowed as Sarah, Mara, and Pastor Wells all connected from their separate homes.

It was Mara's idea, actually—a late-night text to Sarah had sparked the thought:

"Do you think your pastor would talk to both of us sometime? I could really use some perspective."

Sarah had texted back instantly.

"Absolutely. I'll set it up."

Now, as the call opened, Pastor Wells greeted them with his signature warmth.

"Good evening, ladies. It's wonderful to see both of your faces, even if I wish it were under lighter circumstances."

Mara smiled weakly.

"Thank you for making time for us."

Pastor Wells nodded.

"Of course. Sometimes it helps simply to sit together...even virtually...in the presence of God and not carry the weight alone."

After a few minutes of small talk, the conversation turned to their waiting.

Mara spoke first.

"It's just...so hard not to compare. Everyone around me seems to blink and get pregnant. And month after month, the disappointment builds."

Sarah nodded quietly beside her.

Pastor Wells spoke gently.

"The world makes pregnancy feel like it should be effortless—but many people silently carry this same ache. That's why your honesty matters."

Sarah added softly,

"Sometimes I feel like we're both standing at locked doors, knocking—but hearing nothing."

Pastor Wells smiled with compassion.

"And yet you are still knocking. That's faith."

He continued.

"Let me remind you of something I've said before...but it is so foundational. From the very beginning of creation, God spoke His will clearly: *'Be fruitful and multiply.'* That command wasn't simply a biological function—it was a blessing. A divine invitation into His creative design."

He leaned forward slightly.

"Which means this: the desire in your hearts to bear children is not outside of God's will. It's rooted in His very first words over humanity. The enemy may try to distort, delay, or steal that promise—but God's will remains unshaken."

Mara's eyes brimmed with tears as she whispered, "So it's okay to keep believing that?"

Pastor Wells smiled tenderly.

"More than okay. You *should* keep believing it. You should pray boldly, stand on His promises, and speak life over your bodies and your futures."

Mara added softly,

"But what if the outcome looks different?"

He nodded.

"Even if His path surprises you, His will to bring life remains the same. Whether by natural conception, by medicine, by surrogacy, by adoption—the fruitfulness He speaks over you will still bear witness to His faithfulness."

He closed their time in prayer, his voice steady and full of authority.

"Lord, strengthen these women as they wait. Guard their marriages. Protect their hearts from bitterness. And when You are ready—in Your perfect wisdom—fulfill the desires You have planted in them for motherhood. We trust You. We trust You still. Amen."

Both women whispered, *"Amen."*

After the Call

As the screen went dark, Sarah texted Mara immediately.

"Thank you for doing this with me."

Mara replied seconds later.

"Thank YOU. That helped more than I can explain. I feel lighter tonight."

Sarah smiled through tears.

"Me too."

After The Counseling Call—Back in Dallas, Late Evening

The house was quiet. The glow of the small lamp on Mara's nightstand illuminated her open journal and worn Bible.

Her husband, Jared, had already fallen asleep, but Mara sat up in bed, unable to shake the heaviness that still lingered after the video call with Pastor Wells.

Sarah was carrying so much.

Mara closed her journal softly and laid her hand gently over the closed cover.

She whispered aloud, barely more than a breath.

"Lord...I know You see her."

The tears came unexpectedly as her words flowed—not rehearsed, not polished, but raw.

"God, You promised fruitfulness. You declared it from the very first words You spoke over us, '*Be fruitful and multiply.*'
And yet...she waits. And I wait. And some days it feels like the weight of waiting is too much."

Mara paused to steady her voice, wiping her tears.

"But You're not a God who teases or torments. You're the God who writes better endings than we can imagine."

She squeezed her eyes shut, feeling the swell of her own longing mingled with Sarah's.

"Lord, protect her heart. Keep bitterness far from her marriage. Guard Abe and Sarah as they walk this road. And even when she feels like her faith is slipping, hold her steady."

Mara opened her eyes and whispered softly,

"I believe You, God. I believe Your promise over her still stands. And I declare that Sarah Abrams will hold the child You have written for her."

She exhaled slowly, her chest rising and falling, finally releasing the burden she had been carrying for her friend.

"Do what only You can do, Lord. And let me stand in the gap while she waits."

The room grew still again.

Mara laid her Bible gently back on the nightstand and whispered one final prayer as she turned off the light:

"You're still writing, God. And I trust Your pen."

As darkness filled the room, peace finally settled over her, knowing Heaven had heard.

After The Counseling Call—Manhattan, Late Evening

Sarah stared at the ceiling, her Bible unopened beside her on the bed.

I trusted God for a career...and He gave me one. I trusted Him for a husband...and Abe came. Then why can't I trust Him with my womb?

The question didn't bring peace.

Instead, it tightened in her chest.

Maybe this was different. Maybe this was where faith came to die.

Three Months After Testing—Manhattan Fertility Center

Sarah sat on the edge of the exam table, paper gown rustling softly beneath her as she anxiously twisted her wedding ring around her finger. Abe sat across from her in the consultation chair, legs crossed, hands calmly folded—but she knew him well enough to see the quiet tension in his jaw.

Dr. Malik entered with her usual warm, composed presence. She smiled gently as she pulled her rolling stool closer.

"Good afternoon," she said softly, eyes full of both empathy and clinical confidence. "Thank you for your patience with all the tests."

Sarah nodded, her heart racing as she searched Dr. Malik's face for clues.

"Do you have answers?" Abe asked gently.

Dr. Malik nodded.

"We do. And while some pieces remain unexplained, we have enough data to give us a clear sense of where you are."

She paused for a moment before continuing.

"Sarah, your ovarian reserve is lower than we'd expect for your age. And your uterine lining shows some irregularities that may be interfering with implantation."

Sarah inhaled sharply, her pulse pounding.

"Is it...permanent?" she whispered.

Dr. Malik softened her voice even further.

"Nothing is absolute. But it does explain why you've had so

many unsuccessful cycles. And unfortunately, it means that even with aggressive treatments like IUI or IVF, your chances remain significantly lower than average."

Sarah felt Abe's hand reach for hers, his grip steady as always.

Dr. Malik continued, carefully watching their faces.

"However, this does not mean you can't have a child."

Sarah's head snapped up at that glimmer of hope.

"There are alternative options," Dr. Malik said gently. "Many couples in your situation consider using a gestational carrier—a surrogate—who would carry your embryo created through IVF. This allows you to have a biological child while reducing the physical complications that would come with carrying the pregnancy yourself."

Sarah's head swirled at the terminology.

"A surrogate."

"Yes," Dr. Malik nodded. "We would walk you through every step. Legal support, emotional counseling, matching services—if that's the path you feel led to consider."

The room fell quiet.

Sarah's breath was shallow as she whispered, "I never thought we'd get here."

Abe rubbed slow circles into her palm.

"We knew God might take us on a different path," he said softly.

Dr. Malik smiled warmly but professionally.

"You're not alone. And this is not a failure. This is simply a different door opening."

After pausing to let the news sink in, Dr. Malik suggested "Go home. Take it all in, and then let me know what you decide. We can take it from there."

"Thank you, Dr. Malik," Sarah said with disappointment written all over her face.

Six Months Into Infertility—Jordan's Apartment, Midtown

The guys gathered like they did every few months—an unspoken rhythm that had developed over years of friendship.

Tonight was simple: pizza, playoff basketball, and a lot of catching up. Abe sat quietly through the first half of the game, laughing at their usual banter but mostly lost in his own thoughts.

Finally, during halftime, Marcus muted the TV and looked over at him.

"All right, man. You've been way too quiet tonight."

Jordan nodded.

"Seriously. Talk to us."

Abe exhaled, staring down at the bottle of water in his hands.

"We've been trying for over a year now," he finally said softly.

"Still nothing."

The room grew still.

"No pregnancy yet?" Eli asked gently.

Abe shook his head.

Marcus leaned forward, his voice steady.

"Where are you guys emotionally?"

Abe's voice cracked slightly.

"Some days we're hopeful. Some days..." He paused, swallowing hard. "It feels like we're losing tiny pieces of hope each month."

Jordan spoke quietly.

"Are you guys seeing doctors yet?"

"We've started testing," Abe replied. "There are some complications on Sarah's side, but we both know it's not anyone's fault. It's just...complicated."

The guys nodded quietly, absorbing his honesty.

"It's not easy watching your wife carry that weight," Abe added.

"I want to fix it. And I can't."

Marcus leaned in slightly, voice calm and grounding.

"You're not supposed to fix it, Abe. You're supposed to walk through it with her. And you are."

Abe blinked hard, grateful for Marcus's steadiness.

Then he added, almost under his breath, "Lately, I keep wondering... what if this isn't God's plan for us? What if we're praying for something He never intended to give?"

The room went still again—not from awkwardness, but from reverence. The spiritual weight of the question hung heavy.

Eli spoke carefully.

"You really think God would put that desire in your hearts just to mock it?"

"I don't know," Abe admitted. "That's the thing. I used to be sure. But now, I don't always know which thoughts are mine...and which ones are lies."

Jordan nodded.

"The enemy is subtle, man. He won't come at you with pitchforks. He comes with quiet doubts. Ones that sound almost spiritual."

Marcus looked him straight in the eye.

"That voice isn't God's. The God I know doesn't dangle hope just to snatch it away. If He's delaying, it's not because He's cruel. It's because He's building something you can't see yet."

Abe didn't say anything, but he felt the words settle into his chest.

Then, without needing to be asked, the guys instinctively moved closer, forming a small circle. Each placed a hand on his shoulders—anchoring him, covering him.

Marcus spoke first.

"Lord, You are the God who sees. You heard Abraham. You heard Sarah. Just like You hear Abe and Sarah now."

Jordan continued.

"We ask for Your perfect timing, Lord. But we also ask boldly for a child. You're still the God of miracles."

Eli closed.

"And while they wait, give them strength. Guard their marriage. Guard their hearts. And let them know You are never absent in the waiting."

Abe swallowed hard, whispering,

"Amen."

As they sat back down, nothing more needed to be said.

Abe finally smiled.

"Thanks, guys."

Marcus patted him on the shoulder.

"We've got you, man. However long it takes."

The game resumed quietly in the background, but the real work of the night had already been done.

CHAPTER 15

The Waiting Continues

Nine months into Infertility—SoHo

Sarah sat in the corner booth at The Mercer Kitchen, fingers tapping the rim of her coffee cup while Abe scanned headlines on his phone. The morning bustle of SoHo barely reached them here—the clatter of dishes and soft jazz filled the silences.

"Listen to this," Abe said, eyes still on his phone.

"Another record investment in renewables. Maybe it's time to push the proposal out of beta."

Sarah didn't answer. She was counting days. Twelve days late.

Once it had filled her with hope. Now it mocked her.

"Sarah?"

She smiled thinly. "Just a weird week."

Abe studied her face, sensing there was more, but let it go. He lived by signs and coincidences, always trusting the invisible threads.

"I had a dream," he said. "You were holding a baby boy. He had your eyes."

She laughed softly. "You and your dreams! Prophecy by REM cycle?"

"Maybe." He shrugged. "Could be something."

She sipped her coffee, the warmth soothing the knot in her chest.

Sarah was no stranger to waiting. But this—waiting for a child was different. It gnawed at her in a way no business deal or promotion ever could.

Outside, spring crept in, the kind that still demanded a scarf but promised warmth by noon. She once loved this time of year. Now it marked another cycle, another 'maybe.'

"Still okay with...options?" Abe asked. "Remember Dr. Malik said we can get there with surrogacy, adoption...we have choices."

"Do you feel like...we're surrendering?" she whispered.

Abe shook his head.

"I feel like we're trusting."

Sarah swallowed hard.

After a long pause, she whispered, "What if it's not just about a baby? I always dreamed of carrying my own child. To feel him, or her, grow inside me? What if I never stop feeling like a borrowed mother otherwise?"

"I know," Abe said gently. "But your dream was to be a mother, Sarah. And that dream isn't gone." Abe reached for her hand.

"We keep hoping. Even if it's laughable. Even if we're Sarah and Abraham waiting on a miracle!"

She let him hold her hand. But she didn't laugh. Not yet.

The Office—Midtown Manhattan

The morning buzzed like any other—conference calls stacked back-to-back, emails flashing nonstop, and a dozen small fires burning quietly around the edges.

Hagar stood near Sarah's office doorway, observing carefully. She had been with the firm only a few months, and while she was catching on quickly, today she found herself marveling at Sarah's ability to navigate chaos with calm precision.

Inside, Sarah sat at her desk, headset in place, multiple screens open in front of her as she flipped between financial models, legal contracts, and vendor disputes. Her tone was steady, measured—even as the voices on the call grew tense.

"No," Sarah said firmly, cutting through the noise.

"That number doesn't reconcile because you're calculating off last quarter's projected allocation, not the revised spend authorization. Look at line 82."

There was a pause on the call.

"You're right," the voice finally admitted, a little sheepishly.

Sarah softened her tone but remained in control. "Let's update the file. I'll approve the amendment once the corrected version hits my inbox."

She clicked off, exhaling quietly, then glanced up to see Hagar watching. Sarah smiled faintly. "You look like you've seen a magic trick."

Hagar blushed slightly. "Honestly? That was amazing. The way you spotted the error that fast...I don't think I'd even made it to line 10."

Sarah laughed softly. "Years of practice. And caffeine."

Hagar smiled. "You make it look so effortless."

"It's not," Sarah said quietly, her voice tinged with something deeper. "But it helps when you learn how to separate noise from truth."

Before Hagar could respond, Sarah's phone buzzed again. Another meeting was starting.

"Let's grab lunch later," Sarah said as she stood, slipping back into professional gear. "You can sit in on the client call this afternoon too."

"Of course," Hagar nodded, still slightly in awe.

Later That Week

The day started normally. Meetings scheduled, reports delivered, coffee in hand.

But as Hagar arrived at the office that morning, she immediately noticed something different. Sarah was pale, her movements slower, her usual energy missing.

Hagar knocked lightly on her open door. "Good morning."

Sarah looked up with a tight smile that didn't quite reach her eyes. "Morning."

"Is everything alright?"

Sarah hesitated, then stood abruptly and walked over to her desk. She stared at her phone for a moment, then finally spoke—her voice quiet but sharp. "I thought I could be here...please clear my calendar for the rest of the day."

Hagar blinked. "Everything? You have the quarterly review at two..."

"Everything, Hagar." Sarah's voice cracked, and she quickly looked away. "I need to go home. I'm taking a sick day."

"Of course." Hagar stepped back gently. "I'll take care of it."

Sarah grabbed her coat, avoided eye contact, and hurried out of the office. Hagar watched her leave, sensing that whatever was wrong had nothing to do with illness.

Sarah & Abe's Apartment—That Evening

Sarah curled up on the couch, a heating pad pressed against her abdomen, tissues scattered across the coffee table. The cramping had started hours earlier, and with it, the wave of grief she hated admitting still crushed her.

Ten days late.

Ten days of hope building in secret.

And now, another month buried with the others. Each month that passes without getting pregnant feels like mini funeral...over and over again.

Abe had texted that he was running late, so she was alone for now with her disappointment. In her aloneness, she ached to call her mom, who had died when she was in college.

And then, like a wave she hadn't seen coming, the thought hit her:

Any child I bring into this world will never meet my parents. Never know my grandparents. And I will have to walk this road without them.

The familiar ache was not just physical. It was the dull, relentless grief of waiting, hoping, and failing yet again.

She moved to sit on the floor of the spare bedroom—the one they had once imagined would become the nursery.

The soft glow of the hallway light barely reached her. She pulled her knees to her chest, her Bible open in her lap but unread for the past hour.

The tears came before she could stop them—hot and sudden, catching her off guard. It wasn't the possibility of losing another baby that overwhelmed her. It was the ache of knowing that if life was forming, she wouldn't be able to share it with the two people who would have celebrated it most.

Her mom would have cried. Bought books. Told stories. Made casseroles and fussed over paint colors for the nursery.

Her dad would've been quieter about it, but she could already picture him standing awkwardly in the baby aisle, trying to pick out a "My First Cowboys" jersey for his future grandchild.

They should be here for this. For all of it.

She pressed the heel of her hand to her eyes and took a shaky breath.

"Lord..." she finally whispered, her voice trembling.

It was the prayer she had prayed so many times before, but tonight it carried a deeper ache.

"I don't understand why this is so hard. I don't understand why something You created my body to do feels impossible."

She swallowed, her hands gripping the fabric of her pajama pants.

"I want to believe You haven't forgotten me. I want to trust

Your timing. But God...it's getting harder."

Her voice cracked under the weight of the months of disappointments, stacking like bricks in her chest.

"I believe You're good. I believe You give good gifts. And I believe You're the God who opens barren wombs."

She closed her eyes tightly, clinging to the promises she barely had the strength to recite anymore.

"But I need You to strengthen my faith. Because I'm tired of hoping and being disappointed."

Her eyes fell to Genesis 15, her Bible now open to the covenant God had spoken to Abraham:

"Look now toward heaven and count the stars if you are able to number them...so shall your descendants be."

The irony stung, but at the same time, a quiet whisper settled into her spirit: *This promise is still true.*

She wiped her tears, her voice soft but steady now.

"God, if there's still a child You've promised us, I surrender it back to You. However You choose. However You will. But please, Father...don't let me walk this road alone."

It was in that quiet moment—filled with both longing and imagined joy—that the memories began to surface.

The call.

The hospital.

The funeral.

And the aching truth that she had learned to live with, but never really stopped grieving.

Flashback to Six Years Earlier—Dallas, Texas

The call came at 2:11 a.m.

Sarah bolted upright in bed, heart pounding, as her phone buzzed sharply on the nightstand. The glow of the screen lit up the dark room—Mom, it read.

She grabbed it quickly, already bracing herself. Something was wrong.

"Mom?" she answered, voice groggy and dry.

But it wasn't her mother's voice.

"Ms. Sarah Cohen?" a man said calmly. "This is Officer Talbot with the Dallas Police Department. I'm sorry to call at this hour. There's been an accident."

Everything inside her stilled.

She swung her legs off the side of the bed, grounding herself against the hardwood floor.

"What…what kind of accident?" she whispered.

The officer hesitated. "A drunk driver crossed into oncoming traffic. There was a collision involving your parents' vehicle."

Her breath caught. Her body turned cold.

"I'm so sorry to tell you this…your father was pronounced dead at the scene. Your mother was taken to Presbyterian Hospital but…"

He paused, his voice gentling. "She passed shortly after arrival."

Silence.

Sarah's hand flew to her mouth. A soft, strangled cry escaped her lips as the world around her cracked wide open.

She couldn't breathe. Couldn't think. The walls of her bedroom suddenly felt like they were closing in.

"No. No, no, no…"

Tears blurred her vision as she dropped the phone to the floor, collapsing beside it. Her chest heaved with sobs too deep for words—animal, raw, uncontainable.

In the span of a single phone call, she had become an orphan.

Later That Morning—The Hospital

Sarah stood frozen in the sterile hospital hallway, arms wrapped tightly around herself as if sheer will could hold her together. Her coat was still half-buttoned, soaked from the storm outside, the rainwater mingling with tears she hadn't even noticed falling.

A physician in blue scrubs stood before her, gentle-eyed and practiced in delivering the worst news of people's lives. He spoke with careful clarity—but the words struck like hail against glass.

"…I'm very sorry, Ms. Abrams. Your mother arrived with extensive internal bleeding. We did everything we could, but the trauma was…it was too severe."

Sarah didn't respond. She couldn't. Her lips trembled, but no words came out.

"And your father…I'm afraid he was pronounced at the scene."

A drunk driver.

A rainy intersection.

A red light run.

No time to brake.

No goodbye.

The facts floated above her like smoke, impossible to grasp. The words replayed in a loop—slow, surreal, dreamlike.

Gone. Both. Gone.

Behind the doctor, nurses walked briskly past, clipboard in hand, the rhythm of hospital life moving forward as if nothing had happened. As if her entire world hadn't just been reduced to a before and after.

"Would you like to see them?" the doctor asked gently.

Sarah shook her head. Or nodded. She didn't know which. Her limbs felt like lead, her stomach twisted in grief.

She stumbled into a chair, numb, shaking. The overhead lights buzzed softly, sterile and too bright. Her throat burned, but no sobs came now—just an aching hollowness pressing in on all sides.

A chaplain came by. Someone offered her water. A nurse brought a blanket. She barely noticed.

She was twenty-two. And she had no parents.

The storm outside continued, as if the skies themselves wept with her.

The Funeral in Dallas—Three Days After the Accident

The sanctuary was packed with people—friends from childhood, neighbors who brought casseroles they couldn't bear to deliver, distant relatives Sarah hadn't seen since she wore braces. Each face offered kindness, sympathy, love. But none of them could touch the void.

It was too vast.

Too immediate.

Too permanent.

The caskets stood at the front of the church, side by side, draped in white roses and soft lilies. Her parents. Together in death, as they had been in life. The sight of them broke something loose inside her every time she looked up.

Sarah clutched the wrinkled pages of her eulogy with trembling hands. She had written them in the middle of the night, surrounded by the deafening silence of her childhood home—every creak of the floorboards reminding her they were gone. She had called Lottie and Mara to come over the day before and just sit with her while she wrote. They didn't say much. They didn't have to.

And now, here she was, standing behind a podium that had never felt so far from solid ground.

She cleared her throat and began.

"My parents were not perfect people," she said, her voice already cracking, "but they were my home. My foundation. The ones who always saw me...even when I didn't see myself."

She paused, her breath catching as a wave of grief slammed against her chest. Lottie, seated in the front row, gave a gentle nod of encouragement, her hand already gripping Mara's. Both cried with her through the sleepless nights since the accident. Both were here now, holding her up without standing beside her.

Sarah continued, voice quieter but steadier.

"They were the kind of parents who showed up. For piano

recitals I botched. For science fairs I forgot until the night before. For every heartbreak, every triumph…every ordinary day."

She glanced out at the sea of faces, blurred by tears.

"And now, they're part of my future in a different way…not as parents I can call, but as legacy I carry forward."

A long pause. The pages fluttered slightly in her hands.

"I don't know how to live without them," she admitted softly.

"But I know how to live because of them."

She stepped down slowly, unsure how her legs carried her back to the pew. Mara reached for her hand. Lottie slipped an arm around her shoulder. The choir began to sing a quiet hymn—Amazing Grace, one her mother loved. Sarah closed her eyes.

It still didn't feel real. But for the first time since the call, she let herself cry—not just for what she'd lost, but for the strength it would take to keep living. And the friends who would help her do it.

Present Day—Sarah & Abe's Apartment

Sarah sat on the nursery floor, barefoot in her pajamas, clutching a photo album across her lap. Pictures of family vacations, Christmas mornings, birthdays—scenes now sealed in the past.

Abe knelt quietly beside her.

"I don't know how to do life without them," she whispered.

"You'll never have to do life without love," he said gently. "Their love is in you."

Sarah shook her head.

"But they'll never meet our children. They'll never be grandparents."

Abe's throat tightened, knowing how much she longed for a child— even then, before their infertility journey had fully begun.

"They'll see them through you," he whispered. "And I'll hold their legacy alongside you."

The Memory's Grip

Now six years after their death, sitting quietly in the apartment nursery, Sarah often felt her parents' absence as she stared into the empty nursery that waited for a child who still hadn't come.

They would have loved this child fiercely. No question. No hesitation.

The ache doubled—not only for the child she longed for, but for the parents who would never hold him.

And so, with every whispered prayer for a baby, there was always a second, unspoken plea tucked beneath:

I want my child to know unconditional love—the way my parents loved me.

Fertility Clinic—Five Months After Their First Consultation

Sarah sat on the edge of the exam table, staring at the ceiling tiles, her fingers twisting the fabric of her blouse in her lap.

Abe sat beside her, trying to appear calm, but his knee bounced almost imperceptibly, betraying his nerves.

Dr. Malik entered quietly, holding the thin manila file that now represented months of bloodwork, hormone panels, injections, and meticulously timed procedures.

Sarah sat up straighter, heart pounding. This was the moment they had waited for.

"Sarah, Abe," Dr. Malik began, her voice gentle but serious. "I have your results."

She paused slightly, and Sarah already knew. She could see it in her eyes.

"I'm so sorry," Dr. Malik said softly. "The embryo didn't implant. The cycle wasn't successful."

Sarah's stomach dropped. She heard the words but couldn't fully absorb them.

"No heartbeat?" she whispered, her voice barely audible.

"No implantation," Dr. Malik clarified. "It never progressed that far."

Abe exhaled deeply, blinking hard as he reached for Sarah's hand. She stared straight ahead, numb.

"We did everything right," Sarah finally whispered.

"You did," Dr. Malik nodded. "But unfortunately, even when all conditions are ideal, IVF doesn't guarantee success. There are so many factors beyond our control."

Sarah swallowed hard, feeling the familiar sting rise in her throat—the one she had tried to suppress for months.

"Is it... is it me?" she asked softly. "Is it my body?"

"There's nothing you did wrong," Dr. Malik assured her gently.

"You responded well to the medications. Your egg retrieval was strong. The embryos looked promising. Sometimes, even with the best science, there's still mystery."

Sarah clenched her jaw, willing herself not to cry in front of the doctor. Abe spoke quietly, trying to steady the moment.

"What are our next steps?"

Dr. Malik exhaled, choosing her words carefully.

"We can try again. Another IVF cycle is possible, but each round carries additional emotional, physical, and financial strain. I encourage you both to take some time before deciding."

Sarah nodded stiffly, her throat closing.

The Parking Garage

They walked to the car in silence.

Sarah slid into the passenger seat and stared blankly at the dashboard as Abe turned the key. The engine hummed quietly beneath them.

The silence stretched, thick and heavy, until Sarah finally broke it.

"I can't do it again, Abe."

He looked over gently.

"We don't have to decide right now."

"No." Her voice cracked. "I mean—I can't do it again. My body, my mind...I feel like I've been carved open, piece by piece. And for what? Another empty chart? Another nurse giving me that same look?"

Abe reached for her hand.

"Then we won't. Not if it's too much."

Tears slipped down her cheeks as she whispered, "I feel like I failed."

Abe's voice broke now too.

"You didn't fail, Sarah. You've endured more than anyone should have to. God's promise isn't gone. It just may not come the way we expected."

She closed her eyes, breathing through the ache.

"I don't know if I can hope anymore."

Abe squeezed her hand firmly.

"Then I'll hope for both of us."

Long after Abe fell asleep that night, Sarah lay awake, her hand resting flat across her empty stomach.

She whispered through tears:

"God...if You still see me, if Your promise still stands...please show us another way."

She didn't know then that another way was already forming—and that it would come from someone entirely unexpected.

Sarah's Office—Midtown Manhattan

The fire alarm started as a faint beep, then escalated into a staccato wail that echoed across the glass halls of Harbor Creative Group. People rose from desks with varying degrees of urgency—some rolling their eyes, others grabbing laptops, a few shrugging into coats out of instinct. Hagar had just returned from the print room when it started. She moved quickly toward Sarah's office, unsure if this was real or one of those scheduled drills HR forgot to warn anyone about.

"Sarah?" she called, knocking as she pushed the door open.

Sarah stood frozen at her desk, her phone to her ear, eyebrows pinched.

"…I understand, but I can't just—yes, but—fine, fine," she snapped, hanging up. She turned to Hagar, her composure visibly shaken. "That was the fertility clinic. They lost my lab work. All of it." The alarm shrieked again.

Hagar blinked. "Do we need to evacuate?"

Sarah grabbed her coat but not her bag. "Yes, we do. And no, it's not a drill. Apparently, someone burned toast in the break room. Let's go."

They moved with the crowd, but outside, among the crush of staff and passing pedestrians, Sarah pulled away from the noise and into the side alley beside the building. Hagar hesitated, then followed.

Sarah exhaled deeply, resting her head against the cold brick. For a second, she looked ten years older.

"Sorry you had to see that," she said. "Not the best 'leaderly' impression, huh?"

"Actually," Hagar said quietly, "it made you real."

Sarah looked at her, surprised.

Hagar continued, "I know what it's like to wait for news that decides everything."

There was something in her tone—calm, understanding, no pity. Sarah saw, maybe for the first time, the resilience behind her assistant's ambitious drive.

"I'm not ready to talk about it," Sarah said. "I'm just exhausted."

Hagar nodded. "I'm here to help. Whatever you need."

Sarah studied her for a long moment. Then, she finally said, "Thank you."

It was the beginning of trust.

Sarah's Office—Later that Day

They were back inside after the fire alarm, the office now quieter than usual—some employees had taken advantage of the disruption to grab a long lunch. Sarah stood at the espresso machine, grinding beans she didn't need to grind, her mind elsewhere.

Hagar leaned on the doorway.

"You okay?"

"I will be," Sarah said, then paused. "I meant what I said. I trust you. And not just because you're efficient. There's…more."

Hagar stepped inside. "Can I tell you something personal?"

Sarah turned. "Please."

"When I was seventeen," Hagar began, her voice steady, "I was living with my aunt and uncle in a small town in Pennsylvania. My mom was in and out of treatment—addiction. My dad disappeared when I was a baby. I used to think stability was something other people had. Like a Netflix password you weren't allowed to share."

Sarah said nothing, just listened.

"I was on my own by the time I hit college. Worked two jobs. Slept four hours a night. Got into college on a scholarship and clawed my way through every semester."

"That's incredible," Sarah said softly.

"I tell you that not for sympathy," Hagar added, eyes sharp.

"But so you know—I don't break easily. I know how to hold things together when everything feels like it's falling apart. So if you ever need more than just an assistant, I'm here."

Sarah nodded, swallowing the lump in her throat. "I think I've needed that for a while."

The silence between them now felt like a pact.

Bitter Faith: Sarah's Journal Entry

Lord, You said You give good gifts to Your children. So why does this feel like punishment?

I don't know how to keep hoping without hating hope itself. I see babies in strollers and feel like I'm watching someone else's promise walk by.

And still, I pray. Not because I believe right now. But because I used to.

CHAPTER 16

The Escape Plan

Hagar's Flashback to Seven Years Earlier—Small Town, Pennsylvania

The rain pelted the thin tin roof as thirteen-year-old Hagar sat curled up on the edge of the worn sofa, hugging her knees to her chest. Her aunt and uncle argued in the kitchen—again. Voices muffled but sharp. The words blurred together, but the tone was all too familiar: exhaustion, resentment, and unspoken regret for having taken in one more relative when they could barely support themselves.

"She's not even ours."

"We can't keep doing this."

"She's your sister's problem, not ours."

Hagar closed her eyes tightly and whispered into the crook of her arm:

"I'll be gone soon. You won't have to keep me."

She had lived here on and off since she was eight, bouncing between relatives after her mother lost her battle with addiction. Her father had never been part of her story. There was always someone temporarily willing to house her, but never anyone eager to keep her.

Never anyone who said: You belong here.

At School—Lunchtime

Hagar sat alone at the far end of the cafeteria, picking at the dry sandwich wrapped hastily in a paper towel. She'd grown accustomed to her own company. Safer that way.

She watched groups of girls laughing together across the room—sleepover invitations, whispered secrets, friendships that stretched back to kindergarten. She longed to be seen but had long since stopped expecting it.

One teacher occasionally sat with her, Mrs. Rayner, the kind English teacher who noticed when Hagar stayed late after class or missed lunch entirely.

"You're bright, Hagar," Mrs. Rayner told her one afternoon.

"You could have a very different future, you know."

Hagar offered a faint smile, trying not to hope for anything too big.

"Maybe."

Mrs. Rayner leaned in.

"You don't have to stay here. There are scholarships. Programs. If you want it badly enough, you can make your own way."

Hagar looked down at her sandwich, then back up at Mrs. Rayner, her voice barely above a whisper.

"What would I have to do?" she asked.

Mrs. Rayner smiled gently, but her eyes were serious.

"Work harder than everyone else. Keep your grades up, write your heart out in those essays, and start picturing yourself somewhere new. Somewhere that makes you feel alive."

Hagar nodded slowly, her throat tightening with emotion she didn't dare show.

"I can do that," she said.

"I know you can," Mrs. Rayner replied. "I'll help you. But you have to decide this is what you want—not just to leave, but to build something better."

Hagar glanced around the cafeteria again: the noise, the cliques, the invisible walls. Then she looked at the woman beside her, the only one who had ever truly seen her.

"I do," she said. "I want something more."

Mrs. Rayner reached over and squeezed her hand.

"Then let's begin."

Senior Year—The Escape Plan

Hagar had never been one to dream out loud. But by seventeen, the quiet determination that Mrs. Rayner had planted in her heart years earlier had slowly replaced the fear.

She applied to every scholarship, every program she could find. She worked part-time at the grocery store after school, stuffing tips into an old envelope she kept hidden in her closet.

New York City.

The idea sounded absurd at first. But the more she thought about it, the more it became her finish line. A place where nobody would know her story—where she could finally write something new.

The Day She Left

The morning air in rural Pennsylvania was crisp and gray, the kind of quiet that clung to your coat and made you question everything. Hagar stood on the porch steps, her single suitcase resting beside her like a silent witness. It was still early, the sun barely skimming the tops of the trees, but she'd been up for hours—packing, repacking, and waiting.

From inside the kitchen, Aunt Delia's voice cut through the thin screen door.

"College in New York," her aunt muttered. "We'll see how long that lasts. New York will chew you up and spit you out, you know that, right?"

Hagar didn't respond. She knew this speech by heart.

Delia stepped out onto the porch, arms crossed beneath her fraying cardigan. Her dark eyes scanned the suitcase, then her niece. "City girls don't last long when they've got no backup."

"I'm not looking for backup," Hagar said evenly. "I'm looking for a future."

Delia gave a snort and looked out over the yard, as if the answer might be hiding in the frost-covered grass. "Plenty of girls want more. Doesn't mean they get it."

"I'm not them," Hagar said, standing taller.

A door slammed inside. Uncle Rob emerged, pulling a flannel jacket over his shoulders as he stomped toward his truck in the gravel driveway. "Bus comes, it comes," he grumbled. "Don't need a send-off for someone who's already got one foot out the door."

Delia flinched slightly but didn't correct him. She never did.

Hagar watched her uncle disappear into the truck, engine turning over with a guttural growl. She turned back to her aunt, softening just a little.

"I know you don't get it," Hagar said. "But I need to try. I need to know what else is out there."

Delia's face didn't change, but her voice did. Just enough.

"Tryin' ain't the same as stayin'. You've always had ideas too big for this house."

"Maybe," Hagar said. "But if I don't go now, I'll never know if they were just ideas…or if they were seeds."

Delia looked at her then…really looked. There was something like pride buried in the tightness of her jaw, though she'd never admit it.

"You call me," she said finally. "No matter what. If things go bad. If you lose your way."

"I will," Hagar promised. "And I'll visit. I'm not vanishing."

The bus came in a cloud of diesel and winter dust. Hagar didn't cry as she climbed aboard. She took a window seat, her hand pressed lightly against the glass, watching as her Aunt Delia stood there, arms crossed, face unreadable.

As the bus pulled away, Hagar whispered something to herself, so soft it was barely breath.

"I'm not running away."

She looked out toward the highway that stretched far beyond the edge of her old life.

"I'm running toward."

Toward purpose.

Toward becoming someone.

I'll build something different.

I'll matter.

Earning Her Place

The glow of the desk lamp was the only light in her cramped studio apartment, casting long shadows across stacks of textbooks and class notes. Hagar's eyes burned, not from fatigue, but from focus...a kind of laser determination that had taken root deep in her bones since the day she left Pennsylvania.

She scribbled the final line of her economics paper, then glanced at the clock: 3:17 a.m.

Her shift at the café started in less than four hours. She leaned back, pressing her palms into her aching lower back and allowing herself a brief smile. This life—the ramen noodles, the double shifts, the endless reading—it was *hers*. No one handed it to her, no one made room for her. She carved it out with elbow grease and sheer will.

At her job that afternoon, wiping down a corner table, she didn't notice Professor Levin enter until his shadow fell across the register.

"Hagar," he said warmly. "Lovely running into you! Got a minute?"

She nodded, startled. Her apron still smelled like coffee grounds.

"I read your midterm paper yesterday. Twice," he added, smiling.

"Your analysis on macroeconomic trends was impressive. Have you ever considered a mentorship or research program?"

She blinked. "Me?"

His eyes crinkled. "Yes, *you*. You've got a sharp mind. You ask the right questions. People notice."

Hagar watched him go, heart pounding, wiping the counter again with shaky hands. It wasn't just about proving something to the aunt who doubted her or the uncle who barely said a word. This was *her*. Making space. Being seen.

Later that night, back at her desk, she added something new to the sticky note on her wall—right under *Make it count and Don't go back:*

I have something to offer.

The Advisor's Office—What's Next for Hagar

The office smelled like peppermint tea and paper, a strangely calming scent that always seemed to settle Hagar's nerves. She sat across from Dr. Eliza Monroe, the head of the business department and her unofficial mentor for the last two years.

"So," Dr. Monroe began, flipping open a well-worn notebook. "One week to graduation. You ready for the real world?"

Hagar smiled, twisting the strap of her shoulder bag in her lap.

"Ready and terrified."

Dr. Monroe chuckled. "That's the right answer. So, what's next? Any leads?"

Hagar nodded. "I have a job interview next week—executive assistant role at a firm called *Harbor Creative Group*."

"Harbor?" Dr. Monroe raised her eyebrows. "That's one of the top media firms in Manhattan."

"I know," Hagar said, voice trembling slightly. "I still can't believe they responded to my application. I've been doing interview prep and mock scenarios. I even borrowed a blazer."

Dr. Monroe leaned forward, smile softening. "I've seen your progress over the past four years, Hagar. The way you handled your course load, your job, everything. You're not just smart, you've got resilience. The kind that can't be taught."

Hagar blinked quickly. "Thank you."

Dr. Monroe slid a folded piece of paper across the desk. "Just in case. It's a recommendation letter. If they need it, or if the job doesn't pan out and you apply elsewhere."

Hagar held it like it was a golden ticket.

"You've got the instincts of a leader," Dr. Monroe added.

"Even if the job title says 'assistant.' You'll rise."

Hagar nodded, heart full. "I want to matter," she whispered.

"Not for anyone else. Just...for me."

"You already do."

Graduation Day—Her Name Called

The campus lawn was blanketed with rows of folding chairs and rows of proud families holding up signs and cameras. Hagar stood in line with her cap slightly tilted, gripping the program with her name listed—
Hagar Eliana Daniels, B.S. Business Administration, Honors.

She didn't know where her aunt and uncle were, or if they even came. But she didn't scan the crowd for them. She looked forward.

The dean stepped to the podium. "And now, please join me in celebrating our graduates from the College of Business..."

Names were called. Applause echoed. Then:

"Hagar Eliana Daniels!"

She walked, slow and steady, to the sound of strangers clapping—but it still felt like thunder in her ears. She shook the dean's hand, accepted the scroll, and paused at the edge of the stage for a split second.

This was the moment. The culmination. The hinge between everything she had survived and everything she was about to become.

As she returned to her seat, Hagar whispered to herself, "I'm going to get that job."

Present Day—Sarah's Office Lobby

As Hagar stepped into the towering Manhattan building on her first day working for Sarah Abrams, she didn't know yet how deeply this job would change her life.

She only knew one thing:

This is my chance.

CHAPTER 17

The Invitation

Sarah's Office—7:15 PM

The office was finally quiet, most of the staff had gone home hours ago. The only sounds left were the hum of the HVAC system and the faint clicking of keyboards as Sarah and Hagar wrapped up a brutal end-of-quarter crisis.

Hagar knocked lightly on the open door.

"Hey, do you need me to finish up the Jenkins proposal?"

Sarah smiled. "You've done enough today. Go home, Hagar."

Hagar hesitated.

"Are you sure? You've been carrying a lot lately."

Sarah sighed and set her bag down. She looked at Hagar, noticing her concern—not as an employee, but as a friend.

"I'm fine," Sarah offered automatically. Then she softened.

"Well... mostly fine."

Hagar walked in, closing the office door behind her.

"Talk to me," she said gently. "I know something's been

weighing on you these past few months."

Sarah hesitated. She hadn't told many people yet. Only Lottie, Mara, and a small circle of prayer warriors knew about their fertility journey. But Hagar had quietly become more than an assistant. She had become a steady presence—calm, wise beyond her years, full of quiet compassion.

Sarah exhaled deeply.

"Abe and I have been trying for a baby for over two years now."

Hagar's face immediately softened.

"I didn't know. I'm so sorry."

Sarah nodded, blinking back unexpected tears. "We didn't want to say much early on. I thought maybe if we just stayed positive, it would happen."

"And the doctors?" Hagar asked gently.

Sarah swallowed.

"They've run all the tests. It's...complicated. There are some issues with my body that make carrying very difficult. The doctor recommended we consider...surrogacy."

Hagar blinked, absorbing the word.

Sarah continued quietly.

"It was never how I pictured it. I always imagined I'd carry my own child, feel them growing inside me. But now, I'm trying to open my heart to other possibilities."

Hagar sat across from her, hands clasped in her lap.

"Would it still be your child?" she asked carefully.

"Yes," Sarah nodded. "It would be our embryo, our genetics. We just...may need someone else's womb to carry the pregnancy."

Hagar absorbed that, her mind already racing gently in the background.

"That must be so hard to wrap your head around."

Sarah smiled weakly. "You're not wrong. But at the same time, I don't want my pride to get in the way of becoming a mother. I just...I want a family."

Hagar nodded slowly, thoughtfully.

"Sometimes God writes stories differently than we imagined. But He still writes them."

Sarah's eyes filled again at the quiet truth in Hagar's words.

As they stood to leave for the night, Sarah gathered her bag while Hagar gently offered:

"If you ever need to talk about it more...I'm here."

Sarah smiled gratefully, her voice catching slightly.

"Thank you, Hagar. That means more than you know."

They walked toward the elevator together in comfortable silence, but as the doors closed behind them, Hagar's mind stirred quietly for the first time:

Could I be the one to help?

The seed had been planted.

Lottie's Visit—Sarah & Abe's Manhattan Apartment

The kettle whistled as Sarah poured two mugs of tea, trying to steady her hands. Lottie had flown in from Dallas for a long-overdue visit. They sat curled on the couch, city lights twinkling outside the oversized windows like stars taunting Sarah with promises she couldn't touch.

Lottie studied her friend's face. "You look...tired," she said gently.

Sarah laughed hollowly. "I'm tired of being tired."

They sipped in silence for a moment.

"You want to talk about it?" Lottie finally asked.

Sarah set her mug down, her voice barely above a whisper. "It's been two years, Lottie. Two years of trying, testing, hoping. Every month starts with optimism, and every month ends like a tiny funeral."

Lottie reached for her hand. "I'm so sorry."

"I'm angry," Sarah admitted, her voice cracking. "At my body. At God sometimes. At how unfair it feels. I've done everything right. The doctors, the treatments, the prayers...and still nothing."

Lottie's eyes softened, her voice steady. "You haven't done anything wrong, Sarah."

Tears finally spilled down Sarah's cheeks. "I feel like less of a woman, Lottie. Like I'm failing him. Failing Abe."

"You're not." Lottie squeezed her hand. "You're walking through a valley, yes. But this doesn't define you. It never has and it never will."

Sarah sobbed quietly, releasing months of held-in grief. Lottie simply sat with her, holding space for the heartbreak words couldn't touch.

"I keep thinking maybe I've misunderstood God's will for me," Sarah whispered.

Lottie shook her head. "God's will isn't confusion, Sarah. His timing might not make sense right now, but His promises never fail."

For the first time that evening, Sarah allowed herself to breathe deeply. Lottie smiled softly. "And when His promise comes—however, it comes—you won't have any doubt that it was Him who delivered it."

Sarah & Abe's Apartment—Late Night

The apartment had quieted into that peculiar kind of hush that only comes after midnight—the kind not born from sleep, but from thought, and the weight of everything unsaid. Lottie had retired to the guest room hours earlier, the door pulled gently shut behind her, a soft lullaby humming from her phone until even that faded into stillness.

Now, Sarah sat curled on the edge of the couch, wrapped in a cardigan she didn't remember putting on, the nursery catalog spread across her lap like a folded dream. Its glossy pages shimmered under the lamplight, filled with promises of what could be: plush animals, handwoven mobiles, moon-and-star bedding, a rocking chair nestled beneath a painted quote that read, *You are our greatest adventure.*

But Sarah wasn't flipping the pages. She was just…staring.

When Abe came in, he didn't speak right away. He simply walked over and sank down beside her, his body warm and steady. He slipped an arm around her shoulders, fingers brushing the edge of her sleeve. She leaned into him slightly, as if her body remembered how to find comfort even when her heart didn't.

"Couldn't sleep?" he asked, his voice low, like he didn't want to wake something fragile between them.

She shook her head slowly. "I keep thinking about everything this child will never have."

He turned, his brow drawn. "What do you mean?"

Sarah inhaled deeply, but her voice still came out thin. "No grandparents. No warm laps or cookie tins hidden in kitchen cabinets. No bedtime stories that begin with, 'Back when your mom was small...'" She paused, blinking rapidly. "No photos of generations gathered. No one to share old family songs or tell them who they look like."

Abe's mouth tightened. He didn't interrupt. He just listened, his hand circling gently over her back.

She turned her face toward him, eyes shiny. "I want them to know where they come from. And instead, it feels like...like we're starting with nothing. No parents. No children. Just the two of us, standing on a blank page."

He nodded, the movement slow and pained. "I've thought about that too," he said, voice cracking at the edges. "More than once."

Sarah looked down again at the catalog in her lap. A pair of tiny shoes on the page stared back at her, laced and perfect and painfully untouched.

"It feels unfair," she said softly. "That everything begins with absence. That there's a space waiting to be filled, but no one left to fill it but us."

He pressed a kiss to her forehead, lingering there longer than usual, as if the touch could say everything words could not.

"But maybe that's exactly why we'll fill it with something beautiful," he murmured. "Maybe it's because we know the ache of empty places...that we'll cherish what we build even more."

Sarah closed her eyes.

"I just wish they could see it," she whispered, her voice catching, a single tear slipping down her cheek. "I wish they could know how much love is waiting here."

Abe tightened his hold, cradling her against his chest.

"Maybe they will," he said quietly. "Maybe they're already watching. From somewhere higher than we can reach."

Abe's Flashback to Fifteen Years Earlier—Dallas

The garage buzzed with the hum of cicadas and the faint crackle of a ballgame on the old radio. The Texas heat made the air thick, but inside the garage, it always felt like a sanctuary—a place where time slowed and unspoken things had space to breathe.

Abe, barely eighteen, perched on a folding stool nearby, chin resting in his hand, watching his father fiddle with the carburetor. Tools clinked, a wrench turned, and sweat beaded on both their brows. The silence between them wasn't awkward—it was familiar.

"Pass me the socket wrench, son," his father said without looking up.

Abe obeyed instinctively, passing it over without breaking rhythm. This was how they talked—side by side, saying little, but sharing much.

"You ready for graduation?" his father asked, eyes still under the hood.

"Yeah," Abe said. "Sort of. It's coming fast."

His father chuckled. "The best things usually do."

Abe continued, "I've been thinking a lot about college. NYU called last week—they've got a spot for me in their business school if I want it."

His father paused, slowly backing out from under the hood, resting his forearms on the frame as he looked at Abe.

"New York, huh? That's a long way from here."

Abe nodded. "Yeah. But something about it just feels right. I can't explain it, Dad. Like I'm meant to go."

His father smiled faintly, wiping his hands on a towel. "Then go. We don't raise sons to keep them parked in the driveway."

Abe chuckled softly, but the look on his face turned serious.

Abe hesitated, turning the question in his mind like a key in a lock. "Dad...did you always want to be in the energy business?"

"I started in the oil fields, moved into clean energy before it was even a buzzword. Not because it was the obvious choice—but because it was the right one. The future needs people who aren't afraid of being first. That seed in you? That's legacy calling."

Abe met his father's eyes. "Legacy? What do you mean?"

"I mean it's a seed," he said. "And you can either bury it and call it fear, or you can plant it and call it faith."

"A seed?"

He nodded.

"Some men live their whole lives afraid of planting it. But seeds are meant to become trees. Your life—your family—the ones who come after you—that's the tree."

His father smiled faintly.

"And when God places a legacy seed in you, you don't bury it—you plant it."

His father reached over and placed a hand on Abe's shoulder.

"You're not just choosing a school, son. You're stepping into a story. One your kids might not see yet, but one they'll benefit from someday. That's what legacy does. Legacy isn't always about how. It's about who."

A moment passed, thick with something sacred.

"Now," his father said, picking up a rag and tossing it to Abe, "help me finish this thing up. If you're gonna head off to New York, I want this truck working right so I can come visit."

They both laughed, the moment tucked quietly into memory, one that would shape Abe for decades to come.

Present Day—Remembering the Seed

Years later, sitting at his desk after another long fertility consultation, Abe sat in silence as Sarah rested upstairs.

The doctor's words still echoed:

"We may need to start considering alternative paths."

Abe closed his eyes, hearing his father's voice again: Legacy isn't always about how. It's about who.

A soft prayer rose inside him:

Lord, I don't care how You do it. Just let me plant the seed.

The calling to be a father—to carry the family name forward—never left him. But how God would fulfill it was no longer in his hands.

Evening—Video Call

The screen flickered as Sarah answered the video call. Mara's smiling face appeared, framed by soft lamplight and her always-present open Bible nearby.

"Hi, Sarah!" Mara's voice was warm, steady.

"Hi, Mara. Thanks for making time tonight." Sarah smiled weakly.

"Of course. Lottie told me you've been having a tough season." Sarah exhaled deeply. "It's not new, Mara. It's just…starting to crush me in ways I didn't expect."

Mara nodded gently, listening without judgment. "Talk to me." Sarah's voice trembled. "We've tried everything. Doctors. Specialists. Treatments. And every month, another 'no.' It feels like God's forgotten me."

Mara's eyes softened. "Oh, Sarah. God hasn't forgotten you. He never forgets His daughters. You know that."

"Sometimes I believe it in my head but not my heart."

Mara flipped her Bible open. "You're not the first woman who's walked this road. Sarah, Rachel, Hannah—they all waited. And when God moved, He moved in a way that no one could mistake His hand."

Tears filled Sarah's eyes. "What if I never get my miracle?"

Mara's voice grew firm, filled with authority. "That is not your portion, Sarah. God's promise to be fruitful and multiply still stands. The enemy may try to delay, but God's word never returns void."

Sarah wiped her face, her voice a whisper. "Pray for me."

Mara closed her eyes, bowing her head. *"Father, in the name of Jesus, we declare Your promise over Sarah's womb. Every assignment of the enemy that seeks to steal, kill, or destroy is canceled. We release Your perfect will—life, fruitfulness, and healing. Let Sarah's testimony become one that glorifies You, Lord. In Jesus' name. Amen."*

"Amen," Sarah whispered, her voice steadier than before.

"Keep standing, Sarah," Mara smiled. "Your miracle is closer than you think."

CHAPTER 18

The Planted Seed

Two Years into Infertility—Manhattan, Early Spring

The conference room buzzed with controlled energy as Sarah wrapped up the quarterly strategy review.

Her team sat around the polished table, eyes glued to the sleek presentation on the screen behind her: growth metrics, revenue projections, partnership opportunities. She delivered it flawlessly, as always.

"And if we move aggressively into Q3, we should exceed year-end projections by another 8%," Sarah concluded.   "Any questions?"

A few polite nods. One or two clarifying questions about resource allocation. But overall, another win.

When the meeting adjourned, Hagar approached quickly, tablet in hand.

"Great job, Sarah. That landed perfectly with the board. Want to review the speaking engagement requests before you head to your luncheon?"

Sarah forced a smile. "Let's move them to this afternoon. I need a moment."

Hagar's eyes softened slightly—she had learned, by now, to read the subtle tension beneath Sarah's polished exterior.

"Of course."

Sarah slipped quietly into her private office and closed the door behind her. For a moment, she just stood there, staring out the floor-to-ceiling windows at the Manhattan skyline.

So many would trade anything for this: power, prestige, the view from the corner office.

But the gnawing emptiness inside her didn't care how impressive her life appeared to others.

Later That Afternoon—Phone Call with Abe

Sarah sat on the leather sofa, phone pressed to her ear, shoes kicked off to the side.

"Another flawless quarterly?" Abe teased gently.

"Flawless," she replied flatly. "The kind they'll write about in the annual report."

He caught the hollowness in her voice instantly.

"But?"

She exhaled, rubbing her temples.

"I walked out of that room and thought, 'What's the point of all this if I'm still empty everywhere that matters?'"

Abe's voice softened.

"I know, sweetheart."

"I can lead companies, manage millions, build teams," she whispered. "But I can't build the one thing I actually want."

Her voice cracked now, raw.

"Do you know what's worst?" she continued. "Everyone assumes I'm choosing this—that I'm one of those women who didn't want kids so I could climb the ladder."

Abe was silent for a moment.

"They don't know your heart."

"No. They don't. And I'm tired of pretending I'm okay with any of it."

Abe let her words breathe before answering softly.

"You've carried this for so long, Sarah. You don't have to pretend. Not with me. Not with God."

Sarah swallowed hard.

"I thought I'd be fulfilled by now. I've achieved everything I ever set out to do…except the one thing I can't manufacture."

A pause. Then her voice dropped to barely a whisper.

"Sometimes I wonder if God forgot me."

Abe's voice was steady now, like an anchor.

"He hasn't."

Sarah wiped her eyes.

"Then why does it feel like He has? You know what I need? A drink. Wanna meet me at Bar Vera later?"

"Of course, babe, how about 7:45 pm after my last meeting?"

Late Evening at the Office

The office lights had mostly dimmed as Hagar sat at her desk, hunched over spreadsheets and glowing monitor screens. She rubbed her temples, eyes stinging from the long day.

"Still here?" Sarah's voice floated gently from the doorway.

Hagar startled slightly and smiled.

"Just wanted to finish the McAdams analysis before tomorrow morning."

Sarah leaned against the doorframe, studying her.

"You really don't have to work this late every night."

Hagar shrugged lightly.

"Better to stay ahead."

Sarah stepped in a little closer, lowering her voice.

"Or maybe you're just avoiding going home to that empty apartment again."

Hagar smiled, caught.

"Maybe."

Sarah hesitated for a moment, studying her assistant—no, not just her assistant anymore. Hagar had become more than that. Reliable. Loyal. Sharp. And, unexpectedly, someone she felt safe with.

"You know what?" Sarah said, standing and grabbing her coat.

"You've more than earned a drink tonight. Abe's meeting me at Bar Vera in twenty minutes. Why don't you join us?"

Hagar blinked, surprised. "Really? Are you sure?"

"Absolutely," Sarah smiled. "You need to see there's life outside this office. And Abe would love to finally meet the person keeping me sane."

Hagar grinned. "Alright. Let me just run home and change?"

"No need. Come as you are. We're all half-dead anyway."

Bar Vera—7:45 PM

The warm amber lighting of Bar Vera wrapped around them like a soft blanket, contrasting the sharp edges of their corporate world. It was a favorite spot for Sarah and Abe—intimate but unpretentious.

Abe was already seated when they arrived. He stood and smiled warmly as Sarah approached.

"There she is," Abe said, kissing Sarah gently on the cheek.

Then he turned to Hagar, extending his hand. "And you must be the legendary Hagar."

Hagar blushed slightly, shaking his hand. "Legendary? I feel like Sarah's oversold me."

Abe chuckled. "She hasn't stopped talking about how much you've helped her hold it all together."

Sarah waved her hand. "It's true."

Hagar glanced at Sarah with a playful smirk.

"She doesn't exactly let things slow down around here."
Sarah laughed, flagging down the server.

"Work hard, play hard," she joked. "First round's on Abe."
They ordered drinks, and the conversation quickly moved from work to lighter topics—travel, favorite books, even bad reality TV.
After a while, Abe turned to Hagar, his tone curious but kind.
"So, Hagar—what about you? What brought you to New York?"
Hagar hesitated for just a moment before answering, her voice carefully even. "I came to start fresh, actually. Grew up mostly bouncing between relatives—not much stability. New York always felt like a place where you could build something for yourself, you know? Start clean. Be whoever you want to be."
Sarah watched her carefully, sensing there was more beneath the surface but respecting Hagar's guarded answer.
Abe nodded thoughtfully. "That takes courage."
Hagar smiled softly. "Sometimes I think it's less courage and more desperation. But I'm grateful to be here. And grateful to have found my way into Sarah's world. She's…well, she's taught me a lot."

Sarah felt a lump rise in her throat—a mixture of pride, humility, and affection for the young woman sitting beside her.

"Well, I'm lucky to have you," Sarah said, her voice softer than usual. "And I'm glad you're here tonight."
For a few minutes, they simply sipped their drinks in comfortable silence, a small circle of unlikely connection forming beneath the city's quiet hum.
Later, as Abe stepped away to take a call, Hagar and Sarah found themselves briefly alone at the table.

"Thank you for inviting me tonight," Hagar said quietly.
Sarah smiled warmly.

"You're more than just my assistant, Hagar. You've become a friend. I trust you."

Hagar's throat tightened slightly at the unexpected tenderness in Sarah's voice.

"I admire you, Sarah. What you've built. The way you lead. The way you carry so much...and still find time to care about people." Sarah exhaled, her voice soft.

"I don't always carry it well. Some days I feel like I'm barely holding it together. Especially with everything going on."
Hagar gently reached for her hand on the table. "You're doing better than you think."
Neither of them knew it yet, but this night marked a turning point—the quiet beginning of a fragile trust that would soon carry all of them into uncharted territory.
As they left the restaurant and walked toward their cars, Sarah squeezed Hagar's arm.

"Thank you for staying so late all the time. I don't say it enough—you've become a huge part of our lives."
Hagar smiled, blinking back an unexpected sting of emotion.

"I'm grateful to be part of it."
But as Sarah and Abe walked ahead hand-in-hand, laughing softly beneath the streetlights, Hagar lingered just a step behind—her heart quietly stirring with the beginning of something dangerous:
Would I give anything to help them?
The seed planted earlier began to quietly take root.

The Obedience Sermon: Pastor Wells' Sermon
Cornerstone Church was packed that morning, the air expectant. Sarah and Abe sat mid-row, fingers intertwined but hearts distracted.
Pastor Wells stepped up to the pulpit and opened to 1 Samuel 15.

"Obedience is better than sacrifice," he said, his voice clear and firm. "And delayed obedience can become disobedience in disguise."
Sarah blinked.

"Sometimes we rush ahead because God feels slow. We try

to help Him fulfill His own promises. Like Abraham and Sarah with Hagar—what began in hope became a detour in pain."

Abe leaned forward slightly, brows furrowed.

"Even good intentions," the pastor continued, "can be dangerous when they override God's instruction."

Sarah swallowed hard. Later that night, neither mentioned the sermon. But both lay awake longer than usual.

Hagar's Apartment

The hum of the city floated faintly through the thin windows of Hagar's tiny studio apartment. She sat cross-legged on her worn couch, staring at the blank television screen in front of her. Her takeout container sat untouched on the coffee table.

Her mind wouldn't quiet.

The evening with Sarah and Abe replayed over and over in her mind for days after—the warmth of their kindness, the genuine way they both listened to her story without pity or judgment. She hadn't expected to feel so...seen.

But beneath the comfort of new friendship was a stirring she couldn't shake.

Sarah's eyes that night still haunted her: kind, strong, but tired. The kind of tired only people who have carried too much for too long wear in their faces.

She wants a child so badly.

They both do.

Hagar exhaled, feeling her chest tighten.

In her own quiet moments, she often wondered why life had landed her here—young, healthy, single, without ties. She had no family pulling at her, no partner to consult. She was free—but in that freedom was a strange loneliness she rarely admitted aloud.

And yet...hadn't she always longed for a chance to matter? To give something that meant more than reports or spreadsheets?

What if this is why I met her?

Her stomach twisted at the very thought.

Could I really do it?

The practical voice inside her listed all the complications: emotional entanglements, physical risks, legal contracts. She wasn't naïve about how delicate surrogacy could become. But louder than the risks was something else—something holy, almost unsettling.

A tug.

A pull.

What if this is a way I can give life?

Tears welled unexpectedly as she whispered to the empty room.

"God...is this You? Or am I crazy?"

The idea had started as a fleeting thought months ago, but after tonight, it bloomed into something heavier. Something she couldn't easily dismiss.

She had never seen Sarah so open. And in that openness, Hagar saw the cracks beneath Sarah's polished surface. Cracks that only those who had wrestled with disappointment could recognize.

Hagar reached for her Bible—a practice she had only recently started again since working for Sarah. She thumbed through the pages until she landed in the book of Esther.

"Perhaps you were born for such a time as this."

Her breath caught.

She wasn't Sarah's family. She wasn't her equal. But perhaps—just perhaps—she could be part of her redemption story.

Hagar closed her eyes, whispering through tears now. "If this is what You're asking, give me the courage to offer it."

Wednesday Night—Church Small Group

The folding chairs were arranged in a loose circle, the coffee was weak, and the fluorescent lights buzzed faintly overhead—but none of that mattered.

This space had become something sacred for Abe: a place where he didn't have to pretend. A space where he met friends like Marcus, Jordan and Eli—who had become so important to him.

Seven men sat scattered around the room, Bibles and journals in their laps, nodding as Pastor Wells wrapped up the devotional.

"Sometimes the greatest test of faith isn't whether God *can* do something," Pastor Wells said, "but whether we can trust Him when He hasn't done it yet."

The words landed hard on Abe's chest.

As the group shifted into open sharing, Pastor Wells looked toward him.

"Anything on your heart tonight, Abe?"

Abe hesitated, then exhaled deeply.

"We've been trying to have a child for about two years now."

Several heads nodded. A few already knew the story. A few didn't.

"We've done everything we can medically. Prayed every prayer we know. Some days I feel full of faith. Other days..." His voice cracked slightly. "Other days I feel like God has gone silent."

Pastor Wells spoke gently.

"Do you believe He's still good?"

Abe swallowed hard.

"I want to."

He paused, eyes brimming.

"But watching Sarah break under the weight of waiting—it's the hardest thing I've ever walked through. I'm supposed to be her covering. Her protector. And I can't fix this."

The room was quiet. No one rushed to fill the silence.

Another man, older, finally spoke.

"I lost two children years ago. Stillborn." He cleared his throat.

"I remember thinking the same thing: 'Why even pray if He's not going to listen?' But looking back, I learned something I couldn't have known then—unanswered prayers are sometimes delays, not denials."

A younger man chimed in softly.

"And sometimes they're preparations."

Pastor Wells nodded.

"Your pain doesn't intimidate God, Abe. He can handle your anger. He can handle your questions. And I promise you—He hasn't stopped writing your story."

Abe stared down at his hands, voice barely above a whisper.

"I'm afraid Sarah will lose hope before I do."

"Then you hold hope for both of you," Pastor Wells said gently.

"That's part of your covering, too."

The men circled up, placing hands on Abe's shoulders.

As they prayed—quietly, humbly, deeply—something inside Abe finally softened. Not because he suddenly had answers, but because he wasn't carrying the ache alone anymore.

Later That Night—At Home

Sarah was already asleep when Abe slipped quietly into bed.

He watched her for a moment—the rise and fall of her breath, the silent weight she carried even while resting.

He whispered softly in the dark:

I'll keep hoping, God. Even when she can't. I'll keep hoping for both of us.

CHAPTER 19

The Offer

Sarah's Office—A Week Later

The late afternoon sun dipped behind the skyline, casting long shadows across Sarah's office. She sat behind her desk, staring blankly at an email she wasn't reading, her thoughts miles away.

Another month.

Another negative test.

She didn't even cry anymore, at least not at work. She was learning how to compartmentalize her grief into neat, professional boxes.

A soft knock pulled her out of the spiral.

Hagar stepped inside, her voice gentle. "Everything okay? You seemed…somewhere else in the meeting earlier."

Sarah forced a tired smile. "Long week. Long year."

Hagar hovered for a moment, hesitant. She had rehearsed what she was about to say a hundred times since their night at Bar Vera. Each time it still felt terrifying.

"Sarah..." she finally began, her voice soft but steady.

"Can I ask you something? Or maybe...share something?"

Sarah looked up, genuinely surprised by Hagar's serious tone.

"Of course. Sit."

Hagar sat across from her, folding her hands in her lap, steadying herself.

"I've been thinking a lot since we had drinks. About everything you've shared over these past few months."

Sarah's smile faded slightly, her guard lowering. "It's...been a hard season."

"I know," Hagar said quietly. "And I know I don't fully understand what it's like, but I've seen how much these past two years have weighed on you."

Sarah swallowed, her throat tightening. She rarely allowed herself to be vulnerable at work, but something about Hagar's sincerity disarmed her.

"I appreciate you saying that. I don't always talk about it, but yes—it weighs."

Hagar exhaled slowly, the words finally rising to the surface.

"I've prayed about this. And I know it's not my place, but...if you and Abe ever consider surrogacy...I would be willing."

Sarah blinked, momentarily frozen by the weight of what she had just heard.

"I mean it, Sarah," Hagar continued quickly, her voice shaking slightly. "I'm young, I'm healthy, I've done the research. And most importantly—I trust you. I trust Abe. I know how much you want this child. And if I can help bring that into your life, I would count it as an honor."

Sarah's mind raced. She hadn't expected this—not from Hagar. Not from anyone.

"You've...thought about this?" Sarah whispered, almost unable to find her voice.

"I have. A lot." Hagar's eyes glistened now. "This isn't something I'm offering lightly. I know it's complicated. And you don't have to answer. But...it's something I feel led to offer."

For a long moment, Sarah sat in silence. She felt the storm inside her—hope, fear, shock, gratitude—all swirling together.

"You don't feel...pressured? Or obligated because you work for me?" Sarah finally asked, her voice trembling.

Hagar shook her head. "No. I promise. This is from my heart. But only if you and Abe would ever want to even consider it."

Sarah studied her. There was no pity in Hagar's eyes—only clarity.

Sarah's hand instinctively covered her stomach, the weight of the years pressing against her chest. Could this really be a door God was opening? Or was it another dangerous hope waiting to break her heart again?

She inhaled deeply, steadying herself. "I...I need to talk with Abe. This is...a lot."

"Of course," Hagar said quickly, standing. "Take as much time as you need. I just—I needed you to know."

Sarah nodded, tears pooling in her eyes. "Thank you, Hagar. Truly. For even being willing."

Hagar smiled softly, backing toward the door. "Whatever happens, I'm praying for you both."

As the door closed gently behind her, Sarah let her tears fall freely for the first time in weeks—not just grief this time, but something she hadn't felt in a long time.

Possibility.

Sarah & Abe's Apartment—That Evening

The city lights flickered outside as Sarah stirred a pot of soup on the stove, though she wasn't really paying attention to it. Her mind had been spinning since Hagar walked out of her office hours ago.

Abe walked in from the bedroom, loosening his tie. "Hey, babe."

She smiled, trying to appear calm. "Hey."

He kissed her cheek and glanced at the stove. "Smells good."

Sarah turned the burner off, her hands trembling slightly. "Can we sit for a minute? I...need to talk to you about something."

Abe's face shifted instantly, reading the seriousness in her tone. He followed her to the couch and sat beside her, waiting patiently.

Sarah took a deep breath, her fingers twisting the hem of her sweater.

"Hagar came to me today," she began slowly. "She...made an offer."

Abe's brows furrowed slightly. "An offer?"

Sarah's voice wavered. "She offered to be our surrogate."

The words hung in the air, heavier than either of them expected.

Abe blinked, trying to process. "She...what?"

"She's serious, Abe." Sarah's eyes filled. "She said she's prayed about it. She knows our struggle. And she offered. Completely unprompted."

Abe sat back slightly, running a hand through his hair. "Wow."

"I know." Sarah's voice cracked. "I didn't know what to say. I told her we'd need to talk."

Abe exhaled, his mind already racing through a thousand questions. "Did she feel pressured? I mean...she works for you."

"No. She was clear. This was her idea. She said it would be an honor to help."

Abe sat silent for a long moment, processing the weight of it all.

"Do you trust her?" he finally asked.

Sarah nodded slowly. "I do. She's young, healthy, responsible. But more than that...I believe she cares about us. And she's seen how much we've suffered."

Abe's jaw tightened as he stared at the floor. "It's a huge decision."

"I know."

He looked up at her, his eyes softening. "How do you feel?"

Sarah wiped a tear. "Hopeful. Terrified. Conflicted."

"Same," Abe whispered, "I guess I assumed a surrogate would be a stranger...someone we don't already know."

They sat together in silence for a moment, the gravity of it all sinking in.

Abe reached for her hand, his voice steady but gentle. "I don't want to say no out of fear. But I don't want to say yes lightly either."

"Me neither," Sarah whispered.

"Have you prayed about it?" he asked softly.

"Constantly. And I keep hearing...*Maybe this is the door God is opening. Just not the door we expected.*"

Abe exhaled deeply. "Then let's pray together. And we'll take it one step at a time. No pressure. No rushing. We'll only move forward if God gives us peace."

Sarah squeezed his hand, tears falling freely now. "Thank you."

"For what?" Abe asked gently.

"For walking this with me," she whispered. "For not giving up."

Abe kissed her forehead, holding her close. "We're in this together. However long it takes."

And for the first time in a long while, Sarah allowed herself to hope that maybe—just maybe—God's promise was closer than it had ever been.

Act III - Ishmael

Hagar and Sarah

When she knew she was pregnant, she began to despise her mistress. Then Sarai said to Abram, "You are responsible for the wrong I am suffering. I put my slave in your arms, and now that she knows she is pregnant, she despises me. May the Lord judge between you and me." "Your slave is in your hands," Abram said. "Do with her whatever you think best." Then Sarai mistreated Hagar—so, she fled from her. The angel of the Lord found Hagar near a spring in the desert—it was the spring that is beside the road to Shur. And he said, "Hagar, slave of Sarai, where have you come from, and where are you going?"

"I'm running away from my mistress Sarai," she answered.

Then the angel of the Lord told her, "Go back to your mistress and submit to her." The angel added, "I will increase your descendants so much that they will be too numerous to count."

The angel of the Lord also said to her: "You are now pregnant and you will give birth to a son. You shall name him Ishmael, for the Lord has heard of your misery.

He will be a wild donkey of a man—his hand will be against everyone and everyone's hand against him, and he will live in hostility toward all his brothers."

She gave this name to the Lord who spoke to her: "You are the God who sees me," for she said, "I have now seen the One who sees me." That is why the well was called Beer Lahai Roi—it is still there, between Kadesh and Bered.

So Hagar bore Abram a son, and Abram gave the name Ishmael to the son she had borne. Abram was eighty-six years old when Hagar bore him Ishmael.

Genesis 16: 4b-15 (NIV)

Holly Bogdan

CHAPTER 20

The Decision

Abe's Uncertainty

A week had passed since Hagar's offer. Neither of them had brought it up again, waiting for the other to take the lead. Abe and Sarah sat on opposite sides of the couch. Not because they were angry, but because neither knew what to say.

"I got the draft paperwork today," Sarah said quietly, referring to the surrogacy agency. Abe nodded, not looking at her.

"You haven't said much since we met with Hagar."

He inhaled deeply. "I'm still...praying about it."

"We've prayed, Abe. For years. Maybe God is answering in a different way."

Abe turned toward her, his voice soft but uncertain. "Or maybe we're forcing it."

Sarah blinked. "So, you don't want to move forward?"

He hesitated. "I'm not sure. I just don't want to call something faith when it's really fear in disguise."

Silence fell between them. Then Sarah stood. "I can't wait forever for you to feel peace. I need to act before the door closes."

She stormed out of the room.

Sarah's Breakdown

Days later, the silence between them continued to grow. The church bathroom that Sunday echoed with silence. Sarah locked the stall, rested her head against the cool metal, and let the tears fall.

Worship had just ended. The pastor had preached on "faith that waits," and Sarah had smiled and nodded like the good believer she was supposed to be. But now, behind the stall door, her faith fractured.

"Where are You?" she whispered, teeth clenched. "Why do You ask me to believe when You stay silent?"

Her hands curled into fists. "I trusted You. I tithed. I prayed. I fasted. And still...nothing. I'm tired of pretending I'm okay with Your timing." Her sobs grew louder, raw and hollow. She pulled a tissue from her purse and stared at her reflection in the mirror a few moments later— mascara streaked, face pale.

"Do You even see me?" she whispered.

The silence that followed didn't feel cruel. It just felt...empty.

Their Apartment—Several Weeks Later

Several weeks later, the apartment was eerily quiet. The stack of medical paperwork still sat untouched on the dining table. Legal documents. Surrogacy agreements. Counseling referrals. Every logistical step carefully outlined—all that remained was their decision. Sarah sat curled up on the corner of the couch, staring out the window into the Manhattan night. Abe paced nearby, silent but present, giving her space.

Finally, he spoke softly. "You're very quiet."

Sarah's voice cracked slightly as she answered. "Because I'm torn."

Abe sat beside her, close but careful, sensing her inner storm.

"Me too. We don't have to force anything, Sarah."

"I know," she whispered.

She turned to face him fully now, her eyes shining with unshed tears.

"I know Hagar means well. I believe her offer is genuine. And part of me is so incredibly grateful. This could finally be...our answer." Her voice wavered.

"But?"

Sarah swallowed hard. "But I'm struggling with how much of us I have to give away to make it happen."

Abe's brow furrowed gently. "What do you mean?"

Her voice dropped to a whisper. "Pregnancy...it's not just biology. It's supposed to be one of the most intimate, private things we experience together. To see her—another woman—carry your child while I stand on the outside..." She shook her head, wiping at her tears. "I'm afraid it will break something inside me I can't fix."

Abe reached for her hand, steady but tender. "Sarah, nothing could replace you. Nothing. I've been praying non-stop since she offered, and God is opening my heart to the idea of our future baby. Hagar may carry the child physically, but it's our child, our family, our promise. You'll still be the mother—from the very beginning."

Her voice cracked. "But she'll feel the first kicks. She'll hear the heartbeat. She'll experience it in ways I never will."

Abe pulled her gently into his arms. "And yet, none of that will change the fact that this child is yours, Sarah. You're the one who has waited. You're the one who has prayed. You're the one who has held onto hope when everything inside you wanted to give up."

She buried her face into his chest, finally allowing the tears to fall freely.

"I don't want to resent her," she whispered. "I don't want to lose myself in bitterness."

"Then we'll guard your heart together," Abe whispered. "We'll walk it one step at a time, with boundaries and wisdom and God's grace."

They sat together in the quiet for a long moment, as the weight of years of waiting pressed down like a heavy fog.

Finally, Sarah exhaled deeply. "I've asked God for a miracle. Maybe I need to trust that He's allowed it to come in a way I never expected."

Abe kissed the top of her head. "Then we say yes?"

She nodded through her tears. "We say yes."

They held each other tighter, not because all the fear had disappeared—but because they had decided to trust something greater than themselves.

Initial Counseling Appointment—One Month Before Surrogacy Decision

The office was warm, intentionally comforting—soft ivory walls, textured rugs, floor-to-ceiling bookshelves filled with titles Sarah recognized but had never read.

The therapist in charge of the surrogacy appointment, Dr. Whitaker, sat across from her, notebook in hand, glasses resting low on her nose, her voice gentle but direct.

Sarah twisted the corner of her scarf in her lap—the same way she used to wring her hands before high-stakes board meetings. But this wasn't business. She couldn't control this.

"You've already tried IVF, adoption research, and medical consultations," Dr. Whitaker summarized softly. "Now you're here because someone close to you has offered to carry a child for you."

Sarah nodded, her voice tight.

"Yes. My assistant. Hagar."

"And how do you feel about her offer?"

Sarah exhaled, staring down at her lap.

"I feel...guilty."

"Because?"

"Because I'm grateful—and also jealous."

Dr. Whitaker's voice was calm.

"Jealous of Hagar?"

Sarah nodded, her throat tightening.

"She'll experience what I can't. The first flutters. The kicks. The birth."

Tears slipped quietly down her cheek as she added, "I want to hold my baby from the moment life begins. And I won't get that. She will."

Dr. Whitaker nodded gently.

"Both gratitude and grief can live side by side."

Sarah looked up, voice cracking now.

"Is that even fair? To feel both?"

"It's honest. And necessary," the therapist replied.

"Ignoring either won't make the other disappear."

Sarah blinked back fresh tears.

"I'm terrified of what this will cost me emotionally. What if I resent her later? What if I feel like I borrowed motherhood instead of earning it?"

Dr. Whitaker wrote something briefly, then looked at her kindly.

"Sarah, motherhood isn't earned. It's received."

Sarah swallowed hard.

Dr. Whitaker continued.

"Think of it this way: Hagar's offering you the chance to carry motherhood in your heart, even if not in your body."

The words settled heavily in Sarah's chest.

"But it still feels like a loss," Sarah whispered.

"Yes," Dr. Whitaker agreed softly. "Because it is. You're grieving the pregnancy experience you dreamed of. And that grief deserves space."

Sarah exhaled shakily, voice small.

"I don't know how to hold both."

The counselor offered a gentle smile.

"You don't have to hold them alone."

Later—Leaving the Office

The cold Manhattan air stung Sarah's cheeks as she stepped outside. She felt lighter and heavier all at once—like the grief had been named, but not yet resolved.

Abe waited in the car parked across the street, his hand resting on the steering wheel as she climbed in.

"How'd it go?" he asked gently.

Sarah paused, staring out the window for a moment before answering.

"She said I don't have to hold it all alone."

Abe reached for her hand as they pulled away from the curb.

"That's a good point...what did Lottie and Mara say?"

"Oh, I haven't told them yet," Sarah replied.

"Well, there you go...you know what to do next then."

Abe knew her so well.

The Late Evening Phone Call

Sarah sat on the edge of her bed, staring at the city lights glowing outside. Abe was asleep in the next room, but her mind wouldn't stop spinning. Finally, she grabbed her phone and hit the familiar contact.

Lottie answered on the second ring, her voice sleepy but concerned. "Sarah? Everything okay?"

"I didn't mean to wake you."

"You can always wake me."

Sarah hesitated, her voice trembling. "Something has transpired. And I...I need your advice."

"I'm listening."

Sarah took a breath. "Hagar...my assistant...she offered to be our surrogate."

Silence hung for a moment on the line before Lottie spoke, calm but surprised. "Wow."

"Yeah. Wow." Sarah laughed nervously. "She's young, healthy, kind. She knows everything we've been through. And she offered. Voluntarily."

Lottie stayed quiet for a few beats. "And how do you feel?"

"That's the problem. I don't know. Part of me feels like this might be God's provision. Another part feels… terrified."

"Because it's not how you imagined the promise being fulfilled?"

Sarah wiped her eyes. "Exactly."

Lottie's voice was steady. "Sarah, God's promises don't always arrive wrapped the way we expect. But you also need to search your heart. Can you handle the emotional complexity that comes with this? Can Abe? Can Hagar?"

"I'm afraid of what it might do to all of us," Sarah whispered.

"That's wisdom talking, not fear. But listen…you've prayed for years. If this is God's provision, He'll give you peace as confirmation. If it's not, that uneasiness won't leave."

Sarah exhaled. "I just don't want to mess up what God might be orchestrating."

Lottie smiled gently through the phone. "You can't ruin God's plan. You can only trust or delay it. Pray. Wait. And listen for His peace."

Sarah closed her eyes, tears forming again. "Thank you, Lottie."

"I'm right here, always. You don't have to carry this alone."

Several Weeks After Hagar's Offer—Late Night Phone Call

The apartment was quiet except for the hum of the refrigerator and the soft tick of the kitchen clock. Abe had already gone to bed, but Sarah sat at the table, turning her phone over and over in her hands.

Finally, she pressed Mara's name.

Mara answered quickly, sensing the urgency. "Sarah? Are you okay?"

Sarah's voice was soft, almost hesitant. "I need you, Mara. I need your prayers—and your wisdom."

"Of course, always. What's going on?"

Sarah inhaled deeply. "Hagar offered to be our surrogate."

Mara was quiet for a moment, processing.

"She offered?" Mara asked gently.

"Yes. She knows everything we've been through. She wants to help. And on paper, it seems…right. But I'm scared."

Mara's voice was calm. "Scared of what?"

"Of the emotional toll. Of what it might do to my marriage. Of losing something even while receiving what I've begged God for."

Mara exhaled slowly. "Sarah, God can use unusual vessels to fulfill His promises. Look at Abraham and the first Sarah. But you're wise to pause. The right door doesn't mean an easy door."

Sarah wiped a tear. "Exactly. I don't want to get ahead of God."

Mara's tone softened into deep compassion. "Then let's bring this to Him right now."

Sarah closed her eyes as Mara's voice shifted into prayer:

"Father, we come before You, laying Sarah's decision at Your feet. You know her heart's desire. You see every tear she's cried. If this is Your provision, confirm it with Your peace. If it's a distraction, close the door gently but firmly. We trust Your perfect will, Lord. You are not a God of confusion but of order and grace. Let Sarah hear Your voice clearly in the days ahead. In Jesus' name, Amen."

"Amen," Sarah whispered, feeling a small unsteady but undeniable sense of peace settle over her.

Mara smiled through the phone. "You'll know, Sarah. He'll make it plain."

Sarah nodded, tears falling freely now. "Thank you, Mara. I don't know what I'd do without you."

"You won't have to find out," Mara said softly. "I'm not going anywhere."

CHAPTER 21

The Agreement

Abe and Sarah's Apartment—Saturday Morning

The three of them sat around the dining table—Sarah, Abe, and Hagar. The stack of paperwork between them felt both heavy and surreal. Draft legal documents, medical protocols, counseling recommendations. The path ahead now had official terms, but the weight of what they were agreeing to couldn't be fully captured in contracts.

Hagar sat quietly, her fingers tracing the edge of her coffee mug, waiting.

Sarah cleared her throat, her voice steady but softer than usual.

"We want to begin by saying…thank you."

Hagar smiled nervously. "You don't need to thank me."

"We do," Abe added gently. "This is not a small thing. We've prayed. We've sought counsel. And we feel peace moving forward—as long as we're all committed to protecting one another along the way."

Hagar nodded quickly. "I am. Completely."

Sarah inhaled deeply, choosing her words with care. "I want to be honest about something before we go further."

Hagar looked up, her eyes attentive.

"This process...it's beautiful, but complicated. I've wrestled with what it means to allow another woman to carry the child I've prayed for. To carry Abe's child."

Hagar's face flushed slightly, sensing the vulnerability behind Sarah's words.

"I don't want there to be any unspoken tension between us," Sarah continued. "This isn't just medical. It's emotional. And we need boundaries to keep everyone's hearts safe."

"Absolutely," Hagar whispered, her voice full of respect.

"I want you to feel safe through all of this. I don't want to overstep. This is your family, your child. I'm simply honored to help bring him or her into the world."

Sarah's eyes watered. "That means more than you know."

Abe leaned in now, his voice steady. "We've spoken with the agency's counselor about everything: roles, medical decisions, finances, contact agreements—everything that might come up. We want to make sure you feel fully protected too, Hagar. You should have support through this process as well. That is the point of the meeting on Monday, to make sure you understand everything."

Hagar smiled gratefully. "Thank you. I appreciate that."

Sarah reached for her hand across the table, surprising them both a little. "We can only do this if we do it as a team. Open communication. No unspoken fears."

Hagar nodded, tears forming in her eyes now too. "I promise."

But there was a moment, a small moment, when her gaze lingered just a bit too long on Abe. She admired his presence, his voice, the way he looked at Sarah with hope beneath his worry. She looked away quickly. But something had stirred. Something that would complicate everything.

Abe finally broke the silence, his voice light but sincere.

"Well…shall we pray before we officially sign our lives away next week?"

They all chuckled softly through the emotion, grateful for the tension break.

Abe took both women's hands and bowed his head.

"Father, we don't take this lightly. You've brought us here through pain, waiting, and unexpected doors. We ask You to guard this journey—protect our hearts, protect Hagar's health, and protect the child we believe You are preparing even now. Let Your peace guide every step. In Jesus' name, Amen."

"Amen," Sarah and Hagar echoed together.

Hagar's Journal Entry—Borrowed Womb

They call it a gift. This womb of mine.

Sarah smiles at me like I'm helping God. Abe avoids eye contact now, like if he looks too long, he'll see the shame we're all pretending isn't there.

No one asks how I feel. No one wants to know what I lost when I said yes.

But I write it here, because if I don't, I'll forget who I am.

Not a vessel. Not a contract. A woman. A person. One whose story matters, even if it doesn't end in love.

Downtown Manhattan—Attorney's Office

The conference room was sleek, modern, and unsettlingly sterile—a far cry from the raw emotions that had brought them here.

Sarah sat on one side of the long, polished table, her hands folded tightly in her lap. Abe sat beside her, steady but visibly anxious. Across from them sat Rachel Porter, the surrogacy attorney recommended by their fertility clinic—polished, calm, and efficient.

Hagar sat slightly apart, her fingers laced tightly in her lap, eyes flicking between the contract packet and the attorney.

Stacks of legal documents were neatly arranged between them.

The surrogacy contract.

Everything about it felt clinical. Medical. Legal. A transaction wrapped around something deeply personal.

Rachel spoke gently but firmly.

"My job today is to make sure all parties fully understand the legal complexities involved and take you through the final documents to answer any remaining questions you may have. You are about to enter into a highly personal and emotionally charged agreement. It is my responsibility to ensure that, God forbid, if anything goes wrong, everyone is protected."

Sarah inhaled slowly, forcing her shoulders back as if that could hold in the anxiety swelling beneath her ribs.

Rachel continued.

"Now, I've reviewed your surrogacy plan with the clinic, and from a medical standpoint, you're excellent candidates. Hagar, you've been fully screened. But legally, this requires more."

She slid several documents across the table.

"Here's what we're covering today: pre-birth orders, parental rights, compensation structure, medical decision-making authority, and post-birth custody transfer."

Hagar's face flushed slightly.

"Just to be clear...I'm not doing this for money."

Rachel nodded professionally.

"And that's exactly why these documents exist—to ensure that your intentions are honored, and that no one feels manipulated, coerced, or financially vulnerable. Even voluntary surrogacy needs boundaries."

Abe spoke gently.

"We want everyone to feel safe."

Rachel nodded again.

"Exactly. For example, Sarah and Abe will cover all medical expenses related to the pregnancy—including prenatal care, delivery, and any complications that arise. There's a modest stipend built in for your time off work, Hagar, but you're not being paid for the baby itself. That distinction is critical in New York state law."

She paused, letting that settle.

"Next, medical decision-making. While you carry the child, you retain control over your own body—but decisions regarding the fetus must be made jointly. If emergencies arise, the attending physicians will consult both parties as appropriate."

Sarah felt her stomach tighten.

Control over my child—but not in my body.

She still couldn't fully grasp the magnitude of what Hagar was offering. This young woman, barely out of college, stepping into their brokenness. Willingly carrying their child.

Abe's hand reached under the table to squeeze hers gently.

Rachel continued.

"And finally, parental rights. Upon birth, Hagar, you will voluntarily surrender all legal claim to the child. Sarah and Abe will be immediately designated as the sole legal parents."

Hagar swallowed hard but nodded, her voice steady.

"That's what I want."

Rachel looked kindly toward her.

"You may feel very differently once the baby arrives. That's why this paperwork exists—to protect everyone, including yourself, from emotional complications that sometimes arise."

The words hung heavy over the table.

For a moment, no one spoke.

Hagar smiled softly, her eyes gentle. "I understand."

Finally, Sarah exhaled and answered on behalf of her and Abe.

"We understand."

Sarah bit her lip, searching Hagar's face for any trace of hesitation, fear, or second thoughts. But she radiated calm confidence.

Rachel sat back, her tone softening now.

"This isn't just a contract. It's a covenant of trust. And I strongly recommend that each of you speak privately with your own independent counsel before signing."

Abe nodded.

"We will."

Hagar whispered, "I will too."

Rachel folded her hands.

"If you move forward, know that what you're attempting requires courage from all sides. Most intended parents underestimate the emotional strain, and most surrogates underestimate how hard it is to say goodbye."

Sarah's throat tightened again.

Rachel's voice was kind but unflinching.

"You are building something beautiful. But it will cost you."

And with that, they leaned forward to sign—the ink drying on a decision that would change all of their lives.

Hagar signed first. Her signature was neat, deliberate.

Sarah signed next, her fingers briefly trembling as the pen met paper.

Abe signed last, his hand steady, but his mind briefly clouded by that fleeting moment of unspoken energy between him and Hagar. He pushed the thought away, ashamed it had even existed.

As the meeting wrapped, Sarah reached across the table for Hagar's hand and squeezed it, her eyes glistening with cautious hope.

When the paperwork was complete, the lawyers shook hands. The clinical business of it all was over.

Later—Outside the Office

They stepped into the cool afternoon breeze, the weight of the appointment settling over them.

Hagar spoke first, breaking the silence.

"Are you both still...comfortable? After hearing everything?"

Abe spoke gently.

"We are. Are you?"

Hagar nodded quickly, but Sarah noticed the faint flicker of nerves behind her eyes.

Abe added, "Whatever happens from here, I want to say thank you. Both of us do."

"Yes, thank you for giving us this chance," Sarah whispered.

Hagar smiled as she looked at Sarah. "Thank you for trusting me. This is a gift for all of us."

Sarah forced a warm smile, swallowing her own anxiety.

"We'll take it one step at a time, walking this path together as God leads us."

And for the first time, Sarah fully understood:

This miracle would require surrender long before birth.

For now, everything was still hopeful.

But beneath that hope, something fragile and dangerous had begun to stir.

As they drove home, Sarah finally allowed herself to whisper what she hadn't dared to hope for:

"Maybe this time, it will finally happen."

Abe reached over, squeezing her hand. "Maybe this time, it will."

Fertility Clinic—Counseling Office

The room was intentionally cozy. Soft chairs arranged in a circle. A small lamp in the corner. Tissues placed delicately on a side table, as if acknowledging they'd likely be needed.

Sarah sat on one side of the circle, hands clasped tightly. Abe sat beside her, his posture upright but tense. Hagar sat across from them, quiet but composed.

The counselor—Dr. Rebecca Klein—smiled warmly as she opened her notebook and explained the objective of the session.

"First," she said gently, "thank you all for being here. I know this isn't easy. But your willingness to sit here today tells me you're committed to doing this well—emotionally, legally, spiritually."

No one spoke, but all three nodded.

Dr. Klein continued.

"Surrogacy can be one of the most beautiful acts of compassion. It can also surface deeply complicated emotions—for all involved. This space is for you to name those things before you're living in them."

She looked directly at Sarah.

"Would you like to start?"

Sarah swallowed hard, her voice tight.

"I think my biggest fear…is losing something I can't get back."

Dr. Klein nodded softly.

"Losing what, exactly?"

Sarah's eyes glistened as she exhaled.

"My chance. My experience of carrying my child. Of bonding before birth. Of having this life grow inside me."

Her voice cracked as tears slipped down her cheek.

"I'm grateful. So grateful. But every time I picture the pregnancy, I still see Hagar instead of me. And I feel guilty for resenting something I asked God for."

Dr. Klein gently handed her a tissue.

"Sarah, grief and gratitude often live side by side. What you're describing isn't uncommon."

Sarah smiled faintly through her tears.

"Some days it feels like I'm surrendering motherhood before it even begins."

Abe gently placed his hand on Sarah's knee, grounding her.

Dr. Klein turned to him.

"And you, Abe? What emotions are surfacing for you?"

Abe exhaled slowly, his voice steady but low.

"I feel the weight of protecting both of them. Making sure Sarah feels safe, but also making sure Hagar isn't isolated or overwhelmed." He looked toward Hagar with genuine tenderness.

"I never want her to feel invisible or used."

Hagar's eyes glistened as well.

Dr. Klein nodded. "And Hagar, how are you processing everything?"

Hagar paused, her voice quiet but clear.

"I want to do this. With my whole heart, I want to help. But I worry..."

She glanced briefly at Sarah, searching for permission to continue. Sarah nodded softly.

"I worry I'll bond too much. That I'll feel something I shouldn't. That I'll fall in love with this child who won't be mine."

Her voice cracked slightly.

"And that I'll hurt Sarah in ways I never intended."

Sarah reached across the space between them, taking Hagar's hand for the first time that day.

"You're giving us a gift I can't even put into words," Sarah whispered. "And if you bond with him, I won't resent you for it. That just means he's loved from the very start."

The room was quiet for a long moment.

Dr. Klein let the silence breathe before gently concluding.

"You're already doing the most important work: speaking what's real. That's what protects your relationships as you move forward."

She closed her notebook softly.

"My only advice is this—as the pregnancy unfolds, you will all feel things you didn't expect. That's normal. Stay honest. Stay humble. And keep talking."

Later—Leaving the Office

As they stepped into the crisp Manhattan air, the mood felt lighter somehow. Not easier—but lighter.

Hagar smiled nervously.

"Thank you…for letting me say all that."

Sarah squeezed her hand.

"Thank you for your honesty. We'll keep walking this together."

Abe added quietly,

"One step at a time."

And for the first time in weeks, all three of them felt something they hadn't dared to hope for.

Peace.

CHAPTER 22

The Waiting Room

Hagar's Procedure—Fertility Clinic

The medical protocol began almost immediately. The waiting room was bathed in soft light, the kind that tried too hard to be calming—beige walls, muted art prints, and the faint aroma of lavender from a nearby diffuser. But no amount of artificial peace could quiet Sarah's nerves.

She sat between Abe and Hagar, pretending to read an outdated magazine while her foot tapped an uneven rhythm against the tile floor. Hagar sat perfectly still, hands folded in her lap, gaze forward. She looked serene, but Sarah noticed the tightness in her jaw. Abe, meanwhile, glanced periodically at the digital board announcing appointment numbers, his fingers occasionally brushing Sarah's knee in quiet reassurance.

They were here for the embryo transfer.

A culmination of weeks of tests, hormones, signatures, and

conversations that felt simultaneously clinical and intimate.

The nurse finally appeared at the doorway. "Hagar Daniels?"

Hagar stood, smoothing the front of her soft blue dress.

"You can come back now," the nurse smiled. "One support person may accompany you."

Hagar turned toward Sarah, but before Sarah could speak, Abe gently touched her shoulder. "You go, sweetheart. This is your moment with her."

Sarah smiled tightly and nodded, grateful for the gesture. She followed Hagar into the procedure room, leaving Abe behind in the muted waiting room light.

The procedure itself was quick. The doctor walked them through every step, his voice gentle but efficient.

Sarah sat at Hagar's side, gripping her hand.

"You okay?" Sarah whispered.

"I'm fine," Hagar whispered back, voice steady. "I want this to work. For you."

Sarah's throat tightened. There was something deeply humbling about watching another woman carry your most fragile hope inside her body.

When the embryo transfer finally happened, it was both miraculous and terrifying. The procedure was quick, almost anticlimactic for how significant it was.

The doctor smiled and said, "Now we wait."

Back in the waiting room, Abe stood when they emerged.

"Everything went well," Sarah said softly, forcing a hopeful smile.

"Good," Abe said, his gaze immediately falling to Hagar.

"How are you feeling?"

"A little crampy, but fine," Hagar answered. "They said that's normal."

He smiled at her, a tenderness passing through his eyes that Sarah caught—but pretended not to notice.

"Let's get you home to rest," Sarah offered.

They walked out into the late afternoon sun together. As they waited for the car, Hagar paused, glancing at Abe. The sun caught her features just so, and for a second, their eyes locked again.

A flicker of something unsaid. Quickly broken.

Sarah opened the car door, her voice light but firm. "Come on. We've got weeks of waiting ahead."

And wait they did.

As they drove off, the city humming around them, none of them spoke what they each privately carried:

Hope.

Fear.

Temptation.

The Next Few Weeks

There were endless appointments—screenings, medications, hormonal cycles, monitoring. Sarah attended each one, standing quietly beside Hagar, marveling at her calmness. The blood draws, the ultrasounds, the shots and injections, the constant schedule—Hagar took it all in stride. She never once complained.

One afternoon, as they sat waiting for the next appointment, Sarah broke the silence.

"You don't have to do this for us, you know. If you change your mind at any point…"

Hagar smiled gently. "I know. But I won't."

Sarah studied her, feeling both gratitude and guilt swelling inside.

"You're so young," Sarah whispered. "You have your whole life ahead of you."

Hagar's voice was steady. "And part of my life's story will be this. Helping you."

CHAPTER 23

The First Signs

4 weeks—Sarah's Outburst

The news came through a short text from Hagar: "I just took a home pregnancy test. I'm pregnant!" Sarah stared at the screen, numb. Then she tossed her phone across the kitchen. It clattered to the tile.

Abe entered seconds later. "What was that?"

Sarah's voice cracked. "She's pregnant."

He paused. "Sarah…"

"Don't." Her tone cut. "You don't get to act like this is all fine."

"She's helping us…"

"She's replacing me," Sarah snapped.

The silence that followed was heavy.

Abe took a step toward her, but she backed away.

"I wanted to be enough," she whispered, eyes blazing. "I wanted to give you this. And now she has given you something I never could."

She turned and walked out.

Some hours later

Sarah curled up on the couch, staring blankly at the city skyline through the floor-to-ceiling windows. Her untouched tea had gone cold. The news should have brought joy…it did, at first. But now, hours later, all she felt was a slow, aching grief she couldn't name.

She dialed Lottie.

"Hey, love," Lottie answered quickly. "How are you holding up?"

Sarah didn't waste time pretending. Her voice cracked before the second word.

"I'm just so tired and frustrated", Sarah said on the phone with Lottie. "I knew I wanted this, but I don't like how I am feeling knowing that Hagar easily got pregnant for Abe."

Sarah exhaled sharply.

"Yes, I should be thankful. I prayed for this. I agreed to this. But still, knowing another woman got pregnant with Abe's child so easily? It feels… too intimate, and very unfair. Like something sacred happened without me. And I'm just standing outside the glass, watching it all unfold."

There was silence for a moment. Then Lottie spoke with quiet clarity.

"No, Sarah. She is not pregnant *for* Abe. She is carrying *your* child. You and Abe's. You gave the seed. She's giving the soil."

Sarah blinked fast, trying to keep the tears at bay.

"God is still the author here," Lottie continued. "He didn't abandon you. He just rewrote the chapter. Hagar isn't replacing you— she's helping you fulfill the call that's always been on your life to be a mother."

Sarah let the words soak in but didn't respond.

Lottie softened. "Listen…I know it feels like you're losing something.

And maybe you are. Maybe you're losing the version of motherhood you pictured. But you're *not* losing motherhood itself. God hasn't changed His mind about you."

Sarah let out a long breath. "I just...I never imagined it would be her. That my body wouldn't be the one."

"I know," Lottie whispered. "And it's okay to grieve that. You're allowed to. But don't confuse grief with failure. You didn't fail. Your body didn't fail. This isn't punishment, it's provision. It's God saying, 'I still plan to fulfill My word to you, even if it looks different from what you expected.'"

There was silence again, this time heavier, more sacred.

Sarah's voice broke.

"So what do I do with the part of me that still feels...replaced?"

"You bring it into the light," Lottie said gently. "You name it, and you let God speak truth over it. The enemy wants you to see this as a betrayal. But it's not. It's a miracle. And it's *still yours.*"

Sarah closed her eyes as the first tears finally fell.

"I don't know if I'm strong enough for this."

"You don't have to be," Lottie said. "You just have to stay soft. Stay honest. Keep your heart open. The strength will come."

Sarah nodded slowly.

"Okay. I guess I just...need to accept my fate."

"No," Lottie replied gently but firmly. "Don't just *accept* it. *Own* it. Receive it as grace. This isn't the end of your story, Sarah. This is still the unfolding of your miracle."

Sarah wiped her face, trying to absorb it all.

Lottie added softly, "And when you finally hold that baby in your arms, you'll realize none of it was wasted. Not a single step."

Sarah whispered, "Thank you, Lottie."

"I'm always here," Lottie said. "Keep walking. Even when it hurts."

They hung up. And for the first time that day, Sarah let herself believe that maybe, just maybe, this different path was still holy ground.

Later That Night—Sarah's Prayer
After the call with Lottie, Sarah sat alone in the dimly lit nursery, the one she'd started decorating a year too early and avoided ever since. The soft hum of the city buzzed outside, but inside, everything felt painfully still.

She rested her hands in her lap and whispered into the quiet:
"God…I'm trying to be okay with this.
I said yes. I said I trusted You.
But tonight, I don't feel grateful. I feel… left out.
Like the miracle is happening in someone else's body while mine stays silent.
I know Hagar's doing something kind. Brave.
But if I'm honest…really honest…I wish it didn't have to be her.
I wish it didn't have to be anyone but me.
And I hate that part of myself.
The part that can't just be joyful.
The part that still wonders if You forgot me first before You chose her.
But I still believe You're good.
Even when it hurts.
Even when it doesn't make sense.
Please don't let this bitterness grow.
Please help me stay open to the beauty I can't yet see.
And when I can't carry hope anymore…just carry me."
She didn't say *amen.*
She just sat there, eyes full of tears, heart half-closed, but still holding on.

6 Weeks—Sarah & Abe's Apartment
The soft hum of city traffic drifted through the windows as Sarah arranged a platter of fruit and pastries on the coffee table. It had become

a new weekend ritual—Hagar visiting for tea and quiet check-ins. Today was their first meeting outside the office since the transfer.

Hagar arrived right on time, wrapped in a pale sweater, her cheeks flushed from the cool spring air. Sarah greeted her at the door, instantly scanning her face for any signs—of discomfort, of change, of news.

They settled onto the sofa. Sarah poured tea, trying to disguise her nerves beneath polite chatter.

"So," Sarah finally ventured, "how are you feeling?"

Hagar offered a small smile. "Honestly? Tired. And...hungry. Constantly. Which is strange, since it's so early. But I guess my body's working overtime already."

Sarah exhaled, her lips curling into a hopeful grin. "That's a good sign."

"Maybe," Hagar said carefully. "But we won't know for sure until the bloodwork."

Sarah nodded, but couldn't help herself from asking, "Do you feel... different? I mean, besides tired?"

Hagar hesitated for a moment. "It's hard to explain. Like my body knows something before my mind does. Like...waiting for something to arrive that's already started."

Their eyes met, and for a brief moment, Sarah's hope flickered into something close to joy.

The door opened behind them. Abe had just returned from his morning run, towel draped around his neck. His hair was damp, cheeks flushed from exertion.

"Hey," he said, stepping inside and immediately brightening when he saw Hagar. "How are you feeling?"

Hagar smiled. "Good. Tired. Hungry."

Abe chuckled, the warmth in his voice unmistakable. "All the right symptoms, then."

Sarah watched the exchange, noticing again the way Abe's gaze lingered just a second longer than necessary. Hagar looked down quickly, her cheeks flushing slightly, not from the spring air this time.

The air in the room shifted. Subtle. But Sarah felt it. Like the faintest tremor beneath her feet.

"Let's not get ahead of ourselves," Sarah said gently, reclaiming the room with a tone that was both light and intentional. "We'll know more after the blood test."

"Of course," Abe agreed, stepping back, giving his wife a reassuring smile.

They sipped their tea and talked about neutral things: work, movies, the best place for prenatal yoga. But underneath, something was beginning to pulse between the three of them—hope, yes. But also something far more dangerous.

Something unspoken.

Something that none of them were ready to name yet.

One Week Later—Manhattan Apartment

The clinic's phone call came early, too early for Sarah to pretend she hadn't been waiting for it all night.

She answered on the first ring.

"Mrs. Abrams? This is Danielle from Dr. Malik's office. We have Hagar's blood test results."

Sarah's breath caught. "Yes? Please."

"It's positive. The numbers look excellent for this stage. Congratulations."

Sarah sank into the kitchen stool, one hand pressing to her chest as her eyes welled. "Thank you. Thank you so much."

The call ended, but the moment hovered. She sat there, alone in the soft morning light, letting herself feel it: hope without reservation. The fragile miracle had taken root.

That evening, Sarah and Abe invited Hagar over for dinner—not at a restaurant or in some polished neutral space, but home. Intimate. Personal.

The table was set simply. Comfort food. Candlelight.

Sarah's excitement radiated from her like warmth from the oven. "We got the call this morning."

Hagar's face lit up. "Already?"

Sarah nodded, unable to contain her grin. "It's official. You're pregnant."

For a moment, all three of them simply smiled—relief, joy, wonder mixing in the silence.

Abe raised his glass. "To beginnings."

They clinked gently.

Hagar placed a hand protectively over her stomach, still flat but already holding their hope. "I'm really happy for you both."

Sarah reached across and squeezed Hagar's free hand. "I hope you know how much this means to us. I don't have words for it."

"You don't need words," Hagar whispered. "I feel it."

Abe watched her carefully, admiring not only her strength, but something softer—her quiet grace under pressure. Once again, his gaze lingered longer than it should have.

Hagar felt it. A brief charge in the air between them.

She looked away.

Sarah didn't notice, still caught in her happiness.

"We're going to schedule the first ultrasound in a few weeks. I want you to feel like part of everything, not like you're on the outside."

"I'd like that," Hagar said softly.

Abe nodded. "We're in this together."

The words hung there, true on the surface but hinting at deeper, unspoken complexities. The bond forming between the three of them was strong—but growing dangerously intimate.

Fertility Clinic—Eight Weeks Later

The technician dimmed the lights as Sarah, Abe, and Hagar crowded around the small monitor. The cool gel had already been applied to Hagar's stomach, and Sarah squeezed her hand gently while Abe hovered behind, his other hand resting lightly on Sarah's shoulder.

"All right," the technician said cheerfully. "Let's take a look."
The room fell into a tense silence, broken only by the gentle swish of
the probe moving across Hagar's skin. Then, there it was. A flickering,
pulsing light in the center of the screen.
Abe stood behind Sarah, his hand resting gently on her shoulder, both
of them staring at the monitor with wide, cautious eyes.

"There we go," the technician said softly, adjusting the angle.
"There's the heartbeat."

Sarah gasped, her free hand instinctively covering her mouth as
tears filled her eyes. Abe tightened his grip on her shoulder, his voice
thick. "That's…that's incredible."
The faint, rapid flutter filled the room like music Sarah hadn't dared
hope to hear for years: *thump-thump-thump-thump.*
Hagar turned her head slightly, watching Sarah's reaction more than
the screen. The weight of what she was doing settled heavily in her
chest—more than just carrying a child, she was carrying their hope,
their future.

"There's your baby," Hagar smiled to Sarah.
Sarah wiped her tears and whispered to the monitor, "You're really
here."

Abe leaned forward slightly, his face illuminated by the glow of
the screen. "You're strong, little one."
For the first time, the pregnancy no longer felt theoretical. It was real. A
life was growing—their child—inside someone else's body.
Hagar smiled faintly but felt the familiar flicker inside again—the way
Abe's voice softened when he spoke. The way his hand occasionally
brushed Sarah's back, protective and tender. The quiet intimacy they
shared made Hagar feel both deeply honored and unexpectedly isolated.
The technician printed several images and handed them to Sarah.

"Everything looks perfect for this stage. Congratulations."
As the gel was wiped away and the room lights brightened, the mood

shifted slightly. The intensity of the moment had passed, leaving an odd stillness between them.

As they walked back to the car, Sarah tucked the ultrasound photos into her purse like a fragile treasure. Abe opened the passenger door for Hagar first.

"Thank you again," Sarah said, her voice filled with gratitude. "I don't think I'll ever have the words."

"You don't need words," Hagar answered softly, her eyes briefly meeting Abe's once more. "I'm happy to be part of this."

Abe returned her gaze with a polite but unreadable smile, then turned back to Sarah. "Let's get home."

As they pulled away, the city moved around them—alive, bustling, indifferent. But inside the car, three people sat bound by hope, love, and a quiet, growing tension that none of them dared to name.

Later That Afternoon—Coffee Shop

The three of them sat together in a quiet corner of a coffee shop, decompressing after the appointment.

"I still can't believe how fast that little heartbeat was," Abe said softly, stirring his tea.

Hagar smiled, one hand absentmindedly resting on her lower belly. "It's surreal, even for me."

Sarah watched her, feeling a mixture of gratitude and discomfort she couldn't quite name. She was thankful—overwhelmingly so—but every little moment like this also highlighted what she wasn't experiencing firsthand.

She wanted to be the one feeling those flutters. She wanted the doctor's hand on *her* belly.

But instead, she smiled and said, "You're doing amazing, Hagar. Thank you for taking such good care of our little one."

Hagar smiled warmly, sensing the unspoken tension but choosing not to press it. "I'm honored."

There was an easy quiet between them, but Sarah felt her chest tighten as she watched Abe ask Hagar, "Are you feeling okay? Nausea still bad?"

"A little better today," Hagar said. "Mostly just tired."

Sarah nodded politely, but inside, the question stung. *That should be me he's concerned about.*

Abe caught Sarah's eye, reading her subtle change in expression. His gaze softened, and he reached for her hand under the table, gently squeezing it in reassurance.

That Evening—Sarah and Abe's Apartment

Sarah stood in the doorway of what would soon be the nursery, staring at the empty space. The soft glow of the city lights spilled in, casting shadows across the blank walls.

Abe appeared behind her, wrapping his arms around her waist.

"I saw you pulling back a little today," he whispered.

Sarah leaned into him, her voice quiet. "I'm trying, Abe. I'm so grateful. I really am. But sometimes I feel like I'm watching someone else live my dream for me."

"I know." His voice was tender. "It's okay to feel both things."

Tears slipped down Sarah's cheeks. "I hate how jealous I feel sometimes."

Abe turned her to face him, gently cupping her face. "This is still your story, Sarah. Your miracle. Your child. The way we get there may not look like we imagined, but it's still *ours*."

Sarah rested her forehead against his chest, allowing herself to exhale the grief she didn't want to carry into the next stage.

In the quiet, she whispered, "Please don't stop reminding me of that."

"I won't," he promised. "We'll keep waiting together…just like we always have."

Outside, the city pulsed on, unaware that inside this apartment, faith was learning again how to breathe.

Hagar's Journal Entry—14 Weeks

I still wake up some mornings wondering if I've made the biggest mistake of my life.

Not because I regret helping them. I don't. But because every day I feel this baby inside me, and every day I have to remind myself: He's not mine.

The appointments are beautiful and bittersweet. Sarah holds my hand. Abe asks gentle questions. They're kind, respectful, present. But sometimes…

Sometimes when Abe smiles at me, I wonder if I'm imagining something more. And then I feel terrible for even letting the thought form.

This was supposed to be simple.

CHAPTER 24

The Shift

Second Trimester

The second trimester brought with it a mixture of cautious hope and quiet fear. The weeks unfolded like a fragile dream. The doctor's appointments were full of good news: a steady heartbeat, perfect growth measurements, healthy labs. Every check-in brought Sarah relief. And yet, beneath the joy, an undercurrent hummed quietly—unspoken but undeniable.

The first shift came subtly.

Hagar handled the pregnancy with grace, but Sarah could sense the subtle changes already beginning.

It was no longer just a medical process—it was real now. A baby was growing. And Hagar was carrying it.

One afternoon, as they left another appointment, Sarah finally voiced her fear.

"Hagar…may I ask you something?"

"Of course."

"Do you ever…feel attached? To the baby?"

Hagar smiled softly. "Sometimes. But I always remember why I'm doing this. This baby is yours and Abe's. I'm simply helping him arrive."

Sarah blinked away tears. "You're incredibly selfless."

Hagar reached over and squeezed Sarah's hand. "You've waited a long time for this, Sarah. I see how much you love him already."

For a brief moment, Sarah allowed herself to believe it—to fully feel the joy instead of the fear.

But as they stepped outside into the early spring air, something in Hagar shifted. She paused at the curb before getting into the car, her eyes catching a young woman walking by, holding a toddler's hand. The boy's laughter rang through the street like a bell, and Hagar smiled faintly—but the smile didn't quite reach her eyes.

In the car ride home, Sarah chatted softly about nursery colors and pediatrician recommendations, but Hagar grew quieter. Her responses were still kind, but delayed. Measured.

When they pulled up to Sarah and Abe's building, Hagar hesitated before getting out.

"Everything okay?" Sarah asked gently.

"Yeah," Hagar said quickly, forcing a smile. "Just tired, I think. Things are…starting to feel a little heavy."

Sarah nodded sympathetically. "That's totally normal. Let me know if you need anything."

"I will," Hagar replied.

But she didn't.

That night, she lay awake staring at the ceiling of her apartment, her hand resting lightly on the curve of her growing belly—and for the first time since agreeing to carry the child, she didn't feel steady. She felt… displaced.

By morning, the decision was made. She packed a bag, turned off her phone, and rented a car to start the drive for Pennsylvania.

Hagar's Disappearance

It started with a missed meeting.

Sarah had texted Hagar that morning to confirm their usual check-in at the office, but the message sat unread. By noon, Hagar hadn't responded to any emails. Calls went straight to voicemail. By 4:00 p.m., Sarah's tone had shifted from mildly irritated to unnerved.

"She's probably just sick," Abe said that evening, setting down his laptop. "Or forgot to charge her phone."

Sarah didn't look convinced. "Even when she had strep last fall, she still emailed me from her bed with a project update. This isn't like her."

The next morning, there was still nothing.

Sarah showed up at Hagar's apartment building during her lunch break, buzzing the door repeatedly. No answer. She stared up at the darkened windows of Hagar's third-floor unit and felt a knot form in her chest.

By nightfall, panic had fully set in.

"She wouldn't just disappear, right?" Sarah paced their kitchen, gripping her phone like it might come alive. "I mean...she knows what's at stake."

"She's carrying *our* child," Abe said softly, jaw tight.

"And she signed the agreement."

"But agreements don't stop people from changing their minds."

Abe didn't respond to that. Instead, he grabbed his coat. "I'm going over there."

Ten minutes later, he stood in front of Hagar's apartment door, knocking hard, then calling out her name. When there was no answer, he bent slightly and peered through the small window at the top of the door.

The apartment looked tidy, eerily so. No sign of anything disturbed—but also no sign of life. He spotted her favorite pair of flats neatly placed by the door, and the coat rack was empty.

He called Sarah. "She's not here. I don't know where she is."

Silence crackled on the line. Then Sarah whispered, "Abe…what if she left? What if she's going to keep him?"

The Visit—Pennsylvania

The small gray house on the corner of Walnut and 5th looked the same as it had when Hagar left for New York almost six years ago—a worn porch swing, a ceramic rooster in the yard, and the curtains in the front window permanently drawn halfway. It smelled faintly of rain and lemon-scented floor cleaner, the scent of childhood Saturday chores.

Her Aunt Delia was already at the door when Hagar stepped onto the porch.

"Well, well," Delia huffed, arms folded across her chest.

"Look who blew in with the storm."

"Hi, Aunt Delia."

Delia stepped aside without smiling. "Come in, I guess. You hungry?"

"I could eat," said Hagar, while bracing herself for what insults would come her way next. Why did she come?

Inside, the kitchen felt even smaller than Hagar remembered. Her uncle sat at the table, reading the newspaper, glasses low on his nose. He looked up once, then down again.

"Uncle Rob," Hagar said gently.

"You're showing," he replied, not looking at her belly.

Delia slid a plate of roast chicken and potatoes in front of her. "I assume you came here to explain why your face is suddenly all over that town gossip vine?"

Hagar sat carefully. "I didn't think it would reach here."

"Young woman, single, not married, living in New York, carrying someone else's baby'? Oh honey," Delia said, sitting across from her. "You might as well have painted it on a billboard."

"I'm not doing this for money or attention," Hagar said quickly.

"They're my friends. Sarah can't have children. I offered to be their surrogate. That's all."

Uncle Rob looked up then. "That's all? That's everything, Hagar. You're a pawn in their story, Hagar. Once that baby comes, they won't need you anymore."

Delia shook her head. "You always had a bleeding heart. But this is more than just noble. It's personal."

Hagar lowered her fork. "What do you mean?"

Delia's gaze softened for the first time. "I think you're trying to fix something you never could—what happened with your mom, and then bouncing around until we took you in. You were always chasing stability. Maybe now you think if you give someone else a family, it'll make up for not having yours."

Hagar blinked fast. She was surprised her aunt had softened, almost like a caring mother.

"I'm not judging you, sweetheart," Delia added. "But I need you to be honest with yourself. After this baby is born…what then?"

"I go back to my life," Hagar whispered.

"And what is that life, Hagar?" Rob asked, folding his paper.

"Because from what we can see, your whole identity is wrapped around theirs."

Hagar stood up abruptly. "I shouldn't have come."

"You *should* have come," Delia corrected gently, standing too.

"But I want you to leave here with a plan for your own future— not just theirs. Don't let this be the only thing that defines you."

Hagar nodded, throat tight. "Maybe I should leave."

Delia followed her to the door and hugged her tightly. "You've got strength, girl. I just want to see you use it for yourself, too."

After they discussed, she went back to her car, where Hagar sat in the driver's seat for a long time, her hands resting on her stomach.

She whispered aloud, "I'm still figuring it out, little one. But we're going to be okay."

And with that, she started the car and pointed it back toward New York.

Roadside Motel—Nightfall

The neon "VACANCY" sign blinked against the darkening sky, flickering pink and orange over the damp pavement. Hagar pulled into the gravel lot, the same roadside motel where she had stopped two nights ago on her way to Pennsylvania. It was the kind of place people passed without noticing—half-forgotten and quiet. Tonight, it felt like a liminal space, neither here nor there.

She handed the tired clerk her ID and a twenty-dollar bill for the deposit, then stepped into Room 6.

The walls were still painted that strange, seafoam green. The comforter had the same faded floral pattern. But everything felt heavier now.

She dropped her duffel bag by the door and collapsed onto the bed, staring at the ceiling as if it might offer some answers.

Her uncle's words echoed like thunder inside her:

"You're a pawn in their story, Hagar. Once that baby comes, they won't need you anymore."

She blinked hard, trying to shake the sting. The worst part? A small part of her wondered if they were right.

She picked up her phone and saw the missed texts:

SARAH: *Please call me.*

ABE: *We're worried about you. Just let us know you're safe.*

SARAH: *We can talk through this. You don't have to disappear.*

ABE: *Hagar. Please.*

She put the phone face down on the nightstand. Her thumb hovered over it for a moment, then stilled. She couldn't reply. Not yet.

Tears welled in her eyes as she whispered, "God, why did You let me get this far if I was just going to be disposable?"

She curled up on the bed, blanket pulled to her chin. Eventually, exhaustion overtook her.

The Dream

She was a little girl again—barefoot in a sunlit field, a gentle wind brushing through tall grass. And there, across the field, stood a woman. Her mother.

Not frail or lost the way she had been at the end, but radiant. Whole. Her eyes, steady and clear, locked onto Hagar's with fierce love.

"You haven't been forgotten," her mother said softly.

"God sees you."

"I don't know who I am anymore," Hagar whispered.

Her mother stepped closer. "Yes, you do. I named you Hagar because I wanted you to remember: even when people overlook you, God doesn't. You are seen. You are called."

The breeze lifted again, as if Heaven itself breathed on the moment.

"You are not a pawn," her mother continued. "You are a vessel. And you were chosen for this."

Then, just before the dream faded, her mother smiled. "Walk in that truth, baby girl. Even when it costs you."

Morning—Motel Room

Hagar sat up, breath catching in her throat. Morning light filtered in through thin curtains. The clock read 6:47 a.m.

The dream still pulsed in her chest, like a divine echo.

She reached for her phone—not to scroll, not to respond. But to pray.

"God...thank You. I see it now. This isn't about being used. It's about being chosen."

She stood slowly, pulled her hair into a bun, and started packing her things. Her heart wasn't fully healed, but it was steadier. Resolved.

She turned in the key at the front desk, stepped back into her car, and aimed her wheels toward New York City.

Back toward purpose.

Back toward the promise.

Back toward the family she was helping build—one that would forever carry a piece of her.

The Call

It was just after 9 a.m. on the third day when Sarah's phone rang.

She stared at the screen for a beat too long, like her mind didn't trust her eyes.

HAGAR (Mobile)

Sarah answered on the first ring, putting the call on speaker as Abe moved to her side.

"Hagar?" she said, breath catching. "Where are you? Are you okay?"

There was a long pause on the other end. When Hagar spoke, her voice was quieter than they'd ever heard it—small, almost fragile.

"I'm in Pennsylvania. I'm sorry I didn't say anything…I just…I needed to get away for a few days and wanted to visit family. I should've told you."

"You think?" Sarah said, harsher than she intended.

"We've been worried sick, Hagar. You vanished."

"I know," Hagar said quickly. "I wasn't thinking clearly. Everything started to feel… heavy."

Abe leaned in. "Heavy how?"

Hagar took a shaky breath. "Everywhere I go, people look at me like I'm the mother. They ask questions. They touch my stomach. I get congratulated. And I know it's *your* baby, but for nine months…I'm the one carrying him. I'm trying so hard to stay in the right headspace, but I'm scared of getting too attached…or not attached enough. It's confusing."

Sarah's throat tightened. "You could've told us that."

"I didn't know how," Hagar admitted. "And I thought maybe if I went back to where I came from, to my aunt and uncle, maybe I'd feel more grounded."

"How'd that go?" Abe asked, though his tone was careful.
A heavy silence filled the line.

"It didn't," Hagar said flatly. "Let's just say they weren't thrilled about the situation. They think I'm making a mistake…again."
Sarah frowned. "Again?"
There was another pause. "It's complicated," Hagar said. "But I'm coming back, I should be home later today."

"Promise?" Sarah asked, the desperation slipping through.

"I promise," Hagar said. "I just needed to remember who I was before all of this. Before the appointments and the whispers and the 'what ifs.' I still want to do this. I just…I need you both to remember that I'm human too."
There was a long beat before Abe said quietly, "We're learning as we go, too. We'll be here when you're ready."

"Thank you," Hagar whispered. "I'll see you tomorrow."
The call ended. The silence in the room stretched, full of relief, guilt, and a new awareness of how fragile this entire arrangement really was. Sarah reached for Abe's hand and didn't let go.

Back in the City

By the time Hagar arrived back in New York, the sun was setting behind a stretch of Manhattan skyline, casting long shadows across the East River. She sat in her car for a few extra minutes before climbing out, the familiar buzz of the city both comforting and overwhelming after the quiet of Pennsylvania.

She let herself into her apartment, dropped her bags, and exhaled slowly. The plants on the windowsill were somehow still alive. A pile of unopened mail greeted her on the counter. Everything looked the same. But Hagar knew something inside her had shifted.

Her phone buzzed again. Another message from Sarah:

"Just let us know you're okay."
And one from Abe, earlier that day:

"We're not mad. We just need to know you're home."

Hagar hesitated, then picked up the phone and dialed Sarah's number. Sarah answered on the first ring. "Hagar?!"

"Hey…I'm back. I'm okay."

Silence. Then the sound of Sarah exhaling deeply. "You had us terrified."

"I'm sorry," Hagar said quietly. "I just needed to think."

There was a pause. Then Sarah said gently, "Can we see you tomorrow?"

Hagar nodded even though Sarah couldn't see her. "Yeah. Tomorrow's good."

Hagar's Return—Back at Sarah & Abe's Apartment

Hagar started spending more time at the apartment. Sarah insisted after Hagar's "disappearance". And it made sense, on paper. She was carrying their child, after all.

Sarah suggested she join them for dinner more often. Abe offered to drive her home. Occasionally, she stayed over in the guest room when evening appointments ran late.

The next evening, she stepped into Sarah and Abe's apartment cautiously. The tension that had crackled between them the last few days had settled into something quieter, not quite peace, but not volatility either. Sarah pulled her into a hug that was firmer than Hagar expected.

"We thought maybe…" Sarah trailed off.

"I know," Hagar said. "I should've told you I was leaving. I just…I needed space to think. And talk to the people who raised me."

Abe walked in from the kitchen, his arms crossed, concern still on his face.

"You're not just carrying our child," he said. "You're a part of our lives, Hagar. Disappearing scared us."

"I know," she repeated, this time with more weight.

"And I'm sorry. It won't happen again."

They sat around the kitchen island, coffee brewing behind them, the smell oddly grounding.

"I'm going to finish this pregnancy strong," Hagar said, meeting both their eyes. "But I also know that once this is over, I need to figure out who I am outside of...all this."

Sarah reached across the counter and took her hand. "I hope you know...you can always be part of our lives. If that's what you want."

Hagar smiled faintly. "Thank you. I might. But I also know I have to build something of my own."

Abe nodded slowly. "Then we'll cheer you on. Just like you did for us."

The three of them sat in a rare moment of mutual understanding—complicated, yes, but honest. And from that moment on, a quiet shift began. Boundaries became clearer. Emotions settled. The road ahead still held uncertainty, but it was no longer rooted in fear. It was rooted in choice.

Monday Morning—The Shift at the Office

The elevator doors opened with a soft chime, and Hagar stepped into the twelfth floor of the office. The buzz of Monday morning meetings, ringing phones, and the tapping of keys filled the air like a familiar hum. It was the same place...but she didn't feel quite the same walking into it.

She glanced toward Sarah's corner office. The door was open, but the lights were off. Hagar exhaled—grateful for a few moments to settle in before facing her boss...or whatever Sarah was now. Something more complicated.

Her desk had been cleared by someone in her absence—papers neatly stacked, inbox reset. The interns had clearly been briefed to stay out of her way. She appreciated the gesture.

A moment later, Sarah walked in from the elevator bank, coffee in one hand, phone in the other. She paused when she saw Hagar.

"You're here," Sarah said softly.

Hagar stood. "Yeah. I wanted to come back. To keep things normal."

Sarah nodded. "Let's try that."

They didn't say more—didn't need to. Sarah walked toward her office, pausing in the doorway to add, "There's a staff meeting at ten. Join us if you feel up to it."

"Of course."

The day ticked forward—emails, edits, meetings. Hagar took diligent notes and offered a few ideas but kept her head down. She didn't want to become the center of office gossip, didn't want people whispering about "the boss's surrogate" over breakroom coffee. Today, she just wanted to work.

But something felt different.

At lunch, she sat alone in the café downstairs with a salad she barely touched. She scrolled her phone aimlessly, then paused on a job listing someone had forwarded her weeks ago—a program for women entrepreneurs. She'd laughed at it then. Now...it didn't seem so far-fetched.

Later that afternoon, when most of the office had cleared out for the day, she knocked on Sarah's open door.

"I'm going to head out," she said. "But I just wanted to say thanks. For giving me the space... and for letting me come back."

Sarah set down her pen and looked up.

"I'm proud of you, Hagar. Not just for the pregnancy...for how you're finding your voice."

Hagar smiled faintly. "I think I'm starting to hear it again."

Sarah nodded slowly. "Well, when you figure out what you're going to do next...I'll be the first one cheering."

"And, oh, the clinic called to remind us about the anatomy scan tomorrow," Sarah added on, "you're back just in time."

"Of course," Hagar responded, "I wouldn't miss it. Can't wait to see him again."

"Him?" Sarah inquired?

"Just a feeling." Hagar said with a smile.

As Hagar walked out of the office, her steps felt lighter than they had in months. She wasn't sure what was next—but for the first time in a long time, it didn't feel like she was running. It felt like she was walking toward something.

The Anatomy Scan

The waiting room was quieter than usual. Sarah sat stiffly, arms folded, her designer handbag tucked neatly in her lap. Beside her, Abe checked his watch again, then glanced at the hallway where Hagar had gone to fill out paperwork. No one spoke.

"Twenty weeks," Sarah finally said, more to herself than anyone else. "Halfway there."
Abe gave a soft smile. "Feels longer."
Sarah didn't respond. Her eyes were fixed on the "OB Imaging" sign above the door.

When Hagar returned, she held the clipboard like it was a fragile truth she didn't know how to carry. "They said the tech will call us back in a few minutes."
Sarah nodded. The silence stretched again.

It wasn't that they hadn't spoken since Hagar's trip to Pennsylvania—they had. But nothing felt quite the same. No one said out loud how much it had rattled them, how deeply it shook the trust that had been holding their arrangement together. And yet here they were, pretending they were one team again.
A nurse finally called Hagar's name. Sarah and Abe stood at once.

"You're both welcome to come," the nurse added politely.
The ultrasound room was dim and cool, a calming blue light glowing softly from behind the monitor. Hagar climbed onto the table, tugging her maternity blouse above her rounded belly. Sarah instinctively moved to the side of the bed. Abe took the corner near the monitor.
The tech, a kind woman named Olivia, applied the gel and began gliding the probe over Hagar's abdomen. The flickering black-and-white image

appeared almost instantly.

"There's baby," Olivia said, smiling. "Nice strong heartbeat. Let's get some measurements."

The three of them stared at the screen. Sarah blinked back sudden tears. She had seen ultrasound images before, but this time—seeing arms, legs, the spine—it felt different. Real.

Abe cleared his throat. "Is everything looking okay?"

"So far, so good," Olivia said cheerfully. "Let me just measure the femur length…and there's the profile shot. Baby is very cooperative today."

"Do you want to know the sex?" Olivia asked.

Hagar turned to look at Sarah.

Sarah hesitated. They hadn't talked about this yet—not since the trip, not since things felt... uncertain.

Abe stepped in. "Only if Hagar's okay with it."

Hagar nodded slowly. "I think…yes. Let's know."

Olivia smiled. "Well, congratulations. It's a boy."

A long pause followed.

Sarah let out a breath she hadn't realized she was holding. Abe's hand found hers for just a moment, squeezing it. Hagar's eyes were fixed on the screen.

"I already knew," she whispered. "Somehow I already knew."

Sarah glanced at her, surprised by the tenderness in Hagar's voice.

There was still a long road ahead. But for now—in this dark, quiet room filled with flickering light and fetal heartbeats—they were three people witnessing a miracle in motion.

The Journey Home

The subway ride back uptown was unusually quiet. Abe and Sarah sat side by side, their knees touching, but neither had spoken since they left the clinic. The image of their son—their son—had been printed on a strip of black-and-white paper now tucked into Sarah's bag, beside her phone and lip balm, like a secret treasure.

It should have been enough.

But it wasn't.

Once they stepped out onto the sidewalk near their apartment, Abe gently reached for her hand.

"That was something, huh?" he said. "Seeing his little face like that."

Sarah nodded. "Yeah."

Abe glanced at her. "You okay?"

"I'm trying to be," she said honestly. "It's a lot. Today was… beautiful. And strange."

They passed the little French bakery on the corner—the one Sarah used to stop by for coffee before her schedule got too packed and her mornings got too full of doctor appointments and emotional landmines.

"She already knew," Sarah added quietly.

Abe blinked. "Who?"

"Hagar. Yesterday at the office she called the baby "Him". She said she suspected."

Abe stayed quiet, listening.

"It's just one of those things, I guess," Sarah continued.

"She can feel him. She's with him all the time. I'm still… catching up. Still convincing myself this is real, even with ultrasound pictures and shared calendars and a full maternity file with my name on it."

Abe slowed their pace, giving her space to breathe.

"It's okay to feel that way," he said. "You're the mom, Sarah. Whether you're carrying him or not."

She smiled faintly but didn't respond.

"I'm just saying," he added, squeezing her hand. "You're doing this. We're doing this. And one day…when he's crying in the middle of the night or painting dinosaurs on the wall…he's going to come running

to you, not because you carried him, but because you're his mom."
Sarah stopped walking. Abe turned toward her.

"I know you're right," she said. "But sometimes it still hits me.
Like…this ache. That I didn't get to feel him flutter for the first time.
That I'll never know what that's like."

Abe leaned forward and kissed her forehead. "You're allowed to grieve
what you're missing, and still celebrate what you're gaining."

Tears welled in her eyes. She nodded.

"Besides," he said, trying to lighten the mood, "this kid is
already spoiled. Two parents, an overqualified assistant, and a name we
haven't even agreed on yet."

That made her laugh—finally.

"Just promise me we won't name him 'Junior,'" she said.

"No promises," he teased. "You saw his chin. That's my chin."
Sarah elbowed him gently, and for the first time all day, it felt like the
joy could outweigh the ache.

Hagar's Journal Entry—20 Weeks

The anatomy scan was perfect.
Everything is measuring right on track. They cried when they saw his
tiny face on the screen. I smiled too. How could I not?
But afterward, when I went home alone, I sat on the couch and sobbed
until my chest hurt.
The baby kicked for the first time that night.
It felt like he was comforting me. But it also terrified me, because it
reminded me how much I already love him.

CHAPTER 25

The Scare

Twenty-One Weeks into Hagar's Pregnancy—Sarah & Abe's Apartment

Sarah stood in the bathroom staring at the pregnancy test, her heart pounding so hard she thought she might hear it echo. Two pink lines. For a full minute, she couldn't breathe.

Later That Night—Abe Comes Home

Abe walked in from work, loosening his tie, smiling—but the moment he saw Sarah sitting on the edge of the bed, pale and wide-eyed, his stomach dropped.

"Sarah? What's wrong?"

She held up the test, her hands shaking.

"I... I think I'm pregnant."

Abe froze for a second, trying to process the words.

"But…" His voice caught. "…we've never had a positive test before."

Sarah nodded quickly, tears already gathering in her eyes.

"I know. I know. That's why I don't even know how to feel right now."

Abe crossed the room quickly, kneeling in front of her and taking her hands.

"Are you sure?"

"I've taken three." Her voice cracked. "All the same."

He exhaled slowly.

"We need to call Dr. Malik first thing tomorrow."

Sarah nodded, already overwhelmed by the collision of fear and hope swirling inside her.

At the Clinic—The Next Morning

Dr. Malik scanned the early ultrasound, her face professional but cautious.

"There's a gestational sac, but it's measuring smaller than we'd expect at this point," she explained gently. "Your bloodwork suggests this may be what we call a chemical pregnancy, or potentially a non-viable early pregnancy."

Sarah's face fell, Abe's hand tightening around hers immediately.

"So it may not progress?" Sarah whispered.

Dr. Malik offered a compassionate smile.

"There's still a small chance, but I want you to prepare yourselves emotionally. These types of early pregnancies often resolve themselves naturally in the first few weeks."

Sarah blinked back tears, gripping Abe's hand tighter.

The Emotional Crash

That night, as they lay in bed, Sarah whispered into the dark.

"I almost wish I hadn't known. I almost wish I never saw those lines."

Abe pulled her close, holding her tightly.

"It's okay to feel that way. This isn't fair."

Tears streamed down Sarah's face.

"It was like God dangled hope in front of me for 24 hours…and then snatched it back."

Abe kissed her forehead, his own voice thick.

"No matter what happens, we'll get through it. Together."

The Resolution

A week later, the bleeding started.

Sarah sat alone on the cold bathroom floor, knees pulled to her chest, forehead resting against the edge of the tub. The dull cramping in her lower back pulsed in waves, but it was nothing compared to the hollow ache beginning to spread through her chest.

It's over.

The two words echoed like a bell inside her, reverberating through every breath.

The light overhead buzzed quietly, indifferent to her unraveling. She stared down at the faint specks of blood on the tissue—small, almost forgettable, but unmistakable. Like her body was slowly erasing a dream.

The test she had once clung to sat on the counter above her, its two pink lines faded now, but still visible. A cruel artifact of hope—mocking in its silence.

She reached for it, her fingers trembling. Just days ago, she had whispered prayers over it. Tucked it in her top drawer like it was a promise she didn't want the world to touch.

She pulled her robe tighter around her and bit down on the sleeve, stifling the sob that broke loose anyway. It wasn't just the loss of the baby—it was the loss of what she'd allowed herself to believe again: that maybe, just maybe, this time would be different. That God had finally said yes.

Abe was out running errands. He didn't know yet. And for a fleeting moment, Sarah felt a strange guilt that it was happening without him. Like her body had chosen to break quietly while she was alone.

She looked down again, whispering into the silence.

"I wanted you so badly. I already loved you."

And in that moment, a tear finally fell—not just for what was lost, but for the version of herself that had dared to hope again.

Later That Evening

Abe found her sitting on the couch, wrapped tightly in her blanket, staring blankly at the muted television.

He sat down beside her, placing a gentle hand on her back.

"It's officially over," she whispered, her voice hollow.

"The cramping, the bleeding..."

Abe swallowed hard, his own eyes glistening.

"I'm so sorry, baby."

She finally turned toward him, her face flushed and tear-stained.

"I didn't even get to imagine," she said bitterly. "I didn't have time to picture names or tiny fingers or nursery colors. I didn't get a moment to dream—and still it hurts like I lost something."

Abe took her hand, his voice thick.

"You did lose something. And it's okay to grieve that."

She shook her head, wiping angrily at her cheeks.

"And I feel guilty... because we're already expecting a baby with Hagar. That should be enough. What kind of person grieves one pregnancy while another one is already happening for her?"

Abe's voice was steady but full of tenderness.

"You're a human person. That's what kind."

She finally let out a broken sob.

"I hate this waiting, Abe. I hate feeling like I'm constantly one breath away from hope…and one breath away from heartbreak."

Abe pulled her into his chest as her body trembled.

"I know. I know, love. And I hate it too."

After a long silence, Sarah whispered a fear she hadn't yet voiced.

"What if this was my only chance? What if that tiny spark was my miracle…and now it's gone?"

Abe kissed her temple, his own voice catching.

"It wasn't your only chance. God doesn't deal in one-shot miracles. His promises aren't that fragile."

Sarah closed her eyes tightly, clinging to his words but feeling the fragile tremor of doubt still lingering beneath them.

In the Days That Followed

The physical symptoms passed quickly, but the emotional residue clung longer.

Sarah found herself struggling to concentrate at work, her emotions simmering just beneath the surface of every meeting and email.

Lottie and Mara called but Sarah never answered the phone.

At night, Sarah would often sit up after Abe had fallen asleep, staring into the dim glow of the city lights filtering through their apartment windows.

Some nights she prayed fiercely. Other nights she simply sat in silence.

The Quiet Turning Point

One night, as she sat curled on the couch beneath a blanket, her Bible open but unread in her lap, she finally whispered:

"Lord… I still believe You."

Tears streamed down her cheeks as she continued.

"I don't understand You. I don't know why You let me hope for 24 hours only to take it away. But I believe You still write good stories. I believe You haven't forgotten me."

Her voice cracked as she added,

"I don't know how to keep waiting… but I will. Just don't let me stop hoping."

The tears kept falling, but this time they weren't only grief—they were release.

Somewhere deep inside her spirit, something softened. Not resolved. Not healed. But surrendered.

CHAPTER 26

The Distance

Second Trimester—With the Girls in Dallas

The Texas sun beat down as Sarah stepped out of the rideshare at Lottie's suburban home outside of Dallas. Lottie was already at the door, arms wide open.

"You made it!" Lottie beamed, pulling Sarah into a long embrace. "Come inside, I've got your favorite coffee waiting."

They settled into Lottie's cozy living room, sunlight streaming through wide windows, soft praise music playing faintly in the background. It was exactly the kind of peaceful space Sarah needed.

Lottie studied her friend's face. "You're glowing—but not in the good way."

Sarah laughed weakly. "I can't hide anything from you, can I?"

"You don't have to."

Sarah's shoulders slumped as she stirred her coffee.

"Well, Hagar's in her second trimester now. Everything's going smoothly… physically."

"But emotionally?"

Sarah swallowed hard. "It's complicated, Lottie. Hagar's been amazing. Selfless. But I can't ignore how close she and Abe have gotten. They laugh together at appointments. Share these quiet looks when she talks about the baby kicking. And I…I feel like I'm outside my own miracle."

Lottie reached over, taking her hand gently. "Sarah, listen to me. The bond between a pregnant woman and the father of the child is natural. But that doesn't change who the child belongs to."

"I know that in my head," Sarah whispered. "But in my heart, I sometimes feel replaced. Like she's giving him something I can't."

Lottie's voice softened. "You've waited for years, carried this dream longer than anyone knows. Don't let temporary emotions steal your joy."

"I want to trust Hagar. I want to trust Abe." Sarah's voice cracked. "But I'm scared."

Lottie squeezed her hand. "Fear has no place in promises, Sarah.

You're not an outsider. You're the mother. You're the one God whispered this promise to long before Hagar ever came into your life."

Sarah exhaled deeply, blinking back tears. "I needed to hear that."

"And you'll need to keep hearing it," Lottie said, smiling.

"So I'll keep saying it. As long as you need."

Sarah stirred her coffee slowly, then smiled faintly. "We found out it's a boy."

Mara's eyes lit up. "A boy! Oh, Sarah, that's amazing."

Lottie leaned over the table. "Does it feel more real now?"

Sarah hesitated, then nodded. "Yes…and no. Hagar actually guessed it weeks ago. Said she just knew it was a boy. And she was right."

The girls went quiet for a beat before Sarah added, "I'm happy. I really am. It's just hard sometimes…knowing someone else is carrying your son."

Mara reached across the table and squeezed her hand. "He's still yours,

Sarah. He always will be."

Sarah clearly had something else on her mind.

"I know I should be happier...but there's something else. I haven't told anyone this part yet."

Lottie simply nodded, waiting.

Sarah took a long breath before the words spilled.

"After everything with Hagar...after finally deciding to move forward with the surrogacy...I had a positive pregnancy test. It was two pink lines. After everything. And for about 24 hours, I let myself dream. I imagined telling Abe, telling you, seeing a heartbeat, holding a tiny hand."

Lottie's eyes widened.

Sarah's voice cracked. "For one beautiful, terrifying day, I thought...maybe my body was finally catching up. That God might still give us this miracle...one I could carry."

Lottie reached for her hand but said nothing yet.

Sarah's tears came quickly now.

"And then it was gone. Barely had time to settle into hope before it slipped right through my fingers."

Lottie gently squeezed her hand, her own eyes glistening, "Was that the week you wouldn't answer our calls?"

"Yes, I'm so sorry. I could barely breathe, much less talk. And now," Sarah whispered, "I feel like I don't even know how to grieve it. I mean...Hagar's carrying our baby right now. And I should be grateful. I *am* grateful. I should feel full. But I feel... hollow."

Lottie whispered,

"Because it wasn't just about having a baby. It was about being part of it. Experiencing it."

Sarah nodded, her shoulders shaking.

"I've spent years surrendering my timeline to God. But this... this felt cruel. Like He dangled it in front of me just long enough for me to remember how badly I still want it."

After a long pause, Sarah whispered,

"I'm so tired of waiting."

Lottie was quiet for a moment, then spoke softly but firmly.

"Sarah, listen to me. God's will for you to 'be fruitful and multiply' didn't disappear with one loss. His promises are not so fragile. Your grief doesn't disqualify you from gratitude…or from continuing to believe."

Sarah's voice was barely audible. "I feel like I'm failing at trusting Him."

"No," Lottie said gently. "You're walking through the mess of waiting. And He's not asking for perfect trust. He's asking you to stay in it with Him. Even when it hurts."

Sarah finally rested her head on Lottie's shoulder, exhausted from holding it all in for so long.

"Thank you for always being here."

"Always," Lottie whispered, her voice breaking slightly.

They sat that way for a long time—no more words, just two friends sitting together in the sacred, aching space between heartbreak and hope.

Five Months into Hagar's Pregnancy—Guy's Night, Brooklyn

The guys had gathered at Jordan's place—his tiny slice of backyard in Brooklyn, strung with café lights, a grill sizzling, and music playing softly in the background.

Burgers flipped. Drinks poured. Laughter circled easily.

But even beneath the lightness, Abe knew the real conversation was coming.

After they ate, Marcus broke the silence gently.

"How's Sarah holding up, man?"

Abe smiled faintly.

"She's strong. She's handling it better than I think I would if roles were reversed."

Jordan nodded, but glanced at him carefully.

"We heard she went to Dallas for a few days."

Abe's expression tightened for a beat, then he exhaled slowly.

"Yeah. She just needed some air. With Hagar this far along now, emotions have been... heightened."

Eli leaned forward a little.

"Did she…" He caught himself. "She didn't leave, did she?"

Abe's response was immediate, firm.

"Of course not. She just needed space to breathe. And where better to breathe than Texas, right?" He forced a soft laugh.

"Dallas has Lottie and Mara, her safe people. It helps her reset."

Jordan nodded.

"Honestly, that sounds pretty healthy, all things considered."

Abe smiled faintly.

"She and I are solid. It's just a complicated season, that's all."

Eli added carefully,

"Complicated's an understatement."

Marcus spoke softly, grounding the moment.

"But you're both still anchored."

"Absolutely," Abe said firmly. "Always."

"It's complicated sometimes," he admitted. "On the surface, things are good. But there are moments where it's awkward. Emotional lines get blurry. Sarah's trying not to show it, but I know how much it hurts not carrying the child herself."

Eli chimed in carefully.

"And for you? Is it awkward being around Hagar? Especially with how close she is to both of you right now?"

Abe paused, choosing his words with care.

"There are moments, yeah. But I set very firm boundaries early. Sarah's trust means too much to me to let anything cross that line."

Marcus nodded approvingly.

"Good man."

Jordan added softly,

"But it's okay to say it's hard. You're watching another woman carry your first child. That's not something anyone grows up preparing for."

Abe smiled, grateful for the honesty.

"You're not wrong. There are days I feel helpless watching Sarah wrestle with emotions I can't fix. And then there are days I feel this overwhelming gratitude that Hagar was even willing to do this for us."

They sat in silence for a moment, the weight of it hanging like mist between them.

Finally, Marcus said quietly, "You know, brother... this is still God's story. Even when it's messy. Sometimes miracles don't look as neat as we imagine."

Abe whispered,

"Sometimes they're messier."

"But no less miraculous," Marcus finished.

Eli raised his glass slightly.

"To the mess that God still uses."

They clinked quietly, a simple brotherhood prayer disguised as a toast. Later, as they packed up to leave, Jordan pulled Abe aside for a final word.

"You're doing better than you think," he said. "But if you ever need to talk...like, really talk...we've got you."

Abe smiled, heart lighter.

"Thanks, man. That means more than you know."

The Next Evening—Manhattan Apartment

The apartment smelled of roasted garlic and fresh basil as Abe stirred a pan on the stovetop. Cooking had become his small therapy in recent weeks—something predictable, something safe.

The doorbell rang.

He glanced up, surprised.

When he opened the door, Hagar stood there with her usual tote bag over her shoulder.

"Hey," she smiled. "I figured I'd drop off the contracts Dr. Malik's office emailed today."

Abe stepped aside to let her in.

"Thanks. Come in."

As she stepped inside, she paused, glancing around.

"Where's Sarah?" she asked casually.

Abe wiped his hands on a towel.

"She's still in Dallas. Visiting Lottie."

Hagar froze for a second, her smile faltering.

"Right. Of course. I scheduled that time off for her. Pregnancy brain, I guess."

Abe offered a sympathetic smile.

"You're carrying a small watermelon around constantly...I think you've earned a little forgetfulness."

Hagar laughed, resting a hand gently on her belly.

"Fair enough." But something unreadable flickered behind her eyes.

"Smells amazing in here."

"Pasta night," Abe said, lifting the pan slightly. "Way too much for one person."

Before she could respond, Abe continued, "You might as well stay and eat. Otherwise, I'll be eating leftovers all week."

Hagar hesitated briefly, then smiled.

"If you're sure."

The two sat across from each other at the small kitchen island, sharing the meal while soft jazz played in the background. The apartment was quiet—too quiet without Sarah humming from the kitchen or her laugh echoing down the hall.

For a while, the conversation stayed light—pregnancy updates, work anecdotes, casual talk.

But slowly, the ease of the conversation shifted. Hagar's gaze lingered longer across the table. Her voice softened slightly.

"You're really going to be a great dad, you know," she said. Abe smiled, brushing it off humbly.

"Sarah and I both will."

Hagar nodded, but then added quietly, "You've been so...kind. To me. Through all of this."

He looked up, sensing the shift.

"It's been important to us that you feel safe. That this feels... respectful."

Hagar's voice softened further.

"Sometimes, I feel closer to you than anyone. This process... it's so personal."

Abe straightened slightly, his posture tightening.

Hagar continued, voice almost a whisper.

"I don't think I fully realized how much intimacy there would be, she said.

Abe turned toward her, brow furrowed.

She rushed to clarify. "Not physical. I don't mean that. I just mean... emotional. Spiritual even. This life growing inside me...it feels like I've been invited into something private. Like I'm trespassing without meaning to."

A pause hung thick between them.

Abe cleared his throat.

"Hagar..."

Before he could finish, she stood and stepped closer to him, not in a rush, but with an aching vulnerability that made it hard to look away.

"I just wanted to say...thank you. For everything," She whispered.

Her hand brushed his arm. He didn't move at first.

Then she leaned in, hesitating, almost asking permission. Her lips grazed his cheek, then lingered, shifting gently toward his mouth.

Abe didn't respond right away. For half a second, less than a breath, he didn't pull away. The air between them sparked with something undeniable.

Then he stepped back—abrupt, clear, and final.

"Hagar." His voice was low but firm.

She froze, realizing too late that she had crossed a line.

"I…I'm sorry," she stammered. "I wasn't thinking. Maybe it's the hormones, or... I just…"

"I think it's best you head home for tonight," Abe said, the gentleness in his tone layered over something resolute.

The air grew thick with unspoken tension.

She grabbed her bag, flustered, embarrassed. Abe walked her to the door.

She turned once more before leaving.

"Please, don't tell Sarah."

Abe looked at her evenly, the weight of the moment pressing down like gravity.

His voice remained steady.

"Goodnight, Hagar."

The door clicked shut behind her.

He stood there in the silence for a long time—hand on the doorknob, heart racing in his chest. Not because he wanted more. But because, for one terrifying second—he hadn't wanted to stop.

The Next Afternoon—Abe's Office

Abe sat behind his desk, eyes locked on his laptop screen, trying to bury the discomfort from the night before beneath a mountain of work.

A knock startled him.

The door cracked open, and to his surprise—and frustration—Hagar stepped inside.

"Hagar. What are you doing here?"

She shifted nervously, clutching her purse.

"I...I just wanted to apologize for last night. In person."

Abe stood, his voice firm but quiet.

"We don't need to revisit it."

"I know," she said quickly. "I just didn't want things to feel... weird."

"They're not weird," he lied. "As long as we both stay professional and focused on what matters."

Hagar nodded quickly, trying to mask her embarrassment.

"I respect you and Sarah. Truly. Last night was...a lapse."

Abe offered a curt nod, but his eyes carried weight.

"Thank you for saying that. But please don't show up here again without scheduling something. This isn't appropriate."

Her face flushed.

"Of course. You're right."

A beat of silence.

"Take care of yourself, Hagar."

She gave a small nod and slipped out as quickly as she had arrived.

Abe sat back down, pressing his fingers against his temples.

Lord, I need Sarah back here.

The Sanctuary

She didn't wait for the elevator. Her body wouldn't let her.

Hagar took the stairs, breath catching in her throat, the sting of marble against her heels barely registering. Her hands trembled at her sides as she gripped the railing for balance—not because she might fall, but because everything else already had. Her dignity. Her job. The fragile peace she'd once kept with Sarah.

She had come to apologize. That was all. To take responsibility, to offer whatever threadbare humility she could gather. But when Abe opened the door and looked at her—not with rage, not even anger, but that quiet, soul-deep disappointment—something inside her caved.

He didn't have to say much. The look alone said enough: *You crossed a line. And there's no way back from here.*

By the time she burst through the glass doors to the street, the crisp spring air slapped her skin like a sentence. She didn't think. She didn't slow down.

She ran.

Past the cafés where they once laughed about nursery names. Past the bus stop where she used to stand with a book in hand, believing her life still had clean lines and bright beginnings. The city blurred around her—all color and motion and noise—until even her breath betrayed her.

She didn't stop until her legs demanded it.

The church doors were unlocked.

She didn't pause at the threshold, didn't care who might see. She stepped into the cool hush of the sanctuary and slipped inside like a woman seeking refuge—or punishment. She wasn't sure which.

Sunlight slanted through the stained glass in golden fragments. Dust danced in the stillness, suspended in time. And in that silence, her body finally gave up.

She dropped to her knees halfway down the aisle—not gracefully, not dramatically, but as one undone. Her hands trembled as they gripped the smooth wood of the pew. Her head bowed.

"God…" she whispered.

It wasn't a prayer, not yet. Just a reaching.

"I'm sorry."

Her voice cracked. The words were small, crushed under the weight of her own shame.

"I never meant for it to go that far. I never meant to…to take what wasn't mine. I just…" Her voice faltered. "I wanted to feel something real. To feel chosen, even for a moment."

The tears came fast, blurring the light and warping the stained glass until even the saints seemed to look away.

"I crossed a line. I know that. I broke something sacred. I broke trust." Her hands pressed into her face as if to silence the weeping. "I hate that I did."

The soft creak of footsteps echoed behind her, careful, reverent. She turned slightly, startled, and saw him—Pastor Wells, his Bible tucked beneath one arm, concern etched into the corners of his eyes. He said nothing at first. He simply approached, knelt beside her, and waited.

She couldn't meet his gaze. "I messed up," she said, her voice hollow. "And I don't know how to make it right."

He nodded slowly, not with judgment but understanding.

"Repentance doesn't erase the past," he said. "But it realigns your future."

Her lips quivered.

"Will God even forgive me for this?"

He placed a steady hand on her shoulder, his touch grounding.

"You're not the first person to run from a mistake into the arms of grace," he said. "And you won't be the last."

Her breath hitched. Something loosened.

"You came to the right place, Hagar. God is full of mercy, His grace is new every morning."

And they stayed there—just that way. No spotlight. No dramatic music. Only the quiet, holy company of a broken woman and a shepherd who understood what mercy sounded like when it whispered into shame.

When Hagar finally stood, her eyes were red and swollen, but her back was no longer bent by the weight she'd carried in. She wasn't sure how Sarah would look at her again. Or if Abe would ever forgive her.

But she knew—without question—that God still could.

And that was something.

Two Days Later—Manhattan Apartment

The moment Sarah stepped through the front door, Abe pulled her into his arms.

He held her tighter than usual, breathing her in.

"You okay?" she whispered, noticing the intensity.

He kissed her temple, whispering,

"Better now."

They sat together on the couch later that night, Sarah's head resting on Abe's chest.

"I missed you," he said softly.

"I missed you too."

A brief pause.

"You seemed...off when I got home," Sarah said gently.

Abe exhaled.

"There's a lot I need to tell you. Nothing terrible...but... important."

She sat up slightly, looking into his eyes.

"Hagar stopped by while you were gone."

Sarah's brow furrowed slightly.

"For what?"

Abe swallowed.

"She came by the apartment. Says she didn't realize you were out of town. I invited her to stay for dinner. It was innocent... but near the end of the night, she crossed a boundary."

Sarah's breath caught.

"She crossed a boundary how?"

Abe's voice remained calm, but serious. He measured his next statements very carefully, so he didn't cause more damage than their marriage could stand.

"She got too familiar. Emotional. Nothing happened, but it was...uncomfortable. I asked her to leave."

Sarah processed in silence, her stomach tightening.

"She apologized the next day. Showed up at my office."

"She went to your office?"

"I made it clear she crossed a line. I shut it down. But I didn't want to hide it from you."

Sarah nodded slowly, swallowing the lump rising in her throat.

"Thank you for telling me."

"I would never risk what we have," Abe said softly, his voice breaking now. "You. This child. Our life."

Sarah's eyes welled, but she reached for his hand.

"I know. And I trust you."

They sat in silence, both knowing this wouldn't be the last complicated emotion they would face—but knowing they were still firmly anchored to one another.

CHAPTER 27

The Anniversary

Two Months After the Pregnancy Loss—Their Manhattan Apartment

Abe had insisted on handling the plans for their anniversary this year. After all the emotion, the medical appointments, the tears—he knew Sarah didn't need fancy. She needed something steady. Sarah stepped out of the bedroom, surprised by the simple scene waiting for her.

The dining table was set with candles flickering softly. Takeout containers from their favorite little Italian place sat neatly arranged—the same restaurant where they'd first celebrated their engagement. Abe stood by the table, smiling.

"Happy anniversary, babe."

Sarah smiled, her eyes immediately misting.

"This is perfect."

He pulled out her chair for her.

"I figured you didn't need some five-course chef's tasting menu tonight. Just your favorites."

Sarah chuckled softly.

"You know me too well."

After dinner, Abe reached into a small bag beside the table and handed her a tiny, wrapped box.

Sarah carefully opened it to reveal a delicate gold necklace with a single charm: a tiny mustard seed, encased in glass.

Her breath caught instantly.

"Abe…"

He smiled gently.

"If you have faith as small as a mustard seed…" he quoted softly. "You've carried more faith than you know, Sarah. Even when it's been shattered, you've kept choosing to believe."

Tears filled Sarah's eyes as she whispered,

"But sometimes it feels like I'm barely hanging on."

Abe reached for her hand.

"That's why Jesus didn't say you needed a mountain of faith. Just this much."

Sarah closed her fingers around the charm as if it were a lifeline.

Lord, I still believe You.

After a quiet moment, Sarah broke the silence.

"Do you ever wonder if God still has more for us?" she whispered.

Abe's voice was steady.

"Every single day. And I still believe He does. But even if this is all He gives us, I'll be grateful. Because I have you."

She smiled through her tears.

"And I have you."

They sat that way for a while—no more striving, no more fixing—just resting in the fragile beauty of love that had been refined in the fire.

Before bed, as Sarah gently placed the necklace in her jewelry box, she whispered to herself,

"You're not done writing, God. I still trust You."

For the first time in weeks, the weight in her chest felt just a little bit lighter.

The Next Week—Sarah & Abe's Apartment

The next Friday night, they all sat in the nursery, poring over fabric swatches and paint samples. Sarah ran her fingers across a pale sage green. "This one feels peaceful."

"It's soft but fresh," Hagar agreed. "Fitting for a boy."

Abe nodded. "It's perfect."

As Sarah lifted the fabric swatch and held it against the nursery wall, her eye caught a flicker in Abe's gaze—the way it paused, however briefly, on Hagar. It wasn't overt. But there was something there—a soft familiarity, the kind that grows quietly between people who have shared too many days, too many silences. A comfort that hadn't been there before. Not dangerous, but no longer neutral.

Later that night, Abe found her in the nursery, staring at the empty crib. "It's really happening," she whispered, while at the same time a quiet voice whispered in the back of her mind: *This may not feel like yours.*

"It is," Abe said, wrapping his arms around her from behind.

Sarah closed her eyes and breathed deeply. For the first time in years, hope felt like something she could actually hold.

Another Week Passes—Sarah & Abe's Apartment

A week later on a rainy Saturday afternoon, Sarah had excused herself for a virtual client call, leaving Hagar and Abe in the living room. When Sarah returned, she stood quietly for a moment before announcing herself, watching as they worked together to assemble the new crib.

"Left side's higher," Hagar said, laughing.

"I told you these instructions are evil," Abe replied, smiling.

Hagar knelt to tighten a screw, and when she looked up, Abe offered his hand to steady her. Their eyes met. The air pulsed briefly.

Sarah cleared her throat. "How's it coming in here?"

Abe stepped back. "We almost have it."

"Teamwork," Hagar added quickly, glancing away.

Sarah forced a smile and nodded, but her heart fluttered with something harder to name.

They had gathered on the sofa after dinner when Hagar suddenly gasped softly, pressing her hand to her belly.

"What is it?" Sarah asked quickly.

"He's kicking," Hagar whispered, eyes wide. "Here, feel."

Without hesitation, Abe placed his hand gently beside hers.

"There," Hagar breathed. "Do you feel that?"

Abe's eyes softened. "Incredible."

Sarah moved closer, reaching in as well, but the moment between Abe and Hagar had already settled like a quiet secret. She pushed the unease away. This was joy. This was what they had prayed for.

And yet.

That night, as Sarah lay beside Abe in bed, staring at the ceiling, her mind replayed those small exchanges. The shared smiles. The inside jokes. The way Hagar's voice softened when speaking to Abe, and how his eyes sometimes lingered on her a second too long.

She closed her eyes tightly. "Stop it," she whispered to herself.

But the shift was real. Invisible, yes. Subtle. But undeniably real.

CHAPTER 28

The Fracture

End of Second Trimester

The months passed, and the pregnancy progressed smoothly. Sarah felt herself growing more confident, more hopeful. The nursery was nearly complete, and every ultrasound photo found its place on the refrigerator, like tiny sacred snapshots of the promise finally unfolding.

But with time the fracture between her and Abe felt like it continued to widen. Hagar and Abe talked so easily with each other during appointments, they laughed at little things and shared inside jokes about the baby's movements.

It made Sarah felt like a bystander to her own miracle.

Sarah busied herself with work, appointments, nursery details. But her mind increasingly circled back to the moments she couldn't unsee.

26 Weeks—Midtown Coffee Shop

One afternoon, after a routine check-up, they stopped for coffee. Hagar had ordered a decaf latte and was sharing a story about the baby kicking during a staff meeting.

"He's most active right after lunch," Hagar laughed, pressing a hand to her growing belly. "It's like he knows when I've had tacos."

Abe chuckled, leaning forward. "Already opinionated. Just like his mother."

Hagar smiled, but for a moment, Sarah wasn't sure which "mother" Abe meant.

The warmth of the moment tightened Sarah's chest unexpectedly. She forced a smile, but the edges of her heart ached.

That night, she sat on the balcony, staring at the city lights, when Abe found her.

"You've been quiet," he said softly.

Sarah took a long breath. "I'm afraid."

"Of what?"

"Of being replaced," she admitted, her voice cracking.

"By the woman carrying our child."

Abe pulled her into his arms. "Sarah, you are his mother. No one else."

"But sometimes…it feels like you're sharing something with her that I'll never get to share."

Abe was silent for a long moment before answering. "It's complicated. But nothing changes what you mean to me. Or to him. This child wouldn't exist without your hope. Without your faith."

Sarah closed her eyes and leaned into him. "I want to believe that."

Abe kissed her temple. "Then believe it. Because it's true."

A Few Days Later—Sarah & Abe's Apartment

Later that same week, Sarah returned home earlier than planned. She paused just inside the apartment, hearing voices drifting from the kitchen.

"…and you like the name Ethan?" Hagar's voice, soft, almost playful.

Abe chuckled. "I do. Strong. Solid."

"But not Ishmael? After your father?" Hagar asked.

Abe looked up at her, surprised. "Ishmael?"

Hagar nodded slowly. "It was your father's name, right? I thought maybe…"

Abe exhaled, the sound caught between nostalgia and reverence.

"Yeah. My dad was named after the biblical Ishmael…it means '*God hears*.'"

"That's beautiful," Hagar said, her voice softer now.

He nodded, eyes distant. "My grandmother chose it because she said she prayed for a child for years. When my dad finally came along, she named him Ishmael to remind herself that God hadn't forgotten her."

A silence stretched between them for a beat too long.

Hagar finally whispered, "Then maybe it's the perfect name…for this one too."

"Well, we're still negotiating." Abe's voice held warmth.

Sarah froze. She hadn't even known Hagar had opinions about names. The tenderness in their banter tightened something inside her chest.

When Sarah entered, both turned quickly, the air in the room shifting.

"Hey, you're home early," Abe said, his tone overly casual.

"Traffic was light," Sarah replied, forcing brightness. "What are we discussing?"

"Just name ideas," Hagar answered quickly, glancing at Abe.

Sarah smiled politely. "Of course."

Sarah tried to dismiss her unease. After all, nothing had *happened*. Abe was loving, attentive, present. Hagar was respectful, grateful, professional. And yet, the three of them had formed a strange, intimate triangle—one that no contract or agreement could fully govern.

Same Evening—Sarah & Abe's Apartment

That evening, Sarah sat on the edge of their bed as Abe changed into his pajamas. The tension between them buzzed like static.

"Abe," she began carefully, "do you ever feel like the lines are getting…blurry?"

He paused, looking up. "Between who?"

"Between you and Hagar. Between all of us."

Abe exhaled. "Sarah—"

"She's in our home constantly. You two spend more time together than you realize."

"She's carrying our child."

"I know that." Sarah's voice wavered. "But you laugh together. You have private conversations. You pick up her favorite pastries before appointments. You remember things she tells you that I don't even know."

Abe sat beside her. "I care about her, yes. She's given us a gift we couldn't give ourselves. That doesn't mean I feel anything inappropriate."

"Not yet," Sarah whispered.

He looked wounded. "Do you really believe that of me?"

"I don't know what to believe anymore." She swallowed, voice cracking. "And that's the problem."

The Next Day - Sarah's Office

The next day, while sorting emails, Sarah saw the message.

Hagar had forwarded Abe a confirmation for a birthing class—one Sarah hadn't known they'd scheduled together. Her fingers hovered over the keyboard, stomach churning.

It wasn't the class. It was the tone.

"Thanks for arranging it. You're always taking care of me."

Three harmless sentences. And yet.

Sarah closed the laptop gently, breathing through the sudden wave of nausea. This wasn't jealousy. This was something else. Something harder. Something closer to betrayal.

And it was spreading.

Abe's Work Crisis

Abe sat at his desk, eyes locked on the financial projections spread across his monitor. The numbers weren't adding up. Or rather, they were adding up to exactly the problem he feared.

A knock at his office door broke his focus.

"Come in."

His VP of Operations, Greg, stepped inside, closing the door behind him—never a good sign.

"We've got to talk about the Delmar contract."

Abe rubbed his temples.

"I know."

"They're backing out entirely."

Abe exhaled.

"Which leaves a $3.4 million hole in Q4. And potential layoffs."

Greg nodded grimly.

Abe stared at the ceiling for a moment, feeling the tightrope stretch even thinner beneath him. His mind pinged between financials, legal meetings, Hagar's OB appointments, Sarah's quiet sadness, and the growing tension that seemed to hover in their home since the surrogacy began.

"I'll call a meeting with Legal and Finance this afternoon," Abe said quietly. "Let's put together contingency options."

Greg hesitated before leaving.

"Hey seriously. Are you okay?"

Abe forced a smile.

"Yeah. Just... a lot right now."

Greg offered a knowing nod and quietly closed the door.

Later That Night—At Home

Sarah found Abe sitting alone in the dark living room, glass of water in his hand, staring at nothing.

She crossed the room quietly, sitting beside him.

"You're carrying something," she said softly.

Abe shook his head.

"It's nothing you need to worry about."

"Abe."

He exhaled, finally surrendering.

"The Delmar contract collapsed. It's going to ripple through the entire quarter."

Sarah squeezed his hand gently.

"We'll get through it. Like we always do."

Abe shook his head again, voice cracking slightly now.

"It's not just the money. It's...everything. The business. The baby. The surrogacy. Hagar. You."

Sarah's voice was steady.

"You've been trying to protect me from all of it, haven't you?"

Abe stared at her, eyes filled with quiet ache.

"I feel like I'm failing all of you."

Sarah leaned her head onto his shoulder.

"You're not. You're fighting for us. And you don't have to carry it alone."

They sat there for a long time, wrapped in shared silence—two people both desperately trying to hold their fragile world steady.

"Abe?" Sarah finally broke the silence, drawing his gaze.

"Yeah?"

"I've been thinking about something... something I overheard a few days ago. Hagar mentioned a name to you—one you didn't say much about at the time."

His brow furrowed. "A name?"

"For the baby." She paused, then smiled gently.

"Ishmael."

Abe looked surprised, almost hesitant. "Yeah, she said it reminded her that God hears. I didn't want to bring it up in case...I don't know, in case it felt strange."

Sarah reached out and rested her hand on his. "It doesn't feel strange. It feels right."

He studied her, searching her expression. "Really?"

She nodded. "I know we're still figuring everything out. But I love that it's your father's name...that it means something. And I think it could be healing, for all of us, to name him after someone who meant so much to you."

Abe's eyes welled unexpectedly, the moment cracking something inside him that had been under pressure for too long.

"Ishmael Abrams," Sarah said quietly. "That sounds like someone strong. Someone who's been heard."

Abe swallowed hard. "My dad would've loved that."

She gave his hand a gentle squeeze. "Tell me something about him. Something I don't know."

Abe leaned back, a soft smile flickering at the corner of his mouth. "He used to whistle when he worked. Loud and off-key. Drove my mom crazy. But when I was a kid, I used to sit under his desk while he worked on client proposals, just listening. That whistle meant everything was okay."

Sarah rested her head on his shoulder. "I think our son should know that story. And that sound."

Abe chuckled, emotion still thick in his voice. "Then I better start practicing."

Outside, traffic rolled on. Deadlines and crises still waited for Abe tomorrow. But for now, he let himself breathe—really breathe—with Sarah beside him and a name spoken aloud that felt like both honor and redemption.

Ishmael.

He could see it now.

27 Weeks—The Apartment

The apartment felt smaller now, crowded with things they once believed would bring them joy—bassinet, nursing chair, piles of neatly folded onesies. But for Sarah, the joy was increasingly edged with dread.

The confrontation didn't come in a burst. It simmered for days. Sarah wrapped herself in work and tasks. Abe tried to pretend everything was normal. Hagar, sensing the tension her presence caused, grew quieter, more careful. But the unspoken truth lingered between them, thickening the air.

It came to a head one late afternoon.

Sarah walked into the apartment and found Abe and Hagar sitting close at the dining table, reviewing the birthing plan on a laptop. They didn't hear her enter. She watched as Hagar leaned in to point at something on the screen, her hand brushing Abe's arm. Neither pulled back immediately.

Sarah's heart pounded.

When Abe finally looked up and saw her, his expression shifted too quickly from relaxed to guarded.

"Oh…hey, sweetheart. We were just…"

"Making plans?" Sarah finished, her voice too calm.

"Yes," Hagar said softly. "We were finalizing the birthing class schedule."

"I see." Sarah walked in slowly, closing the door behind her. "Without me."

There was silence.

"It wasn't intentional," Abe said. "We were just trying to stay ahead of things."

Sarah's eyes burned. "Is that how it's been? The two of you 'staying ahead of things'?"

Abe stood, concern rising. "Sarah—"

She held up her hand. "No. We need to say it. Right here. Right now."

Hagar's eyes welled, but she said nothing.

Sarah turned fully toward Abe, her voice shaking. "I trusted both of you. And somewhere along the way, the boundaries blurred. You don't even see it. The stolen glances. Private texts. Inside jokes. The quiet moments you don't think I notice. And who really knows what transpired when I was in Dallas."

"It's not like that," Abe said quickly, defensive.

"Isn't it?" Sarah's voice broke. "You're bonding with the woman carrying our child. You're sharing pieces of yourself that belong to us." Hagar whispered, "I never meant—"

"You didn't mean to, but you did," Sarah said, turning to her.

"You are not the villain, Hagar. You've given us something sacred. But this…" she gestured between them, "…this is no longer safe."

Tears slipped down Hagar's cheeks. "I'm so sorry, Sarah. I never wanted to cross a line."

Sarah exhaled shakily. "And yet, here we are."

Abe stepped closer, his voice softening. "Please. Don't let this destroy everything we've built."

Sarah's shoulders sagged. "It already has. At least a part of it."

They stood there, three people bound by hope, love, and now deep regret—the fragile triangle collapsing under the weight of their silence. No one spoke again that night.

28 Weeks—Sarah & Abe's Apartment

Over the next few days, the shifting dynamics between them continued to stir beneath the surface, subtle but undeniable.

Hagar remained gracious, never crossing any obvious lines, but Sarah couldn't shake the feeling that something fragile and unspoken lived between her and Abe. It wasn't intentional—at least not yet—but intimacy has many forms, and proximity was one of them.

One afternoon, as Hagar sat in Sarah's living room, the conversation shifted to more personal territory.

"Sarah," Hagar began hesitantly, "I want to be honest with you about something."

Sarah tensed. "Of course. You can tell me anything."

"I know this situation is…complicated," Hagar said softly.

"And I want you to know I never meant for any of this to feel confusing or to make you uncomfortable."

Sarah's stomach tightened. "Go on."

Hagar looked down, folding her hands nervously. "When we first started this, I thought I could completely separate myself from it emotionally. But as the pregnancy has progressed…sometimes I find myself feeling more connected than I should."

Sarah swallowed, her throat suddenly dry.

"Connected to the baby?" she asked carefully.

Hagar hesitated. "To everything. The baby. You. Abe."

The weight of the admission hung in the air.

"I would never try to come between you and Abe," Hagar continued quickly. "I respect your marriage. But…carrying his child, seeing him care so deeply…it's made me admire him even more."

Sarah's chest ached with the complicated mixture of gratitude, fear, and something bordering on jealousy.

"I appreciate your honesty," Sarah finally said, her voice trembling slightly. "And I believe you. But I also need to be honest with you, Hagar."

Hagar looked up, her eyes wide.

"This arrangement was never going to be easy," Sarah said softly. "And I've tried so hard to see this only as a blessing. But it's also hard…feeling like an outsider in my own miracle."

Hagar's eyes welled with tears. "I never wanted you to feel that way."

Sarah reached over and gently squeezed her hand. "I know. And I'm trusting both of us to guard each other's hearts. For the sake of this child. For the sake of all of us."

Hagar nodded, her voice breaking. "I promise."

They sat together for a long time after that, both feeling the weight of what they had just spoken aloud—both knowing that while words had been said, much still remained unspoken.

Hagar's Journal Entry—28 Weeks

People at work keep asking when I'm due, if I have a nursery ready, if I've picked names.

How do you explain to strangers that your child is someone else's?

That you're a vessel, but not a mother?

The hardest part isn't their curiosity. It's the assumptions.

I answer politely. I always say: "It's complicated."

But the truth is, my heart is what's complicated.

CHAPTER 29

The Final Stretch

The Office—Conference Room, Third Trimester

S arah had barely stepped off the elevator when she heard the unmistakable burst of applause and laughter erupting from the conference room down the hall. Before she could fully process what was happening, Hagar appeared at her side, grinning and pulling Sarah gently by the arm.

"Come on," Hagar said excitedly. "They have a surprise."
Sarah's stomach twisted slightly. She hadn't planned for any kind of baby shower—not at the office, not like this. She hadn't even wanted one. The thought of standing in the spotlight while someone else carried her child had felt... complicated.
But it was happening.
As they entered the conference room, the entire team erupted into cheers.
"Surprise!"

The long table was decorated with soft blues and yellows, pastel balloons floating in bunches. A diaper cake sat in the center, surrounded by neatly wrapped gifts, tiny baby onesies hanging from a makeshift clothesline.

Another assistant, Leslie, grinned, "We couldn't let you two go through this without celebrating you and the little miracle!"

Sarah's smile tightened as cameras flashed and coworkers gathered around.

"Look at this," Hagar whispered to her, eyes wide with genuine delight. "They did all this?"

"They did," Sarah forced herself to say, her voice light.

The team quickly surrounded Hagar, offering hugs, placing hands carefully on her baby bump, asking eager questions.

"How are you feeling?"

"Any names yet?"

"Look at that beautiful belly!"

Sarah stood slightly off to the side, plastering on a smile as Hagar soaked in the attention—her face glowing, her hand instinctively resting on the curve of her stomach. The bump that should have been Sarah's.

She was genuinely happy for Hagar. She was.

And yet.

Each comment, each lingering touch, each "you're glowing" felt like a fresh little paper cut—not deep enough to cry over, but sharp enough to sting.

Abe had wanted to come but was tied up in meetings. Sarah secretly wished he were here—if only to anchor her through the awkwardness.

As the gift opening began, Sarah caught snippets:

"Oh, Hagar—you'll be a natural!"

"You're such a blessing to this baby."

Sarah nodded politely, adding an occasional "thank you" when appropriate, but every compliment directed at Hagar reminded her again of what she wasn't experiencing.

When it was finally over and the team began filing out, Sarah helped gather the gifts into bags. Hagar turned to her, still glowing.

"I hope this didn't make you uncomfortable."

Sarah swallowed the lump rising in her throat, forcing a soft smile. "No, not at all. You deserve to be celebrated."

Hagar's voice lowered slightly, serious. "This baby is yours and Abe's, Sarah. I know I'm carrying him, but you're still his mother."

Sarah's voice broke slightly as she whispered, "Thank you for saying that."

Hagar reached out and gently squeezed Sarah's hand. "We're almost there."

Sarah nodded, blinking back tears. "Yes. We're almost there."

Obstetrics Office—Third Trimester

The exam room was brighter than usual, sunlight pouring through the high windows as the doctor finished measuring Hagar's growing belly.

"Everything looks great," Dr. Malik smiled. "Baby's measuring right on track. Strong heartbeat, excellent fluid levels. We're right where we want to be."

Sarah stood quietly near the window while Abe sat closer to Hagar, glancing at the chart as the doctor reviewed the numbers.

"Good job, Hagar," Abe said with genuine warmth. "You're handling all of this like a pro."

Hagar smiled, brushing a stray hair behind her ear. "Well, this little one seems pretty content in there."

They exchanged an easy laugh—friendly, natural, familiar.

Sarah forced a small smile as she folded her arms, watching their interaction from just a few feet away, yet somehow feeling outside of it. Like a guest observing her own life.

As the doctor stepped out to prepare the next set of labs, Abe turned back toward Hagar. "Any more nausea? Still sleeping okay?"

"Sleeping is harder now," Hagar admitted, resting a hand on her stomach. "But I've been reading all the tricks. Extra pillows, warm tea before bed. Your wife gave me some great tips."

Abe chuckled, glancing over at Sarah. "She's done her research."

Sarah smiled faintly but said nothing.

Abe continued, still addressing Hagar, "You really have handled this with so much grace. We're beyond grateful."

Hagar's eyes softened. "It's been an honor."

Their eyes lingered a moment too long for Sarah's comfort—not romantic, not inappropriate—but connected. The kind of shared experience that had grown deeper over the months of doctor visits, prenatal classes, and baby preparation that Sarah often couldn't attend because of her work schedule.

Sarah inhaled quietly, forcing the breath into her chest. She looked away, pretending to study a brochure about postpartum care as the faint sting of jealousy pricked her heart.

The Car Ride Home

They drove in silence for several blocks. Abe was behind the wheel, Sarah staring out the window as Manhattan blurred past.

Finally, Abe spoke gently. "You've been quiet."

"I'm just tired," Sarah replied.

"You sure that's all?"

She hesitated, debating whether to speak the thing she hadn't yet voiced. The ache she feared would sound petty if spoken aloud.

"She's spending a lot of time with you," Sarah said softly.

Abe glanced over, his face filled with both concern and caution.

"You mean the appointments?"

"The appointments. The conversations. The way you two just… click sometimes."

Abe exhaled. "Sarah, we've been over this so many times. I promise...I would never—"

"I know," she interrupted, closing her eyes briefly. "I'm not accusing you. It's just hard to watch sometimes."

She turned to him now, her voice trembling. "This whole process was supposed to bring us closer. And some days...I feel more distant from you than ever."

Abe reached across and gently took her hand. "We're in uncharted territory, Sarah. But we'll stay grounded. You and me. Always."

Sarah swallowed, blinking back tears. "I need you to keep seeing *me*, Abe. Not just her. Not just the baby."

"I see you, Sarah." His voice was firm but tender. "I see you."

Hagar's Journal Entry—29 Weeks

Sarah surprised me today with a massage gift card and a long lunch.

She keeps thanking me. Always thanking me.

I wish she knew that sometimes her gratitude only makes it harder. Because every time she thanks me, I remember that one day soon...I have to let go.

I tell myself: This is what love looks like. Love gives.

But love also hurts.

30 Weeks—Coffee Shop

The final trimester brought both anticipation and tension.

The baby was thriving. Each doctor's visit confirmed steady growth and strong development. The nursery was complete, and Sarah had even allowed herself to start organizing baby clothes, folding and refolding the tiny outfits with trembling hands.

But beneath the excitement, the emotional strain tightened like an invisible rope between them.

One evening, Hagar invited Sarah to join her for tea. It was rare for them to spend time together without Abe present, and Sarah sensed the conversation ahead would not be easy.

They sat across from each other at a small café table, steam rising from their cups.

The baby kicked softly beneath Hagar's hand, and both women glanced instinctively at the gentle movement.

"He's active tonight," Hagar smiled.

"He knows something's coming," Sarah whispered.

They shared a small, knowing laugh—the kind born not from humor, but from vulnerability.

The silence stretched, but it wasn't uncomfortable.

Finally, Hagar broke it.

"I wanted to talk before things get…harder," Hagar said softly.

Sarah nodded, bracing herself.

"I've been thinking about what happens after the delivery."

Sarah swallowed. "Yes."

Hagar looked down for a moment, her fingers stroking her rounded belly.

"I know legally everything is in place," Hagar continued.

"And emotionally, I've tried to stay in the right headspace. But I'm scared because I also know that giving him to you won't be easy. Even though I've always known it's the plan."

Sarah's heart ached. She had rehearsed these fears in her mind many times but hearing Hagar voice them made the reality feel heavier.

Sarah inhaled softly, nodding, but allowing Hagar to keep going.

"I know this baby isn't mine," Hagar whispered. "I've always known. But I also know that I've carried him. I've felt him. I've talked to him every night. And I worry that when I hand him over, I'll lose a part of myself I didn't even realize I was giving."

Her voice cracked.

"I don't want to grieve something that was never supposed to be mine."

Sarah swallowed, her heart breaking as she reached over to place her hand gently over Hagar's.

"I don't expect you to pretend it won't hurt," Sarah said gently.

"This is an enormous gift, and it carries enormous sacrifice."

Hagar's eyes filled. "I just don't want you to worry that I'll change my mind. I won't. I'm committed to this."

"I don't pretend to know exactly what you're feeling," Sarah whispered. "But I do know what it feels like to want something so badly it hurts. And then fear that when you finally have it, you'll break under the weight of it."

Tears slipped quietly down Hagar's cheeks.

Sarah continued, her voice trembling now.

"And honestly…I've been scared too. Scared that I'll love this child so much but always feel like I missed something because I couldn't carry him myself."

The room thickened with shared tears, silent and sacred.

"Do you resent me?" Hagar whispered.

Sarah's answer came immediately, without hesitation.

"No. I'm grateful for you. I know what you've given up for us…for me. But I'd be lying if I said this has always been easy."

Hagar gave a weak smile.

"Me too."

They both laughed softly now—a strange, almost exhausted relief to finally speak the things they'd tiptoed around for months.

Sarah tightened her grip on Hagar's hand.

"When he's born, I won't forget you, Hagar. Not ever. You'll always be part of his story. Of ours."

Hagar wiped her cheeks and nodded, voice breaking again.

"Thank you."

For the first time, they sat together not as an employer and assistant, or even as intended parent and surrogate—but as two women who had learned to hold both gratitude and grief inside the same fragile miracle.

32 Weeks—Hagar's Apartment

The rain tapped softly against the windows as Hagar sat cross-legged on the couch, hands resting protectively over her swollen belly. The soft hum of the white noise machine played in the background—something her midwife had suggested to help her sleep, though tonight, it wasn't working.

Sleep had become harder these past few weeks—not because of the physical discomfort, but because of the growing ache inside her chest.

She rubbed slow circles across her belly.

"You're safe," she whispered. "You're growing strong. Almost there."

The baby kicked gently in response.

And as always, the moment was both beautiful and deeply painful.

The Duality

Her apartment felt emptier these days.

The boundaries between Sarah's life and hers had grown strangely blurred as the pregnancy advanced.

She attended appointments with them.

She texted updates to them.

She smiled at their gratitude.

But every night, she came home—alone.

You're not his mother, she kept reminding herself.

But as the days passed, her heart refused to fully cooperate with that reality.

She whispered again:

"I won't get to see your first steps. Or hear your first word. Or comfort you when you're sick."

Her throat tightened.

"That's not my role."

The Weight of Isolation

Hagar stood and wandered toward the nursery she had *not* allowed herself to create. No crib. No clothes. No signs of the child growing inside her—a protective strategy advised by her counselor.

But the absence of those things didn't lessen the ache. If anything, it made it worse.

She paced, her mind racing.

Maybe I made a mistake.

The thought hit like a lightning bolt.

No—*don't think that.*

But once the door cracked open, it refused to close again.

What if I can't do it? What if I can't let go?

The Tension with Sarah

Her phone buzzed—a message from Sarah.

"Just checking in—any new kicks tonight?"

Hagar stared at the screen, her stomach flipping.

She loved Sarah. Admired her. Respected her.

And yet...she resented her too.

Sarah would get to hold him forever.

Hagar would only hold him for a few more weeks.

Her fingers hovered over the keyboard as tears filled her eyes.

She typed:

"He's moving lots tonight. Strong little guy."

Then hit send—choosing love over truth.

The Quiet Breakdown

She finally collapsed onto her bed, curling around her stomach protectively, letting the tears fall freely now.

"God, help me," she whispered into the darkness.

"Help me release him."

Hagar's Journal Entry—32 Weeks

I'm starting to have dreams. Vivid ones.
Sometimes I'm holding him. Sometimes Sarah is. Sometimes both of
us.
I wake up crying.
I pray every night now:
Lord, protect my heart. Protect my motives. Protect this child.
Help me release him with grace when the time comes.
And help me not confuse my sacrifice with ownership.

Sarah & Abe's Apartment—Late Evening

The city was unusually quiet that night, as if even Manhattan sensed the fragile tension filling their apartment.

Sarah sat at the dining table, scrolling absentmindedly through her phone, though she wasn't reading anything. The half-finished dinner sat untouched on the kitchen counter behind her.

Abe came out of the bedroom, loosening his collar. He paused when he saw her still sitting there.

"Sarah."

She looked up, forcing a small smile. "Hey."

"You've barely eaten."

"Not really hungry."

Abe stepped closer, sensing the weight behind her words. He pulled out a chair across from her, sitting down, folding his hands on the table.

"Let's talk."

Sarah hesitated for a long moment. She was tired of pretending, tired of smiling through a pain she was afraid to name.

Finally, she whispered, "I feel like I'm losing you."

Abe's eyes widened slightly. "Sarah…"

She shook her head quickly, blinking back tears. "I know you love me. I don't question that. But ever since Hagar started carrying the baby,

I feel like I've been watching you connect with her in ways you've stopped connecting with me."

Abe exhaled slowly, his voice gentle. "She's carrying our child. Of course I've grown close to her in some ways. But it's not what you think."

Sarah swallowed hard. "I don't think you're having an affair, Abe. That's not what I'm afraid of. I'm afraid that emotionally, you're drifting... that this experience is bonding you to her in ways I can't reach."

Abe reached across the table, his hand covering hers. "I never wanted any of this to create distance between us. You know that."

She nodded, voice barely audible. "I do. But I can feel it anyway."

For a moment, they sat in heavy silence.

"I don't know how to fix it," Sarah finally admitted. "I want to be grateful. I want to be strong. But sometimes I feel like a bystander in my own miracle."

Abe's face softened, his own eyes glistening now. "You are not a bystander. You are the reason we even have this miracle. You carried the years of waiting. You carried the heartbreak. You carried the prayers. This child exists because of your faith."

Sarah's shoulders shook as tears finally spilled freely.

"I need you to stay close to me in this, Abe. Don't let her experience—" she paused, choking on the words, "—don't let *her pregnancy* pull you further from me."

Abe stood and moved around the table, kneeling beside her chair. He gently took her face in his hands.

"I promise you, Sarah. My heart belongs to you. It always has. It always will. We are so close to the end of all of this. I promise it will get back to being just you and me very soon."

She closed her eyes as he rested his forehead against hers. For a moment, their breath synchronized—two hearts recalibrating after months of quiet drift.

"I don't want to lose us," she whispered.

"You won't," Abe vowed softly. "We're not finished. God's not finished."

Hagar's Apartment—Late Night

The city hummed faintly outside her tiny window as Hagar sat cross-legged on her bed, the dim light of her bedside lamp casting soft shadows across the room. The baby shifted inside her belly—a gentle kick reminding her once again that time was running short.

She rested her hand over the curve of her stomach, exhaling.

"This isn't mine," she whispered softly to the empty room.

But no matter how many times she repeated it, the words landed heavier with each passing week.

At the start, it had felt so simple. Selfless, even. A way to give back. A way to help Sarah—her mentor, her boss, her friend—receive the miracle she had longed for. Hagar had stepped into this with confidence, believing it was the right thing.

And yet...she hadn't anticipated the ache.

She hadn't anticipated how easy it would be to enjoy Abe's gentle concern at appointments, his kind words, his protective questions about her health. She hadn't anticipated how much she would begin to long for someone to care for her that way—not as a surrogate, but as a woman.

It wasn't romantic. It wasn't even inappropriate. But it was dangerous in ways she hadn't understood before now.

Her phone buzzed on the nightstand—a text from Sarah:

"Don't forget—final OB appointment Friday. I'll meet you there after my morning meeting. Rest well tonight, sweet girl"

Hagar's stomach twisted. Sarah had always gone out of her way to include her, honor her. And yet, the more Sarah included her, the more excluded Hagar sometimes felt—as if she was being asked to both belong and not belong at the same time.

This child isn't yours. But you're carrying him.
This family isn't yours. But you're living in their center.

Tears pricked her eyes as the baby kicked again—as if responding to her thoughts.

She whispered into the quiet. *"I don't want to feel this. I don't want to want more."*

She pulled her Bible from the nightstand—the one Sarah had gifted her when she first started attending church—and flipped aimlessly until she landed on *Psalm 51*.

"Create in me a clean heart, O God, and renew a right spirit within me."

Hagar closed her eyes and prayed softly, tears slipping down her cheeks.

"God...guard my heart. Don't let me desire what isn't mine. Help me honor Sarah. Help me release this child fully to her."

The baby shifted again, settling.

Hagar breathed deeply, cradling her belly one more time before lying back down.

"I am only the vessel," she whispered, almost as a mantra. *"This is not my story to steal."*

But as sleep finally pulled her under, the ache remained quietly inside her—unresolved.

Sarah & Abe's Apartment—Two Weeks Before the Due Date

The tension had been building for months—layer upon layer of unspoken fears, fragile gratitude, and quiet distance. Tonight, it finally cracked.

Sarah stood in the nursery, folding tiny clothes into neat piles on the dresser. The room was ready: crib assembled, bottles sanitized, rocking chair positioned near the window.

The only thing missing was the part she'd always dreamed would come first—the experience of carrying the child herself.

Abe entered the doorway, watching her work. "You've been nesting all afternoon."

Sarah smiled faintly but didn't look up. "Keeps my hands busy."

A long pause hung between them.

"We got the hospital paperwork back today," Abe offered gently.

"They're ready when we are."

Sarah kept folding. "That's good."

But her voice cracked slightly as the words left her mouth.

Abe stepped closer, sensing the weight behind her quietness.

"Talk to me."

Sarah finally stopped folding and turned to face him, her eyes already glistening.

"I thought I was stronger than this."

"Stronger than what?"

"Stronger than...this jealousy." She swallowed hard, tears slipping down her cheeks. "I've tried, Abe. I've tried so hard to be grateful. To be gracious. But watching her carry our child...it's killing me."

Abe's face softened, his own heart breaking at her honesty.

"She's been incredible," Sarah continued, her voice trembling.

"But I can't deny what it feels like every time I see her hand resting on my baby. Every time she talks about the kicks, or the cravings, or the contractions starting."

She shook her head, biting her lip. "And then I see how close you two have become. The way you comfort her, the way you check on her, the way you laugh with her."

Abe reached for her hands. "Sarah—"

"I know you love me," she whispered. "I don't doubt that. But I feel like this pregnancy belongs to the two of you...and I'm just waiting to be handed the child when it's over."

Abe's eyes filled. "I hate that you feel that way."

Sarah's voice cracked into sobs. "I feel like she got to experience something with you that I never will."

Abe pulled her into his chest, holding her tightly as her shoulders shook.

"I wish I could take that pain from you," he whispered.

"I wish there was another way."

For a long moment, they stood like that—both grieving what couldn't be changed.

Finally, Sarah whispered into his chest. "I need you to choose me again, Abe. After this is over. After the baby comes. I need to know we'll still be us."

Abe gently lifted her chin so their eyes met. "We will be. I swear it, Sarah. You are my covenant. She's part of the process, not part of our story."

Sarah's tears slowed as she breathed deeply.

"And I need to release this bitterness," she whispered.

"Because if I carry it into motherhood, I'll destroy the very blessing I've prayed for."

Abe nodded gently. "Then let's release it together."

In the quiet nursery—fully prepared for the child who hadn't yet arrived—they bowed their heads together and whispered their fragile prayer: for peace, for grace, for healing.

Holly Bogdan

Act IV - Isaac

The Covenant

"As for me, this is my covenant with you: You will be the father of many nations. No longer will you be called Abram; your name will be Abraham, for I have made you a father of many nations. I will make you very fruitful; I will make nations of you, and kings will come from you. I will establish my covenant as an everlasting covenant between me and you and your descendants after you for the generations to come, to be your God and the God of your descendants after you. The whole land of Canaan, where you now reside as a foreigner, I will give as an everlasting possession to you and your descendants after you; and I will be their God."

Then God said to Abraham, "As for you, you must keep my covenant, you and your descendants after you for the generations to come.

God also said to Abraham, "As for Sarai your wife, you are no longer to call her Sarai; her name will be Sarah. I will bless her and will surely give you a son by her. I will bless her so that she will be the

mother of nations; kings of peoples will come from her."
Abraham fell facedown; he laughed and said to himself, "Will a son
be born to a man a hundred years old? Will Sarah bear a child at the
age of ninety?" And Abraham said to God, "If only Ishmael might live
under your blessing!"
Then God said, "Yes, but your wife Sarah will bear you a son, and you
will call him Isaac.

Genesis 17:4-9, 15-19 (NIV)

CHAPTER 30

The Delivery

Delivery Day

The contractions came early. It wasn't supposed to happen this way—not yet. The baby was only thirty-four weeks, and Sarah had barely finished packing the hospital bag she kept near the door. The phone call came just after midnight.

"Sarah's eyes flew open as her phone buzzed on the nightstand. She fumbled for it, her heart already racing before she answered. Hagar's voice was thin, panicked:

"Sarah…my water broke. I'm at the hospital. They're saying I'm in labor."

Sarah sat bolt upright. "What? But—you're only 34 weeks."

"I know," Hagar's voice cracked. "They're trying to stop it but…it's happening fast."

Sarah was already out of bed, flipping on the light and pulling on her jeans.

As she shouted for Abe, she told Hagar, "We're on our way. Stay calm. We'll be there in ten minutes."

Abe was already pulling on jeans beside her. His face was pale but steady. "I'll call the hospital. Let's go."

The drive to the hospital was a blur of city lights and rain-streaked windows. Sarah's heart pounded against her ribs, a sick mixture of fear and helplessness twisting inside her.

When Hagar's water broke, all the tension that had built between them was stripped away by urgency. There was no time for resentment or regret—only the raw, primal reality of what was about to happen.

Hospital—Labor & Delivery

The car ride flew past in a haze of sirens and whispered prayers. Abe gripped Sarah's hand tightly as they sped through the quiet, glowing streets of the city.

When they arrived at Manhattan General, a nurse quickly ushered them to the maternity floor.

Hagar was already in a delivery room, monitors beeping steadily around her. She looked small and overwhelmed in the wide hospital bed, an oxygen tube resting beneath her nose, sweat clinging to her brow.

Her eyes lit up when she saw them. "You made it."

Sarah rushed to her side. "Of course we did."

"The baby's coming fast," Hagar whispered. "They said he's in distress."

Sarah swallowed hard, trying to stay calm for both of them.

"You're doing great. Just keep breathing."

A nurse entered briskly. "We're preparing for delivery now. The NICU team is on standby since baby is early."

Sarah's stomach clenched at the words. NICU. Neonatologist. Premature.

"Breathe with me," Sarah whispered. "Just like the class."

"I don't know if I can do this," Hagar gasped through gritted teeth.

"Yes, you can," Sarah said, her voice firmer. "You already are." Abe's voice was low as he leaned toward Sarah. "We trust God. Just like we have been…in every step."

She nodded quickly, gripping his hand tighter.

The Delivery

The hours blurred. At one point, during a brief lull between contractions, Hagar reached for Sarah's hand.

"I never wanted to hurt you," Hagar whispered through tears. "I know we crossed lines we shouldn't have. I know I…confused things." Sarah's own tears spilled freely now. "I forgive you. You've given us life. You've carried our miracle. That will always matter more."

They both sat in the sacred space between brokenness and grace, holding hands as another contraction built.

Abe stood nearby, watching, his face pale but filled with gratitude—for both women.

Contractions intensified. Nurses swirled around them. Monitors beeped in sharp, steady tones. The OB, Dr. Malik, arrived and quickly assessed the situation.

"We don't have time to wait. Baby's heart rate is dropping between contractions. We're delivering now."

The delivery team snapped into position. Sarah stood near Hagar's head, holding one trembling hand while Abe stood behind her, offering steady strength, as he said a quick prayer, *"Lord, we have seen you do miracles time and time again. We ask that you grant us a safe delivery in Jesus' name."*

"Amen. You're doing amazing," Sarah whispered, though her own voice trembled.

Hagar nodded through gritted teeth, sweat pouring down her face. "I'm scared."

"I know," Sarah whispered, stroking her hair. "But you're not alone. We're right here."

"Big push, Hagar!" Dr. Malik called.

Hagar pushed with every ounce of strength left in her body. Tears streamed down her face as she fought through the pain.

Another push. And another.

The process was raw and violent. Screams, sweat, tears—a mixture of agony and hope. Sarah whispered encouragement with each push, her hand never leaving Hagar's.

"You're almost there. Just a little more. You've got this."

Finally, a small, sharp cry pierced the air.

"He's here!" Dr. Malik called out.

The tiny baby was rushed immediately to the NICU team stationed nearby. The umbilical cord was cut quickly—there was no leisurely first cuddle.

Sarah's breath caught as she watched the neonatologists work.

"Is he okay?" she whispered, her voice breaking.

A nurse turned and offered a tight but hopeful smile.

"He's breathing. He's small, but he's breathing."

Sarah collapsed into Abe's arms, sobbing in relief.

Minutes later, a nurse brought the tiny, swaddled bundle over to Sarah, her voice gentle. "He's stable enough for a few minutes of skin-to-skin before we take him upstairs."

Sarah and Abe stood frozen, awe-struck.

The pediatrician turned to them. "Would you like to meet your son?"

Sarah's hands shook as she reached out for him, her breath catching completely when she felt the warm, fragile weight settle onto her chest. Tiny. Perfect. Hers.

His skin was flushed pink, his breath quick and shallow but steady. His fingers curled instinctively around the edge of her hospital gown.

Sarah whispered through her tears. "Hello, my sweet boy."

Abe joined her, wrapping his arms around both Sarah and the baby. His voice broke as he whispered, "Ishmael, you're really here."

"He's perfect."

Abe kissed her forehead, his own tears falling freely.

In the corner of the room, Hagar lay exhausted, watching them silently, her face a complicated mixture of exhaustion, relief, and something unspoken. She smiled softly, but her eyes glistened.

She watched as Sarah and Abe became parents before her eyes—and she let go.

Sarah glanced at her, their eyes locking across the space that had always existed between them.

"Thank you, Hagar" Sarah whispered, her voice breaking.

"Thank you for bringing him into the world."

Hagar nodded, her lips trembling. "He's yours. You're his mother now."

And with that simple sentence, the line between them was drawn—and crossed—all at once.

The nurse gently lifted the baby after a few precious minutes.

"We'll get him settled upstairs now."

Sarah's eyes never left her son as they wheeled him away.

Abe wrapped his arms around her tightly, holding her upright as her knees threatened to buckle.

"We did it," he whispered.

"No," Sarah said softly. "God did it."

And for the first time in years, Sarah felt the weight of waiting finally lift, replaced by the fragile but undeniable weight of answered prayer.

NICU—Day One

The day following the birth were a whirlwind. Doctors, nurses, lactation consultants, and social workers moved in and out of the hospital room with careful routines.

Because the baby was premature, he was sent directly to the neonatal intensive care unit. Sarah and Abe took turns sitting beside the small incubator, watching his tiny chest rise and fall beneath the soft hum of machines. Tiny wires and tubes attached to Ishmael's fragile body traced his every heartbeat, every breath. His eyes fluttered beneath paper-thin lids.

Sarah stood beside the isolette, her hand gently resting on the side of the incubator.

"He's a fighter," one of the NICU nurses had whispered earlier that morning. "He's stronger than we even expected for 34 weeks."

Sarah wiped away another tear as she stared at her son. *Her* son. Sarah felt the deepest kind of love she had ever known—but also a quiet ache that hadn't fully gone away.

Abe stood behind her, his hands resting gently on her shoulders.

"Look at him," Abe whispered. "Perfect."

Sarah exhaled shakily. "I still can't believe he's really here."

A knock on the NICU door interrupted the moment.

It was Hagar.

She stepped inside cautiously, her face pale, her movements still slow from the delivery. She hadn't yet been back to see Ishmael. The doctors had urged her to rest, but Sarah knew there was more than just physical exhaustion keeping her away.

Guilt. Fear. Grief.

"Hi," Hagar whispered.

Sarah turned, her voice gentle. "Come in."

Hagar approached slowly, standing beside Sarah now. She peered through the incubator's clear wall, her breath catching as she saw him up close for the first time since the delivery.

"He's strong," Hagar whispered.

Sarah nodded, swallowing the lump in her throat. "Yes. He is."

For a long moment, neither of them spoke.

Finally, Hagar turned toward Sarah, her voice trembling. "I want you to know…I never thought this would be so hard."

Sarah's eyes filled. "I know."

"I've given him to you freely. But that doesn't mean my heart isn't breaking."

Tears spilled down Sarah's cheeks. "I can't imagine the sacrifice you've made."

Hagar smiled softly, blinking quickly to contain her own emotions. "I'll be okay. I have to be."

Sarah swallowed hard, searching for words.

"Would you… like to touch him?"

Hagar's eyes welled with tears instantly. "Are you sure?"

Sarah nodded, her voice breaking. "Yes."

A nurse nearby opened one of the access ports, guiding Hagar's hand gently inside. Her fingertips brushed his tiny arm, and she gasped at the warmth and softness.

"Hi, little one," she whispered. "You've already done more than I ever have in my whole life."

Tears slipped down her face freely now as she gently withdrew her hand.

Sarah reached out, pulling Hagar into a gentle embrace. They stood that way for a long time, bound together by something neither of them could have fully predicted when this journey began.

As Hagar pulled away, she looked one last time at the sleeping baby.

"Take care of him," she whispered.

Sarah nodded, her voice breaking. "I will. With everything I have."

After Hagar left, Sarah sat beside the incubator once again, placing her hand gently against the glass.

The storm of waiting, hoping, fearing—it was over. And yet, something new was beginning—something just as fragile and uncertain.

Abe entered quietly, wrapping his arms around Sarah's shoulders.

"He's ours," he whispered.

Sarah nodded, tears falling freely. "He's ours."

But even as she said it, she knew that the story between her, Abe, and Hagar wasn't fully finished. Some things linger beneath the surface, waiting for time to heal what words alone cannot.

NICU—Night One

The beeping was constant.

Monitors blinked in steady rhythms as Sarah sat beside the tiny incubator, her chair pulled as close as the cords and equipment would allow.

Ishmael lay inside, swaddled in a nest of soft linens, a tiny oxygen cannula resting beneath his nose. His chest rose and fell with short, quick breaths. Machines carefully recorded every beat, every breath, every fluctuation.

Sarah rested her hand on the incubator wall, her palm flattening against the clear plastic as if trying to transmit her love directly through it.

Abe had gone home to shower and rest—a choice they made so at least one of them could function in the morning. But Sarah couldn't leave.

Not yet.

Not while he was fighting.

Sarah's Whispered Prayer

She closed her eyes, whispering just above the machines:

"Lord, I know this child is Your promise. You knit him together. You opened this door."

Her voice cracked.

"But why now, Lord? Why so soon? Why the fight? Haven't we waited long enough already?"

Tears dripped silently onto her lap.

"I trust You. I do. But I am so afraid."

The monitors beeped in steady response—their own kind of lullaby.

"Protect him," she whispered. "I rebuke every plan of the enemy. You said, 'Be fruitful and multiply.' You said, 'I have come that they may have life.' I speak life over him now."

She closed her eyes, repeating softly:

"He shall live and not die. He shall live and not die."

Her hand trembled against the incubator wall.

"I will not hand him over to fear, Lord. Not tonight."

Hospital Legal Office—The Following Morning

The conference room was sterile and quiet, a far cry from the NICU.

A social worker, an attorney, and a hospital administrator sat across the table. The formalities felt cold, but necessary.

On the table lay a stack of legal documents: final consent forms, parental rights assignments, and legal confirmation of Sarah and Abe's sole parentage.

Hagar sat across from them, her hands clasped tightly in her lap.

The attorney spoke first, gently but firmly. "Hagar, these documents will permanently relinquish any parental rights to the child. You're signing voluntarily, and you're under no obligation. Are you certain you wish to proceed?"

Hagar nodded, though her voice quivered. "Yes. I'm certain."

The attorney slid the paperwork toward her. "When you're ready."

For a moment, Hagar's hand hovered above the pen. Her eyes flicked briefly toward Sarah, and then Abe. Both were watching her, hearts pounding in their chests.

Sarah whispered softly, her voice breaking, "Only if you're ready."

Hagar smiled weakly. "He was never mine, Sarah. He was always yours."

Her voice barely held steady as she signed the papers, one line at a time. When it was finished, the attorney gathered the forms and spoke quietly. "Congratulations, Mr. and Mrs. Abrams. Your son is officially yours."

Sarah exhaled deeply, relief and sorrow crashing together inside her.

Hagar stood to leave, pausing for a moment.

She turned to Sarah. "Promise me you'll tell him one day...that he was always wanted."

Sarah nodded, tears falling freely now. "I promise."

Abe stepped forward, pulling Hagar into a gentle, respectful hug. "We're grateful for you—more than we'll ever be able to say."

Hagar smiled through tears as she whispered, "Take care of him."

Then, quietly, she left the room.

Sarah stood frozen for a moment, overwhelmed by the finality of it all.

Abe took her hand. "He's home now, Sarah. In every way."

Sarah closed her eyes, breathing deeply, before whispering back, "Let's go to him."

NICU—Night Three

The days blurred. Sunrises and sunsets melted into one long vigil of monitors, doctors, whispered updates, and carefully measured ounces of formula.

But tonight was different.

The doctor had pulled her aside that afternoon:

"He's stable. Breathing stronger. He's improving, Sarah."

The words had brought instant relief, but now that the immediate fear was fading, a new weight settled in, the emotional fallout.

Sarah sat in the glider across from his isolette now, exhausted but unable to leave. She pulled her Bible from her tote bag and opened it at random.

Her eyes fell on *Romans 4:18:*

"Against all hope, Abraham in hope believed and so became the father of many nations, just as it had been said to him, "So shall your offspring

be."

Tears filled her eyes.

Abraham's hope.

Her Abraham.

Their child.

"Being fully persuaded that God had power to do what He had promised."

She exhaled shakily, whispering through her tears.

"I am trying to be fully persuaded, Lord. Help my unbelief."

NICU—Night Five

The nurse approached quietly.

"Would you like to hold him tonight, Mama?"

Sarah's breath caught in her throat.

"Yes. Please."

The nurse gently lifted Ishmael from the isolette, carefully arranging the wires and tubes before placing his tiny frame into Sarah's waiting arms.

The warmth of his body against her chest unlocked something inside her.

She wept openly now, unable to hold it back.

He was here.

He was alive.

He was hers.

"Thank You, Lord," she whispered. "Thank You."

For the first time since his birth, Sarah exhaled fully.

The fear was not gone, but faith was louder.

Manhattan General—Postpartum Room

The room was still. Quiet.

No more monitors, no more teams of specialists.

Just Sarah, Abe, and the tiny bundle sleeping peacefully in the bassinet beside the bed.

For the first time since his arrival, Ishmael was finally with them—discharged from NICU observation after five nights that felt like an eternity and placed fully in their care.

Sarah sat upright in bed, exhausted but wide awake, unable to take her eyes off the baby.

Abe moved quietly around the room, refilling her water cup, tidying small things just to keep his hands moving. The adrenaline that had carried them for days was finally crashing, but neither of them wanted to sleep.

Sarah's voice was quiet, almost reverent.

"He's smaller than I imagined."

Abe smiled softly, looking down at their son.

"He's perfect."

The baby's tiny fist flexed as his lips pursed in soft little sucking motions. His skin was pinker now, the nurses having removed most of the wires and monitors earlier that morning.

Sarah reached gently into the bassinet and lifted him to her chest. She cradled him there, listening to his breath, the rise and fall of his tiny chest against hers.

Tears slipped down her face as she whispered, "You're really here."

Abe sat beside her on the bed, wrapping one arm around her shoulder as they sat together in awe of the life they had waited so long to hold.

A Few Hours Later—Visitors

Lottie arrived first, her eyes already filled with tears before she even crossed the room.

"Oh, Sarah," she whispered, pulling her into a careful hug while eyeing the sleeping baby.

Sarah handed Ishmael to her gently.

"Meet your nephew."

Lottie's breath caught as she cradled the tiny boy.

"Look at you. You're a miracle."

She looked up at Sarah, voice thick.

"I've prayed for this moment for years."

Sarah smiled softly, feeling the lump form in her throat.

"Me too."

Mara arrived soon after, her own arms full of takeout bags and bright balloons.

"I figured you two hadn't eaten anything real since all this started," she joked as she carefully placed the bags on the counter. "Also...these balloons were not optional. I saw them and couldn't help myself."

Sarah laughed softly, grateful for the lightness.

Mara's expression turned more serious as she approached the baby.

"May I?"

"Of course."

Mara gently stroked the baby's head as she whispered a quiet prayer under her breath:

"Father, thank You for this life. Protect him. Use him. May his name be known for Your glory."

Sarah closed her eyes briefly, deeply moved by her friends' presence—friends who had prayed, believed, and carried hope with her for so long.

Later That Night—Quiet Again

Abe was finally asleep on the couch across the room, his arm slung over his eyes, completely spent.

Sarah sat awake once again, rocking Ishmael gently as moonlight filtered through the window.

The ache she thought would disappear after birth remained—but it was different now. Not the ache of waiting, but of fragility. Of knowing how much could still go wrong. Of knowing how deeply she loved this child already.

She whispered softly to the sleeping baby:

"I'll probably fail you sometimes. But I promise you, little one, I will never stop fighting for you. I'll never stop thanking God for you." The tears came again, but not like before. These were not the tears of waiting.

These were the tears of having finally arrived.

CHAPTER 31

The Homecoming

One Week After Ishmael's Birth—Their Apartment

The moment Sarah stepped across the apartment threshold carrying Ishmael in her arms, something inside her cracked open.

This was the moment she had imagined for years. The nursery they had decorated months ago was now complete—not just with furniture, but with the child who belonged here.

Abe followed behind her, setting down bags while carefully watching both mother and baby. His movements were protective, almost reverent.

"Welcome home, little one," he whispered softly.

Sarah stood in the center of the living room for a moment, unable to move.

"I almost don't want to put him down."

Abe smiled gently. "You don't have to. Not yet."

She finally exhaled and slowly carried Ishmael into the nursery. The soft colors, the rocking chair, the sunlight streaming through the pale curtains—everything was exactly as they'd planned. And yet, standing there with him now felt surreal.

She laid him gently in the bassinet, her hand resting on his tiny chest. His breath rose and fell in steady little puffs.

Abe appeared behind her, wrapping his arms around her waist.

"You did it, Sarah."

Sarah's voice trembled. "We did it."

That Evening

Dinner sat untouched on the kitchen table, both of them too exhausted to eat. Sarah paced back and forth in the nursery, checking on Ishmael every few minutes even as he slept peacefully.

Abe watched her from the doorway.

"You've been standing for hours."

Sarah gave a weak smile. "What if something happens while I'm not looking?"

He stepped inside, his voice soft but steady.

"He's safe. You don't have to stand guard every second."

She shook her head slightly.

"I waited so long for him, Abe. I just...I don't know how to fully let myself relax."

Abe took her hand, guiding her gently to the rocking chair.

"Sit. Breathe. You're allowed to enjoy him."

As she sat, her voice cracked under the weight of her emotions.

"Sometimes I still feel like I borrowed him. Like this isn't fully real. Like God could still take him back."

Abe knelt in front of her, steadying her gaze.

"He's ours, Sarah. Fully. Completely. You are his mother."

Tears filled her eyes as she whispered, "But I didn't carry him."

"No," Abe said softly. "But you carried this promise for years.

You carried every loss. Every disappointment. Every prayer. You carried this family long before today."

She sobbed now, releasing the grief she hadn't allowed herself to feel fully in the hospital.

"I'm afraid, Abe."

He held her tightly.

"I know. But you're not alone."

Two Weeks After Ishmael's Birth—Marcus's Rooftop

The night air was cool but comfortable as the four men gathered on Marcus's rooftop—one of their favorite unofficial hangouts above the city skyline.

A small outdoor heater glowed beside them as Marcus handed out the cigars he had been saving for this exact occasion.

"This isn't just any cigar, gentlemen," Marcus declared.

"This is a 'miracle baby' cigar."

The guys chuckled as they each accepted one.

Abe turned the cigar slowly in his fingers, smiling.

"Ishmael's finally home. That alone feels surreal."

Jordan lit his and blew out a slow stream of smoke into the night sky.

"How's Sarah doing now that you're home and settled?"

Abe smiled genuinely for the first time in what felt like months.

"She's amazing. Exhausted, but amazing. She's bonding with him beautifully. It's like the last two years of struggle have finally softened into something peaceful."

Eli nodded.

"And Hagar? Everything go okay after...everything?"

Abe exhaled carefully.

"She's back to her own life now. We've all worked hard to keep boundaries respectful, but it's still complicated emotionally. She'll always be part of his story—but not part of our home."

Marcus glanced over, his voice steady.

"And you, man? You've carried so much through all this. How are *you*?"

Abe stared quietly at the glowing ember on the tip of his cigar.

"I'm good," he said softly. "Really good. For the first time in a long time, I feel like I can finally breathe. I've been holding my breath for so long."

Jordan raised his glass.

"To answered prayers."

"To God's timing," Eli added.

Marcus smiled, lifting his own.

"To miracles we couldn't have written better ourselves."

Abe raised his glass last, his voice thick with quiet emotion.

"To Ishmael—proof that God hears."

They clinked their glasses gently, the sound echoing under the starlit Manhattan sky.

For a moment, no one spoke—all simply letting the weight of the journey settle into the night like the smoke that swirled above them.

The Next Morning—Hagar's Visit

Hagar stood at the apartment door, small gift bag in hand, her face a mixture of peace and grief.

Sarah opened the door slowly, pausing for a beat before stepping aside.

"Come in."

The apartment smelled like lavender and baby powder. Ishmael was asleep in his bassinet.

Hagar's eyes immediately drifted toward him.

"He's grown already."

Sarah nodded, her voice cautious but kind.

"He's thriving."

For a moment, neither spoke.

"He's beautiful," Hagar whispered. "You and Abe...you're already amazing parents."

Sarah swallowed hard. "Because of you."

They stood in silence for a long moment, both aware this would likely be their last private moment together.

Finally, Hagar extended the small bag.

"Just a little something—a blanket my grandmother made years ago. She always said it was for my first child...but I think maybe she didn't know what that would mean."

Sarah took the bag gently, her throat tightening.

"Thank you."

Hagar's eyes glistened.

"He's where he's supposed to be. I know that."

Sarah studied her for a moment before finally stepping forward and embracing her gently.

"We couldn't have done this without you."

Hagar whispered into the hug.

"And I couldn't have found peace without you."

When they pulled apart, Sarah offered a small, grateful smile.

"You'll always have a place in his story."

Hagar nodded, her voice thick.

"And you'll always have my prayers."

Finally, Hagar stood up to leave. "Well, I'll take my leave now."

Sarah glanced back down at Ishmael, then up at the young woman who had carried him into the world.

"You'll always be part of his story, you know."

Hagar smiled faintly, her voice breaking. "And you'll always be his mother."

Sarah stepped forward and wrapped her arms around Hagar. They stood locked in an embrace that was both release and blessing, both bittersweet and deeply sacred.

"Thank you," Sarah whispered. "For everything."

Still breathing.
Still open to the idea that this story didn't end with goodbye.
Someday, I'll build something of my own.
But tonight, I let myself feel the loss.
Because love—even the borrowed kind—always leaves a mark.

The Following Weeks

The weeks after bringing Ishmael home were filled with the small chaos of new parenthood. Feedings every few hours, diaper changes, late-night pacing through the apartment—all the moments Sarah had long dreamed of were now real.

And yet, shadows still lingered.

Though Hagar had kept her distance, her presence seemed to echo through Sarah's thoughts. She hadn't reached out since her last visit several weeks ago. There had been no texts, no calls, no polite check-ins. Just silence.

Abe was patient and gentle, always careful not to mention Hagar unless Sarah brought her up first. But the unspoken tension between them simmered.

One night, while rocking Ishmael to sleep, Sarah whispered softly into the dimly lit nursery, "You're finally here, little one. You're mine."

She said it as much for herself as for him.

Abe stood at the door, watching quietly before speaking. "You don't have to keep proving that to anyone."

Sarah glanced up, exhaustion heavy in her eyes. "Sometimes I wonder if I'm still trying to prove it to myself."

Abe walked over and placed a hand gently on her shoulder.

"Hagar gave us this gift, but you are his mother, Sarah. That has never been in question."

"I know," Sarah whispered, but the words sat heavily in her

chest.

As the weeks passed, Sarah slowly found her rhythm as a mother. The sleepless nights became more manageable—the baby's coos and smiles brought fresh joy to each day. She poured herself into the role she had prayed for, desperate to silence the lingering doubts.

But some nights, when the apartment grew quiet, Sarah's mind drifted to Hagar—wondering if she was hurting, if she regretted, if she felt abandoned.

And in those quiet moments, Sarah prayed not just for herself, but for the young woman who had given her everything.

Three Months After Ishmael's Birth—Sarah and Abe's Home

Months passed, and the silence between Sarah and Hagar held.

Then one afternoon, unexpectedly, Sarah's phone lit up with a message.

Hagar: *Hi. I hope you and the baby are doing well. I've been thinking about you both a lot. If you're open to it, I'd like to come see him sometime. But only if you're comfortable.*

Sarah stared at the message for a long time. Her stomach twisted with emotion—gratitude, fear, hesitation.

Abe noticed her stillness and looked up from across the room.

"Everything okay?"

Sarah handed him the phone. He read the message carefully, his brow furrowing slightly.

"She waited a long time to reach out," he said softly.

Sarah nodded. "I know."

"What do you want to do?"

Sarah exhaled slowly. "I don't know."

In the end, Sarah texted back.

Sarah: *We would be open to seeing you. Why don't you come by next weekend?*

The Next Saturday

Sarah found herself anxiously rearranging the living room in anticipation of Hagar's visit. She dressed Ishmael in his softest onesie, brushing his fine hair gently with trembling hands.

When the doorbell rang, Sarah's heart pounded.

Abe opened the door, and Hagar stood there, her face flushed, eyes already welling.

"He's so beautiful," Hagar whispered as she stepped inside.

Sarah smiled nervously, rocking Ishmael gently. "He's grown so much since you last saw him."

Hagar stepped closer, her eyes wide, drinking in every tiny detail of the child she had once carried.

"May I?" she asked softly.

Sarah hesitated for only a second before nodding. "Of course."

Hagar held him delicately, as though cradling a piece of her own soul. Tears rolled down her cheeks as she gently rocked him.

"I'm so grateful he's healthy...and loved," Hagar whispered.

Sarah swallowed, watching the moment with complicated emotions swirling inside her.

"We're grateful for you," Sarah said, her voice breaking.

Abe stood quietly, allowing the two women space as they navigated the fragile reunion.

For the first time since Ishmael's birth, the unspoken tension began to ease. They were no longer simply women on opposite sides of a transaction, but two souls forever intertwined by grace, sacrifice, and something neither of them could fully name.

Boundaries

The reunion with Hagar had gone better than Sarah expected—but afterward, a subtle unease lingered.

In the following weeks, Hagar began visiting more often. At first, it was brief: dropping off a small gift, offering to hold Ishmael while Sarah ran a quick errand. She was always polite, always respectful.

But slowly, Sarah began to feel the delicate line between gratitude and intrusion blurring.

One evening, after Hagar had visited again, Sarah sat quietly in the living room, watching Ishmael sleep in his bassinet while Abe scrolled through his tablet.

She broke the silence.

"Abe, do you think…she's coming around too much?"

Abe looked up. "Hagar?"

Sarah nodded. "I'm grateful for her, truly. But sometimes it feels like… she's trying to reclaim something."

Abe was quiet, choosing his words carefully. "It's natural for her to feel connected. But you're right…it's important we don't confuse her kindness with shared custody."

Sarah looked down, her voice tightening. "I'm afraid if we don't set boundaries now, it'll become harder later."

Abe reached over, taking her hand. "Then we'll do it together."

The following week, Sarah invited Hagar for coffee, determined to speak gently but firmly.

Sitting across the café table, Sarah took a deep breath.

"Hagar, I need to talk to you about something."

Hagar's eyes immediately grew cautious. "Of course."

"I'm so grateful for everything you've done…for who you are. You'll always have a special place in our lives. But for now…I need a little more space as I bond with Ishmael."

Hagar's face flushed. She nodded quickly, biting her lip. "Of course. I didn't mean to overstep."

"I know you didn't." Sarah reached for her hand. "I value you. I just need time to fully step into my role as his mother."

Tears welled in Hagar's eyes. "I understand. I really do."

They sat in heavy silence for a few moments before Hagar spoke again.

"Sarah… I never realized how complicated this would feel. For all of us."

Sarah squeezed her hand gently. "Neither did I."

And in that moment, there was not anger, but mutual ache—and a small thread of grace binding them once again.

CHAPTER 32

The Departure

Six Months After Ishmael's Birth—Sarah's Office

arah sat at her desk sorting through contracts and proposals when a gentle knock interrupted her focus. Hagar stood in the doorway, holding a white envelope. Her eyes were steady but glossy, like she'd rehearsed this moment a hundred times but still wasn't ready.

"Got a second?" she asked.

Sarah nodded, suddenly alert. "Of course. Come in."

Hagar stepped into the office slowly, the same one where she had once fetched coffees, color-coded briefs, and helped organize every detail of Sarah's ambitious pitch meetings. It felt like a lifetime ago.

She handed Sarah the envelope.

Sarah glanced at it, then back at her. "What is this?"

"My resignation." Hagar's voice was calm, but it quivered at the edges. "Effective in two weeks. I wanted to tell you in person."

Sarah sat back, stunned. "I...Hagar, are you sure? You've been such a vital part of this team, of my life. You…you're family."

"I know," Hagar said softly. "And that's why I have to go."

Sarah's brows furrowed. "Why?"

Hagar drew a breath. "Because somewhere along the way, I stopped knowing who I was. I became someone's assistant. Someone's surrogate. A helper. A vessel. But I need to find out who I am apart from all of this."

She looked around the office—at the glass windows, the framed awards, the life she had built in the margins of Sarah's world. " I didn't come here looking for any of this. I just needed a job. And fate… or maybe God…brought me to you. You were an answer to a prayer I didn't even know how to pray."

Sarah's throat tightened. "And you were an answer to mine."

There was a long silence between them, full of everything they couldn't say—the years, the heartbreak, the miracle in the middle.

"What will you do next?" Sarah finally asked, trying to keep her voice from cracking.

Hagar smiled faintly. "I already accepted an offer in Boston…something different. I'll see where it takes me. Maybe I'll find…my own version of a family. My own answered prayer."

Tears welled in Sarah's eyes. "You deserve all of that. And more."

"Ishmael will always know who his mother is," Hagar added quietly. "But he'll also know he was loved by both of us. That matters to me."

"It matters to me, too," Sarah whispered.

They stood there for a moment—mentor and assistant, mother and surrogate, sisters by circumstance. Then Sarah walked around the desk and embraced her.

"Thank you for carrying what I couldn't," Sarah said. "Not just the pregnancy. Everything."

Hagar held her tightly. "Thank you for letting me."

As Hagar turned to leave, Sarah called after her, voice breaking just slightly: "Wherever you go next…don't be a stranger. In fact, don't leave like this...come by tonight, have dinner with us, say goodbye to Ishmael."

"I'll think about it...that's a good idea actually," Hagar said, pausing in the doorway. "Yes. I'll come."

And with that, she stepped out of the office—ready to begin the journey of becoming her own.

The Call to Abe

Sarah closed her office door gently behind her, the envelope still resting on her desk like an unopened memory. She sat in her chair, staring at the space where Hagar had stood just moments ago.

A strange stillness settled in the room.

Without thinking, she reached for her phone and dialed Abe.

He answered quickly. "Hey, everything okay?"

Sarah hesitated. "She resigned."

A pause.

"Hagar?"

Sarah nodded, then remembered he couldn't see her. "Yeah. Just now. She came in, handed me a letter, said she needs to figure out who she is apart from...this life."

"Wow," Abe said. "Are you okay?"

"I don't know," Sarah admitted, her voice quieter now. "It hit harder than I expected. I knew she couldn't stay in this...orbit forever, but I thought I had more time to prepare for it."

"She's been a part of our lives for a long time," Abe said gently. "More than just work. She carried so much with us."

"I know," Sarah said. "But I think she's right. She needs her own story now."

There was a pause before Abe added, "You helped her find that strength. Don't forget that."

Sarah swallowed, blinking back the emotion. "I just hope she finds what she's looking for."

"She will," Abe said. "And we'll be cheering her on. Quietly. From a distance."

Sarah gave a small, bittersweet laugh. "It's the end of an era."

"Yeah," Abe said. "But maybe it's the start of another one, too.

For all of us."

She looked out the window, the city pulsing with motion and meaning beyond the glass.

"Thanks," she said softly, "and before I forget, I invited her over tonight for dinner so she can say goodbye to Ishmael."

"Well, that was nice. How about we meet for lunch so we can keep talking about it? I'll cancel my 1 o'clock."

Sarah smiled. "I'd like that."

Hagar's Goodbye—Sarah & Abe's Apartment

The nursery glowed with a kind of quiet mercy—the soft hush of early evening pooling along the floorboards, bathing the crib in amber light. The curtains fluttered gently in the breeze, a lullaby without music.

Hagar stood at the crib's edge, watching Ishmael sleep. He had filled out—the fragile child she once carried now warm and strong, his chest rising in steady rhythm, a tiny fist curled near his cheek. There was even a smile, faint but sure, playing on his lips as if he were dreaming of something kind.

She didn't touch him.

Not this time.

Her fingers hovered above the rail, brushing the smooth wood like it could hold the weight of her affection without crossing any boundary.

From the doorway, Sarah watched—not interrupting, not breathing too loud, simply standing still in the shadow of the moment. Then, with a softness born of hard-earned grace, she stepped inside.

"He's grown so much," Hagar whispered, her voice thick as wool. "So fast."

Sarah nodded. "He is. He's already trying to crawl out of our arms like he's got somewhere important to be."

They shared a smile, brief but genuine, and stood in silence as the room wrapped itself around them—not cold or awkward, just full of things that couldn't be said easily. Memory. Pain. Gratitude. Regret. All of it lived in that space between two women who had loved the same child, differently, but fiercely.

"I'm glad you asked me to come," Hagar said finally.

"To say goodbye."

Sarah's throat tightened. She pressed her hand against her chest to keep her voice from breaking.

"Are you sure?" she asked. "That you have to go?"

Hagar looked at her—really looked—with eyes that had once been unsure, but now were steady with peace. She gave a quiet smile, sad at the corners.

"I think it's time."

She glanced back down at Ishmael, her voice dropping to a hush.

"This was always temporary. And though part of me will always live in him...I know I can't stay at the center of your lives. Not forever. It wouldn't be fair—not to you, not to him, and not to me."

Sarah nodded, though her heart didn't want to agree.

"You gave us everything, Hagar," she said softly. "I hope you know that."

"I do."

The words hung there, gentle but full, like a candle between them.

A long pause. Not because they didn't know what to say, but because some things deserved stillness.

Then Sarah asked what had haunted her quietly for weeks.

"Do you regret any of it?"

Hagar's answer came without hesitation.

"Not for one second." Her eyes glistened. "If I had to choose again, I would still say yes. Even knowing the ending."

Sarah stepped forward, arms trembling before they wrapped around Hagar—and for the first time, the two women held each other with nothing in between.

"Thank you," Sarah whispered. "For your courage. For your obedience. For helping me become a mother."

They clung for a moment, tears mingling, sorrow and love coexisting in the space between their shoulders. When they pulled apart, they wiped their eyes with the quiet intimacy of women who had survived something sacred and unspeakable together.

"You'll tell him, right?" Hagar asked. "When he's older?"

Sarah reached for her hand, squeezing it. "I promise. He'll know how loved he was. From the very beginning. By all three of us."

Hagar smiled faintly, her voice splintering.

"That's all I want."

Behind them, Abe appeared in the hallway, leaning gently against the doorframe. He didn't interrupt, didn't intrude. He just nodded once, his eyes warm with gratitude.

"Thank you, Hagar," he said.

She returned the nod with a soft wave, her hand lingering just a little longer before she turned toward the door.

At the threshold, she paused.

Looked back one final time.

"Take good care of him."

Sarah's voice cracked. "We will."

And then the door closed behind her—not like an exile, but like a release.

Her footsteps faded down the hall, but her presence lingered. In the scent on the baby's blanket. In the quiet lullabies still echoing in the walls. In the miracle that now slept, unaware that he had been the bridge between two women and one God-woven story.

Hagar's part was over.

But her legacy would remain—not in the pages of a birth certificate, but in the marrow of a boy who would one day ask where he came from.

And who would be told the truth.

With love.

One Month After Hagar's Departure

The office hummed with its usual energy as Sarah stepped off the elevator, balancing her coffee in one hand and her tote in the other. Conference calls, market reports, and quarterly goals had slowly reclaimed their space in her daily routine.

From the outside, everything looked normal again.

But normal had changed.

The New Assistant

"Good morning, Ms. Abrams."

Kelsey—her new assistant—smiled brightly from behind the desk. She was sharp, efficient, polite. She took initiative, anticipated needs, kept the office humming.

In every professional sense, Kelsey was excellent.

But as Sarah glanced at her—her carefully curated outfits, her color-coded notebooks, her eagerness to impress—a quiet ache stirred inside her chest.

The Absence

Hagar had occupied this desk once.

Hagar, with her nervous energy that had slowly given way to quiet confidence.

Hagar, who had once brought her morning coffee without being asked, who learned to read Sarah's mood before she even spoke.

Hagar, who had crossed an impossible bridge—from employee, to confidante, to something Sarah still struggled to fully define.

And now, she was gone.

The Unexpected Grief

Sarah retreated into her office, closing the door softly behind her. The ache pressed heavier as she settled into her chair, letting the weight of it settle over her.

She missed Hagar.

Not just as her surrogate.

Not even just as the woman who had carried Ishmael.

She missed *her*.

Her laugh.

Her surprising wisdom.

Her vulnerability.

Her willingness to enter Sarah's private grief without judgment.

Hagar had entered Sarah's most broken spaces—and though complicated, her presence had been real.

Now, that absence sat quietly inside Sarah's chest—not loud or dramatic, but steady.

The Honest Admission

Later that evening, as she and Abe sat quietly after dinner, Sarah finally spoke it aloud.

"I miss her."

Abe glanced up from his laptop, understanding immediately.

"Hagar?"

Sarah nodded, her voice tight.

"I know it's complicated. I know boundaries had to be set. But she was...part of it all. Part of the waiting. The hope. The miracle."

Abe reached across the table and squeezed her hand gently.

"It's okay to miss her...but I think it's for the best."

Sarah exhaled, allowing the tears to finally come.

"There's a part of this story that will always belong to her, Abe. And sometimes...that feels like a void no one else can fill."

Abe nodded softly, his voice steady.

"Because it is."

They sat together, hand in hand, letting the quiet grief exist right alongside their joy—the beautiful, bittersweet reality of complicated miracles.

Nine Months After Ishmael's Birth—Sarah and Abe's Home

Weeks turned into months. Ishmael grew strong, thriving under Sarah and Abe's care. His first smiles, his first giggles, his first wobbly attempts at rolling over—every milestone filled Sarah's heart with wonder and gratitude.

But despite the joy, Sarah still felt the quiet space that had opened between her and Hagar widening with each passing day.

The text messages grew less frequent since she left for Boston. Hagar seemed to retreat into her own world, and though Sarah had longed for boundaries, the growing distance now felt oddly painful.

One afternoon, Sarah sat with Abe on the balcony, the city humming quietly below them. Ishmael napped peacefully in his crib inside.

"Have you heard from her?" Sarah asked softly.

Abe shook his head. "Not for some time now."

Sarah stared out over the skyline. "I thought space would help. And it has, in some ways. But…I don't want her to disappear completely."

"She probably needs this time to heal, Sarah," Abe said gently.

"To find her own life again."

Sarah nodded, but her heart was heavy.

"She gave up so much for us," Sarah whispered.

"Sometimes I wonder if I've been selfish."

Abe turned to her, his voice steady. "You've done everything with love. With grace. You honored her. You honored this gift."

Sarah sighed, leaning her head against his shoulder.

"I just wish I knew she was okay."

"Then maybe you should tell her that," Abe said softly.

That evening, after Ishmael was asleep, Sarah sat at her kitchen table, staring at her phone for a long time before finally typing:

Sarah: *Thinking of you tonight. Grateful for you. Always. I hope you're doing well.*

She hit send and waited.

For a long while, nothing came.

But just as Sarah was about to turn off the light and head to bed, her phone buzzed.

Hagar: *Thank you, Sarah. I'm okay. Healing. And I'm grateful too.*

Sarah stared at the screen, tears pooling in her eyes. For the first time in months, she felt peace.

The threads of their story were not severed, but gently loosening, as they each stepped into the next chapters of their lives.

Saturday—Four Months Later

The café patio was alive with the gentle chaos of spring—the clinking of iced tea glasses, a low hum of laughter from the far corner, and sunlight that danced lazily across the table linens. Children shrieked in delight from a nearby playground, and the scent of blooming jasmine floated past as if summoned just for the occasion.

Sarah arrived with her hands full—a diaper bag sliding off one shoulder, her oversized tote threatening to tip from the other, and Ishmael blinking up at the world from his stroller as though deciding whether he approved of this noisy Saturday afternoon. She looked like every other mother on the patio—slightly flustered, slightly late, and already apologizing with her eyes before she'd even spoken.

Lottie was the first to wave, rising from her seat beside Mara and opening her arms as if she'd been waiting all morning just for this moment. The hug was tight and grounding.

"You made it," Lottie said, her smile wide, her iced tea already halfway gone.

"Barely," Sarah replied, her breath half-laugh, half-confession.

"I almost canceled twice. It's... hard to leave the house. Harder than I thought."

The three women sat together under the striped awning as the waitress brought menus and a round of water. Ishmael let out a delighted squeal at the sight of a golden retriever slinking past, and Sarah instinctively reached for him, but Lottie had already scooped him up, bouncing him with the ease of someone who'd surprised even herself.

"I get it now," Lottie said, eyes never leaving the baby's face. "I get why you're obsessed. He's...he's something else."

Sarah smiled—tired, genuine, full of the kind of joy that only comes when love outweighs exhaustion. "Even on the hard days," she murmured, "he's still the best part."

"He looks like Abe when he furrows his brow," Lottie mused. "Like he's calculating toddler taxes."

That made Sarah laugh—a sound that sounded like her old self for a moment. "You're good with him."

Lottie looked surprised, as if only just realizing it. "Maybe because he's yours. Or maybe because...he's him. I don't know."

The menus were opened but not read, eyes scanning more out of habit than hunger. The conversation drifted, as it always did, to the quiet things. The unspoken questions that hovered beneath the surface.

"Do you ever think about it?" Sarah asked, eyes on Lottie, voice soft. "Having your own?"

There was a pause, and then another. Lottie passed the baby back carefully, brushing a kiss over his crown, before turning her gaze toward the playground in the distance. A father was lifting his daughter onto a swing, his laughter loud and easy.

"I don't think I'm wired that way," she said finally. "At least, I never thought so. But sometimes...sometimes I wonder what it would be like. To have someone look at you the way he looks at you. Like the world begins and ends in your arms."

Sarah nodded, not with persuasion but with peace. "It's okay not to know. Or to change your mind. You don't owe anyone a fixed answer."

"That's what I love about us," Lottie said. "You've never made me feel wrong for not being you."

"Maybe the path isn't different," Sarah offered. "Just longer. Or loopier."

They laughed, and Ishmael babbled something half-formed, a jumble of syllables that made both women lean in, eyes wide.

"Did he just say 'Lottie'?" Sarah asked.

"No, I think he said 'latte,'" Lottie replied, grinning. "Which, honestly, is on brand."

Something in Lottie softened then—something that had stayed guarded for years. The kind of soft that doesn't come from answers but from being seen.

"So," she asked gently, "how is it really? Being back at work. Doing it all again."

Sarah paused, her finger tracing the rim of her glass. Her voice came slowly, not rehearsed.

"It's...strange," she said.

"Strange good, or strange hard?" Mara asked, her tone as soft as the linen napkin resting in her lap.

"Both," Sarah admitted. "Some days, I feel like I'm me again.

The version of me who could own a boardroom, close a pitch, make the world bend a little. And then other days, I stare at a spreadsheet and wonder what Ishmael's doing at daycare. I wonder if he misses me. If he knows I miss him."

She blinked quickly, trying not to let the words catch in her throat.

"It feels like I'm living between two lives. The one I had, and the one I have now. I'm not sure who I am in either."

Mara reached across the table, her fingers warm and certain.

"Guilt doesn't mean you're doing it wrong," she said.

"Sometimes it's just the heart's way of showing up."

Sarah nodded, tears threatening.

"And the other part?" Lottie asked, her voice quieter now. "The part that used to include... Hagar?"

Sarah's expression shifted—a shadow passing across her features. The laughter from earlier dulled into memory.

"I think about her more than I say out loud. She's not here. She probably won't ever be again. But I feel her. Sometimes in the way Ishmael sleeps with one hand curled near his cheek. Sometimes in the spaces where we don't speak her name."

She swallowed hard. "I miss her."

Lottie's eyes shone with understanding. "Because she carried part of your promise."

Sarah exhaled. "She carried part of me." The table went quiet. Mara's voice came last, woven with wisdom and something holy. "That's what grace feels like, Sarah. It's not clean. It's not tidy. It lets you hold gratitude and grief in the same hand."

Sarah didn't answer right away.

But when she did, her voice was soft and sure.

"That's exactly what it feels like."

The waitress arrived then, salads in hand, her bright smile unintentionally offering a pause—a breath—a gentle way to return to the world.

But the heart of the conversation lingered, tucked into the spaces between bites and laughter, where love and loss could live side by side without explanation.

The Laughter Returns

As they ate, the heaviness gradually lifted, replaced by easy laughter and old rhythms. They teased Lottie about her latest dating app misadventure. Mara shared stories from a recent counseling retreat.

For a brief moment, Sarah felt normal again—not just as a mother, or wife, or boss—but as *herself.*

As they stood to leave, Mara paused and looked at Sarah with quiet certainty.

"Do you remember what I prayed for you all those years ago? When this journey first started?"

Sarah nodded, smiling through misty eyes.

"That God would fulfill His promise."

Mara smiled.

"And He did."

Sarah whispered,

"Every single piece of it."

They hugged tightly, lingering in the embrace—three women who had walked through waiting, loss, miracles, and grace together.

And as they stepped back into the swirl of city life, Sarah felt the sacred weight of it all—not heavy, but holy.

Some weeks later—Friday Evening

Sarah stood frozen at the front door, purse on her shoulder, keys in hand, while the babysitter, Denise, bounced Ishmael gently in the living room.

"You're going to be late, honey," Abe said gently, standing beside her with an encouraging smile.

Sarah glanced at him, then back toward Ishmael.

"What if he wakes up while we're gone?"

Denise smiled warmly.

"Then I'll rock him back to sleep, just like I did with my son when he was his age."

Sarah swallowed.

"I know. I know you've got it."

"And what if he gets fussy?" she added, voice rising.

"Then I'll cuddle him and hum worship songs until he quiets down," Denise said, unbothered. "You've walked me through his routine more times than I can count."

Abe gently took Sarah's hand.

"He's okay. You're okay."

Sarah's voice cracked slightly.

"It's just...this is the first time."

"I know."

The Drive

In the car, Sarah clutched her phone like a lifeline.

Abe glanced over with a small grin.

"Do you want me to call home?"

"No...not yet."

He reached across and squeezed her hand gently.

"I promise, if anything happens, Denise will call immediately."

Sarah smiled weakly, exhaling slowly.

"Did you feel like this when you left for work that first week?"

Abe nodded honestly.

"Absolutely. But every time I came home and saw him safe and happy, it got a little easier."

Sarah wiped a stray tear, finally laughing softly.

"I feel like part of my heart is sitting back there in that apartment."

"That's exactly where it is," Abe said with a smile.

"And the other part's sitting right here next to me."

The Restaurant

By the time they reached the small Italian bistro, Sarah's pulse had finally slowed.

The candlelight flickered between them as they scanned the menu.

Abe smiled playfully.

"I love that we're on a date and you're still staring at your phone."

Sarah laughed, placing it face-down on the table.

"Okay, I'm officially present."

Abe leaned forward, his voice tender.

"You've been amazing through all of this. The waiting. The NICU. The adjustments. Motherhood."

Sarah's eyes filled again, but this time with peace rather than panic.

"Sometimes I still feel like I'm holding my breath."

Abe nodded.

"And every day we exhale just a little more."

The Check-In

Halfway through dessert, her phone buzzed.

Sarah snatched it up instinctively, heart fluttering—only to see a text from Denise:

"All good here. Ishmael is asleep."

Sarah laughed softly, handing the phone to Abe.

He chuckled, raising his glass.

"To surviving the first date night."

Sarah clinked her glass against his.

"To surviving motherhood."

The Quiet Drive Home

As they pulled into the garage later that night, Sarah exhaled fully for the first time all evening.

Abe smiled as he parked the car.

"See? We did it."

Sarah grinned.

"Now can I go hold him for just a minute?"

Abe chuckled.

"You'll never hear me say no to that."

CHAPTER 33

The Move

Short Hills, New Jersey—Local Park

The apartment was long behind them now. Life had slowly shifted from the tight corners of Manhattan into a cozy home in Short Hills, New Jersey nestled on a quiet cul-de-sac just outside the city—room to breathe, a backyard, a swing set, and the gentle rhythm of early parenthood.

"The warm spring air carried the sound of giggles and squeaky swings as Sarah settled onto a park bench, her iced coffee balanced precariously on her knee. Ishmael, now eighteen months old, toddled around the sandbox, determined to dump as much sand into his small bucket as physically possible.

Around her sat three other moms—women she was just beginning to get to know since the move out of the city.
Lindsey glanced at Ishmael with a smile.

"He's adorable, Sarah."

"Thanks," Sarah said with a grin, eyes tracking his every move. "And busy. Very, very busy."

The Conversation

Megan, bouncing her baby girl on her hip, smiled warmly.

"How long have you guys been out here now?"

"Just a few months," Sarah replied. "We moved after Ishmael was born. We wanted a little more space—and less honking outside the window."

The group laughed knowingly.

"Do you miss the city yet?" Lindsey asked.

Sarah paused, glancing at Ishmael stacking sand carefully.

"Sometimes. We still go in for work, and some weekends. But honestly? After everything Abe and I went through to get to this season...quiet feels like a gift."

The other moms nodded, sensing there was a deeper story behind her words.

The Quiet Reflection

Megan leaned forward gently, her voice low but threaded with genuine curiosity. "You mentioned once...that it took a while to have him?" It wasn't the kind of question that pried, just the kind that women ask each other when they've shared enough coffee and stories to know the silences between the lines.

Sarah nodded, slowly, her fingers brushing crumbs off her lap more out of instinct than thought. "Yeah," she said quietly.

"Years, actually. Years of waiting. Praying. Hoping. Months marked by disappointment instead of due dates. We tried everything we knew how to try...and when nothing worked, we waited. And somewhere in that waiting, I started thinking maybe the promise was for someone else." She glanced over her shoulder, eyes landing on Ishmael toddling nearby, arms flailing with joy as if he were testing gravity for the first time. Her voice thinned, just slightly. "But God was faithful. In His time, not mine."

There was a silence then—not awkward, but respectful. A stillness that passed like a prayer across the circle. Lindsey was the first to speak, her smile soft and knowing. "That's beautiful," she said simply. There was nothing else that needed to be added.

Megan nodded slowly, her own gaze drifting toward the playground where children shrieked in delight over something as simple as a plastic slide. "It's funny, isn't it?" she said. "How motherhood resets your entire definition of what matters. It shrinks the world and expands it at the same time."

Sarah let out a small laugh, dry and genuine. "I used to win campaigns. Negotiate with CEOs. Manage million-dollar launches without blinking." She lifted her iced coffee, took a slow sip, then smiled. "My biggest accomplishment today was managing to pack the diaper bag correctly on the first try."

The group erupted into that kind of laughter only mothers can share—the laugh that says me too, even if the specifics are different. It wasn't loud or attention-seeking, just warm and rooted. It filled the space between them like sunlight.

As if summoned by the joy, Ishmael came tumbling back toward her—a tiny, uncoordinated whirlwind of curls and giggles and grubby hands. Sarah opened her arms instinctively, catching him in a swoop that had become second nature. She buried her face in the softness of his neck, kissed the top of his head, and inhaled the scent of sunscreen and graham crackers.

"You're my favorite answered prayer," she whispered into his curls, the words more sacred than poetic, spoken not for the group, but for the boy in her arms.

The sun warmed her face as she leaned back against the chair, her son now nestled against her chest, his tiny hand clinging to her necklace. Around her, the voices of her friends continued—stories, laughter, shared aches, and joys—weaving themselves into the fabric of this new season.

Once, this life had felt impossibly far. A distant shore she couldn't reach, no matter how hard she swam.

But now, here it was—wrapped in sticky fingers and stolen moments of peace. Not perfect, not easy.

Just real.

Just hers.

That Afternoon—Returning to the New Nest

The sun had begun its slow descent behind the maple trees lining the quiet street as Sarah pushed open the front door to their house in Short Hills. The faint scent of lavender cleaner greeted her—the trace of the housekeeper who had come earlier that morning—but the rest was still, quiet.

She set her bag down on the mudroom bench and slipped off her shoes, calling softly, "We're home, little man."

Ishmael, toddling beside her with his sippy cup, giggled at the echo of his own footsteps on the hardwood floors. Sarah smiled, kneeling down to unbuckle his coat.

She still couldn't quite believe this was theirs.

The house, with its arched doorways and crown molding, was more than a home—it was a symbol. Of grace. Of survival.

Of the family they were becoming. The nursery upstairs still smelled faintly of fresh paint, and the kitchen bore marks of warm meals shared with Abe late into the evening. This was where her motherhood had begun—messy, unexpected, sacred.

Sarah carried Ishmael into the living room and settled into the oversized armchair by the bay window. Afternoon light filtered through sheer curtains, casting golden shadows across the oak floor.

"You were so brave today," she whispered to Ishmael, brushing his curls back from his forehead. "Meeting those kids at the park. I think you're going to love it here."

He babbled something in response—nonsensical, beautiful baby talk—and pressed his cheek to her chest. Sarah held him close, heart full.

"Abe and I wanted to build something lasting," she continued, her voice more to herself now than to her son. "And this...this is the beginning of it, Ish. This house, this street, this life."

She looked out the window, where the sun had dipped lower, setting the sky ablaze in amber and coral. She pictured Abe riding the train back from Manhattan, tired but satisfied, chasing his own legacy—just like he always dreamed.

"I hope you grow up knowing this was built for you," she whispered. "For family. For faith. For love."

And as Ishmael's breathing slowed, Sarah closed her eyes, holding him tighter, a quiet thank you rising from her chest to the heavens.

That Evening—The Commute Home to NJ

Abe leaned his head against the cool glass of the train window as the Midtown skyline blurred past, giving way to the calmer rhythm of the suburbs. The steady clatter of the NJ Transit train offered its own kind of music—a welcome contrast to the day's noise: back-to-back meetings, market projections, and phone calls that left little room to breathe. This, right here, was the hour he cherished most—not because it was quiet, but because it led him home.

He loosened his tie, rolled his shoulders, and glanced down at the folder balanced on his knee. Quarterly projections. He closed it without reading. Numbers could wait. There was a boy waiting to tell him about a rock he found in the backyard, a wife who would greet him with that look she only wore for him, and the steady warmth of a house that had become the answer to a prayer neither of them had dared to speak too loudly.

Somewhere between Secaucus and Summit, the landscape began to stretch open—buildings giving way to trees, sidewalks to driveways, the world unspooling into softness. Short Hills.

Every time the train pulled into the station, he still marveled that they'd made it here. Not just the geography of it, but the life itself: a yard that smelled like cut grass in spring, neighbors who waved from porches, a rhythm slower and more deliberate than the city would ever allow.

This wasn't just about real estate. It was about roots.

And now, roots were what they had—a son with wild curls and endless questions, and a home stitched together by moments so ordinary they felt sacred. Abe smiled as he pulled out his phone and sent a quick message:

Train's pulling in now. Be home in 10. You need anything?

The reply came almost instantly.

Just you.

He grinned, pocketing the phone, already feeling the pull of evening light and soft voices. As the train slowed and hissed to a stop, he stood and joined the flow of commuters, though part of him felt separate— held aloft by gratitude.

Not every man got to live the life he imagined when he was twenty-five. Not every man got to build something that outlived ambition—a legacy not carved in steel and salary, but in bedtime stories, refrigerator drawings, and tiny shoes by the door.

The Welcome Home

The front door clicked shut as Abe stepped into the soft quiet of the house. The scent of lavender and something warm from the oven greeting him like a gentle embrace. He dropped his briefcase gently by the entry table, already removing his tie.

From the hallway, the sound of little feet pattering on the hardwood floor grew louder—uneven, joyous, and fast.

"Dada!" Ishmael appeared, chubby arms lifted in the universal toddler request to be scooped up.

Abe dropped to his knees just in time. "Hey there, buddy! Miss me today?" he said, catching him in a tight hug. Ishmael giggled, burying his face into Abe's neck.

"Quack-quack!" Ishmael shouted gleefully. "Ducks!"

Abe pulled back slightly, smiling. "You saw ducks today?"

"Quack!" Ishmael nodded, eyes wide and earnest.

Sarah leaned against the hallway archway, one hand resting on her hip, the other tucked into the front pocket of an old NYU hoodie. Her hair was in a messy bun, and her socks didn't match—but to Abe, she looked like peace itself.

"Ducks, grass, a muddy shoe, and a very loud snack request," she said, walking toward them. "But we survived. Barely."

"Hey, you," she said, her voice low and warm.

Abe stood and crossed the space between them, pressing a kiss to her forehead. "You look like a dream," he murmured.

Sarah raised a brow. "A dream that needs a nap and a foot massage."

"Deal," he said, grinning.

She turned toward the kitchen. "Lasagna's in the oven. And I poured you a glass of wine. Figured you might need it."

"I always need it more when I'm coming home from the city," he joked, following her in. "That commute is starting to feel like a second job."

"Long day?" she asked.

"Productive," he said, leaning his forehead against hers for a moment. "But this…this is the best part."

She smiled, then turned toward the kitchen. "Let me get you some lasagna. I figured carbs and cheese are a good way to celebrate surviving another Tuesday."

Ishmael squirmed in his arms and pointed toward the dining table. "Eat!"

"Yes, sir." Abe set him down gently. Ishmael toddled off, humming to himself as he grabbed a nearby wooden spoon and began banging it softly on a cushion.

Sarah pulled plates from the cabinet, moving a little slower than usual. Abe reached around her to grab the silverware.

"He was sweet today," she said. "After he had his meltdown over the wrong sippy cup color. He picked a flower for me in the park." Abe's eyes softened. "That's my boy."

They moved easily around each other—a well-practiced rhythm of domesticity that neither of them had imagined five years ago. And yet, here it was.

As they sat at the table, Ishmael in his booster seat, holding his toddler fork like a sword, Sarah watched Abe quietly.

"You know," she said softly, "I had a moment today…just walking through the park. I realized this…this messy, duck-watching, lasagna-filled life…is exactly what I prayed for."

Abe reached for her hand across the table. "Me too."

From the highchair, Ishmael raised his arms triumphantly.

"More 'zagna!"

"Coming right up, little king," he said.

And for a while, there was only the clink of forks, the squeal of toddler joy, and the quiet, holy hush of home.

The Quiet Rooms

The dishwasher hummed softly in the background, the last dish tucked away and the counters wiped clean. Upstairs, Ishmael had finally fallen asleep after a round of bedtime stories, a sippy cup of warm milk, and one very specific request for his fuzzy blue blanket.

Sarah curled up on the sectional sofa with her knees tucked beneath her, a throw blanket draped across her lap. Abe entered from the kitchen with two mugs of chamomile tea, setting one gently in front of her before lowering himself onto the couch beside her.

"You're good at this," she murmured, accepting the mug.

"Good at what?"

"This," she gestured around the room—the soft lighting, the quiet stillness, the warmth of a family lived-in home.

"Making it feel like we belong here."

Abe leaned back and sighed, arm stretched behind her shoulders.

"Takes two."

They sat in companionable silence for a few moments, the kind that only comes from deep knowing.

Sarah finally spoke. "Ishmael's room feels so full. Of life. Of memories already."

Abe smiled. "It's because he throws half his toys on the floor."

She chuckled, then turned serious. "But the other rooms…they're quiet. Almost waiting."

He glanced at her, sensing the shift. "Waiting for what?"

She looked down into her mug, gathering the words gently. "I don't know. Maybe for a brother or sister to chase him down the hallway. For laughter echoing off the stairwell. For…life to multiply."

Abe tilted his head. "Are you saying what I think you're saying?"

She nodded, slowly. "I want to start looking into adoption."

His eyes didn't flinch. Instead, he reached for her hand and held it.

"I want to fill the rooms too," he said simply. "I've been waiting for you to say when."

Sarah looked at him, emotion rising. "I don't want Ishmael to grow up alone. He's such a gift, but it still feels like we're holding our breath. I want him to know the kind of love only a sibling can bring. And…I haven't let go of what God spoke over us either."

Abe nodded. "'Be fruitful and multiply.'"

"Exactly," she whispered. "Even if it doesn't look the way we once pictured it."

He squeezed her hand. "Then let's start. One step at a time."

The house was quiet but no longer waiting.

Ishmael Age Two—Suburban New Jersey

Time moved forward.

Ishmael grew into a bright, curious little boy—full of questions, full of energy. Sarah's days were now filled with school drop-offs, bedtime stories, scraped knees, and endless snacks. She had started the long process of researching adoption agencies, overwhelmed by the options. The quiet ache that once haunted her to carry a child in her womb had softened into something tender, like an old scar. She marveled at the way God had woven their story together—not perfectly, but purposefully.

Her relationship with Hagar settled into a distant, respectful rhythm. Occasionally, they would exchange brief messages—simple check-ins, polite and kind—but the deep entanglement they once shared had gently dissolved. Each woman carried her own version of the story now.

Sarah sometimes wondered if Ishmael would one day ask about how he came into the world—about Hagar, about the complexity of it all. She prayed for wisdom when that time came.

One evening, as Ishmael curled beside her on the couch, his little hand wrapped around her finger, Sarah whispered softly, almost to herself.

"You were worth every tear. Every wait. Every impossible prayer."

Abe watched from across the room, his eyes warm with understanding. "God's promises never fail," he said.

Sarah smiled, her heart full. "Even when they feel delayed."

Sarah sat cross-legged on the couch, her laptop open, surrounded by a sea of brochures, articles, and sticky notes.

"Still researching?" he asked, settling in beside her so he could see her laptop.

She nodded, her expression both focused and tender. "There are so many agencies. Domestic, international, private…I didn't realize how many paths there were."

Abe leaned over, scanning the screen. "What are you leaning toward?"

Sarah sighed. "Domestic. I keep reading that open adoption is more common now—birth moms can choose the family."

Abe placed a hand on her knee. "So, we'll build a profile and trust God to connect us with the right story. Just like He did before."

Sarah looked at him, tears in her eyes. "It's different this time. I'm not broken like before, just…hopeful. But scared."

He squeezed her knee. "Let's walk it together."

They sat in the soft glow of the room, wrapped in quiet contentment—unaware that their story was not yet finished.

Because even now, deep within Sarah's heart, God was preparing a new miracle—one she never dared to imagine.

A month later—New Jersey Home

The decision had been made—not in a single, dramatic moment, but in a series of quiet conversations and gentle prayers whispered in the dark. It wasn't about replacing what they'd lost or forcing a miracle into being. It was about hope. About growing their family in whatever way God made possible.

And so, the journey began—not with a joyful phone call or a nursery being painted, but with…paperwork.

"Medical history, financials, background checks, parenting philosophy…I feel like I'm applying for a government job and sainthood all at once," Sarah muttered, flipping through yet another form.

Abe chuckled as he scribbled a signature. "Some of these questions are intense. 'How would you discipline a child with oppositional defiance disorder?'"

Sarah raised her eyebrows. "I don't know, probably call Mara and cry?"
They both laughed. Ishmael popped up with a block tower and beamed.

"I want baby," he said, plopping the tower in Sarah's lap.
Sarah's heart swelled. "Me too, buddy."

Ishmael, Age Four—Suburban New Jersey

Ishmael, now a vibrant four-year-old, sprinted through the house in a blur of pajamas and dinosaur slippers.

His laughter filled the space that once felt so painfully empty. Sarah marveled at him daily—his steady feet, his bright curiosity, the way he would squeal with joy whenever Abe lifted him into the air.

"Mommy! Daddy! Watch me!" he shouted as he leaped from the ottoman onto a pile of pillows he'd stacked like a fortress.
Sarah laughed from the kitchen, placing dishes in the drying rack.

"That's the third time, buddy."

"It was higher this time!" Ishmael beamed.
Abe walked in, catching the tail end of the leap.

"Gravity's still working, I see."
Ishmael giggled and took off toward his room again, a blur of joy and endless energy.
Sarah stood quietly for a moment, watching him disappear down the hallway.

"Can you believe how fast he's growing?"
Abe wrapped his arms around her from behind.

"I still remember the first time you held him."
She leaned into him, exhaling softly.

"It feels like a lifetime ago. But also…like yesterday."
Sarah stared at the empty coffee cup in her hands. The kitchen was quiet except for Ishmael humming to himself in the playroom.
Abe was reluctant to bring it up as he heads out the door for work but asked anyway. "Anything from the adoption agency?"
She shook her head slowly. "Another 'we loved your profile but chose

someone else' email last night."

Abe kissed her forehead. "You okay?"

She smiled faintly. "Yeah. Just tired. Of waiting."

He paused. "We're not forgotten, Sarah."

"I know," she whispered. "It's just...I thought I had more patience. But this waiting is different. Quiet. Heavy."

Abe wrapped his arms around her. "So was the last one...until everything changed in one moment."

Sarah nodded. "You're right. It only takes one yes."

For a few moments, they simply stood there—no longer the desperate couple fighting month after month for a child, but parents who had settled into a different kind of waiting.

The old ache had dulled over the years but never fully disappeared. Sarah had accepted that Ishmael might be her only child—her miracle, her promise fulfilled in an unexpected way.

And yet, deep inside, the quiet whisper still lingered:

What about the child You promised me, Lord? The one from my own body?

She rarely spoke that prayer aloud anymore, but it never quite left her spirit.

Later That Evening—The Whisper Returns

After Ishmael was asleep, Sarah curled up on the couch with her journal, something she still kept by habit even after all these years.

She flipped through old entries:

I'm still waiting, Lord. I trust You. Even if never.

Her pen hovered for a moment before she finally wrote in soft, careful strokes:

Thank You for Ishmael. My heart is full. But if You're still willing...I remain open.

She closed the journal and whispered softly into the quiet room, barely loud enough to hear herself speak: *"Even now, God. Even now."*

CHAPTER 34

The Impossible News

Primary Care Office—Routine Appointment

The bloodwork had been routine. A simple annual check-up Sarah had almost rescheduled three times due to work, school drop-offs, and life's usual interruptions.

She wasn't expecting anything unusual. At 42, she was healthy, active, and content.

Which is why she stared at the nurse practitioner now, unsure she'd heard correctly.

"Wait…I'm sorry. Could you repeat that?"

"You're a bit anemic," she said, scanning the chart. "And your hormone levels are…interesting."

Sarah furrowed her brow. "Interesting?"

She glanced up from her tablet. "Sarah, when was your last period?"

She paused. "I'm not exactly sure."

"How long, approximately?"

"Maybe two months? A little more."

The nurse smiled gently, her eyes warm and steady.

"Your bloodwork came back with elevated HCG levels. That's consistent with early pregnancy. I'd like to run a pregnancy test."

Sarah laughed, the sound dry and sharp. "That's not necessary."

"Humor me," she smiled.

The Results

The doctor entered, reviewing her chart.

He looked up gently. "Sarah...you're pregnant. I know this must be surprising, but your labs are very clear. Based on your levels, I'd estimate around nine or ten weeks."

Sarah's pulse roared in her ears.

Pregnant.

Naturally.

After all these years.

"That...that can't be," Sarah whispered, her voice hoarse.

"I haven't even..."

"I know," the doctor said kindly. "But your hormone levels, your ultrasounds, everything confirms it."

Ten weeks. That meant she had already been carrying this child for over two months without even knowing it.

Tears welled in her eyes, but they weren't fully tears of joy yet. They were tears of shock, of fear, of confusion.

"How...?" Her voice broke.

"Medically? Rare. But not impossible. And for you?" He paused gently. "Perhaps...miraculous."

"Is..." she struggled for words, "is the baby okay? Is this dangerous at my age?"

The doctor nodded calmly. "We'll monitor closely. But for now, everything looks perfectly normal."

Sarah sat still, barely able to breathe as a strange mix of joy and terror swirled through her chest.

Pregnant.

At forty-two.

The Drive Home

Sarah drove in silence.

No music. No podcast. Just the hum of the road beneath her and the weight of impossible news pressing against her ribs.

As she pulled into their driveway, Ishmael's face appeared in the front window, waving excitedly as Abe stood behind him, smiling.

She stepped out of the car slowly, still stunned. The world around her felt somehow softer, brighter, like something sacred had broken through the ordinary.

Abe opened the door as she approached.

"Hey, love. How was your appointment?"

Sarah's voice shook as she looked at both of them—the family she already had, and the one quietly forming inside her.

She swallowed.

"Abe…I need to tell you something."

His brow furrowed with instant concern.

"Are you okay?"

Tears flooded her eyes now as she laughed softly through her breath.

"I'm…I'm pregnant."

Abe froze, unable to process the words.

Sarah whispered again, this time slower, steadier:

"We're pregnant."

For a moment, neither of them spoke. Abe's mouth opened slightly, eyes wide with awe and disbelief.

"But how?" he whispered, stepping closer.

"I don't know. God. A miracle. I don't have an answer," Sarah replied as she laughed softly through fresh tears.

"After all these years…after everything."

Abe pulled her into his arms, holding her tightly as the realization washed over him, laughter erupting from somewhere deep and holy.

"My God," he chuckled. "After all these years you're carrying our child."

Their child.

Finally.

Sarah nodded, her voice a broken whisper.

"After everything...He still remembered. God has brought me laughter, and everyone who hears will laugh with me." They stood in silence for a long time, just holding each other, until Abe quietly added, "What do we do about the adoption? The portfolio, the agency..."

Sarah pulled back slightly to meet his eyes.

"We put it on pause. For now. It's not a 'no.' But this..." she placed a hand over her belly, "...this is what we've been waiting for. I don't want to miss a moment of it."

Abe nodded slowly, emotion catching in his throat.

"Ishmael's going to be a big brother," he said, glancing over to where their son was sitting on the floor, playing with blocks.

As if on cue, Ishmael looked up and ran toward them, sensing the joy even if he didn't fully understand why.

Sarah knelt down to scoop him into her arms. One child in her lap, another forming inside her.

The promise wasn't dead after all.

The promise had simply been waiting for its appointed time.

They sat there together, overwhelmed by the impossible. By the miracle. And in the quiet, Sarah could almost hear the echo of God's ancient words, spoken long ago to another Sarah:

"Is anything too hard for the Lord?"

Sarah's Journal Entry—10 Weeks

I don't know how to describe what I feel. Gratitude? Yes. Terror? Also yes.

I've waited so long for this—for my body to finally carry life. And yet, every time I feel a cramp or a wave of nausea, I wonder if it's a warning or a gift. I'm afraid to hope too much.

Lord, You've brought me this far. Please don't let me lose him.

Abe's Work Celebration

The upscale lounge in Midtown buzzed with quiet energy, the kind of place where polished marble and velvet banquettes whispered power. Abe had insisted on the venue. Not because of the view or the wine list, but because he wanted his team to feel like royalty. Tonight was a win, not just for him, but for the people who had helped him get there.

Sarah held a glass of sparkling cider, keeping one hand on her belly, while watching Abe navigate the crowd like a true leader—warm, direct, magnetic. She admired how he greeted the junior analysts by name, how he paused to thank the administrative staff, and how his eyes lit up when speaking with the partners. It was one thing to love someone, but another thing entirely to admire them.

As the night reached its crescendo, Abe stepped to the front of the room to speak.

"I won't take long," he began, his voice calm but commanding. "Tonight isn't just about me. It's about vision. About believing in something before you see it. When I first walked through the doors of this firm, I wasn't sure where I fit. But I knew I wanted to build something that mattered."

The room hushed with anticipation. Just two days earlier, Abe's team had successfully led their firm through a landmark IPO— the largest in the company's history—launching a renewable energy company onto the public stage. It had been months of late nights, hard decisions, and unrelenting pressure.

"This IPO wasn't just a business win," he continued, his eyes sweeping across the room. "It was a statement. That we believe in sustainable energy. That we're committed to investing in the kind of world our children will inherit."

He paused, scanning the room until his gaze landed on Sarah.

"And now I know…it's not about buildings or deals or even titles. It's about legacy. It's about building something that outlasts you."

Applause swelled around the room. But for Abe, the real win wasn't just professional. It was the quiet pride in Sarah's eyes, a shared understanding that his work was no longer just about ambition, but about purpose.

Later, when the toasts and laughter had faded into the clink of dessert spoons, Sarah pulled Abe aside.

"You really meant what you said up there, didn't you?" she asked.

He nodded and put his hand on Sarah's stomach. "I want our kids to be proud of the name they carry. I want them to know their dad tried to make the world better, even in small ways."

Sarah squeezed his hand, feeling the weight and warmth of that promise. Ishmael was still so small. Isaac was only just conceived. But Abe already carried the weight of fatherhood like a mantle.

"I'm proud of you," she said softly.

"And I'm proud of us," he replied. "This is just the beginning."

Later in the evening, another partner in the firm, Michael, caught up with Abe near the bar. "You've got the board buzzing," he said with a smirk.

Abe smiled. "That's either a good thing or a terrible thing."

Michael leaned in. "You spoke about legacy tonight. That's rare in this business. Most guys are chasing the next deal, not the next generation."

"I used to be one of them," Abe admitted. "But…something changed. Now I just want to build something that means something… for her, for…whoever comes next."

Michael nodded, casting a glance at Sarah. "That woman's your compass. Hold on to her. And whatever you build, make sure it's worthy of both your names."

Michael raised his glass. "To legacy."

Abe clinked his back. "To legacy."

After the Celebration

It was past 8 p.m. when Abe and Sarah returned home from the celebration. The day had been long—planning for the event, practicing his speech, putting out fires so his project timeline progressed as planned. The kind of day that used to make him feel powerful, untouchable. But lately, it just made him tired.

From down the hall, a giggle echoed.

"Ishmael," Sarah called gently from their bedroom,

"time to settle down and go to bed!"

Abe smiled and got up, moving toward the sound. He found Ishmael sitting on the nursery rug, surrounded by toy animals and wooden blocks, a tiny lion clutched in one hand.

"You still up, little man?" Abe asked.

Ishmael looked up, grinning wide. "Daddy! The lion's the king."

Abe dropped to the rug beside him. "You're not wrong about that."

For a few minutes, they just played—arranging animals in lines, building caves out of pillows, making up stories about wild adventures. Then Ishmael yawned and climbed into Abe's lap, curling against his chest without a word.

The room dimmed as the night crept in around them. Abe held his son close, resting his chin on the soft curls atop Ishmael's head.

"This is it," he whispered aloud, more to himself than to the sleepy child. "This is the real legacy."

In the soft glow of the nightlight, Abe looked around the nursery.

The framed sonogram on the shelf. The tiny footprints stamped on hospital paper. The bookshelf still half empty, waiting for bedtime stories and superhero comics. He thought about IPOs, market wins, all the metrics of success he had once believed defined him.

But now?

If this little boy grew up knowing he was loved, if he grew to be kind and bold and full of wonder—that would be the legacy that mattered.

"I hope you grow up to be better than me, Ishmael" Abe whispered into the silence. "Wiser. Stronger. Braver."

He wasn't sure if Ishmael heard him. But the little hand that curled tighter around Abe's finger said maybe he did.

When Sarah peeked in later, she found father and son fast asleep on the nursery rug, tangled in each other like a quiet promise.

CHAPTER 35

The Laughter

Twelve Weeks—Sarah & Abe's Home

The house was quiet except for the soft rustle of trees outside their bedroom window, the kind of stillness Sarah had come to love in their new life just beyond the city. Sarah lay curled into the crook of Abe's arm, her head resting on his chest, one hand absently tracing gentle circles on her belly.

Twelve weeks. The first trimester milestone. The baby was real, growing, and—according to the last appointment—thriving.

Abe's hand came to rest over hers. "I still can't believe this is happening," he murmured.

"I know," she whispered. "Sometimes I wake up and wonder if it's a dream."

He kissed the top of her head, then said softly, "Have you thought about names?"

Sarah paused. "I…might have."

"Oh?" Abe grinned. "You've been holding out on me?"

She turned slightly to face him, propping herself on one elbow. "I've been thinking about the way our story has unfolded. The waiting. The doubt. The miracle. And I keep coming back to Isaac."

Abe's face lit up, not with surprise, but with quiet agreement. "He laughs."

Sarah nodded. "Because I laughed when I found out. Not because I doubted God could do it, but because I honestly didn't think it would ever be our story."

Abe's voice was thick with emotion. "And now it is."

She smiled. "It feels like...honoring the full circle. Our names. Our journey. Our faith."

Abe reached up and gently tucked a strand of hair behind her ear. "Isaac Abrams. That's a name with history."

Sarah laughed. "It's also a name that sounds like he should be wearing suspenders and quoting scripture by kindergarten."

Abe chuckled. "Or joining the chess club by first grade."

Her smile softened. "Do you think kids will make fun of them? Ishmael and Isaac? It's...a lot of Bible name energy."

Abe grinned. "You mean we sound like we're raising prophets instead of little boys?"

She laughed again, then sobered. "I just don't want them to feel...boxed in by our story."

"They won't," he said gently. "They'll feel rooted in it. That's the difference."

She studied his face, her heart swelling with gratitude. "Isaac?"

He nodded. "Isaac."

And just like that, their promised child had a name.

Sarah's Journal Entry—12 Weeks

We heard the heartbeat today.
Strong. Fast. Alive.

The doctor smiled, but I could barely hear her over the thundering rhythm pulsing through the speakers. It was the sound I feared I would never hear.

Ishmael was born through a miracle of trust. This child—this Isaac— is the fulfillment of Your original promise.

I still don't understand why You waited. But I am learning that waiting and suffering are not the same thing.

First Trimester

The pregnancy unfolded like a gentle surprise wrapped inside each new day. The days that followed were filled with emotions Sarah hadn't expected—not like this.

Of course, there was joy. Unspeakable joy. She would lie in bed some mornings, her hand resting on her growing belly, whispering prayers of thanksgiving.

After all these years...You remembered me.

Every milestone—every heartbeat, every sonogram, every kick—felt like a gift Sarah never expected to receive. After years of doctor visits, failed tests, and silent heartbreaks, her body was finally doing what she had always longed for.

She marveled at every flutter of movement inside her.

I'm carrying him, she would whisper to herself.

I finally get to carry him.

And yet, alongside the joy sat fear. Fear that this miracle might slip away as easily as it had arrived. Fear that her body, now older, might not sustain what had finally begun. Fear that the heartbreak of years past might somehow find her again.

The medical team monitored her closely due to her age, but each visit brought good reports. Abe came to every appointment, holding her hand, his eyes shining with awe and gratitude.

It was strange, being both grateful and afraid.

Group Call after 12-week Appointment

The crisp afternoon sunlight streamed through the kitchen window as Sarah poured herself a ginger tea—a small comfort for the waves of nausea that had thankfully started to ease. Her phone buzzed on the counter. A text from Lottie:

Lottie: *FaceTime later? You've been on my mind!*

Sarah smiled. Perfect timing.

She quickly typed back, *FaceTime in 5. Adding Mara.*

Minutes later, the screen lit up with the familiar faces of her two closest friends—Lottie, lounging in her Dallas apartment with a messy top knot and sparkly eye patches under her eyes, and Mara, tucked into the corner of her sectional, a mug of something herbal steaming beside her.

Lottie greeted first. "Okay, I called this meeting because my coworkers are on my last nerve, and I needed real conversation with actual humans I like."

Mara laughed softly. "Amen. What's the emergency, Lottie? Or are we just talking about your dramatic barista again?"

Sarah grinned, then took a steadying breath.

"Actually… I have a bit of news."

Two curious faces leaned in.

Sarah touched her stomach unconsciously and let the words come out in a rush.

"I had my 12-week appointment today…and everything looks great. I'm pregnant."

There was a beat of silence.

Lottie's eyes went wide as her mouth dropped open. "Wait—WAIT—SARAH! Are you serious?!"

Mara's face froze, blinking fast, her hand flying to her mouth.

"Twelve weeks?"

Sarah nodded, tears springing to her eyes. "I wanted to wait until I knew it was really happening. But it is. It's real. I'm going to have a baby."

Lottie squealed, doing a sort of excited shimmy in her seat. "Oh my gosh, this is the BEST news. Oh my goodness—do you know the gender yet? When are you due? Wait—what are you wearing to your own baby shower?!"

Sarah laughed through her tears, overwhelmed with emotion.

Then she turned her attention gently toward Mara, who was quiet.

"Mara," she said softly.

Mara looked up, her eyes glistening but her smile warm. "I'm so happy for you. Truly. You've waited so long. I know what this means."

"I know it's hard," Sarah said, her voice quieter now. "I was thinking about you the whole way home from the doctor. I almost didn't call yet…but I wanted you both to hear it from me. Together."

Mara exhaled deeply, brushing a tear from her cheek.

"It's okay. It really is. There's grief, but there's also hope. And I want to hold both. You deserve this joy."

Lottie spoke up again, gently but firmly. "And Mara, when it's your turn, we're throwing the biggest, most over-the-top celebration Dallas has ever seen. Like, hot air balloons. Or a band. I'm talking Beyoncé-level party."

That broke the tension, and all three women laughed.

Sarah placed a hand over her belly again, grateful beyond words for the love that wove through the screen.

They talked for another hour—about symptoms and cravings, about nursery paint colors, and about how surreal it all still felt. The call ended the way they always did, with promises to check in again soon and a string of heart emojis.

As Sarah hung up, her eyes lingered on the dark screen for a moment.

This baby wasn't just her miracle—it belonged to the village who had waited and prayed with her. And now, the next chapter had begun.

The news spread slowly at first—shared only with close friends and family. The reactions were always the same: wide eyes, disbelief, followed by hesitant congratulations, as if no one quite knew how to process it.

After so many years of infertility, of failed treatments, of waiting, Sarah's pregnancy seemed impossible. But the doctors continued to marvel at how healthy both she and the baby remained as the weeks passed.

"It's nothing short of miraculous," her OB said at every appointment.

Second Trimester

Sarah often found herself waking in the middle of the night, her hands resting protectively on her growing belly, still unable to fully believe it herself.

"This is real," she whispered into the darkness. "This is real."

Abe was radiant, almost childlike in his excitement. He hovered protectively, eager to schedule every doctor's appointment, read every article, monitor every craving. He spoke to her belly each night, his voice tender, as though their unborn child could already hear his whispered promises.

But Sarah kept part of herself guarded.

One evening, as they sat together on the couch, Abe reached for her hand. "Talk to me."

She smiled faintly. "About what?"

"About why you're holding back."

She inhaled slowly. "I've dreamed of this for so long, Abe. And now that it's here...I don't know how to fully receive it."

He waited patiently.

"It's like...part of me is waiting for the other shoe to drop. I feel guilty for being afraid, but I'm terrified to let my heart fully believe."

Abe leaned closer, his voice soft but steady. "Sarah, we've both waited for this child. You don't have to protect yourself from God's goodness. This isn't a cruel trick. This is His promise."

She swallowed back tears. "I'm thankful for the role Hagar played too. She helped me believe when I was on the brink of totally giving up."

Abe's smile faded slightly but remained tender. "I know."

"We asked Hagar to give us what we thought we couldn't have. And now, I carry what we always hoped for. It feels...complicated."

He nodded. "Life is complicated. But this child is not a punishment. It's a gift."

Sarah squeezed his hand, breathing deeply. "A gift."

Sarah's Journal Entry—20 Weeks

The ultrasound showed ten fingers, ten toes, a perfect spine.

Abe cried when they printed the photos. I did too.

We've waited so long, and yet it feels like it's all happening so fast.

Lord, steady my heart. Teach me how to enjoy what I once feared would never come.

26 Weeks—Sarah's Home, New Jersey

The kettle whistled softly as Sarah poured steaming chamomile tea into two oversized mugs. Lottie had insisted on coming to visit—"No more video calls," she'd said. "You need real hugs."

The two women curled into the oversized sectional in Sarah's living room, their mugs resting on the coffee table between them. They'd just finished dinner while Abe handled bedtime with Ishmael.

Lottie glanced down at Sarah's growing belly and smiled.

"You're glowing," she said softly. "Absolutely radiant."

Sarah smiled but exhaled with a trace of hesitation.

"Most days, yes. Some days, I still feel like I'm dreaming."

"Or waiting for the other shoe to drop?" Lottie offered gently.

Sarah's eyes glistened as she nodded.

"Exactly."

Sarah's phone buzzed. *Mara.*

Sarah's heart fluttered—it wasn't unusual to get a call from Mara, but the timing felt…significant. She held up the screen. "It's her. Mind if I…?"

Lottie waved her off, already grabbing her laptop. "Go! I'll be here Googling if spicy food can naturally induce labor."

Sarah answered with a warm smile in her voice. "Hey, you. Everything okay?"

There was a pause, then Mara's voice, quieter than usual.

"Yeah. Yeah, more than okay. I've been meaning to call you all day. Just…wasn't sure how."

Sarah sat up straighter, instincts on alert. "You're scaring me. What is it?"

Another pause. Then:

"I'm pregnant, Sarah."

The silence on Sarah's end was only a second long, but it felt suspended in air—then dissolved into a shocked laugh and a gasp.

"Wait. What?! Say it again!"

"I'm pregnant," Mara repeated, and this time there was a tremble in her voice. "I'm ten weeks. It's super early but it's real, Sarah. I can't believe it."

Tears sprang to Sarah's eyes instantly. She motioned wildly to Lottie, who rushed over mouthing, *What?!*

Sarah mouthed back, *She's pregnant!*

Lottie screamed, even though she wasn't on the phone. Sarah wiped her face, laughing through her tears. "Mara, oh my gosh. After everything you've been through…this is incredible. I'm so happy for you."

"I didn't want to steal your moment," Mara whispered.

"I wanted to wait until I knew everything was stable for you and the baby…"

"Mara." Sarah's voice grew soft but firm. "You didn't steal anything. You just multiplied the joy. We're going to have babies at the same time."

Lottie, still listening in, fist-pumped the air.

"You know what this means, right?" Sarah added, now beaming.

"We're doing a double shower. In Dallas. It's happening."

"I was hoping you'd say that," Mara said through what sounded like her own quiet tears.

"God is so wild," Sarah whispered. "His timing…it's never ours. But man, He's good."

"Yes. So good."

As they hung up, Sarah stared at the ceiling, heart full, then looked at Lottie.

"I've waited so long for this for myself," Sarah whispered, "and now God has given us a double portion of blessings!"

Sarah's brow furrowed as she continued, "Now that it's happening thought, there's a part of me that keeps bracing for bad news—like God somehow made a mistake by finally saying yes. What is this is Mara's moment and not mine?"

Lottie reached over and placed her hand gently on Sarah.

"Sarah, listen to me."

Sarah lifted her eyes.

"This is not God dangling a gift He plans to snatch back. This is Him fulfilling what He promised you long ago—what He's always intended for you."

Sarah swallowed, her throat tightening.

"But why now? After everything? After Hagar…after all of it?"

Lottie smiled softly, her voice steady.

"I don't know *why now*. But I do know this: His timing is never punishment. His timing is preparation."

Tears slipped quietly down Sarah's cheeks.

Lottie continued.

"God waited because He was weaving more into your story than you could see back then. Healing. Surrender. Trust. And now... joy. And the joy of sharing this with Mara."

Sarah's voice cracked.

"But what if something still goes wrong?"

Lottie squeezed her hand.

"Then even then...even now...God will still be good."

They sat there for a long moment, hands clasped, tears shared.

After a while, Sarah chuckled softly, wiping her cheeks.

"I knew you were coming to preach at me."

Lottie grinned.

"Absolutely. That's my job."

They both laughed, the heaviness lifting.

Sarah leaned back into the couch, resting her hands on her stomach, feeling the rhythmic kicks inside.

"I can't believe how far we've come."

Lottie smiled, her eyes full.

"And the best is still ahead."

28 Weeks

Ishmael, still too young to fully grasp the magnitude, was endlessly curious.

"So the baby is in your tummy, Mama? Not like before?"

Sarah smiled each time.

"That's right, sweetheart. This time God placed him right here."

"And when he comes out, will he be my brother?"

She pulled him close.

"Yes. He'll be your little brother."

Ishmael nodded as if he understood everything perfectly.

"Then, I'll take care of him."

Hagar's Journal Entry—28 Weeks

I dreamt last night that Sarah from the Bible sat beside me.
She placed her hand on my belly and whispered, "He is faithful."
I woke up sobbing.
God, I believe You're writing the same story twice—once through her,
and once through me.

CHAPTER 36

The Double Shower

31 Weeks—Dallas, Texas

The Dallas heat was mild for November, but Sarah still felt sticky and winded as she stepped out of the car. Abe hovered behind her with the suitcase, keeping one hand on her lower back. She was 31 weeks along, and the flight had taken more out of her than she expected.

Still, nothing could have kept her from coming. Mara had been her sounding board, her prayer warrior, and now—after years of waiting and loss—they were both expecting. The miracle felt too big to celebrate alone.

Inside Mara's parents' home, pastel streamers and floral balloons lined the entryway. The dining table was covered in sage green and cream decorations, fresh flowers, charcuterie cones, sugar cookies and a large sign hung above the fireplace:

"Double the Joy: Celebrating Mara & Sarah"

Sarah pressed her hand to her chest, touched beyond words.

Mara emerged from the kitchen, radiant and glowing, her bump just beginning to show beneath a soft sweater. "You made it!" she cried, pulling Sarah into a gentle hug.

"I wouldn't have missed this for anything," Sarah said, already teary.

Lottie had been working double duty all morning—organizing the mimosa bar, directing the caterers, and keeping the playlist just right. She'd just stepped away for a breather when a friend of Mara's, arms full with a diaper cake and a wiggly baby, asked, "Could you hold him for a sec?"

"Me? I'm not licensed for this," Lottie quipped, but instinctively held out her arms. The baby—maybe six months old, with a tuft of dark curls—settled in surprisingly fast.

"There," the woman said, relieved. "You've got the touch."

Lottie chuckled. "Tell that to my dating history."

Just then, Mara appeared, holding a half-filled glass of lemonade and catching the moment. She arched a brow and grinned.

"Well, well, look who's caught in the act."

Lottie laughed. "Caught doing what?"

"Looking way too natural," Mara said, stepping closer.

Sarah joined in a beat later, gently elbowing Lottie. "You holding a baby and not immediately handing it back? We're documenting this for evidence."

"Relax," Lottie said, adjusting the baby with ease. "He's cute. Doesn't mean I'm about to start pinning nursery décor."

Mara leaned in. "No judgment if you do. You're allowed to change your mind, you know."

"I haven't," Lottie replied quickly—but her voice lacked its usual edge. She looked down at the baby, who had grabbed a fistful of her necklace and was babbling up at her. "I just…think I'd be the cool aunt. The one who travels a lot and brings weird souvenirs."

Sarah smiled. "You already are. But you'd be an amazing mom, too."

Lottie didn't answer at first. The baby started to doze, heavy and warm in her arms. For a rare moment, her joking exterior fell quiet. Thoughtful.

"Maybe," she said finally, barely above a whisper. "But not today."

Mara and Sarah exchanged a glance…not pushy, not hopeful, just…tender.

"That's okay," Mara said, gently brushing a curl behind Lottie's ear. "We're just glad you're here. All of us."

Just then, the playlist skipped to *"Isn't She Lovely,"* and a wave of guests swelled toward the cake table. Lottie passed the baby back, adjusted her blazer, and exhaled.

"Alright. Back to party captain mode."

As she strode off to corral the crowd, Mara and Sarah watched her go— both quietly wondering if something had just shifted, ever so slightly, in their fearless friend.

The house buzzed with laughter, stories, and warm embraces. Friends from their college days mingled with neighbors and church members. Lottie helped organize a "baby bingo" game, and even Abe was roped into a diaper-changing competition against Jared—Mara's husband— which he lost in spectacular fashion.

During gift opening, two armchairs sat side by side. Mara unwrapped a tiny set of onesies that read *"Answered Prayer,"* and Sarah received a hand-knit blanket embroidered with both boys' initials.

Later, over punch and lemon bars, Mara leaned in and whispered, "Can you believe we're here?"

Sarah smiled and shook her head slowly. "For so long I thought it might never happen. And now…it's happening for both of us. Together."

"God's timing," Mara said. "Not mine. But perfect, anyway."

Lottie appeared beside them, beaming.

"You deserve every single bit of this, sweet friends."

Sarah glanced around the room, swallowing back her emotions.
"It feels strange."

"Strange how?" Lottie asked.

Sarah's voice softened.

"I've thrown so many showers for everyone else over the years. Smiled through every one of them. I dreamed of this moment...but I also convinced myself it might never happen."

Mara reached for Sarah's hand.

"God writes long stories sometimes."

Sarah smiled faintly.

"This one's been long."

"But beautiful," Lottie added gently. "And not over yet."

The Meal

As salads were served, the women easily slipped into conversation— asking questions about each other's nursery colors, baby names, sleep schedules—the kind of normal chatter both Mara and Sarah had always longed to participate in.

But underneath the joy lived a quiet humility. These women knew her story. They understood what it cost to arrive at this table.

"How are you feeling?" one friend asked softly.

Sarah paused for a moment before answering.

"Grateful," she said simply. "And honestly...terrified. But in the best way."

The women smiled knowingly.

"You're allowed to feel both," Mara said. "That's called motherhood."

The Prayer Circle

After dessert, Lottie stood and gently tapped her glass.

"Before we end tonight, I'd love for us to pray over Sarah and Mara as well as Abe and Jared."

The women circled around, each laying a hand on each parents' shoulders, back, or arms.

Lottie began.

"Lord, we thank You for Your faithfulness. For the promise fulfilled. For these two children who carries both Sarah and Mara's laughter and Your glory."

Mara continued.

"May these children's lives be marked by Your favor, Father.

May Sarah feel Your peace in every contraction, every breath, every sleepless night. May this family stand as a living testimony that nothing is impossible with You."

Tears streamed down Sarah's cheeks as each woman prayed softly, the room filled with warmth and the unmistakable presence of grace.

When the prayers ended, Sarah whispered through trembling lips: "Thank You."

And as the women hugged her, one by one, Sarah felt something lift inside her.

For the first time in years, the celebration didn't feel borrowed.

It was hers, both the joy of carrying her own child, and seeing her best friend also get her dream fulfilled.

Introductions—Gravesite of Sarah's Parents

The Texas sun was still low, casting long shadows over the soft hills of Restland Cemetery as Sarah, Abe, and Ishmael stepped out of the rental car a few hours after the baby shower. The quiet was familiar, sacred even—the only sound was the rustle of oak leaves in the breeze and the distant hum of cicadas warming up for the day.

Sarah held Ishmael's hand while Abe carried a small bouquet of white lilies she had picked up that morning. They walked slowly down the gravel path, the three of them moving like they'd rehearsed this. She hadn't been here in years, but she could never forget the path to their headstones.

"Over there," she said softly, guiding them toward the place where her parents lay side by side.

Abe handed her the flowers and gently stepped back, giving her space. She knelt down, brushing a leaf off her mother's headstone before placing the lilies at the base.

"Hi, Mom. Hi, Dad," she whispered, her voice trembling. "I brought someone I want you to meet."

She stood and turned, reaching for Ishmael's small hand.

"This is Ishmael. He's ours. And he's…amazing. You would've loved him. He's full of questions and joy and stubbornness…especially the stubbornness. He's got Dad's eyebrows when he's mad."

A soft laugh escaped her, followed by tears. Ishmael looked up at her with wide eyes, sensing the emotion in her voice.

"And…" Sarah placed a hand on her belly. "There's another one on the way. A little brother. His name will be Isaac."

She paused, then added, "He's a miracle. Just like the doctors said I'd never have."

Abe stepped forward, placing a steadying hand on her shoulder.

"We're doing okay," Sarah said, now speaking more to the air than to the stones. "Life's been full…harder than we expected, more beautiful than we deserved. I still miss you every day. But your girl… she's not alone anymore."

A few quiet moments passed, and then Abe knelt beside her.

"You know," he said softly, "I wish I could've met them. Just once."

Sarah smiled through her tears. "They would've loved you."

He reached into his pocket and pulled out a tiny toy car—Ishmael's favorite—and set it gently on the grass beside the lilies.

"For the grandparents," he said.

As they turned to leave, Sarah gave the markers one last look. Her heart felt both heavier and lighter—grief and gratitude, side by side. Somehow, they could coexist.

"I'll come back when Isaac is born and ready to meet you," she whispered.

And with that, she walked away, her family beside her, the breeze now brushing gently behind them—like a blessing carried on the wind.

32 Weeks—Manhattan General OB Clinic

The exam room was quiet as Dr. Malik studied the ultrasound screen carefully. Sarah lay back, trying to read her face while Abe sat silently nearby, his hand resting gently on her knee.

Dr. Malik finally exhaled softly.

"Sarah, I know you were feeling well enough to travel last week, but your cervix has shortened further since your last visit."

Sarah's stomach tightened.

"Is the baby okay?"

"Yes," Dr. Malik reassured quickly. "Isaac's growth is excellent. His heart rate looks strong. But your body's giving us warning signs."

Sarah glanced nervously at Abe.

Dr. Malik continued, her voice calm but serious.

"We need to shift you to partial bed rest for the remainder of the pregnancy. No more travel. Minimal work if possible…from home if you must. Minimal movement. Strict rest."

Sarah swallowed, her throat tightening.

"I thought I was being careful in Dallas."

"You were," Dr. Malik said kindly. "But even minor exertion can accelerate preterm risk at this stage. This isn't a punishment, it's prevention."

The Emotional Impact

Later that evening, back in their apartment, Sarah stared out the living room window, resting in the chair Abe had carefully prepared for her. The city skyline glittered beyond the glass.

"I shouldn't have gone," she whispered.

Abe knelt beside her, gently rubbing her arm.

"Don't do that."

"I was being stubborn. I wanted one more trip before everything changed."

Abe smiled faintly.

"You're allowed to want things, Sarah. You're allowed to try to feel normal."

Tears slipped quietly down her cheeks.

"But I'm terrified now."

Abe rested his forehead against hers.

"We've walked harder roads than this. And God's brought us through every single one."

The Spiritual Wrestling

In the quiet that night, Sarah whispered into the dark as Isaac shifted softly beneath her hand.

"Lord, I release control. Again. But You know how much I want to hold him. To see him safe in my arms."

She let the prayer hover between heaven and earth as tears ran quietly onto her pillow.

The Strengthening of Surrender

Days turned into weeks.

The couch became her world: books, devotionals, text threads with Mara and Lottie, whispered prayers, soft worship music filling the apartment.

Mara called daily, often simply to read scripture aloud:

"And let us not grow weary while doing good, for in due season we shall reap if we do not lose heart." (Galatians 6:9)

Sarah clung to the words like breath.

"In due season…"

"In Your season, Lord."

Week 33—Sarah & Abe's Home, Short Hills

Sarah shifted on the couch, adjusting the pillows under her feet as best she could. The house was unusually quiet, except for the soft tick of the grandfather clock in the entryway.

Her laptop rested closed on the coffee table, untouched for the last two days—something that still felt foreign to her.

How quickly life can shift from boardrooms to blood pressure monitors, she thought with a small smile.

The doorbell rang.

Abe's voice floated from upstairs.

"I'll get it!"

Moments later, Sarah's assistant, Kelsey, stepped into the living room carrying a canvas tote filled with neatly organized folders.

"Hey boss," Kelsey said with a warm smile. "Delivery service, at your command."

Sarah chuckled.

"I feel like I should tip you."

Kelsey grinned as she set the tote on the table.

"Just make sure the new maternity leave policy sticks—I'll

consider that my tip."

They both laughed as Kelsey took a seat nearby.

"I didn't bring too much," Kelsey said, pulling out a slim stack.

"Just a few contracts that need your signature, two client updates, and your favorite...quarterly budget variance reports."

Sarah groaned playfully.

"You really know how to spoil a girl on bed rest."

Kelsey grinned.

"Gotta keep you sharp for when you come back."

Sarah's expression softened.

"If I come back the same way."

Kelsey tilted her head.

"You're thinking about scaling back?"

Sarah exhaled slowly, running her hand across her rounded belly as the baby shifted inside her.

"Honestly? I might. This little one has recalibrated a lot of my priorities."

Kelsey smiled, her voice kind.

"Whatever you decide, you've earned the space to choose. You built an amazing team."

Sarah smiled back, deeply grateful.

"Thanks, Kels. And thank you for keeping the ship afloat."

As Kelsey packed up the empty coffee cups before heading out, she paused.

"You know...watching you walk through this whole journey... it's been inspiring. You never let the waiting steal your hope."

Sarah blinked back unexpected tears, placing a hand over her chest.

"There were days I came very close."

Kelsey smiled softly, "But here you are."

Sarah whispered, "Here I am. And here he is."

A gentle kick pressed against her ribs, as if on cue.

"Call me if you need anything else," Kelsey said warmly, gathering her tote.

"I will. Thank you again."

As Kelsey left, Sarah leaned back into the pillows, gently rubbing her belly.

Not long now.

And for once, the waiting felt peaceful.

34 Weeks Pregnant with Isaac—Manhattan Center for Advanced Women's Health

After two weeks of non-stop bed rest, Sarah settled back into the exam room chair, placing a protective hand over her very active belly as the monitor beeped softly beside her.

Dr. Malik entered with a warm smile, her tablet in hand.

"Well, Ms. Sarah Abrams—you are officially boring me, which is my favorite kind of patient this far along."

Sarah laughed softly.

"Boring sounds wonderful right now."

Dr. Malik pulled up the latest scan, turning the screen slightly toward Sarah.

"Baby boy is growing beautifully. Measurements are right on track. Fluid levels are back on track. Blood pressure has come back to normal. All your efforts have put us back on track."

Sarah exhaled, releasing some of the tension she hadn't realized she was holding.

Thank You, Lord.

As Dr. Malik typed in a few final notes, she glanced over with a more thoughtful expression.

"You know...you were one of my most complex cases when we first met."

Sarah smiled, rubbing her belly gently, "I remember."

Dr. Malik's voice softened.

"Multiple years of infertility. Pregnancy losses. Surrogacy. Hagar's pregnancy. Then your own chemical pregnancy scare. And now...here you are."

Sarah's eyes misted unexpectedly.

"I still sometimes can't believe it's real."

Dr. Malik reached over, placing her hand gently on Sarah's arm.

"You've fought hard for this child. Spiritually, emotionally, physically. And every single bit of it has brought you here."

Sarah inhaled deeply, her voice small.

"Sometimes I still feel like I'm holding my breath."

"That's perfectly normal."

Dr. Malik gave her a reassuring smile.

"Even patients without your history feel that way in the final weeks. But Sarah...you're in a strong place. And you have an excellent team around you."

Sarah nodded, smiling softly.

"I drive over from Short Hills every appointment because I trust you, Dr. Malik."

Dr. Malik chuckled.

"And we are honored to still have you. Though one day, when you're done expanding this little family, I expect to see you far less."

Sarah laughed gently.

"Deal."

As Dr. Malik stood to leave, Sarah paused.

"Can I tell you something?"

"Of course."

Sarah's voice grew tender.

"I used to pray for this so long that I honestly didn't know if it would ever happen. And now that I'm here...every little movement reminds me that God doesn't forget His promises. Even when it feels like He's taking His time."

Dr. Malik smiled warmly.

"And sometimes He saves His best stories for those who waited the longest."

Sarah whispered softly,

"Amen to that."

Dr. Malik glanced at her schedule.

"Okay, continue with the bed rest and we'll see you back here in two weeks—and then weekly after that. And of course, call me if anything feels off."

Sarah smiled.

"Two more weeks closer."

"Exactly," Dr. Malik said. "We're almost there."

The Final Stretch—36 Weeks

Abe was a constant source of steadiness. He took to reading over her every night—scriptures of promise, of God's faithfulness, of barren women who were made full.

One night, Sarah interrupted him as he read.

"Do you think people will laugh at me?" she asked quietly.

Abe closed the Bible and smiled. "Yes," he said. "But they'll laugh because of joy. Because of how impossible this is."

Sarah smiled softly, her eyes glistening. "Like the first Sarah."

Abe reached over and placed his hand gently on her belly. "Our Isaac." The name had come easily this time.

Laughter.

Not the bitter, forced laughter of years gone by, but the kind that bubbles up from a place of pure, uncontainable joy.

Doctor Visit—36 Weeks

At her next appointment, the doctor's words were still steady and encouraging. The baby was thriving. Strong heartbeat. Steady growth. The bed rest was working.

As she stared at the ultrasound monitor, watching the tiny flicker of life inside her, something inside Sarah finally released.

Tears streamed down her cheeks—not from fear this time, but from peace.

You really are faithful, Lord.

For the first time in years, she let herself laugh. Softly at first, then with growing freedom.

Abe squeezed her hand, smiling. "What is it?"

"Nothing," Sarah whispered, her eyes glistening.

"Everything. *God has made me laugh.*"

And in that moment, the ancient weight she had carried for so long slipped from her shoulders.

This was no longer a borrowed blessing.

This was her promise—fulfilled in God's perfect time.

Sarah's Journal Entry—39 Weeks

Any day now, we meet him!

And after years of empty arms, my arms will finally be full—with both sons You promised.

Thank You for teaching me how to laugh again.

CHAPTER 37

The Arrival

39 Weeks—Manhattan General

The contractions started gently before sunrise. Sarah had barely slept the night before, sensing something had shifted in her body but too nervous to trust it.

By 5:17 a.m., the contractions were regular. By 7:00am, they were undeniable.

Abe helped her into the car as the early morning light crept across the skyline.

"Today's the day," she whispered, clutching his hand tightly.

Abe smiled but kept his voice steady, anchoring both of them.

"Yes. Today."

The past nine months had moved both quickly and slowly. Each check-up, each healthy report, each milestone had brought them closer to this impossible day. And yet, even now, at the edge of delivery, Sarah marveled that it was real.

347

This time was different.

No rushing through midnight streets.

No early water breaking. No NICU team waiting anxiously nearby.

Just peace.

Labor & Delivery Suite

The room was bright, sterile, but oddly calm.

Nurses moved with practiced efficiency. The monitors hummed gently, tracking every beat of Isaac's tiny heart. The contractions built, slow but powerful, like waves pulling Sarah deeper with each surge.

Dr. Malik entered mid-morning, warm and confident.

"You're progressing beautifully, Sarah. Everything looks strong."

The contractions had started steadily that morning, building slowly throughout the day. Sarah's doctor moved calmly, guiding her through every phase with reassuring confidence.

Sarah nodded, breathing through another contraction, her voice soft but determined.

"I've waited so long for him."

Dr. Malik smiled.

"Then let's bring him home."

Early Afternoon—Active Labor

The pain was different than she imagined.

It wasn't just physical—it was emotional, spiritual, even sacred.

Between contractions, Sarah whispered breathless prayers:

"Thank You, Lord."

"Steady me."

"Cover him."

Abe never left her side, wiping her forehead, whispering encouragements, holding her hand as tightly as she needed.

"You're doing amazing, Sarah," he whispered as he wiped her brow.

Sarah gripped his hand tightly as another contraction peaked.

"I can't believe we're here."

Abe smiled, his eyes full of tears.

"I can."

The final hours passed in a blur of pain and sacred anticipation.

Sarah squeezed Abe's hand as he whispered prayers close to her ear.

The pain sharpened, then crested.

Dr. Malik's voice broke through:

"One more push, Sarah. One more."

Then, at last, the room filled with the sound Sarah had waited her whole life to hear:

The strong, healthy cry of her newborn son.

Strong. Full. Alive.

The doctor smiled as she lifted the baby into view. "Congratulations, you did it! He's perfect."

Sarah sobbed uncontrollably as she cradled his warm, slippery body against her chest, staring into the tiny face she'd only imagined for years.

He was real.

He was here.

Her arms, once empty, were now full.

Abe kissed her forehead, his voice thick with emotion.

"You did it."

Sarah whispered through her tears:

"Thank You, God. Thank You."

Post-Delivery

The delivery was smooth—almost gentle—as if the weight of years had been lifted long before Sarah ever entered the hospital.

Unlike Ishmael's early and uncertain birth, this child arrived full-term, healthy, and strong.

A tiny, perfect boy was placed on Sarah's chest, his skin warm and slick against her trembling hands. Tears streamed down her cheeks as she stared into his scrunched, crying face.

She had imagined this moment for so many years—only to have it come in God's timing, not her own.

Her eyes overflowed again as she held him close, her voice breaking.

"Hello, my sweet Isaac."

Abe leaned over, wrapping both of them in his arms, his own tears falling freely.

"Welcome, little one. You've been long expected."

For a long moment, the three of them stayed there—a sacred circle, breathless in the presence of God's extravagant mercy.

"Isaac," Sarah whispered, her voice breaking with awe. "My Isaac."

The name rolled off their tongues with reverence. The fulfillment of a promise that had once seemed absurd, even laughable, now wrapped in soft skin and steady breath. It was no longer a name from ancient stories. It was flesh and blood—living proof of a promise fulfilled.

The nurses worked quietly around them, cleaning, checking, swaddling. But in Sarah's world, everything else faded into the background. Only the tiny life she held mattered now.

Later That Night—Recovery Room

The room was dim now. Quiet. Holy.

Sarah sat upright, Isaac asleep against her chest, his tiny hand resting against her collarbone. Abe sat nearby, Ishmael leaning sleepily against him.

The family was whole now—in every sense.

"Can you believe this?" Sarah whispered.

Abe kissed her forehead. "Yes. Because He promised."

Sarah nodded, her voice tender.

"His timing was never late. Just…different."

They sat together in the quiet afterglow of labor, wrapped in the presence of this long-awaited miracle.

Sarah thought back to the years of tears, prayers, disappointments, and whispered doubts. She thought of Hagar, of Ishmael, of all the turns their story had taken to bring them here.

And she smiled through her tears.

God has made me laugh.

The Hospital—Postpartum Room

Soft morning light poured through the hospital room window. The world outside was waking up, but inside, time seemed to stand still. Sarah sat in her hospital bed, Isaac swaddled tightly in her arms, his tiny chest rising and falling with peaceful rhythm.

Abe sat beside her, his hand gently resting on Isaac's head, his eyes filled with wonder.

"He's here," Sarah whispered again, as if saying it aloud helped her fully believe it.

Before Abe could respond, a quiet knock tapped against the door.

"Come in," Abe called softly.

The door creaked open, and both Lottie and Mara slipped inside, wide smiles lighting up their faces. They stood for a moment, reverent and overwhelmed by the sight of the long-awaited promise cradled in Sarah's arms.

"Oh, Sarah…" Lottie whispered first, her eyes instantly brimming with tears. "He's perfect."

Mara stepped forward beside her, voice full of awe. "The Lord has done it. Just like He said."

Sarah's lips trembled as tears filled her eyes. "You both prayed me here."

"We never stopped," Lottie said softly. "Even when you

couldn't."

Mara nodded, her hand instinctively resting on her rounded belly. "Every time I prayed, I heard Him whisper, *'At the appointed time.'*"

Sarah blinked, then looked at her friend more closely. "I can't believe you came all this way…Mara, you shouldn't have traveled."

Mara smiled through misty eyes. "There was no way I was missing this. I had to see the miracle with my own eyes."

They all stood in reverent silence for a moment, letting the weight of the miracle settle fully in the room.

Abe finally broke the moment with a quiet smile. "Ladies, would you like to meet Isaac?"

Lottie and Mara gently stepped closer as Sarah carefully passed Isaac into Lottie's waiting arms.

Lottie held him like something sacred, fresh tears rolling down her cheeks.

"Hi, little man," Lottie whispered. "You've been a long time coming."

Mara laid a hand gently on Isaac's tiny head, closing her eyes as she whispered a prayer over him.

"Father, may Isaac walk in Your promises all the days of his life. May his laughter be a testimony of Your faithfulness. May every delay, every tear his mother cried, be redeemed in joy overflowing."

Sarah's tears fell freely now. She reached out and took both of their hands, voice breaking. "Thank you for praying when I was weak. For holding faith when mine was gone. For walking every step of this with me."

Lottie squeezed her hand. "You were never alone, Sarah."

Abe's voice was quiet, but full of emotion. "None of us were."

Lottie handed Isaac back to Sarah with care, brushing a tear from her cheek. "He already knows he's loved. You can see it in how calm he is with you."

Sarah cradled him close again, her smile soft and full.

Mara reached out to stroke the baby's tiny fingers—and then paused, her eyes widening slightly. She drew in a small breath and pressed a hand to her belly.

Sarah noticed. "What is it?"

Mara looked up, her expression a blend of surprise and wonder. "He kicked."

Lottie gasped. "Right now?"

Mara nodded slowly. "The strongest one yet."

A moment of sacred stillness fell again. Three women, knit together by years of friendship, ache, and faith, stood witness to not one promise fulfilled—but another awakening beneath Mara's hand.

Sarah's eyes shimmered. "They already know each other."

Mara chuckled softly, her voice catching. "He just wanted to say hi to his big cousin."

They all laughed, breathless with wonder, and for a moment it was as if heaven itself had leaned in to listen.

As Isaac stirred gently, the four of them sat together, wrapped in peace, a small circle of friends who had fought together in prayer, hope, and faith, and now sat together holding the fruit of every impossible promise made beautiful in its time.

Hagar's Visit

Visitors came and went over the next few days, family, close friends, even church members who had long prayed alongside them.

But it was Hagar's visit that Sarah both anticipated and feared the most. When Hagar stepped into the hospital room, she paused just inside the doorway. Her eyes went immediately to Sarah, who sat propped in bed, and then to the small bundle in her arms.

Tears filled Hagar's eyes as she whispered, "May I?"

Sarah nodded, surprised by how calm her heart felt. "Of course."

She carefully lifted Isaac and placed him in Hagar's arms. The baby stirred slightly but settled quickly against the unfamiliar warmth.

Hagar stared down at him, her voice trembling. "He's beautiful, Sarah. Truly. You waited…and God answered."

Sarah swallowed, emotion rising in her throat. "Yes. He answered."

They stood quietly for a moment, two women who had once shared more than they ever expected, now meeting again on the other side of something sacred.

"I didn't know if I should come," Hagar admitted. "But Lottie told me. She called after the baby shower and said you were close. When I heard you'd delivered, I just…I needed to come."

Sarah blinked back tears. "I'm glad you did."

"I didn't want to intrude," Hagar added quickly. "I just thought maybe…I don't know…maybe it mattered that you knew I care. That I'm happy for you."

Sarah reached out and took Hagar's free hand. "It does matter. You do."

They both looked down at Isaac, who made a soft sighing sound in his sleep.

Hagar smiled gently. "I'm still in Boston. I'm working at a nonprofit, nothing fancy, but it's good work. Marketing and fundraising, so I'm doing what I love. It's steady. It's quiet. Feels right."

Sarah squeezed her hand. "That's amazing. I'm proud of you."

Hagar looked up with a flicker of something shy in her eyes. "And… I'm seeing someone. His name's Tobias. He's kind. He knows about everything. About here. About you. And he's okay with it."

Sarah's eyebrows lifted, her face softening with joy. "Wow. That makes me so happy to hear."

A light laugh escaped Hagar. "He's good to me, Sarah. Really good. And it feels…real. I think he might be the one."

Sarah nodded, her eyes stinging again.

They stood that way for a while, Hagar rocking Isaac gently, Sarah watching the two of them, her heart full of things she didn't quite have words for.

When Hagar finally handed Isaac back, she brushed a thumb gently across his cheek. "Thank you for letting me meet him."

"Thank you for coming," Sarah whispered.

As Hagar turned to leave, she paused at the door. "He's going to have a beautiful life, Sarah."

Sarah smiled through tears. "I know. And I hope you do too."

They stood that way, holding both the child and each other's silent prayers—a testimony to promises fulfilled, hearts mended, and grace enough for all of them.

After Hagar's Visit

The room had gone still again.

Isaac stirred gently in Sarah's arms, his tiny fists curling under his chin as if even in sleep, he was holding on to something unseen.

The door clicked open.

Abe stepped in carrying a coffee cup and a small bag of snacks. " H e finally stopped crying?" he asked with a half-smile, setting everything down on the tray table.

Sarah looked up at him, her eyes misty. "You just missed her."

Abe paused mid-motion. "Missed who?"

"Hagar! Lottie told her. She came by for a few minutes."

Abe exhaled and sat on the edge of the bed. "How did it go?"

Sarah leaned her head against his shoulder. "Gentler than I expected. She held him. We talked. She told me she's living in Boston now, has a new job…and a boyfriend. Tobias."

Abe blinked. "Tobias?"

"I know," Sarah said, smiling softly. "It suits her."

He was quiet for a moment. "And you're okay?"

Sarah nodded. "Yeah. I am. It was strange and healing at the same time. She was…kind. Grateful. She said he was beautiful and that she was happy for us."

Abe looked down at his wife and newborn son and reached for her hand. "I wish I'd been here."

"I think it was better this way," she whispered. "Just us two. No old tension, no confusion. Just…closure. A full circle."

Abe let that sink in.

"She needed to see this, Abe," Sarah added. "Not just him. Us. That the promise really came."

He kissed the top of her head. "And I needed to hear that you're okay with it."

"I am," she said. "Because this…" she looked down at Isaac, "…was always the ending God had in mind."

They sat there in silence, the hospital room wrapped in the quiet rhythm of a newborn's breathing and the deep exhale of peace after a long, unfinished chapter had finally closed.

Hagar's Return to Boston

The train ride back to Boston was quiet.

Hagar sat by the window, watching city skylines blur into suburbs, then fields. Her hands were folded in her lap, one thumb brushing lightly over the edge of the hospital visitor badge still tucked into her coat pocket.

She hadn't told Tobias much—just that she needed to go back and say goodbye in her own way.

He was waiting for her at South Station when she arrived, leaning against a column in his usual crisp coat and scarf, holding a paper cup of hot cider.

He spotted her, smiled, and stepped forward. "How was it?"

Hagar didn't answer right away. She let him wrap an arm around her, held onto his warmth for a long moment before whispering, "Good.

Really good. Hard. But right."

They walked quietly to the car, the chill in the air not quite winter but more than fall. Once inside, she reached into her bag and pulled out a small photo.

"She let me hold him," she said softly. "His name's Isaac. He's beautiful. And she looked happy. Really happy."

Tobias glanced at the photo. "You okay?"

"I think...for the first time, I am," she said, her voice steady but thick with emotion. She looked down at her hands, then back out the window as the city lights flickered past.

"I carried so much for so long. Not just the pregnancy...but the confusion, the shame, the guilt, the hope...all tangled together. For a while, I didn't even know where Sarah ended and I began. I was grateful, then bitter. I felt chosen, then disposable. There were days I thought I was part of something sacred, and others I felt like a mistake wrapped in kindness."

She turned to Tobias now, her eyes clear and wet.

"But seeing her today...holding that baby, seeing the peace on her face...it was like watching a door close gently instead of slamming shut. And in that moment, I realized...I'm not the same girl who stepped into their apartment, wide-eyed and aching to matter. I've become someone else. Someone stronger. Someone who survived the breaking and still chose grace."

She drew in a shaky breath and whispered again, firmer this time.

"That chapter is closed. Not because I was written out...but because I chose to walk out whole."

He didn't say anything right away. He just reached across the console and held her hand.

"I'm proud of you," he said finally. "I've seen you wrestle with this. And I've waited for the moment when you could breathe again."

She looked at him, eyes shining. "I think I can now."
He took a breath, then reached into the glove box and pulled out a small velvet box.

"I was going to wait until dinner," he said with a half-smile, "but I can't think of a better moment."

Tobias reached for her hand, his thumb brushing gently over her knuckles as he steadied himself.

"I love you," he said quietly, but the weight behind his words made Hagar look up. He held her gaze with steady warmth. "And I've loved you longer than you probably realize."
He let out a small breath, almost a laugh.

"I still remember the first time I saw you…at that conference in Boston. You were asking this impossible question during the Q&A, pushing back with grace and fire, and I thought, *who is this woman who doesn't shrink back?* You were fearless. And brilliant. And when you smiled afterward…I was done for."
Hagar's breath caught in her throat.

"I know your story," he continued gently. "Not all of it. But enough. I know the valleys you've walked through and the grace with which you've carried yourself. And still, you show up kind, thoughtful, stronger than you give yourself credit for."
He paused, emotion softening his expression.

"I don't need perfect. I don't need easy. I just need *you*. The way you hum while you cook, the way you journal your prayers, the way you love fiercely and forgive slowly. You've taught me what resilience looks like…and what it means to start again."
He continued to nervously fumble with the small, velvet box. His voice trembled slightly.

"I want to build a life with you. One full of laughter and late-night talks and family dinners and…God willing, children of our own. I want you to know the joy you gave to others…tenfold. I want you to *be* the one who's chosen, this time, without condition."

Hagar's breath caught as he opened the box.

A simple ring. Elegant. Timeless.

"So I'm asking…Hagar Eliana Daniels…will you marry me?"

Tears slipped down Hagar's cheeks—not from sorrow, but release. Relief. Hope.

For a long moment, Hagar just stared at *him*—not at the ring, but at him. The man who had seen all her cracks and chose not to flinch. The man who never asked for explanations but always made room for them.

Tears welled in her eyes. Not from fear, not from uncertainty—but from the sheer unfamiliar weight of being *wanted* this deeply, this freely.

She exhaled shakily, her voice barely above a whisper.

"You really want *all* of me? The before. The during. The after. All the broken bits I've been trying to make sense of for years?"

Tobias smiled and leaned forward, touching his forehead to hers.

"I want *you*. Not in spite of the journey—because of it."

A tear slipped down her cheek as something inside her—something long locked away—finally broke open. Not in pain this time. In release.

"I think…I spent a long time believing I was a footnote in someone else's story," she whispered.

He gently cupped her face, "You're the whole story to me."

Hagar gave a small laugh, thick with emotion. She nodded slowly, then more surely, as the words came, "Yes. Yes, I'll marry you."

Tobias slid the ring onto her finger, his hands steady even as hers trembled.

He pulled her into an embrace that said more than words ever could—this was the beginning she hadn't dared to hope for.

And for the first time in a long time, Hagar didn't feel like someone left behind.

She felt…chosen.

Act V - The Laughter Returns
The Birth of Isaac

Now the Lord was gracious to Sarah as he had said, and the Lord did for Sarah what he had promised. Sarah became pregnant and bore a son to Abraham in his old age, at the very time God had promised him. Abraham gave the name Isaac to the son Sarah bore him. When his son Isaac was eight days old, Abraham circumcised him, as God commanded him. Abraham was a hundred years old when his son Isaac was born to him.

Sarah said, "God has brought me laughter, and everyone who hears about this will laugh with me." And she added, "Who would have said to Abraham that Sarah would nurse children? Yet, I have borne him a son in his old age."

Genesis 21: 1-7 (NIV)

CHAPTER 38

Sarah's Dream

Even If You Hadn't

Sarah and Abe were finally home with Isaac. Despite their best planning, his nursery still wasn't finished. For now, Issac slept in a basinet beside their bed.

Sarah, however, couldn't sleep. Instead, she sat cross-legged on the hardwood floor, surrounded by unassembled crib parts and a scattered blanket.

One hand rested absently on her belly, as if her body still hadn't caught up the miracle.

The joy was real. So was the awe. But something else stirred beneath the surface—something unfinished.

She reached for her old journal, the one she hadn't opened in months. Its pages were full of tear-streaked ink and aching prayers from another lifetime.

She turned to a new page and wrote:

Lord, You gave me what I asked for. But tonight, I need to say

something I couldn't say before. Even if You hadn't...You are still good. You were enough, even in the silence. Even in the waiting.
She closed her eyes and whispered, "Thank You—for the promise, and the process."

Then, softly, she sang. A quiet melody, not for anyone else. Just for the One who had carried her through it all.

Three Weeks After Isaac's Birth—The Nursery, 3:12 AM

The house was still.

Only the soft rhythm of Isaac's tiny breath filled the nursery, now freshly painted, furnished, and quiet.

He lay curled against Sarah's chest as she rocked slowly in the corner chair, his tiny body rising and falling in sync with hers.

Moonlight poured gently through the half-closed blinds, casting stripes of pale silver across the walls.

Sarah hummed quietly—not any particular melody, just the instinctive sound a mother makes to soothe both her child and herself.

And then, somewhere between the rhythm of the rocking and the pull of exhaustion, Sarah drifted into a light sleep—not fully awake, not fully dreaming—but somewhere in between.

The promise had come.

But what stayed with her most was how God had met her long before the miracle.

The Vision

She stood in a wide-open field.

The grass was tall and golden, swaying gently in the breeze. The sky above her was endless—bright and open, yet soft.

In the distance, she saw them:

Generations.

Children she did not yet know. Faces unfamiliar, yet somehow hers.

Sons and daughters running and laughing, their voices carrying across the wind.

They stretched as far as she could see—generations sprouting from her like branches from an ancient tree.

And standing quietly beside her was a woman—older, radiant, eyes full of deep knowing.

Sarah instinctively recognized her.

The original Sarah.

The woman smiled, speaking without moving her lips, her voice settling inside Sarah's spirit.

"I *waited too*," the woman said. "*And I laughed too.*"

Tears filled Sarah's eyes.

"*But God fulfilled it,*" the woman continued softly. "*Not just for me. For you too.*"

Sarah tried to speak, but words weren't necessary.

They simply stood there, two women bound across time by the same faithful God, the same long waiting, the same impossible promise fulfilled.

Waking

The chair creaked softly as Sarah's eyes fluttered open.

Isaac stirred gently in her arms, sighing a sleepy breath against her chest.

The dream still shimmered inside her—not fading, but settling into her like a quiet seed of truth.

Abe appeared quietly in the doorway, his voice a whisper.

"You okay?"

Sarah smiled, fresh tears slipping down her cheeks as she kissed Isaac's soft head.

"I am," she whispered. "I finally am."

She glanced up at Abe, her voice full of peace now.

"Our legacy isn't just beginning. It's already unfolding."

Abe crossed the room and wrapped his arms around them both as Sarah breathed in the miracle she was now living.

Nothing had been wasted.

Sarah rose from the rocking chair, to place Isaac in his crib. She was gently patting Isaac's back as he snuggled in. Abe watched her with a quiet smile.

"You're getting good at this," he whispered.

Sarah gave a tired but contented smile. "He finally fell asleep without drama. That's a win."

A soft creak in the hallway made them both pause.

Tiny feet shuffled into the room, and there was Ishmael—his hair tousled from sleep, his dinosaur pajamas wrinkled and clinging to one arm of his favorite stuffed lion.

"Mommy?" he whispered, blinking against the dim light. "I couldn't sleep."

Sarah looked over at Abe, then back at their oldest. She opened her free arm and Ishmael padded over, resting his head against her hip, one hand lightly touching the hem of her robe.

"We have to whisper," she said softly, crouching down so she didn't wake the newborn in her arms. "Your brother is asleep."

Ishmael's eyes widened as he peeked at Isaac. "He's so tiny."

"He is," Abe said, stepping forward with a quiet smile. "And he needs his rest...just like you, little man."

Abe crouched beside Ishmael and gently rubbed his back.

"I've got him," Abe said quietly to Sarah.

She nodded, her hand resting lightly on the baby's chest for a moment before pulling the blanket around him.

Abe scooped Ishmael into his arms, who didn't resist but nestled in with a sigh.

"I'll walk him back," Abe said.

Sarah turned and smiled softly. "I'll meet you back in our room."

Abe kissed her temple before heading down the hall with their firstborn curled against his chest.

Sarah watched them go, heart full and heavy in the best way. Two boys. Two answered prayers.

She lingered for a moment beside the crib, watching Isaac's chest rise and fall.

Then she turned out the light and quietly followed the trail of her family home.

Six Weeks After Isaac's Birth—A Quiet Saturday Morning

The house was still waking up.

Sunlight spilled through the kitchen windows as Abe poured coffee and flipped pancakes. Sarah sat at the breakfast table, nursing Isaac beneath a soft muslin blanket, rocking slightly with practiced ease.

Ishmael padded into the room, still wearing his dinosaur pajamas, hair tousled from sleep.

He rubbed his eyes, then climbed into the chair beside Sarah, watching closely as Isaac made soft, breathy noises beneath the blanket.

"Is he eating again?" Ishmael asked softly.

Sarah smiled.

"He's growing fast."

Ishmael leaned his elbows onto the table, peeking under the edge of the blanket.

"Hi, baby brother," he whispered.

Isaac shifted slightly at the sound of Ishmael's voice, his tiny hand stretching upward in reflex.

Ishmael's eyes widened.

"Did you see that? He knows me!"

Sarah's heart swelled.

"Yes, sweetheart. He knows your voice already."

Ishmael smiled with pride, then grew serious for a moment.

"Can I hold him again today?"

"Of course."

Sarah settled Ishmael onto the couch with a stack of pillows surrounding him for safety, then gently placed Isaac into his brother's small, eager arms.

Ishmael studied Isaac's face with intense concentration.

"His head is smaller than my soccer ball," he whispered, awe in his voice.

Sarah laughed.

"Yes, for now."

Ishmael gently rocked, his voice soft.

"I'll keep him safe, Mommy."

Sarah's throat tightened as she watched the two of them together—the two branches of her promise, living and breathing side by side.

"You already do," she whispered.

Abe stood nearby, his arms crossed, watching his sons with quiet pride.

"You're a good big brother," he said.

Ishmael looked up.

"Do you think God gave him to us because I prayed?"

Sarah's breath caught.

"I think God heard all of our prayers, sweetheart. Yours too."

Ishmael nodded solemnly, then looked back down at Isaac.

"It was worth waiting."

Sarah sat beside them now, running her fingers softly through Ishmael's curls.

She thought back to every night she had cried into her pillow. Every doctor's office. Every disappointment. Every desperate prayer whispered into the darkness.

And yet here we are.
Two sons.
Two promises.
Both born from waiting.
Both wrapped in grace.

Three Months After Isaac's Birth—Sunday Morning

The sanctuary glowed with soft morning light filtering through the stained-glass windows. The choir had just finished singing *Great Is Thy Faithfulness* as Pastor Wells stepped to the front, his voice warm and steady.

The congregation quieted as Sarah and Abe rose from their seats, baby Isaac cradled safely in Abe's arms.

Mara, gently rocking her own newborn against her chest, sat in the pew just behind them. Lottie sat beside her, and even a visiting Hagar was there, each woman holding her own complex mixture of joy, tears, and gratitude.

Pastor Wells smiled gently as the family approached.

"Today," he began, "we celebrate a child of promise."

Sarah's throat tightened immediately.

Pastor Wells continued, addressing the congregation:

"We are witnesses this morning to God's faithfulness. Abe and Sarah have walked through long waiting, through heartbreak and surrender...but never without hope."

The room filled with quiet emotion.

"In Genesis, the Lord promised Abraham that his descendants would outnumber the stars, even when the circumstances looked impossible. And in the fullness of time, God fulfilled His promise."

He smiled down at Isaac now, who squirmed lightly in Abe's arms, his wide eyes blinking beneath the soft glow of the stage lights.

"Isaac means 'laughter,'" Pastor Wells added. "And today, we join their laughter…the kind that only comes after God redeems what once felt lost."

The congregation chuckled softly, many wiping tears.

Turning now to Sarah and Abe, Pastor Wells's tone grew tender.

"Do you promise to raise Isaac to know and follow the Lord? To teach him God's ways? To surrender his life to the One who gave it?"

Sarah whispered, tears brimming,

"We do."

Pastor Wells laid his hand gently over Isaac's tiny head.

"Father, we dedicate Isaac to You today. May he grow strong in wisdom, in favor with God and man. May his life be marked by Your presence. May every day of his journey reflect Your grace, Your timing, and Your faithfulness. In Jesus' name, Amen."

The congregation softly echoed,

"Amen."

The Quiet After

After the final "amen," guests slowly filtered out of the sanctuary, the last notes of the worship music still echoing faintly off the walls. The dedication had been simple, sacred—just as Sarah had hoped.

She held Isaac close to her chest as a soft line of people formed. There were hugs, whispered prayers, gentle laughter, and more than one set of eyes glistening with shared joy.

An older woman from the church—someone who had prayed with them countless Sundays—gently cupped Sarah's face in her wrinkled hands.

"You waited well," she said.

Sarah smiled, eyes swimming. "We didn't always feel like we did."

"But God always knew the ending," the woman replied, patting her cheek.

Lottie swept in next with a bright smile and a teary laugh.

"He is perfect," she said, brushing a finger over Isaac's soft curls. "Even if he did scream through the last song."

"He just wanted to remind everyone he's a miracle with opinions," Sarah joked.

Mara stood behind Lottie, cradling her own son in her arms. Her eyes found Sarah's, and they didn't need to say much. They had both walked the dark valleys.

"This is the fruit of your faith," Mara whispered.

Sarah reached for her hand, squeezing it. "This is the fruit of God's faithfulness."

Behind them, Abe was helping gather cards and folded programs but paused and walked back to her side. He leaned down and kissed Isaac's forehead with a quiet reverence.

"You are living proof, little one," he murmured. "Living proof that the God who promises is the God who delivers."

Eventually, the crowd thinned. The lights dimmed. Someone from the team began stacking chairs.

Sarah let herself breathe then. Not the shallow breath of hope mixed with fear—the full kind. The kind that reaches down into your ribs and says, *you've made it.*

She stepped outside into the golden dusk, Abe at her side, holding Ishmael on his hip, and Isaac nestled peacefully in her arms.

As they crossed the church parking lot, Sarah looked up at the fading sky.

"Do you think he knows?" she asked softly.

Abe looked down. "Isaac?"

She nodded. "That he's part of something bigger?"

Abe smiled and wrapped an arm around her shoulder.

"He will. One day."

And for the first time in years, Sarah exhaled fully—her heart quiet, her hands full, her faith complete in a way it never had been before.

Not because the wait was over.

 But because the promise had come.

Three Months After Isaac's Birth—Coffee Shop, Manhattan

The coffee shop was quiet, tucked into its usual corner of 9th and 22nd, where Mara waited with two steaming mugs already on the table.

As Sarah slipped into the chair across from her, she reached for Mara's hand, eyes still glistening from the morning's service.

"Thank you for being there today," Sarah whispered. "You've carried so much of this journey with us. I couldn't imagine dedicating Isaac without you there."

Mara smiled softly, squeezing her hand.

"There was nowhere else I'd be."

They sat in silence for a beat, letting the warmth of the moment settle between them. Then Sarah smirked, glancing toward the window.

"Do you think they'll survive the next thirty minutes without us?"

Mara laughed, taking a long sip of her drink. "Barely. Abe looked like he was gearing up for a military operation when I handed him the diaper bag."

Sarah grinned. "I gave Isaac two extra pacifiers and said a silent prayer."

Mara leaned back with a content sigh. "This might be the hottest date I've had in months—me, you, and a cappuccino without a car seat in sight."

They both laughed, the kind of laughter that only comes after shared stretching and shared joy. Motherhood had changed them—but moments like this reminded them they were still themselves, too.

"Sometimes I think back to the first night you called me to pray. When Hagar first offered."

Sarah nodded, her eyes misting.

Mara continued.

"I remember sitting at my kitchen table after we hung up, staring at my Bible. I was so afraid for you…afraid of what it might cost emotionally, afraid you would carry guilt, afraid of the unknown." She paused, looking at Sarah with deep tenderness.

"And yet God whispered to me that night, 'I'm not finished writing her story.'"

Sarah wiped a tear from her cheek, nodding.

Mara smiled.

"I didn't know then what it would look like. Ishmael. Isaac. The waiting. The ache. The miracle. The double portion."

Sarah's voice cracked.

"Double portion."

Mara nodded, her voice steady.

"That's what you're living, Sarah. You didn't just receive a child—you received a testimony. A legacy that will outlive all of us."

The Watchman's Prayer

Mara exhaled deeply, as if releasing something she'd carried for years.

"I've prayed a lot of intercessory prayers in my life. But yours… yours changed me too. It taught me something about God's timing I never fully understood before."

Sarah reached across the table, taking Mara's hand.

"Thank you for standing watch."

Mara smiled through her tears.

"That's what we do, Sarah. We watch. We pray. We hold up the ones too tired to stand for themselves. And when the promise finally comes…" she glanced down at the photo album, "…we celebrate."

They sat quietly for a long moment, hands still clasped, as the city moved around them.

And both knew, without needing to say it:
The promise had fully arrived.

Two Weeks After Isaac's Dedication—2:13 AM

Abe stood in the nursery, arms crossed, watching Isaac sleep. The soft nightlight cast a warm glow across the crib, illuminating Isaac's tiny, steady breaths.

Abe had always imagined fatherhood would feel like *arrival*—like finally standing on the mountain after years of climbing. But instead, it felt like *stewardship*—a weighty, beautiful responsibility that grew heavier with each passing day.

He pulled the blanket gently over Isaac's feet and whispered softly:
"You have no idea how long we waited for you."

Abe moved to the armchair now, Bible resting unopened in his lap, head bowed as he whispered his prayer.

"Father, thank You for this boy. For both of our boys."
He paused, swallowing the tightness in his throat.

"I used to think the hardest part was waiting. But now I realize... the real weight is *raising* them."
His voice cracked.

"I'm terrified I won't do it right. That I'll fail him somehow. That I won't model Your heart the way he needs."
He exhaled slowly, staring at the ceiling.

"I know You didn't answer our prayers just to hand me this and leave me to figure it out alone. But some nights...I feel so inadequate."

The words hung in the stillness. As Abe sat in the silence, an old verse surfaced in his heart—one his father had read to him as a boy:

"He who calls you is faithful, who also will do it." 1 Thessalonians 5:24

Abe breathed deeply, whispering aloud:

"You didn't just give me this calling—You promised to equip me for it."

His shoulders relaxed as a quiet peace settled over him.

He looked at Isaac once more, his voice full now:

"I may not be enough for you, son...but God will always be."

Before leaving the nursery, Abe rested his hand gently over Isaac's tiny chest and whispered his personal benediction:

"May you always know the God who answered our prayers. And may your life always carry the laughter of your name."

CHAPTER 39

The New Normal

Ten Year Anniversary—Hudson Valley Weekend Retreat

The boutique inn sat tucked into the hills like a hidden treasure—stone cottages, flowering gardens, and wraparound porches with rocking chairs that overlooked miles of rolling green.

Sarah inhaled deeply as they arrived.

"I can't believe you found this place."

Abe smiled as he carried in their overnight bags.

"Ten years married deserves more than takeout and Netflix. Also, I thought we could use something nice and quiet before you head back to work."

Sarah laughed.

"Quiet sounds heavenly."

He laughed. "Which is exactly why I booked the quietest spot I could find. No noise. No schedule. Just us."

"And the boys?" Sarah asked, only half-joking.

"They're in good hands. Denise's got them—and I bribed her with extra PTO and cookies from that bakery she loves."

Sarah laughed, her shoulders finally beginning to relax.

"I could cry from gratitude. I'm so happy we still have her in our lives."

That evening, they sat beneath string lights on the inn's garden terrace. The meal was simple—roasted salmon, local vegetables, warm bread— but the peace was its own kind of luxury.

Sarah sipped her wine and leaned forward, the candlelight soft on her face.

"Ten years, Abe. Can you believe it?"

"Sometimes it feels like we just met. Other times, like we've lived a whole lifetime together already." He reached for her hand. "I'd do it all again."

Sarah nodded, her voice tender. "It's strange how still everything feels tonight."

Abe chuckled. "We forgot what adult conversations sound like."

"Remind me again why we thought two boys under six was a good idea?" she teased.

Abe raised his glass.

"Because God's sense of humor is alive and well."

They laughed, letting the sound fill the night air—free and unhurried. The ache of the early years had softened into something sacred. And here, in this quiet place, their love felt both familiar and brand new.

After dessert arrived, Sarah's tone grew more thoughtful.

"Do you ever think back to...all of it? The waiting...? The heartbreak? Hagar? The surrogacy? The losses?"

Abe nodded slowly, "All the time."

He reached across the table for her hand.

"But I think about it differently now. I used to replay it like a test we barely survived. Now, I see how God wove it all together. Even the parts that nearly broke us."

Sarah's voice softened.

"Sometimes I still struggle with that. The 'why it had to be that way' part."

Abe's eyes stayed steady.

"I don't think we were ever meant to understand all of it. But I do know this…none of it was wasted."

Sarah blinked away the quiet tears that threatened.

"No, it wasn't."

As the night cooled, they stepped onto the walking trail behind the inn, strolling beneath the stars.

Abe tucked Sarah's arm into his.

"Do you ever wonder what's next?" he asked softly.

Sarah smiled, "All the time."

They walked a few steps in silence.

"I'm open," she finally whispered.

"Open to what God writes next…whether that's more children…or just raising these two wild boys…or something completely unexpected."

Abe squeezed her hand.

"Whatever He writes, we've already seen how good He is at redemption."

Sarah exhaled, her voice full of peace.

"And I trust Him now more than I ever did before."

Later that night, as they lay together under crisp white sheets, Sarah whispered into the dark:

"I love this season."

Abe kissed her forehead.

"Me too. We earned this one."

Five Months Postpartum—Short Hills, NJ

The faint sound of Isaac's baby monitor hummed in the background as Sarah adjusted her laptop camera. She glanced down at the tiny bundle sleeping in the bassinet beside her desk.

The house was unusually still—for now.

"Alright, team," Sarah said into the camera, flashing a confident smile to the eight faces staring back at her from the Harbor Creative Group weekly leadership Zoom.

"First, thank you for keeping everything running so smoothly while I've been juggling this little guy. You all are rockstars."

On screen, Kelsey grinned.

"You're the one running meetings on zero sleep, Sarah."

Sarah laughed softly.

"I've discovered that coffee and dry shampoo are the real MVPs of working motherhood."

They dove into updates—client accounts, project timelines, staffing needs. Sarah's sharp instincts remained as sharp as ever, but her pace was gentler now, more collaborative.

At one point, Kelsey mentioned,

"We've had some new business inquiries come in. Once you're fully back, I think we can scale up if you're open."

Sarah nodded thoughtfully.

"I am fully back...but I want us to scale with balance. I'm learning that growth doesn't have to mean burnout. We build strong—and sustainable."

The team nodded in agreement.

Just then, Isaac stirred and let out a soft cry from the bassinet. Sarah instinctively reached over, gently patting his chest to soothe him.

The team smiled.

Lindsey, one of her senior directors, spoke up warmly:

"You're doing it, Sarah. You're showing the rest of us that we can build careers and still hold our babies."

Sarah's eyes misted unexpectedly.

"Thank you. I'm learning as I go."

As the meeting wrapped, Sarah muted her mic, lifted Isaac into her arms, and held him close against her chest.

There was a season when this felt impossible. And now...

She kissed the top of his fuzzy head, whispering:

"You were worth every single email I didn't send."

Through the home office window, the afternoon sun shone gently on the blooming trees outside. Life, both work and motherhood, was full. But for the first time, full didn't feel overwhelming.

It simply felt...right.

CHAPTER 40

The Celebration

Isaac's First Birthday—Saturday Afternoon

The backyard was filled with sunlight and soft laughter as family and friends gathered beneath the white tent that Abe had insisted on renting—"Go big this year," he'd said.

The banner stretched across the fence read:

"Isaac—One Year of Laughter."

Sarah stood for a moment, taking it all in—the balloons gently bobbing in the breeze, children playing under the shade trees, Lottie and Mara chatting with guests, and Ishmael chasing bubbles across the lawn in his "Big Brother" t-shirt.

Two miracles.

Two promises fulfilled.

Sarah noticed the quiet shift in the crowd as Hagar arrived through the side gate. She was alone, holding a small, carefully wrapped gift, looking both eager and uncertain. This was her first visit back since visiting Sarah and Isaac in the hospital—and her time seeing Ishmael since she left years ago. Her first step back into the life she had once been so deeply entwined with.

Their eyes met across the yard. Sarah felt the usual swirl of complicated emotion rise, but this time, there was no sharp edge—only a soft ache.

Sarah moved toward her, smiling as she closed the distance.

"I'm glad you came," Sarah said gently.

Hagar's shoulders seemed to relax slightly.

"I wasn't sure I should."

"You should," Sarah said firmly, taking her hand for a brief moment. "You're part of this story, Hagar. Always will be."

During the Party

The yard buzzed with cheerful noise—kids laughing, parents chatting, balloons swaying gently in the breeze. Hagar stood quietly near the edge of the tent, watching Ishmael play with a group of children near the sandbox.

He was five now—full of energy, joy, and innocence. His tiny hands worked carefully to fill a yellow dump truck with sand, his curls bouncing as he concentrated.

Hagar's chest tightened as she watched him—a strange mixture of pride, love, and unspeakable distance.

After a few minutes, Ishmael noticed her standing nearby. Curious, he skipped over, clutching a plastic toy shovel.

"Hi!" he said brightly, looking up at her with wide, unfamiliar eyes.

Hagar knelt slowly to his level, her heart pounding.

"Hi there," she whispered, forcing a smile.

He studied her face for a moment but showed no sign of

recognition. She was simply another adult at his party.

"What's your name?" he asked with innocent boldness.

Hagar's throat tightened. She swallowed hard but kept her smile steady.

"My name is Hagar. I'm...I'm a friend of your mommy and daddy."

He nodded happily, satisfied with the answer.

"I'm Ishmael. This is my brother's party!" he said proudly, pointing toward Isaac's highchair.

Hagar's eyes filled instantly.

"I know," she whispered. "You're both very special boys."

Ishmael smiled, waving his toy in the air before running back toward the sandbox.

Hagar watched him go, blinking quickly, holding back tears.

Behind her, Sarah had quietly walked up, observing the moment from a respectful distance.

Hagar wiped her cheek before turning slightly toward Sarah.

"He doesn't remember me," she whispered softly, her voice breaking slightly.

Sarah laid a gentle hand on her arm.

"No, but that's okay. He knows all he needs to know. He knows he's loved."

Hagar nodded, her lips trembling, forcing another fragile smile.

"Yes," she whispered. "That's enough."

They stood together for a moment, both silently carrying the strange, beautiful weight of grace.

Hagar glanced around, taking it all in.

"You've built something beautiful here, Sarah."

Sarah followed her gaze.

"We've been given something beautiful."

Hagar smiled, but her eyes glistened.

"There were days I wasn't sure we'd ever get to this part."

Sarah nodded, "Me either."

They stood quietly for a moment, letting the unspoken memories settle between them.

"I think about him sometimes," Hagar finally whispered.

"About Ishmael. Not in a possessive way...I know he's yours. He always was. But...I feel connected to him. Like a thread that will always be there."

Sarah smiled softly, reaching for Hagar's hand.

"You'll always be part of his beginning, Hagar. And I'll always be grateful for what you gave us."

Tears brimmed in both women's eyes, but neither pulled away from the honest tenderness of the moment.

Another Private Moment

A little later, as the cake table was being set up, Sarah quietly pulled Hagar aside again, this time into the kitchen while most of the guests remained outside.

"There's something I've wanted to say for a long time," Sarah began, her voice low but steady.

Hagar waited, curious but open.

"I've spent a lot of this year wrestling with my own pride. With how hard it was to let you carry something that I longed to carry myself. And there were times...I didn't handle that very well."

Hagar's eyes softened.

"Sarah, you never owed me perfection. You trusted me with your dreams. That was enough."

Sarah exhaled, blinking back fresh tears.

"I just want you to know I see it now. All of it. And I'll never forget your kindness...even when it got...complicated."

Hagar smiled fully for the first time that day. "We were both carrying something too heavy for one person to hold alone."

Hagar reached into her purse and pulled out a cream-colored envelope, thick and slightly weighted.

"I've been working on this for a while," she said softly, sliding the envelope across the table. "It's a letter...for Ishmael. For when you and Abe feel he's old enough."

Sarah's eyes misted instantly.

"Are you sure?"

Hagar nodded.

"I won't interfere. I won't confuse him. But I want him to know...one day...that he was deeply loved by everyone involved in his story...including me."

Sarah accepted it carefully, her fingers brushing the unsealed flap. "Do you want us to read it?"

"I wrote it knowing you might," Hagar said softly.

"There are no secrets. Just...my heart."

Sarah slipped it into her pocket, feeling the unexpected weight of it press against her—not from the paper, but from everything it represented.

"Thank you," Sarah whispered. "This is...a beautiful sentiment...I wish I had thought of it. I will make sure to hold onto it until the perfect time."

Hagar smiled through her own quiet tears.

"He deserves to know how fully he was loved. That's all."

Sarah reached across and squeezed Hagar's hand, both women now sharing a peace neither of them could have imagined when this story first began.

Two mothers.

One promise.

Grace between them.

Abe and Hagar's Brief Conversation

Near the grill, Abe found himself unexpectedly alone with Hagar while flipping burgers as guests gathered plates.

"You've got this party running like a well-oiled machine,"

Hagar said lightly, trying to break the initial tension.

Abe smiled.

"Sarah's doing, not mine."

There was a pause. Abe glanced toward the kids playing, then back to her.

"I appreciate you coming today," he said, his tone honest.

Hagar nodded, lowering her voice.

"I wasn't sure if you'd want me here."

Abe met her eyes, his voice kind but firm.

"Whatever happened between us back then...it never changed what you gave us. What you gave my wife. My family."

Hagar nodded slowly.

"Thank you for saying that."

Abe offered a small, genuine smile.

"This is where healing starts."

For the first time, both seemed able to fully exhale.

The Cake Prayer

When it was time for cake, Abe gently tapped his glass to quiet the group.

"I don't have words big enough for what this past year has meant. But I know exactly Who to thank," as he pointed one finger to heaven.

The crowd listened intently as his voice grew tender.

"We serve a God who does not waste waiting...who brings life from broken places, and laughter from the impossible."

Abe turned toward Isaac, who giggled wildly in his highchair.

"Son, your name means laughter, and you've filled this home... and our hearts...with it every day."

He squeezed Sarah's hand as Mara stepped forward for the prayer.

"Father, we bless this child of promise today. We thank You for both of Sarah and Abe's sons...for Ishmael and Isaac...and for the intricate story You've written across these years. May they grow to know You, to trust You, and to carry Your promises even further."

The guests softly echoed, "Amen."

The Exhale

That night, long after the last guests had departed and the string lights glowed softly overhead, Sarah and Abe stood in the backyard watching both boys sleep peacefully on the monitor screen inside.

"You know," Sarah whispered, "I never imagined the story would look like this."

Abe smiled, pulling her close.

"Neither did I."

She exhaled, her heart full.

"But I'm so grateful it does."

"Oh! I almost forgot," she whispered to Abe. "Hagar gave me this, for Ishmael. For when he's older." She held the letter in her hands for a moment, feeling its quiet weight.

Abe glanced at the envelope, his expression softening. "Do you want to read it together now?"

Sarah nodded.

They moved to an outdoor couch and carefully opened the letter— reading Hagar's words as the night closed gently around them.

The Letter

My Dearest Ishmael,

You may not remember me. And that's okay.

One day, your parents may give you this letter, and when they do, I pray you'll read it with peace in your heart—and theirs.

I was honored to be part of your story before you were born. For a season, God entrusted me with the sacred role of carrying you. You were never mine to keep, but you were mine to hold, to protect, and to love as you were knitted together in my womb.

You belong fully to your mother and father—Sarah and Abe—who longed for you, prayed for you, and believed for you even when the wait felt endless. Their love made room for a miracle. I was simply chosen to help bring that miracle into the world.

Know this, Ishmael: you are not the product of chance or circumstance. You were the fulfillment of a promise. The answer to years of tears, hope, and faith. You came into this world wrapped in intention, surrounded by love, and covered in prayer.

Your name means "God hears." And He did. He heard your parents. And He heard me too.

I prayed for you from the moment I knew you were there. I have prayed for your joy, your courage, your kindness. I have prayed that you would know who you are, and more importantly, whose you are. If ever you wonder whether you were loved by me, the answer is yes. Deeply. Completely. From the first flutter of your heartbeat until the last time I whispered a prayer for your future.

With all my tenderness and gratitude for the role I got to play in your beginning,

—Hagar

Sarah read through blurred eyes as she gently closed the envelope again, her hands resting softly over it.

Abe exhaled, his voice quiet.

"She wrote that beautifully."

Sarah nodded, her throat tight.

"She loved him, Abe. She really did. And she never tried to claim what wasn't hers."

Abe reached for her hand, interlacing their fingers.

"I think that's what makes it even more sacred. She gave us a part of herself but never tried to hold onto it."

Sarah stared down at the letter, her voice soft.

"When the time comes, I'll be grateful to give him these words."

Abe nodded. "And he'll grow up knowing not just how much we love him…but how many people God wove into his story to bring him here."

Sarah smiled through the mist in her eyes.

"Grace upon grace."

Abe kissed the back of her hand gently.

"Exactly that."

They sat together beneath the stars—no longer waiting, no longer afraid—fully resting inside the extravagant grace of the God who had not only delivered His promise but had written beauty even in the most complicated parts of it.

CHAPTER 41

The Family Tree

One Year Later—Sarah and Abe's Living Room, New Jersey

The late afternoon sun poured through the tall windows as Sarah placed fresh coffee and pastries on the table. Mara and Lottie had flown in for one of their long-overdue girls weekends—the kind they used to dream about back in college.

The house was full of energy. Ishmael, now seven years old, was busy building an elaborate Lego tower in the corner while two-year-old Isaac waddled happily between Sarah's legs and the toy basket.
Abe peeked in from the kitchen as Isaac squealed.

"Careful, little man…that's your brother's masterpiece you're about to knock over."

"Mommy, Isaac's gonna break it!" Ishmael called dramatically. Sarah smiled, scooping Isaac up before disaster struck.

"Crisis averted," she teased, planting a kiss on Isaac's head.

Mara watched them with a soft, full smile.

"Your boys are getting so big, Sarah."

Sarah beamed.

"They're keeping us busy—but I wouldn't trade it for anything."
Lottie added playfully,

"I can barely keep up with the group texts you send of their latest toddler disasters."

Sarah laughed.

"Ishmael thinks he's Isaac's third parent half the time."

"I'm his big brother," Ishmael chimed proudly from across the room.

"That you are," Sarah said warmly.

As they sipped their coffee, Mara grew quiet. She glanced at Lottie nervously, who simply nodded in silent encouragement.

Sarah noticed instantly.

"Mara? What's going on?"

Mara smiled softly, her eyes already glistening.

"I wanted to tell you both in person."

Sarah's breath caught slightly, sensing what was coming.

Mara reached for her hand across the table.

"Sarah... after all the waiting, after all the prayers... I'm pregnant again. A little girl, a baby sister for Jacob."

For a moment, the world seemed to pause. Then Sarah's eyes filled as she squeezed Mara's hand tightly.

"Oh, Mara..."

The two women fell into each other's arms, tears flowing freely—not tears of pain this time, but of joy and release.

As they pulled back, Sarah smiled through her tears.

"How far along are you?"

"Almost ten weeks," Mara said softly. "It still feels surreal."

Lottie chimed in, wiping her eyes.

"See? He never forgot either of you."

Sarah nodded, her voice thick.

"His timing may not make sense, but His promises always stand."

Mara smiled, whispering:

"I never stopped declaring it. Even on the days it felt impossible. We wait so long for one child and now we are blessed with two!"

Sarah squeezed her hand again, her heart full.

"Ditto! Now we are both blessed with two miracles."

Lottie, stirring her chai, smiled too—but it was the kind of smile that hinted at something behind it. She'd been quieter this morning, and both Sarah and Mara noticed.

Sarah glanced at her. "You good, Lott? You've been awfully reflective for someone who stayed up playing Cards Against Humanity with Abe and Jared until midnight."

Lottie exhaled. "Yeah, I've just been…thinking." She swirled her spoon in her cup.

"And?" Mara asked gently.

Lottie looked between her two best friends. "And I think being around your kids…hearing Isaac call Sarah 'Mama,' watching Ishmael try to teach him how to build Legos…" she paused, swallowing emotion, "it stirred something. Something I wasn't expecting."

Sarah leaned in, concerned but curious. "Tell us."

"I've always said I didn't want a family. And maybe that was true for a long time. But lately…I'm wondering if I was just protecting myself from something I didn't think I could have."

Mara reached across the table and touched her hand. "You don't have to explain. You're allowed to change."

Lottie nodded, eyes misty. "There's someone in my life…Drew.

We've been seeing each other for a while now. I haven't told either of you yet because I wasn't sure where it was going. But…he's different. Safe. Gentle. The kind of man who brings an umbrella even when there's only a 10% chance of rain."

Sarah smiled, eyes wide with surprise and delight.

"You're in love!"

Lottie groaned, half-laughing. "Maybe. I don't know. But I think I might be ready to want more."

Mara grinned. "Did we just witness the fall of the Ice Queen?"

Lottie rolled her eyes. "Easy, it's still a maybe. I haven't told him I'm open to the whole...family thing."

Sarah leaned forward. "You will. When you're ready. And if he's the one, he'll walk through that door with you."

Lottie looked at both of them, warmth flooding her chest. "You know what the wildest part is? Watching you two...all the mess and beauty of motherhood, the heartache and miracles...it's not perfect, but it's... real. And I think I want that kind of real."

Mara lifted her coffee. "To real."

Sarah clinked hers gently. "To surprises."

Lottie smirked. "And to babies who can't pronounce my name but already have my heart."

They laughed again—loud, unfiltered joy—then sat together in a soft hush, three women tethered by years of history, different stories, but hearts that had grown together through it all.

Later That Night—Sarah & Abe's House

The house was finally still.

Isaac had long since fallen asleep, and Ishmael's soft breathing filled his bedroom down the hall. Abe had drifted off beside her, but Sarah remained awake—not from anxiety this time, but from something else entirely. Gratitude.

She quietly slipped out of bed and curled into her favorite chair by the window. The stars sparkled across the skyline like tiny reminders of how far they had come.

Sarah opened her journal—the one she hadn't written in for months—

and gently ran her fingers across the first blank page.

Taking a breath, she began to write:

Lord,

Sometimes I still can't believe this is my life. I sit here tonight with two sleeping boys under our roof—one carried through another's womb, the other carried through years of prayer—and I am overwhelmed by Your kindness.

I remember the ache of waiting. The years of wondering if You were listening. The fear that maybe I had been passed over.

And yet...You were always writing. Even when I couldn't see the next page.

Mara is pregnant now too. After her own waiting season. You didn't forget her either.

Pastor Wells once told me that my waiting could become someone else's comfort. And somehow, You've done that. You've taken all these pieces—the heartbreak, the longing, the confusion—and stitched together something far more beautiful than I ever imagined.

There were days when my faith was smaller than a mustard seed. But even then, You held onto me. You never stopped writing.

And now, when I look at Ishmael's bright eyes, and Isaac's joyful laughter, I see nothing but grace upon grace.

You kept Your promise, Lord. You always do.

And tonight, I rest in that.

Sarah closed the journal softly, pressing her hand against the cover for a long moment.

She whispered into the quiet,

"Thank You, God."

And with that, she finally allowed herself to sleep—not with the weight of waiting, but with the fullness of promises kept.

Three Years After Isaac's Birth—Midtown Cigar Lounge, Manhattan

The low hum of conversation, clinking glasses, and faint jazz created a relaxed rhythm as Abe leaned back into the leather armchair. Across from him sat Marcus, Eli, and Jordan—his crew, his circle, the men who had walked with him through every twist of the last few years. Marcus handed him a glass of bourbon.

"Alright, Dad of the Year—you finally made it out of the house." Abe grinned, taking the glass.

"Barely. It took me and Sarah both forty-five minutes just to get Isaac down tonight. Kid has the energy of a squirrel on espresso." Eli chuckled, puffing his cigar.

"And Ishmael? What's he up to now?"

"Building Lego cities that rival midtown," Abe said.

"And correcting me anytime I pronounce a dinosaur wrong." Jordan raised his glass.

"You've got your hands full, brother."

After a few minutes of the usual banter, the conversation settled into the familiar rhythm of real friendship.

Marcus leaned forward slightly.

"Honestly though, Abe...I've been meaning to say this... watching you and Sarah walk through everything these past few years? The infertility, the surrogacy, Hagar, the delivery, even the post-baby storm? Man...not a lot of people would've made it through all that the way you two have."

The others nodded in agreement.

Abe exhaled slowly, swirling the amber liquid in his glass.

"There were days I wasn't sure we would either."

Jordan spoke gently. "What was the hardest part?"

Abe paused, choosing his words carefully.

"Honestly? The helplessness. Watching Sarah carry all that pain and not being able to fix it for her. And then...when Hagar came into the picture...man, that tested everything."

Eli nodded.

"Most guys wouldn't have handled a situation like that with half the grace you did."

Abe gave a small, humble smile.

"Grace...and a whole lot of prayer. And friends like you who kept showing up."

Marcus leaned back, voice thoughtful.

"You still believe God orchestrated all of it?"

Abe's answer was immediate.

"Absolutely. Even the messy parts. Especially the messy parts."

He looked down for a moment, his voice softening.

"There were nights Sarah and I prayed when all we could say was 'Help.' But somehow...God carried us through. And when I look at Ishmael and Isaac...I see nothing but grace."

Jordan raised his glass again.

"To answered prayers...even the ones that didn't look the way you thought they would."

Eli added with a grin.

"And to wives who somehow love us anyway."

The men laughed as their glasses clinked together.

Abe smiled, feeling the full weight of gratitude in his chest.

"To God's faithfulness...in the waiting, in the storm, and in the promise."

As the conversation shifted back to lighter jokes and old stories, Abe sat quietly for a moment, letting the truth settle deeply:
God had not only fulfilled His promise—He had sustained them through the waiting.

Ishmael, age 8

It started with a school assignment.

"Draw your family tree," the instructions had said.
"Include your parents, siblings, and grandparents. Ask your grown-ups to help."

Sarah found the paper in Ishmael's backpack the evening before it was due, smudged with crayons and a few eraser marks where a branch had been redrawn.

"Ish, do you want help with this?" she asked as they sat at the kitchen island, Isaac playing with wooden blocks on the floor nearby.
Ishmael nodded. "Yeah. But…" He looked up at her, brown eyes serious. "Can I ask something weird?"

"Of course, baby. Anything."

He hesitated. "How come I don't know my real mom?"
Sarah's heart skipped. They had anticipated this moment, talked it through with Pastor Wells and a family counselor. Still, it landed like a small quake under her ribs.

"Well," she said carefully, "you do know your real mom—I'm her. I'm the one who prayed for you and loved you before you were even born. But I think I know what you mean."

Ishmael nodded slowly. "The lady who carried me in her belly. The one who gave me to you and Daddy."
Sarah reached for his hand. "Her name is Hagar. She was someone very special to us…and she loved you, too. She gave us a gift that changed everything."

"Do I look like her?" he asked.

"You have her determination," Sarah said. "But my eyes, and you have your daddy's laugh and your grandpa's name."
That caught him. "My grandpa?"

"Yes," Abe said, walking in with a bowl of apple slices and hearing the tail end of the conversation. "My dad's name was Ishmael, too. We named you after him because we wanted you to carry on the strength of his story."

Ishmael blinked. "Did I meet him?"

Abe crouched next to him. "No, buddy. He died before you were born. But he would've loved you so much. He was strong and wise and believed in building things that lasted. He helped people. Just like I believe you will."

"Can I see a picture of him?" Ishmael asked.

Abe smiled and nodded. "Absolutely. I'll show you tonight."

Ishmael looked down at the family tree. "So I write 'Hagar' and then 'Sarah' under the mom line?"

Sarah smiled gently. "You could write both names. Maybe draw a heart between them…like a bridge. That's what she was. A bridge."

Ishmael nodded, deep in thought. "And grandpa Ishmael goes at the top?"

"Right at the top," Abe said, ruffling his son's hair.

"Where all good legacies begin."

Later That Evening

After dinner, the family tree was spread across the dining table, now dotted with sticky notes and colored markers.

"Okay," Ishmael said, tongue sticking out in concentration as he wrote in blocky letters. "Grandpa Ishmael. What was Grandma's name?"

Abe looked up from where he was rinsing dishes. "Her name was Lillian, but everyone called her Lily."

Ishmael grinned. "Like the flower?"

"Exactly," Abe said. "She was kind. Quiet strength. The kind of woman who made you feel safe just by sitting beside her."

"Did she die too?"

"Yes," Abe said, walking over and drying his hands on a towel.

"She died when I was in college. I miss her every day."

Ishmael wrote "Lily" next to "Ishmael Sr." and then turned to Sarah. "What about your mom and dad?"

Sarah smiled. "My mom's name was Grace, and my dad was Thomas. They were very loving. Mom used to sing me lullabies, and Dad made the best pancakes on Saturday mornings."

"Can I draw pancakes next to him?"

Sarah laughed. "Sure, why not?"

Ishmael sketched a lopsided stack with syrup. Then he looked at both parents. "It's weird that I don't remember any of them. The grandparents."

"That's okay," Abe said. "You carry pieces of them in you. Their stories, their names, the way we talk about them...that's how we remember."

"And we'll always tell you those stories," Sarah added, wrapping an arm around him.

Isaac wandered into the room and clambered onto Abe's lap. "I draw too?"

Ishmael beamed. "You can help color the heart bridge."

Sarah looked at the clock. "Okay, artists, it's bedtime."

"Story first?" Ishmael asked.

"Story first," Abe confirmed, hoisting Isaac into one arm and gesturing for Ishmael to grab his blanket.

They all piled onto the couch, kids sandwiched between their parents.

"What kind of story tonight?" Sarah asked.

"Tell me the one about your dream," Ishmael said. "The one where you saw me."

Sarah blinked, surprised. "You remember that one?"

"You said it before. I want to hear it again."

Abe smiled and began, voice soft, "Before you were born, I had a dream. I saw a little boy with big eyes and a smile that could light up a city block. And when I woke up, I told your mom, 'I think he's coming.'"

"And we waited," Sarah added, brushing a curl off Ishmael's forehead. "We waited a long time. But you came. And you were worth it."

Ishmael nestled deeper between them. "Tell it again tomorrow, okay?"

"Every night, if you want," Sarah whispered.

Isaac was already snoring. Ishmael blinked slowly, holding his blanket close.

Abe looked over at Sarah, eyes meeting in that quiet, sacred way parents sometimes speak without words.

The family tree sat complete on the table.

But the roots? They were right here—in love, in waiting, and in the stories whispered before sleep.

Family Tree Day at School

The next morning, Sarah adjusted Ishmael's backpack straps and handed him the carefully rolled family tree, now protected in a cardboard tube. "Be gentle with it, okay? No sword fights."

Ishmael grinned. "Promise."

Abe handed him a lunchbox. "You ready to show off your masterpiece?"

"Totally," Ishmael said. "Miss Gonzalez said we get to go up one by one and explain who's on our tree."

As they approached the school, Sarah knelt beside him at the car line. "Remember, it's okay to tell them the truth about your family...every family looks a little different."

"I know," Ishmael said seriously. "But mine's awesome. I have two parents, two brothers..."

Sarah raised an eyebrow.

"Okay, fine," Ishmael giggled. "One brother. But Isaac steals my toys, so it's like having two."

Sarah laughed and gave him a kiss on the cheek. "You're going to do great."

Later that morning, in front of his class, Ishmael unrolled the colorful poster.

"This is my family tree," he announced confidently. "My name is from my grandpa, Ishmael. He died before I was born, but I still carry his name so we remember him."

Gasps and nods came from his classmates as he pointed to a little sketch of pancakes. "This is my other grandpa...he made pancakes for my mom on Saturdays. And this," he gestured to a pink flower, "is my Grandma Lily. She was quiet but strong, like my dad says."

A hand shot up. "Where's your mom and dad?"

He pointed to the big red hearts connecting everything. "Right here. Mom and Dad. They're the roots. And my baby brother, Isaac, is the newest leaf."

Miss Gonzalez smiled. "And what does that heart mean?"

"It means our family started with love," Ishmael said proudly.

The room fell into a soft hush—even the fidgety kids paused.

Later, Miss Gonzalez knelt beside him as the class prepared for recess. "That was a beautiful presentation, Ishmael. I think you helped a lot of kids feel proud of their own families, too."

He shrugged, stuffing the tube back in his bag. "Thanks. My mom and dad tell good stories."

The Legacy Continues

The clink of forks and laughter echoed off the kitchen walls. Isaac babbled from his booster seat, triumphantly smearing mashed sweet potato across his tray like it was a canvas.

"I think he's creating his own language," Sarah said, handing him a wipe.

Isaac lifted a spoon and proudly declared, "Tree house!"

Abe tilted his head. "Tree house?"

Isaac nodded with glee. "Family tree live in tree house!"

Ishmael burst out laughing. "That's not how it works, bro."

"Well, technically," Sarah teased, "it's not totally wrong."
Ishmael sat taller than usual at the table, chest puffed with subtle pride as he bit into his grilled cheese. Abe noticed and grinned.

"So, how'd it go today? Did your family tree steal the show?"

"It did!" Ishmael said between bites. "Miss Gonzalez said mine had the most 'thoughtful symbolism.' That means it made people feel stuff."

"Oh, it sure does," Sarah smiled, handing him a napkin.
"I bet your classmates learned a lot from you."

"They did," he nodded.

"One kid said his grandma lives in another country, so I told him it still counts. He drew a plane next to her picture."
Abe chuckled. "You're a natural at this, buddy. And someday, you'll get to help your own kids make their family tree."
Ishmael blinked. "Wait… what?"

Abe leaned back with a teasing grin. "Sure. One day you'll get married, have kids, and pass on the Abrams legacy."
Ishmael's face twisted in horror. "Oh gross! Nooo way. I'm never doing that."
Sarah burst out laughing. "You sound just like your dad did when he was your age."
Abe nodded sagely. "And look at me now…married to the best girl in the world, with two awesome sons."
Ishmael looked skeptical. "Well… maybe. But only if she likes robots and can make grilled cheese without burning it."
"High standards," Abe said, raising his glass of water. "I respect that."
Isaac looked up from his potatoes. "I get married!"
Everyone froze.

"You what?" Sarah asked, eyes wide with a laugh building in her throat.

"I get married! To juice!" Isaac announced, then clapped for himself.

"Married to juice," Abe repeated, raising his brows. "A man of commitment. I respect that."

They all burst out laughing. Isaac joined in, not entirely sure why, but thrilled to be included.

They clinked their glasses—Abe, Sarah, and Ishmael—as Isaac tapped his sippy cup with dramatic flair, spilling a little on the table.

And just like that, another layer of legacy was quietly laid around that dinner table—one filled with stories, sticky hands, and the promise of more tomorrows.

That Night

The house was finally still. The boys had been wrestled into pajamas, read their stories, kissed on foreheads, and tucked into dreams.

The dishwasher hummed faintly in the background, and soft lamplight glowed in the living room where Sarah sat on the couch with her tea, feet tucked beneath her, a blanket draped across her legs. Abe was going through that day's mail at the kitchen counter.

Sarah exhaled deeply. "I can't believe Isaac said he was marrying juice."

Abe laughed, the sound low and warm. "He's got good taste. Organic apple, no sugar added? A fine match."

Abe noticed a letter, buried under a pile of catalogs and bills. No return address—just Sarah's name written in familiar, elegant handwriting. He stared for a long moment, then reached for it.

Abe turned to Sarah with a look of shock on his face.

"What's that?" Sarah asked.

He didn't answer at first, just passed the envelope to her.

Sarah's brow furrowed as she recognized the handwriting.

"Hagar?"

Abe nodded. "I haven't opened it yet."

Together, they moved to sit at the kitchen table, side by side. The only sound was the soft hum of the dishwasher and the gentle tick of the clock on the wall.

With a breath, Sarah opened the envelope.

Inside: a photo and a letter. She looked at the photo first.

Hagar stood in front of a white house with green shutters, her arm around a tall, warm-eyed man. In her arms was a baby—round cheeks, wide grin, dark curls. She looked happy. At peace.

Abe leaned in. "She looks...good."

Sarah nodded, then unfolded the letter.

Dear Sarah,

I hope this letter finds you and your precious family well. I've written it in my head a thousand times, but it never seemed like the right moment until now.

You'll never fully know what working for you meant to me—not just the job, but the invitation into your life. You showed me trust, even when I didn't know how to hold it. And grace, even when I didn't deserve it.

I left New York to find out who I was without you, without the role I had stepped into. It wasn't easy. But I did find myself. Piece by piece. Two years ago, I married a kind man named Tobias...he proposed shortly after I visited you and Isaac in the hospital. He is good in all the ways I didn't know to ask for. And a few months ago, we had a daughter.

Her name is Selah Hope.

Selah because she is my pause, my breath, my sacred turning point. Hope because after everything, she is proof that something beautiful can still grow.

I want you to know I never stopped praying for you and Abe—and

Ishmael and Isaac too. You are their true parents in every way that counts.
You don't need to write back. I just wanted you to know that I'm okay. That I found joy. And that I will always be grateful to you and Abe— for the grace, the forgiveness, and the second chance to start again.
With love,
Hagar

Sarah's hands trembled as she lowered the letter. Abe reached over and took it gently, skimming the lines.

"She did it," he said quietly. "She built a life."

"She did," Sarah whispered.

For a long while, they said nothing. Just sat with the letter, with the picture, with the enormity of what had once been—and what had finally healed.

Sarah traced the edge of the photo, then tucked it and the letter back into the envelope and pressed it to her chest.

"I think I'll hold onto this," she murmured. "For Ishmael. When the time's right."

Abe leaned over, kissed her temple. "He'll understand. One day."

And together, under the soft kitchen light, they sat in the quiet— full of peace, and a surprising sense of closure they hadn't known they still needed.

"Wow, first Ishmael's project and now Hagar's letter..." Sarah said, her voice thoughtful. "Watching him try to make sense of people he's never met...grandparents who are long gone...of a surrogate mother he barely remembers. It made me wish we could give him more answers. Or more time with them."

Abe nodded slowly. "Yeah. I had my dad growing up, but losing him right before college...it left a hole I didn't know how to fill.

Sometimes I still find myself trying to hold onto fragments...

his old letters, things people say about him, the way he used to laugh when he got excited. But it's not the same as having him here."

Sarah leaned her head on Abe's shoulder. "You're giving Ishmael and Isaac what your dad didn't get to give you. That matters."

"I hope so." He rubbed his thumb gently over her hand.

"I just want them to feel rooted. Like they're standing on something solid...even if the people who built it are gone."

"They are," she said. "And someday, they'll understand it even better. Maybe not today, not while they're marrying juice and building tree houses in their minds, but someday."

Abe chuckled, then grew quiet again. "I love our life. It's messy. Unscripted. But it's ours."

Sarah smiled, her eyes closing. "Me too."

He kissed the top of her head, and they sat together, holding the weight and wonder of legacy—not just the one they inherited, but the one they were building brick by brick, bedtime by bedtime, love by love.

Legacy and Mentorship

The woman sitting across from Sarah looked barely twenty-five, fragile, wide-eyed with tears welling as she described her second failed IVF attempt.

Sarah didn't rush to speak. She had learned not to fill silence with noise, especially not empty promises. She simply sat, steady, present, unshaken.

"What if it never happens?" the young woman whispered. Her voice cracked on the last word.

Sarah reached across the small table and took her hand, warm and sure.

"Then you'll still be whole," she said gently. "Still seen. Still chosen. Even in the waiting."

The woman cried harder, not from pity, but from the relief of not being preached to, fixed, or hurried past her pain.

Sarah had once been in that same chair—heart hollowed by

disappointment, faith stretched thin like a thread pulled too tight. But now, with both Isaac and Ishmael asleep at home, miracle upon miracle realized, she understood something deeper than resolution. She carried revelation that her journey could impact the journey of future generations.

Sarah had become someone else's anchor.

"There's a lie we start to believe in the waiting," Sarah said softly. "That maybe we were never meant to be mothers. That maybe God skipped over us when He handed out fruitfulness. But that's not truth. That's fear. That's the enemy."

The woman looked up slowly, searching Sarah's eyes.

"Do you know the very first thing God said to humanity?" Sarah continued, her voice quiet but fierce. "He blessed them and said, *Be fruitful and multiply.* That wasn't a suggestion, it was a blessing. A part of His design. So, no matter how long it takes, don't let go of that truth. Don't trade it for the lie."

The young woman clutched a tissue, nodding slowly through tears.

Sarah, once broken open by grief, now felt the weight of stewardship, to pass on what had been formed in her not just through miracles, but through fire.

They bowed their heads and prayed together. Sarah didn't ask for a baby that day. She asked for peace. For comfort in the not-yet. For the kind of hope that can breathe even in barren places. When the final "amen" settled over them like a blanket, Sarah squeezed her hand once more.

And as the prayer settled into quiet, Sarah's thoughts briefly drifted to Hagar—the young woman who had once carried Sarah's promise when her own body couldn't. There had been so much unspoken between them in those early months: gratitude tangled with jealousy, faith complicated by fear. But grace had carved space for both of them to heal. And in the end, they had both been changed by it.

Sarah looked into the woman's eyes and whispered:

"God hasn't forgotten you. Not your body. Not your prayers. Not your name." And she meant it.

Because she had seen it—not just in the birth of her sons, but in the redemption of a broken friendship. In the sisterhood that was born not through blood, but forged through shared surrender.

Legacy, she had come to believe, wasn't just about the children you raise.

It was the women you walk with.

The truths you pass down.

And the lies you refuse to let the next generation believe.

edge—only a soft ache.

Epilogue

The Fullness of Time

"He makes everything beautiful in its time." Ecclesiastes 3:11 (NKJV)

The park was alive with the sounds of children's laughter, bicycles clattering, and parents calling softly to their little ones. The late afternoon sun painted everything in a warm golden hue.

Sarah sat on the bench, watching Ishmael and Isaac run ahead, their giggles blending like music.

Two brothers—different beginnings, yet equally her sons.

Ishmael, now a vibrant eight-year-old, sprinted barefoot across the grass, chasing bubbles that floated like tiny glass orbs under the afternoon sky. Isaac, at three, followed Ishmael everywhere, mimicking his every move, his laughter echoing like music through every room.

Isaac giggled as Ishmael danced around him, popping bubbles one by one.

"More! More!" Isaac squealed, his toddler voice bright and musical.

Sarah laughed, her heart overflowing as she kissed the top of Isaac's head.

"Your brother has plenty of energy, doesn't he?"

Isaac clapped his small hands, beaming up at her as if agreeing completely.

Abe approached with two cups of coffee, handing one to Sarah as he sat beside her. For a moment, neither spoke. They simply watched.

"They're growing fast," Abe finally said.

Sarah smiled. "Too fast."

Ishmael was protective of his younger brother, guiding him carefully around the playground like a little shepherd. Isaac, still learning to balance his toddler legs, followed closely behind.

As Sarah watched them, her heart swelled—not just with love, but with awe. The years of waiting, the heartbreak, the impossible decisions—all led here. To this.

"I never thought I'd see a day like this," Sarah whispered.

Abe reached for her hand. "I did," he said gently. "Even when you couldn't. God never forgot His promise."

Sarah felt the truth of those words sink deep into her soul. The ache that had once lived deep inside her had transformed over time—no longer sharp, no longer haunting. And now, the joy had come—not because she earned it, but because grace had made room for it.

Every path they had walked, the waiting, the heartbreak, the surrogacy, the fracture, the healing, had led them here.

And though she hadn't seen Hagar in a couple of years, Sarah still prayed for her often. She sometimes wondered if, one day, their paths would cross again—not as rivals bound by brokenness, but as women connected by grace.

Across the playground, Ishmael called out, "Mom! Watch this!"

She smiled wide and waved, her voice warm. "I'm watching, sweetheart!"

Isaac clapped his hands, mimicking his big brother.

Two miracles. Two promises. Two chapters of one impossible, beautiful story.

Sarah leaned her head against Abe's shoulder, the breeze soft against her face.

"Yes," she whispered. "He makes everything beautiful. In His time."

That Evening—Quiet Reflection

After the boys were asleep, Sarah stepped out onto the back porch, wrapped in a light sweater, listening to the soft hum of summer cicadas. Abe joined her, sliding his arm around her waist as they stood in the quiet.

"Do you ever stop and marvel?" she whispered.

Abe smiled.

"Every single day."

She rested her head against his shoulder, her voice soft.

"I used to be afraid I would never laugh again."

Abe kissed the top of her head.

"And now you laugh all the time."

Sarah smiled, tears welling as she whispered,

"Just like He promised."

She thought of the name they had given their son—Isaac—*he who laughs.*

Their story had not unfolded the way she once imagined, but in the end, God had written something far more beautiful than she ever could have scripted.

A miracle in two chapters.

Two sons. Two promises. Both held in God's perfect time.

And beneath the quiet stars, Sarah whispered once more simple prayer into the night—not out of longing, but out of fullness:

"Thank You for remembering me."

The stars above sparkled against the dark canvas of the city skyline—the same stars God once pointed out to Abraham when He first made the promise.

So shall your descendants be.

And now, through unexpected turns and unplanned miracles, that promise lived on—right here in her arms, running through her home, filling her life with joy.

Sarah smiled, her heart finally and fully at peace.

Sarah's Letter to Isaac

The house was quiet—both boys finally asleep, the soft hum of the baby monitor a gentle background melody. Sarah sat at her desk beneath the warm glow of the lamp, her journal open, pen poised.

She had written so many prayers over the years.

Tonight, she was writing a letter.

Not for today.

But for one day.

When Isaac would be old enough to understand where his story began.

Before beginning her letter, Sarah sat quietly at her desk, reflecting on the envelope that still rested in their safe—the letter Hagar had written for Ishmael.

She had read it many times since the party, always moved by Hagar's grace, her honesty, and the quiet love woven through every word.

If Hagar could leave something so beautiful for Ishmael, Sarah thought, then surely I can do the same for Isaac.

With that, she opened her journal and began to write—not out of obligation, but out of the overflow of love, gratitude, and the quiet, complicated beauty that had brought their family into being.

The Letter

My sweet Isaac,

There's so much I want to tell you—things you may never fully grasp until life gives you a season of waiting of your own.

You are a promise. Not just the answer to a prayer—but the culmination of many prayers. Your father and I waited for you longer than we ever imagined. We cried. We questioned. We hoped against hope.

And just when we thought perhaps the answer would always be "no," God whispered "not yet."

I want you to know that waiting does not mean forgotten. Delay is not denial. Sometimes God writes His most beautiful stories through waiting—because He's busy building something even greater than we dared to dream.

Before you came, your big brother Ishmael was born—also a miracle. His life is part of the promise too. You two are the living evidence that God redeems even complicated journeys.
There was another woman involved—Hagar—who helped carry your brother into this world when my body could not. She was part of God's provision, even in the midst of my pain. And for that, I will always be grateful.

There were days I didn't know if I'd survive the ache. But now, when I look at you, I see the kindness of God written across every inch of your life.

Isaac, your name means laughter—and you've brought exactly that into our home. You are joy. You are proof that God's promises are never too late.

I pray that as you grow, you will come to know the God who answered our prayers—not because we were strong, but because He is faithful.

And I pray you'll trust Him with every piece of your story, just like He held ours.

With all my love,

Mommy.

Sarah gently closed the journal, resting her hand over it for a moment, allowing the tears to fall freely now—but this time, they were tears of peace.

Abe appeared quietly behind her, resting his hands on her shoulders.

"You okay?" he whispered.

She smiled through her tears.

"I'm better than okay."

Together, they stood for a moment, watching the monitor screen where both of their sons slept peacefully.

The waiting was over.

The promise had been fulfilled.

Author's Note

When I first imagined *Modern Sarah*, I wasn't simply retelling a story from the Bible. I was writing out pieces of my own journey—a journey of waiting, disappointment, hope, and ultimately, God's faithfulness. God's simple ask of me in putting these words on paper was to reveal His truth against Satan's lies.

Like Sarah in the Bible, I spent many years longing for a child. In my early thirties, my husband and I tried to start a family, only to face the heartbreak of infertility. The first half of my thirties were consumed with trying—the second half, I tried to convince myself that perhaps it simply wasn't God's will.

But as I grew in my faith and understanding of God's Word, I realized something powerful: infertility was never His will. God's first words to mankind in Genesis 1:28 were, "Be fruitful and multiply." And His Word assures us again and again that His will for us is good, pleasing, and perfect (Romans 12:2).

Infertility is a thief—one of many ways Satan tries to steal, kill, and destroy (John 10:10). But God has given us authority through Jesus to resist the enemy and stand in faith for His promises. When I finally understood my authority in Christ, I realized I could speak directly to my circumstances, just as Jesus did—commanding sickness to leave, commanding dead things to rise, and declaring God's will over my body and my life.

During my own journey, God allowed me to share this revelation with others—including a coworker who had been trying to conceive for six years. I encouraged her to declare God's Word daily, command her womb to align with His perfect design of multiplication, and resist the enemy's attempts to steal her miracle. Within three months, she was pregnant. And while I don't take credit for her miracle, I saw once again how God's Word is alive, powerful, and true for anyone who believes.

Still, I thought my own story was closed. My husband and I had made peace with the idea that children would not be part of our future. But God's timing was not finished. After I had given up completely—God surprised us. I became pregnant more than five years after we had stopped trying. God orchestrated a series of events that removed every obstacle in His way. My favorite saying, "Wanna hear God laugh? Tell Him your plans."

Looking back, I see clearly now: Satan may plot, but he remains on a leash. My God's will cannot be withheld (Job 42:2). He restored to me what I thought was lost, just as He did for Sarah and Abraham. And like Sarah, I can say with confidence that God's purposes for my life will stand.

My prayer for you—especially if you are walking through infertility or unanswered prayers—is that you will never doubt God's will for fruitfulness in your life. Stand on His promises. Command the enemy to flee. Speak life to every area that feels barren. And trust that even when we cannot see it, God is always weaving beauty from brokenness.

This story is not just fiction. It's testimony. And it's my honor to share it with you.

"The effective, fervent prayer of a righteous man avails much." —
James 5:16 (NKJV)

Acknowledgments

First and foremost, I give thanks to my Heavenly Father, the Author of every good and perfect gift. Every word of this novel exists because of His faithfulness, His mercy, and His perfect timing. What seemed impossible for so many years, He made possible, in His way and His time.

To my husband, family and friends—your prayers, encouragement, and constant reminders of God's promises sustained me through every disappointment, every tear, and every quiet hope. I especially thank my dad, who never stopped praying for his future grandchild, even when I had given up hope.

To those who are still waiting, you are seen. You are loved. And God has not forgotten you. To every woman whose story echoes Sarah's—whether in longing, in sacrifice, or in joy—may this novel serve as both testimony and encouragement that God is still the God who fulfills promises.

And finally, to every reader, thank you for choosing to journey with me through this retelling. My prayer is that *Modern Sarah* not only entertains but reminds you that no season is wasted, and that in God's hands, even long waits birth beautiful things.

If you enjoyed *Modern Sarah*, please tell your friends and leave a review on Amazon to support independent publishers.

About the Author

Holly Bogdan lives in Dallas-Fort Worth, Texas, where she balances a full career in the corporate world with her calling as a minister of healing through the love and power of Jesus Christ. While she has spent most of her life as a believer, in recent years she's experienced firsthand the miraculous ways God still moves through ordinary people today. Holly shares her stories to encourage others to discover the authority and purpose God has placed within them.

Modern Sarah is her debut novel—a deeply personal, faith-filled reimagining of the biblical story of Sarah, reflecting her own journey through infertility, waiting, and the miracle of God's perfect timing.

5-Week Small Group Guide

A companion guide for book clubs, Bible studies, and women's ministry groups.

Introduction

The story of Modern Sarah is both personal and universal—touching God's faithfulness. The following questions are designed to spark honest, meaningful conversations as you reflect on your own journey and faith.

How to Use This Guide:
- Read the assigned chapters each week before meeting. Use the discussion questions for group conversation.
- Reflect on the scripture anchor and personal application.
- Close each session with prayer for one another's waiting seasons.

WEEK 1—Act I: Chapters 1–10
Theme: Faith in the Wilderness: Trusting God in the Unknown
Discussion Questions:

- How do Sarah's early dreams of legacy and family shape the trajectory of her adult life?
- Lottie and Mara both play critical roles in Sarah's life. What stood out to you about these friendships? Why is it important to have trusted friends during seasons of uncertainty?
- What role do Lottie and Mara play in establishing Sarah's faith and identity?
- How does Sarah's grief over her parents influence her choices and relationships?
- What do you notice about the way Sarah and Abe's relationship builds from the start?
- What wisdom does Scripture offer on protecting marriages and friendships?

Scripture Anchor: The Lord's Covenant with Abram

After this, the word of the Lord came to Abram in a vision:

"Do not be afraid, Abram. I am your shield, your very great reward."
But Abram said, "Sovereign Lord, what can you give me since I remain childless and the one who will inherit my estate is Eliezer of Damascus?" And Abram said, "You have given me no children—so a servant in my household will be my heir."
Then the word of the Lord came to him: "This man will not be your heir, but a son who is your own flesh and blood will be your heir." He took him outside and said, "Look up at the sky and count the stars—if indeed you can count them." Then he said to him, "So shall your offspring be."
Genesis 15: 1-5 (NIV)

Personal Reflection Prompt:
- How have you handled seasons of waiting in your own life?
- Where is God calling you to trust Him more deeply in a season of uncertainty or transition?

Prayer Reflection (Optional)

Close by praying over one another's waiting seasons—whether for children, healing, restoration, or other promises still unfolding.

WEEK 2—Act II: Chapters 11–19
Theme: The Burden of Waiting

Discussion Questions:

- How does infertility challenge a woman's sense of identity, purpose, or worth?
- What lies does the enemy whisper during seasons of delay or loss? What truth does scripture reveal?
- Hagar begins as Sarah's assistant, but their relationship evolves into something much deeper. Why do you think Sarah opened up to Hagar about her infertility? What made Hagar uniquely positioned to play such a significant role in Sarah's story?
- In what ways is Hagar's introduction into their lives both hopeful and complicated?
- What is the emotional cost of infertility as shown through Sarah, Abe, and even Mara?
- How does prayer, community, and professional support show up in their lives?
- When Dr. Malik introduces surrogacy as an option, Sarah wrestles with letting go of her desire to carry her own child. What emotions or cultural expectations might women face today around fertility, motherhood, and surrogacy?

Scripture Anchor: Hagar and Sarah

Now Sarai, Abram's wife, had borne him no children. But she had an Egyptian slave named Hagar—so she said to Abram, "The Lord has kept me from having children. Go, sleep with my slave—perhaps I can build a family through her."

Abram agreed to what Sarai said. So after Abram had been living in Canaan ten years, Sarai his wife took her Egyptian slave Hagar and gave her to her husband to be his wife. He slept with Hagar, and she conceived.
Genesis 16: 1-4a (NIV)

Personal Reflection Prompt:
• Think about a season when God seemed silent. How did you respond, and what did you learn?
• What spiritual cost often comes with following God's plan?

Prayer Reflection (Optional)
Close by praying over one another's waiting seasons—whether for children, healing, restoration, or other promises still unfolding.

WEEK 3—Act III: Chapters 20–29
Theme: Surrender and Complication

Discussion Questions:
• What makes Sarah's decision to accept Hagar's offer both faithful and painful?
• How does the power dynamic between Sarah, Hagar, and Abe begin to shift?
• What moments of vulnerability shape how the characters relate to one another?
• At times, the emotional intimacy between Abe and Hagar blurs boundaries. How did you experience those moments as a reader? What emotions did they stir in you about loyalty, temptation, and emotional fidelity?
• How did Sarah and Abe's faith evolve throughout their infertility journey? Where did you see God's hand in their story even when they couldn't?

Scripture Anchor: Hagar and Sarah

When she knew she was pregnant, she began to despise her mistress. Then Sarai said to Abram, *"You are responsible for the wrong I am suffering. I put my slave in your arms, and now that she knows she is pregnant, she despises me. May the Lord judge between you and me."*

"Your slave is in your hands," Abram said. "Do with her whatever you think best." Then Sarai mistreated Hagar—so she fled from her.

The angel of the Lord found Hagar near a spring in the desert—it was the spring that is beside the road to Shur. And he said, *"Hagar, slave of Sarai, where have you come from, and where are you going?"*

"I'm running away from my mistress Sarai," she answered.

Then the angel of the Lord told her, "Go back to your mistress and submit to her." The angel added, "I will increase your descendants so much that they will be too numerous to count."

The angel of the Lord also said to her: "You are now pregnant and you will give birth to a son. You shall name him Ishmael, for the Lord has heard of your misery.

He will be a wild donkey of a man—his hand will be against everyone and everyone's hand against him, and he will live in hostility toward all his brothers."

She gave this name to the Lord who spoke to her: *"You are the God who sees me,"* for she said, *"I have now seen the One who sees me."* That is why the well was called Beer Lahai Roi—it is still there, between Kadesh and Bered.

So Hagar bore Abram a son, and Abram gave the name Ishmael to the son she had borne. Abram was eighty-six years old when Hagar bore him Ishmael.

Genesis 16: 4b-15 (NIV)

Personal Reflection Prompt:

- Consider something you had to surrender to God. What emotions

came with that decision?
- Is it difficult for you to share vulnerable struggles with others?
- Prayer Reflection (Optional)

Close by praying over one another's waiting seasons—whether for children, healing, restoration, or other promises still unfolding.

WEEK 4—Act IV: Chapters 30–38
Theme: Joy and Restoration

Discussion Questions:
- How does the birth of Ishmael impact Sarah, Abe, and Hagar individually?
- What changes after Sarah learns she is pregnant with Isaac?
- In what ways do friendships (especially with Lottie and Mara) help anchor the characters?
- Abe consistently supports Sarah while navigating his own emotions. How did you view Abe's spiritual leadership and emotional steadiness? In what ways do you see his character reflect biblical Abraham?
- This novel presents infertility not only as a medical struggle, but also a spiritual one. How did Sarah's perspective on God's will shift throughout the book? How do you personally wrestle with trusting God's timing?

Scripture Anchor:
"As for me, this is my covenant with you: You will be the father of many nations. No longer will you be called Abram; your name will be Abraham, for I have made you a father of many nations. I will make you very fruitful; I will make nations of you, and kings will come from you. I will establish my covenant as an everlasting covenant between me and you and your descendants after you for the generations to come, to be your God and the God of your descendants after you. The whole

land of Canaan, where you now reside as a foreigner, I will give as an everlasting possession to you and your descendants after you; and I will be their God."
Then God said to Abraham, "As for you, you must keep my covenant, you and your descendants after you for the generations to come.

God also said to Abraham, *"As for Sarai your wife, you are no longer to call her Sarai; her name will be Sarah. I will bless her and will surely give you a son by her. I will bless her so that she will be the mother of nations; kings of peoples will come from her."*
Abraham fell facedown; he laughed and said to himself, *"Will a son be born to a man a hundred years old? Will Sarah bear a child at the age of ninety?" And Abraham said to God, "If only Ishmael might live under your blessing!"*
Then God said, *"Yes, but your wife Sarah will bear you a son, and you will call him Isaac.*
Genesis 17:4-9, 15-19 (NIV)

Personal Reflection Prompt:
Describe a moment when a long-awaited promise came true. How did it change you?

Prayer Reflection (Optional)
Close by praying over one another's waiting seasons—whether for children, healing, restoration, or other promises still unfolding.

WEEK 5—Act V: Remaining Chapters + Author's Note
Theme: Legacy and Fullness
Discussion Questions:
- What does legacy mean to Sarah and Abe by the end of the story?
- How has each character evolved in how they view family and faith?
- How did you respond to the letter Hagar wrote for Ishmael? Why was it important for Hagar to leave behind her voice for him? What

does this letter teach us about releasing control and embracing grace?

- What does Modern Sarah teach us about how God redeems even the most complicated chapters of our lives?
- This novel reimagines Sarah and Abraham's story in a modern setting. What similarities or contrasts stood out most to you between Modern Sarah and the original biblical account in Genesis?
- How did the real-life testimony woven into the Author's Note shape your understanding of this fictional retelling? Do you believe God still writes miracle stories like this today?

Scripture Anchor: The Birth of Isaac

Now the Lord was gracious to Sarah as he had said, and the Lord did for Sarah what he had promised. Sarah became pregnant and bore a son to Abraham in his old age, at the very time God had promised him. Abraham gave the name Isaac to the son Sarah bore him. When his son Isaac was eight days old, Abraham circumcised him, as God commanded him. Abraham was a hundred years old when his son Isaac was born to him.

Sarah said, "God has brought me laughter, and everyone who hears about this will laugh with me." And she added, "Who would have said to Abraham that Sarah would nurse children? Yet I have borne him a son in his old age."

Genesis 21: 1-7 (NIV)

Personal Reflection Prompts:

- What part of Modern Sarah felt most personal to you?
- What legacy do you hope to leave, and how do faith and perseverance shape that vision?
- How might God use your own story to encourage someone else?

Prayer Reflection (Optional)

Close by praying over one another's waiting seasons—whether for children, healing, restoration, or other promises still unfolding.

Holly Bogdan